What people are saying about Teresa Reasor...

"Love is no match for warring Scottish clans until gutsy Mary Mac Lachlan makes her stand. Teresa Reasor's debut will keep you reading!" ~ Award-winning author Joanne Rock

He kept his tone soft.

"Why did you offer me the bairn, Mary? I know you do not wish to be parted from him."

"'Tis better for him to be accepted into your clan than mine. He'll have the safety of a father to care for him, rather than a grandsire who will use him or abuse him."

"You know Collin well," he said.

"Aye." The huskiness of her tone tinted the word with pain.

Though she kept her head bent, he glimpsed her tear stained cheeks and red nose. He eased closer, driven by a need to comfort her.

She fell silent for a moment then raised her gaze to the stone structure behind him. "He will be a Campbell and he will never have to know what 'tis to have a foot in two clans, and never truly belong to either. He'll know what 'tis to owe his loyalty to only one and be accepted without question."

Something in her expression brought a tightness to Alexander's chest. "I do not wish to raise my son or daughter alone. A bairn needs its mother."

She remained silent.

Grasping her chin with his fingertips, he turned up her face. "Will you allow your hate for me to deprive our child of your care and affection, as you were deprived of your mother's?"

Her blue gaze traced his features with a pain that weighted the pit of his stomach with stones of guilt. "I did not wish to hate you, Alexander. I wanted very much to care for you because you were to be my husband."

The knowledge that she had meant to accept him, struck him with the force of a battle-ax and he drew a deep breath.

She raised her chin. "'Twas a lifetime ago when I was innocent enough to trust you. 'Twill not happen again."

.

Highland Moonlight

by

Teresa Reasor

Highland Moonlight

Cover Art by *Tamra Westberry*

The Wild Rose Press
PO Box 706
Adams Basin, NY 14410-0706
Visit us at www.thewildrosepress.com

Publishing History
First English Tea Rose Edition, March 2007
Print ISBN 1-60154-050-7

Published in the United States of America

Dedication

To my mother, who has unconditional faith in me in all
my endeavors.

Scotland 1328

Chapter One

At the unexpected sound of booted steps in the narrow passageway, Mary concealed herself in the rock wall's craggy surface. The smell of peat smoke hung acrid and strong in the confined space. With every breath, she tasted it. Water trickled like perpetual rain from deep within the hillside. She hoped its movement would cover the uneven sound of her breathing.

"Mary?" The sound of her name echoed through the cave.

She recognized her father's voice and the thick white hair that brushed his shoulders. Another man accompanied him, his face indiscernible in the dim light.

Bracing the weight of the crossbow against her hip, her fingers found the trigger. She stepped from the shadows, careful to keep the fire between herself and the men. "'Tis here I am, Father."

Both turned at the sound of her voice. Recognition sent a tremor of shock racing through her, and she stumbled back, swallowing a gasp. With a practiced jerk, she leveled the crossbow at the larger of the two.

Her father threw out a hand stilling the man's stride toward her. "Loose the arrow, Mary, and you will have murdered an unarmed man," Collin said.

What purpose could he have in bringing Alexander to this place?

Almost as though he heard the thought, Collin said, "He has come to set things aright, lass."

She shook her head, amazed how obtuse her father could be. "Surely you know that can not be done."

"Aye, it can if you will allow it, Mary," Alexander said, his deep voice echoing through the chamber.

Those few words flayed her soul with promises that

1

could not be. Her throat grew tight and thick with instant tears. She blinked quickly to clear her vision.

"You can not stay here alone much longer, lass," Collin said.

"Not now you have seen fit to bring the likes of him about." Her brittle tone was rewarded by the fierce scowls of both men.

"I have signed the betrothal contract with Alexander. I have given my oath. You will marry him."

Overwhelmed by a sense of helplessness, she fell silent. If he were any kind of father, he would not ask this of her. A panicked feeling of being cornered raced through her. Her eyes searched the passageway behind them. The bow dipped as she stepped closer to the dark opening at her left.

When no threat appeared, her gaze settled on the man responsible for her plight. Heavy brows, the same dark chestnut as his hair, came together in a fierce frown over a straight well-shaped nose. Thick auburn lashes surrounded his pale amber eyes, their tawny wolfish hue startling and unusual. The generous curve of his bottom lip promised both humor and passion. A heavy beard colored his lean jaw a rusty hue, underlining the strong masculinity of his features.

A fresh wave of pain assaulted her just from looking at him. "You can not expect me to abide by the contract now."

"You are with child, Mary. He wants to be a father to the bairn."

A short bark of bitter laughter broke from her. "Aye, he would." She drew a steadying breath and straightened her shoulders though she trembled with a combination of reaction and cold. "I will not be his wife."

"I signed the contract. You must honor it."

"Nay! The contract be damned!"

Collin's jaw tensed, his brows puckered in a severe frown. "The marriage has been arranged to prevent a feud, Daughter."

"A feud of your making not mine. 'Twas you who started it, should be you who ends it."

"You will be shamed by bearing a child out of wedlock, Mary."

Alexander's deep, quiet voice scraped at the wound already raw.

"Do not talk to me of shame! 'Twas you and your deceit that has caused this!" She hated the defensive guilt that tormented her. How had she ever thought he cared for her? How could she have trusted him with all she had to offer? She shuddered, causing the bolt in the crossbow to jiggle.

"The child is mine, Mary. You can not deny me my rights as its sire." His jaw set, his dark auburn brows meshed into a fierce frown. The masculine planes of his face held an undeniable strength and determination, on other occasions, she had found almost beautiful. Now the sight of him inspired such feelings of anger and pain she found it hard to stand her ground.

Emotion held her silent a moment, her heart crying out against the events that had brought her to this impasse. Her chin rose in open defiance of him and his claims. "You are not my husband. You have no rights."

Alexander's lips thinned, drawing her attention to them for a moment. Gentle memories brought fresh pain in their wake. He had tasted of cinnamon and smelled of leather and wood smoke and man. She quashed the thoughts before they could go any further.

Her attention shifted to her father, her distrust a living breathing thing within her. A Campbell bastard beneath her father's roof would be used against her, or for his own purposes. She had known that from the first. She would not see her child abused by him.

No matter how he had failed her, Alexander would not fail to protect the child. Tears clogged her throat and for a moment pain threatened to overwhelm her resolve. Her voice sounded hoarse. "You may have the bairn in recompense for the contract."

"You can not be serious, Mary!" Collin stared at her, his features blank with shock.

"Aye, I am serious, Father." Her face felt stiff with the effort to retain her composure when it felt as though her heart were being ripped from her chest. "If a father he wants to be, then I will let him be one." She stepped closer to the fire. "Let us see if he is as good a one as you have been these many years past." The enmity she felt for both of them lay like a stone in the pit of her stomach. "You have both received what you came for, now leave."

"We can not do that, Mary," Alexander said. "You can not remain here. 'Tis not good for you, or the bairn."

She had given him her love, had shared her body without reservation, and he had proven how little she had meant to him. How could he play the concerned lover now? "I have survived worse things."

Alexander's lean jaw clenched. The scar along his cheekbone grew white in the firelight.

"Do not pretend to be concerned for my well-being or the bairn's. I have learned well the ways of men since that night. Your only interest is yourself, and what you can gain from this. Just as it is his." She nodded toward her father.

Collin's jaw moved as though he gritted his teeth his features set in a grimace of fierce displeasure. "You will come home with me."

She ignored his attempt to intimidate her into submission. Even in this he had not acted as a father, but the Chief of his clan. And once again, she felt used and betrayed, just as she had that night. "I will not go with a man so willing to hand me over to the likes of him." She used the bow to point in Alexander's direction. "I shall go to the abbey and reside with the nuns until the bairn is born. Afterwards, I will send the babe to Castle Lorne."

She fastened her attention on her father. "You will leave me out of any future plans you may have, Collin. From this day forward, I will owe you as much loyalty as you have offered me in this matter, or any other." She swallowed against the tears threatening to overwhelm her. "Go now. I have had enough of the both of you to last a lifetime." Backing away, she slipped into the chamber at the back of the cave. From the safety of the shadows, she turned to watch the two men.

****

Collin grasped Alexander's arm when he strode forward to follow her. "She will kill you if she thinks you intend to touch her," he warned. "She will do as she has said. You shall have the child."

Alexander had expected her resistance, but he had not expected Collin to yield so easily to her wishes. He

4

rubbed absently at the stubble along his jaw, wondering how the MacLachlan chief hoped to use this to his advantage.

"She will not accept you, Alexander." Collin's features were taut as he knelt to feed dried peat and small branches to the fire to build up the meager blaze.

"You're her father. She has to obey you."

The man's blue eyes, just a few shades darker than his daughter's, settled on him. "The church will not recognize a marriage where the bride is forced to speak the vows agin her will." He raked his fingers through his thick mane of white hair, his movements angry and impatient.

"Mayhap you should plead the bairn's case, instead of mine," Alexander suggested. "I have no wish to separate the babe from her."

"What would you have me say?"

He studied the older man. He was amazed by Collin's ineptitude. "The bairn needs a mother. If we wed, she will not have to be separated from it and the bairn will have my name to protect him from the slander of being called a bastard. She will not wish that for him."

Collin eyed him gravely. "She will not agree to anything that gives you the right to lay hands on her again."

Alexander fell silent a moment. His attention turned to the impenetrable darkness of the cavern beyond. She had made that plain enough.

"'Tis a fact your entire clan can do little but take, and take, and forever lust for more- more power, more land, and now more of what you had. You had not the patience to wait before. There's no reason why she should believe you will now."

The older man spoke a truth with which he had to agree. There had been a brief moment when he could have stopped, might have even done so. With one taste of her response, the die had been caste. He had done what he had believed was best, hadn't he? He had asked himself that question a hundred times and still could not find the answer. Now she carried his child. She hated him for it, that was plain enough. Perhaps she hated the child as well, and was eager to be rid of it.

He spoke the words he thought might persuade her to accept him. "I will give my word, I will not touch her again until she gives me leave to do so."

Collin grinned with obvious amusement. "You will be in for a long wait, lad, if she agrees."

Alexander ignored the other man's attempts to bait him. "That should please you, MacLachlan, and give her time to exact no small revenge as well. Mayhap you should suggest that to her." He turned and stalked from the cave.

****

Collin squatted near the fire.

Mary watched him from her position just beyond the entrance to the chamber. His mane of hair appeared more white than blond. In the flickering firelight his pale brows shadowed his deep-set blue eyes. She sought and found no similarities in his features to her own. She was her mother's daughter in all, but coloring.

"He is gone, Mary. You have nothing to fear, lass."

Slowly she came forward, checking the darkened areas for movement. She squatted on the opposite side of the fire, careful to keep her distance from him. The skirt of her gown, streaked with moisture from the rocks of the cavern, hung in cloying folds against her legs. She felt chilled and drew her tartan cloak more closely around her, but did not set aside the crossbow.

"You look ill, lass."

She felt ill. Her strength ebbed and flowed upon its own tide as much as the sickness that came to her in unexpected moments. "Your concern is touching, Father."

Collin's jaw tensed at her tone.

She brushed back a stray curl from her forehead. "You are truly a fool if you believe anything he says."

"He is a Campbell. If he offers a pledge he will keep it."

Rage rose up to take her breath and for a moment she could not speak. "Nay! I shan't agree to anything that will bind me to him."

"The bairn will bind you to him, Mary. You'll have to make your peace with him, for the child's sake."

"I shall never have to see him again after this day."

"You can not truly mean to give up your child," he

6

argued, his tone laced with amazement.

"It did not seem to trouble you over much to give up yours," she taunted.

Collin sighed and lowered his eyes to the fire. "We but followed custom, lass."

"Aye, a custom that denies a child its mother, and makes it easier for a father to think of it as a pawn upon the political chessboard of this shire." She drew a deep breath, suddenly so tired she longed to lie down on the hard ground and rest. She forced herself to her feet instead. "Go home, Collin and forget you ever had a daughter named Mary. I will no longer be a party to your plans."

He rose, his features harsh with control. "My only plan now, Daughter, is to protect you from further harm."

She stifled a sound of disbelief. "As you did when you had me beaten?"

"You brought it upon yourself by welcoming him into your bed. 'Twould have been within my rights to do worse."

It had taken weeks for her back to heal and every breath she had drawn had been torture. Fever had brought her close to death more than once. For a moment, she thought how easy it would be to loose the bolt in the crossbow. Collin must have read something in her expression for the muscles of his face tightened and he froze.

"Neither of you shall ever lay hands upon me again."

"'Tis dangerous to be threatening to kill a man." Though his blue eyes grew cold and flat, a tick twitched in his cheek.

"'Tis no threat." She kept her gaze steady on his face. For once she knew what it was to be the one in power and though she knew it wouldn't last, she embraced the headiness of it and the strength it gave her.

He clenched his hands into fists at his sides, his movements careful. "I shall warn him, but 'twill do no more good than talking to you has done."

"What did you expect?"

His features took on a stern look. "You were not raised to be so hard-hearted daughter."

She ignored his attempt at reestablishing himself as

the father he had never been. "You did not raise me. You do not even know me." She shook her head. "I am only a piece of goods with which to barter and form your alliances. Did you think me too ignorant to realize it? If you had looked upon me as more, you would have looked more closely at the man to which you promised me. Instead you saw only the name and the purpose of the deed." Her eyes stung. "I am nothing to you, just as I am nothing to him. 'Twould be a service to me if you would both think no more of me and let me live in peace."

"Giving up your child will not bring you peace."

"You are probably right, but in doing it, I will be free of him, and any debt I might owe you for siring me." The need to weep grew like a tide inside her. She raised her chin instead. "I am not a fool. You are not here to defend a daughter's honor, but to see your plans do not go awry."

He did not deny her accusation. "There is a way in which you might seek your revenge against him."

She studied him, her body growing tense with distrust. "What would you be speaking of?"

"The MacDonalds and Campbells are grave enemies. What greater revenge than to bear the child of one within the clan of another?"

Anxious tremors slithered down her spine.

"Bearach MacDonald could be persuaded to wed you and give your bairn a name, lass."

A quick vision of Bearach with his thick lips and narrow eyes sent a shiver of revulsion through her. The one time she had shared a meal with him at her father's table, he had grasped her hand with a proprietary air that had made her ill at ease. His touch had been sweaty and he had purposely pressed his heavy thigh to hers as they sat on the bench. Something in his expression had made her feel trapped and afraid. It had taken all her will not to bolt from the table.

"Bearach MacDonald is a pig. Do you believe I would suffer him to touch me any more than I would Alexander Campbell?" Her ire rose once again at his lack of care for her and her child. "'Tis my bairn too, my own flesh and blood. Do you believe I would bear him within the jaws of an enemy where he would be abused, just to seek my revenge agin his father?"

8

His sly expression changed to one of impatience. "'Twould save you from dishonor and offer you revenge in one stroke." He turned to leave and added over his shoulder, "'Twould serve you well to think upon it."

She listened to Collin's receding footsteps as he left the cave.

The hint of a threat in his words had fear curling in her belly. She placed a protective hand over the fragile life within her. "Never!" she murmured to herself.

****

Alexander surveyed the two camps stationed close to the cave entrance. Campbell clansmen had claimed the west side of the hillside. While he had been inside the cave, campfires had been lit and the men had organized the camp into stations of food, shelter, and horses. As he watched, men broke away from the main body to stand watch at all four corners of the area.

The MacLachlan men had set up camp on the east side of the craig closer to the cave. Two men stood guard just outside the opening, while others took their watch to the north and south of the camp. Alexander's attention rested on the two guards at the entrance. He wondered if they were there to protect Mary from him or to hold her prisoner for her father. She seemed no more enamored of Collin than she was with him.

"How does she fare, Brother?" Duncan asked as he joined him.

"Carrying the child has made her ill, but her hate for me is strong."

Duncan smiled. "Sounds as though she shall fit well into our family."

Not amused by the comment, Alexander flashed him a frown.

"Mayhap the child will be a girl and you will learn first hand what 'tis to defend a daughter's honor."

His brother's humorous jibes irritated him, for there was no way he could defend himself. His gaze settled on the MacLachlan clansmen who squatted about a campfire a short distance away, then moved to his own men. The two clans were as divided by his actions as they had been before.

"Has she truly been alone up here since that night?"

Duncan asked.

"Nay. She has been cloistered at the abbey. 'Twas only when the good Father saw fit to notify Collin of her condition, she left the kirk to go into hiding here."

"Has it occurred to you, Brother, that you might not be the only one to have had her?" Duncan tossed more peat on the fire. "The countryside is crawling with Scotsmen who would take advantage of a woman."

He focused on Duncan's face and shook his head. "She was a virgin when I took her. The bairn is mine."

Duncan shrugged. "'Twas but a thought. 'Twould give you a way out."

Alexander studied his brother's features, so much like his own. Would Duncan turn away so easily if it were his child of which they spoke? He thought not. "'Twould suit her if I did not claim the child, Duncan. She wants to be rid of me. If she thought she could achieve that by claiming another sire for the bairn, she would have done so already. There has been no one else."

Duncan nodded. "So what are you going to do?"

Alexander looked toward the mouth of the cave. "I am going to hold her to the contract. I shall use the bairn to coax her to Castle Lorne and try to keep her there."

Duncan's gray eyes held a speculative light as he studied him. "Why this lass? What is different about her that she should hold your interest so completely?"

She had belonged to him from the moment he had claimed her virginity. Nay before that. "She carries my child. She belongs to me."

"'Twould seem she does not wish to, Brother."

"Fate has deemed it otherwise, Duncan, and I am going to see it through."

Duncan made a sound of impatient disgust. "Your head is as thick as yon tree." His features creased in a scowl as he gestured toward a huge oak nearby.

Alexander curbed his impatience with an effort. "Would you have me abandon my own child?"

"Nay. You can recognize the child as yours without pressing the lass to wed."

Alexander flicked his hand in a negative gesture. "I will not have my son known as a bastard. She will wed me because she has no other choice."

10

Duncan shrugged his shoulders. "I would not wager on that. Women do not always see things as we do."

"She's a noblewoman. Having her pride split asunder by the judgment of her own clan will persuade her." He spoke with greater conviction than he felt. The reckless anger he had seen in her face did not bode well for an easy end to the matter.

Alexander wrapped the extra fabric of his kilt around his torso and squatted close to the fire. The night had grown chill and his thoughts rested on Mary. She looked pale and thin. Being with child was proving difficult for her. The damp chill permeating the cave could not be good for her or the bairn.

The Chief of the MacLachlan Clan did not trust him, that was plain enough. He watched as several men assumed subtle posts to keep watch over him.

"Why are the two of you so eager to give her what she wants?" Duncan asked with a frown.

"She's like a hurt animal lashing out at anything that moves. She needs time."

"Time for what, Alexander. A bit of swyving did not harm her."

Rage flared hot within him. His gaze swung to his younger brother's face as he lashed out to grab the front of his shirt. "I will warn you to keep a civil tongue in your head. Say one more disrespectful word and you may find yourself unable to say anything for a very long time!" He shoved Duncan away. "This is no common slut you are discussing, but the woman to whom I am betrothed."

"You've been like a hurt boar ever since you had her," Duncan complained as he straightened his clothes, a disgruntled look on his face.

Alexander remained silent. He knew better than Duncan; he didn't have to be told. Regret gnawed at his insides like a festering wound. Every time he thought he had found a way to put it aside it rose back up to smite him.

He had done the thing to protect himself and his men, but it had been to protect her as well. To explain his actions would do no good. She would not believe him without proof.

He raked his fingers through his hair and ran a hand

over the bristly stubble along his jaw. "Morning will be a long time coming. Assign the watch, then turn in."

His brother rose to do as he was bid.

****

To keep watch on the mouth of the cave, and be free of his brother's remarks, Alexander chose a spot midway between the two camps. He positioned himself within the forked roots of a large oak and leaned back against the trunk. Placing his sword beside him, he wrapped the woolen fabric of his kilt around his shoulders and folded his arms. Breathing in the smell of the peat fire, he watched the familiar routine of men digging in for the night.

How many nights had he spent camped beneath the heavens waiting for dawn to come and the next battle to ensue? He had raised his sword in defense of his clan. He had raised it at the behest of his King. His soul was weary of fighting and bloodshed. Of late he had felt the need for some small haven of peace where he could rest his head and his heart. From the first moment he had seen her, Mary had represented that haven to him. Had he destroyed with his own hands what he had wanted the most? His fingers followed the course of the scar that cut down one side of his face to his chin. He was a man of one score and ten years, but had behaved as a callow youth. He had been too eager and had given himself away to Collin. His gaze found the pale hair of the older man. Impotent anger roiled within him. Had he been able to trust the MacLachlan Chief, there would have been no need to pursue such a course.

The men stationed before the mouth of the cave rose in force. Alexander followed suit, his gaze fastening on the entrance where Mary had appeared.

Her gold hair, covered with a red and green tartan shawl, looked pale as moonlight. Soft tendrils escaped from beneath the fabric to curl against the edge surrounding her face. The flickering light of the torches jammed into the ground around the entrance of the cave illuminated her slender form as she stood just inside the opening.

Alexander strode forward to see what had driven her from the safety of the cave.

"Will you not join us closer to the fire, Daughter?" Collin motioned to the fire in invitation.

She shook her head. "If I could trouble you for another tartan, 'tis all I need."

Alexander found himself flanked by two large MacLachlans, intent on keeping a close vigil on his movements. Duncan had no such problem. He had almost reached the opening of the cave before a clansman grabbed his arm. The dark green tartan he carried spilled to the ground. A struggle ensued until Collin stepped forward calling a halt to it.

"'Twas my intent to give the lass what she requested," Duncan said, jerking his arm free of the clansman's grasp. He bent to retrieve the tartan.

Collin's signal had the MacLachlan clansmen backing away. He moved close beside Duncan as he approached the cave entrance.

Mary held the crossbow ready as they approached. "Leave it on the ground and back away." Her voice echoed through the chamber behind her.

Duncan did as she requested.

The aim of the bow never wavered from his chest as she moved forward and crouched to pick up the tartan.

"Would you be needing anything else, Mary?" Collin asked.

"I would know what your intentions are for the morrow. Do you intend to give me over to them?"

Collin shook his head. "Alexander has agreed you should return to the abbey until the bairn is born. You do not have to fear anyone will harm you."

She fell silent for several moments, her head bent. Her face looked pale and drawn when she looked up. "I am grateful for that." She turned away to return to the inner chamber of the cave.

Alexander's gaze met his brother's across the distance between them. Two MacLachlan clansmen dogged Duncan's steps as he returned to the Campbell camp. The anger Alexander read in the men's faces elicited no response. He could not blame them for being angry with him when he felt the same toward himself.

Duncan spoke after a long silence. "I did not expect her to be such a wee lass, nor so wounded by what has happened between you."

Alexander flinched inwardly. "If she stays at the abbey, she'll be cloistered with the nuns and I will not be allowed to speak with her."

"She will not speak with you civilly anyway, Brother."

"It does not matter what she says to me, be it with a civil tongue or not." He would deal with that when they were once again together.

"Do you mean to take her then?" Duncan asked.

"Aye." He nodded after only a brief pause. "There will be no other way. She will not come on her own."

"'Twill be dangerous with so many MacLachlans about. They're feeling less than friendly toward you, if you have not noticed."

A wry smile crossed Alexander's lips. "'Twill be a last measure. Mayhap Collin will be able to change her mind about the marriage on the morrow. If he can not, I will insist on escorting her to the abbey with them. We will take her then."

Duncan's gray eyes probed his face. "Do you value her so much?"

Rarely did he allow his private feelings to be known, not even to his brother. "Aye, I value her."

Duncan gave a nod of ascent. "We will plan with care then. You will not want to put her, or the bairn she carries, in anymore danger than is necessary."

Chapter Two

Collin's white hair stood out against the dark green brush as he spoke to one of the men. To ensure the paleness of her own would not be as easy to identify, Mary wrapped the Campbell tartan more securely about her head and neck.

She watched the men's movements for some time, familiarizing herself with their routine. Several men lay asleep on the ground wrapped in their tartans, while others squatted close to the fire, keeping warm between patrols.

Her legs aching from kneeling, she shifted her weight and the brittle snap of a twig beneath her heel echoed through the darkness. She froze and waited for one of the men on watch to rise and investigate. One of them looked up, but went back to his reverie after a passing show of interest. She breathed an inward sigh of relief.

She eased down the tree-covered bank a step at a time. Her movements cautious, she circled the camp. Neither Collin's nor Alexander's men had found the back entrance of the cave. She had been waiting hours to slip away once the men had settled for the night. With luck, it might be dawn before they discovered her escape. Reaching a safe distance from camp, she quickened her pace.

She stopped to change her apparel under the early morning sky then adjusted the buckle of the wide leather girdle about her waist and arranged the fabric over her shoulder as she had seen the men do. Unaccustomed to the short length of the kilt, her legs felt bare though her boots came to mid-calf.

She appreciated the freedom the shorter garb offered when she climbed the steep incline of the brae without the usual long skirts to hinder her. She shifted the small bundle of possessions she carried from hand to hand.

Since she was traveling alone, the weight of the crossbow hung over her shoulder boosted her confidence, and eased the anxious feeling lodged in the pit of her stomach.

She topped the rise and the abbey stretched out below her. The long roughly hewn stone building, and the small kirk attached to it, looked desolate in the first light of dawn. The nuns began to stir. Several of the women crossed the courtyard, going in the direction of the cookhouse at the back of the structure.

She had thought to sneak down and ask the sisters for food, but decided the risk was too great. Her escape had probably been discovered by now. Alexander's men could be lying in wait to capture her as she came down from the hillside. She squatted behind a clump of heavy brush that afforded her an unobstructed view of the abbey, but offered her cover. She settled in to watch and wait.

Collin and a troop of twenty men galloped over the rise within minutes. The men spread out over the church property to search the kirk and the adjoining buildings.

Father Patrick's tall, shrouded form appeared from the interior of the church. His hands moved in angry gestures and he waved a finger in Collin's face.

The sound of her own appreciative chuckle seemed loud in the quiet of the hillside. Though she couldn't hear a word of it, she relished the angry tirade to which he subjected her father.

Her attention focused on the horses left unattended at the gate of the churchyard and another smile curved her lips. Mayhap she would not have to walk after all. She rose to her feet and started down the slope.

The sound of the men's voices raised in anger reached her, though she couldn't distinguish their words. Hunching down behind the low wall, she circled the courtyard and the adjoining graveyard. By following its course, she reached the gate and the horses without detection.

Her father's large chestnut gelding, arraigned with an ornate saddle and a water bag, stood at the gate. It would be small justice should Collin lose a prized possession for his attempts to give her away so carelessly.

She hazarded a quick glance over the rock wall to

check the position of all the men. The argument between the priest and their chief held their attention. Easing forward, she grasped the reins that dragged the ground.

The closest cover of brush and trees lay across the road. Mary trotted the horse over the open ground, keeping the cover of the gate between her and the men within the courtyard.

Despite the horse's nervous dance, she placed her foot within the stirrup, and managed to swing herself astride its broad back. A flick of the long end of the reins against the animal's haunches, and the gelding leaped forward. She smothered a surge of exuberant laughter as she rode away from the abbey, keeping to the cover of the hillside brush.

****

"She's worthy to be a Campbell bride, Alexander," Duncan said as they watched Mary's escape from the spot where she had stood watch earlier. "A lass bold enough to steal her father's mount may need protection, though."

"Nay," Alexander shook his head. "'Twill be Collin who will need protection from her."

Duncan laughed aloud as did the other men.

"We will follow close enough to offer her assistance should she have a need of it, but far enough behind to make her feel she has nothing to fear. I wish to know where she is going." Alexander motioned for the group to follow. The group of twenty horses surged forward at his signal.

****

After two hours of hard riding, Mary's legs ached with the strain. She left the dirt road to cut upward into a grove of trees. The gelding, though a young horse, needed to rest, as did she.

Fearful of being followed, she dismounted and stood listening, her body tense as she scanned the road below. After some time, she relaxed enough to remove the water bag. She poured water into her cupped hand to offer the horse, then took a small drink herself. Leaving her mount to graze, she withdrew a small loaf of bread from the bundle tied to the saddle. She broke off a chunk from one end and settled on the ground to eat the meager meal.

Believing she would be on foot for some time, she had

taken only what she could carry. Now with the horse to carry the burden, she wished she had attempted to escape with more of her possessions. It was too late and too dangerous to return for them, so the small supply of food and clothing would have to do until she reached Lorne.

Her eyes followed the gentle rolling hills in the distance. It would take two days of hard riding to reach the castle. Two dangerous days. She would have to be constantly alert to the threat of robbers. She had dressed as a lad to disguise her gender, for that in itself was an invitation to harm. Taking her father's mount had been a mistake. A fine saddle would be a temptation to every Scottish highwayman for miles.

Thoughts of her father had her drawing an uneven breath. She had not been fooled by his concession for her to go to the abbey. Eventually, he would find a way to use her or the bairn against Alexander and his Campbell kin. Or worse, he would separate her from her bairn and give it away as he had his own. Without a husband to protect her, he could force her into some other odious union as well. The threat of Bearach MacDonald came to mind. She would never allow that to happen.

Even with a man who professed some small hint of affection for you, the joys that went with such a joining could be used against you. Used to make a woman feel less than what she had been before. Collin had made certain she understood that with every lash he had delivered.

Her father needn't have bothered. Alexander's actions had shamed her before three clans, and he had readily admitted that he had done so deliberately. The pain of his betrayal twisted like a blade between her ribs every time she thought about it, and every time she experienced the pain, she knew how little he thought of her.

Never again would she allow a man to treat her in such a manner. Never again would she lower her shields with such abandon.

Rising, she caught the horse's reins, determination in every step. She would ride to Castle Lorne and petition Laird Campbell himself for protection and shelter until the birth of her bairn. And if he refused—if he refused, she would do whatever she had to protect herself and her babe.

Mary pushed her mount as hard as she dared. Exhausted by late afternoon, she stopped to rest atop a craggy hillside scattered with trees. She nibbled another crust of dry bread to ease the sickness that plagued her, but could not eat the meat she had saved from her evening meal the night before. She decided to rest for a wee bit, and lay on the ground.

A short time later, she awakened to the warm moist breath of the horse as he nuzzled her neck. She laughed at his amorous attentions and raised a hand to stroke the velvety softness of his nose. The queasiness had eased and the short nap had rested her. But as she struggled to her feet, she nearly groaned aloud for her muscles had stiffened and protested every movement.

She straightened with difficulty and turned to check the horse. "The saddle is growing heavy no doubt." She patted his sleek neck. "Let us be on our way and we will soon stop for the night."

Traveling the road was dangerous. Cutting across country strange to her could prove more so. Mary decided to stay on the rocky stretch of road for a while and swung herself gingerly into the saddle.

Several times she thought she heard the beat of horse's hooves behind her and sought cover to wait for them to appear. After the third delay, she decided her fears were playing her for a fool. Lest she saw the brigands on her tail, she would not stop again.

It had grown dark before she came upon the widening slopes of the valley that opened to Loch Awe. In the dusky light, the hills appeared to rise to mountainous proportion in the east. The purplish black expanse of the loch stretched before her. The rising moon reflected on the breeze-rippled surface of the dark water, like the myriad dance of fireflies.

The valley narrowed and the mountains to the east hugged the banks of Loch Awe like some mythical beast come to drink from its waters. She found shelter in the glen beneath a small canopy of trees nestled at the base of a steep hillside.

She lit a small fire to hold the animals at bay then

turned to see to the horse. It took all her strength to drag the heavy saddle from his back and place it close to the fire to use as a backrest.

"'Tis sorry I am that I have no oats for you, for you have toiled hard for me this day." She spoke to the horse as she wiped him down with the tartan pad beneath the saddle. The animal nickered in reply, bringing a smile to her lips. Suddenly, tears burnt her eyes and she rested against the warmth of the animal to draw fresh strength from its closeness. Since discovering she was with child, she seemed to swing between tears and laughter with irrational regularity.

"If 'twas that men showed half so much affection or care for their women folk as they do their horses, I would not mind so much being bound to one." She stroked his nose then turned to guide him forward to the edge of the water to drink. "You are used, but you are valued. Not so we lasses. We are just possessions to be used, without a word of kindness or affection. 'Tis that I can not abide. 'Tis better to be alone for all eternity than to live in such a way."

She sat on a flat stone next to him and dipped the cuff of her sleeve in the water to bath her face. "Men have fought these many years against a tyranny they can not abide. Then they turn their own tyranny against those weaker than themselves. Do you not believe that those who bear their young and ease their hurts deserve better?"

The animal tossed his head, as though in agreement, and she smiled again. A memory of tender, sweet kisses and heated caresses made her smile falter and her anger with it. A hollow ache that had little to do with hunger throbbed beneath her breastbone. It had meant nothing to him. For a moment the loss was almost more than she could bear.

Swallowing against the tears, she straightened her shoulders. She would one day learn to dismiss it as nothing as well. Wiping her face with her shirtsleeve one last time, she grasped the reins and led the horse back to the fire. She hobbled his front hooves so he would not stray while he grazed on the lush grass growing close to the water.

The meat, she had been unable to eat earlier, and another small chunk of bread barely stayed her hunger. If she did not reach Castle Lorne by midday tomorrow, she would have to take the time to hunt. Exhaustion weighted her movements as she curled close to the fire. Using the bowed seat of the saddle as a pillow, she fell asleep in moments.

****

Alexander motioned for Duncan and the rest of his men to circle the camp. Their movements stealthy, they each found a place well covered by brush to stand watch.

If Mary wished to travel to Castle Lorne on her own, Alexander saw no purpose in interfering with her, as long as he could keep her safe.

From his position several feet away, he could see her features clearly. Against the dark fabric she wore as a liripipe to cover her hair, her skin glowed creamy and warm in the firelight. From a distance she could pass for a young lad. On closer view, her face appeared too delicately wrought to be anything but feminine. Her lips, full and finely shaped, were parted, her features relaxed in sleep. She looked very young curled on her side with her hand tucked beneath her cheek

The memory of how she had grasped the tartan about her to hide her nudity from her father's men rose up to smite his conscience and he drew a deep breath. He had known they would be coming, but had not offered her a warning. Her virgin blood had been smeared bright red on the sheets and between her thighs for all to see. He had spared her nothing. Nothing.

He had not just taken her innocence when he possessed her body, he had crushed it beneath his admission of betrayal. He remembered how the color had leached from her skin as though she had received a mortal blow. Shame and regret brought a hollow feeling to his gut. He had been a warrior too long. He had known nothing but fear and death, blood and ruthlessness. But even when he killed in the name of his king and his country, he had believed himself to be an honorable man. But that night, he had not behaved as one. His belief that his actions would force Collin to honor the betrothal contract had given him an excuse to act with as little honor as the Mac Lachlan Laird. And he had done so. He hadn't wanted to lose her, but his own actions had insured he would.

Raking his fingers through his hair and pushing against his temples with the heel of his hands, he bit back the warrior's yell of frustration and pain that built inside him. There had to be something he could do to make amends. Regaining some control, he folded his arms across his chest.

His attention moved back to Mary. It was a miracle she had conceived so easily. It would take another for him to win her back.

Chapter Three

"If I had to bock as often as she, and you were the cause of it, I'd hate you myself," Duncan whispered. "She has spent more time in the brush than she has upon her mount this morn."

Alexander flashed Duncan a warning look. He could see for himself how ill Mary was and how miserable because of it.

"'Tis the way of it sometimes in the beginning, Alexander." Derrick Campbell said from behind him. "'Twill ease in time."

Reappearing from the brush, Mary leaned against her horse for support. She filled her mouth from the water bag then spat it on the ground. With obvious effort she dragged herself atop the gelding.

"Should she fall from her mount, she could bring harm to herself and the bairn." He voiced a concern that had plagued him since she had gotten sick the first time.

Like distant thunder, the rapid rumble of horses approaching from the south sounded. As they appeared from around a bend in the road, the pale gleam of Collin MacLachlan's hair came into sight. Mary whipped the reins against the haunches of her mount, sending him forward with a leap.

Alexander swore and crashed through the underbrush in quick pursuit. "Slow them, if you can," he yelled to his brother.

****

Mary glanced behind her, seeing the large black gelding gaining on her with each steady stride. She swung away from the road and charged up a steep slope, then veered to the left, following the winding trail of a well-used path. The pursuing horse's hooves pounded behind her with the same furious beat as her heart's. She urged the gelding to a faster pace.

Dogs bayed nearby, drawing her attention and she turned her horse in that direction. The path became a rain gully running downward. The horse's footing uncertain, they slid down the bank to a flatter plain. The smell of damp vegetation hung strong in the air. The creek bed proved marshy with only a narrow trickle of water running down the center. The horses splashed through, sending up clots of mud, and then bound up the bank and across a field.

The open spaces allowed her to give her horse full rein. Hazarding a glance over her shoulder, she found the black horse trailing by only a length. Recognition of the man on his back urged her to panicked recklessness. She sawed back on the reins with such force it caused her horse to rear and almost fall.

Alexander prevented the two animals from colliding as he swerved past with only inches to spare.

Turning the gelding into a gully between two rock-strewn hills, she rode back toward the trail and the loch. On the road, the larger group rounded a bend behind her. She grabbed the bow secured on the saddle horn. Turning her mount to face the on-rushing band of horses, she aimed the bow above the heads of the men and loosed the bolt. They scattered for cover on either side of the road.

She turned her horse and kicked it forward and nearly rode into Alexander, as he turned his mount to face her. Whipping past him, she encouraged the horse to stretch out into a full, unfettered run.

They rushed upon a village of stone huts roofed with thatch. Geese and cocks, pups and goats, scattered as they wove with dangerous haste through the stone strewn trail curving down the valley.

Castle Lorne perched atop the center of a narrow strip of land jutting out into Loch Awe. The bare limbed trees surrounding it clawed at the sides of the gray stone structure. She had only seconds to acknowledge the formidable sight before she rode to it. The gates closed against her, she turned her horse to the left to follow the wall of the castle seeking entrance elsewhere. The rock-strewn bank of the loch hugged the west wall. The horses pace slowed, its footing uncertain.

Alexander's shout behind her spurred her on. She

turned the horse toward the loch. The bank grew steep as they approached the water. Her mount balked and she grabbed the crossbow and dismounted.

The bank along the castle was purposely fortified with stones the size of fists or bigger. She hugged the wall as she staggered over the uneven terrain. Coming to a spot where the loch had eaten away the ground she halted and looked over her shoulder. Having dismounted, Alexander followed only a short distance behind. What was his intent should he catch her? Would he hold her prisoner until the babe came? The unrelenting determination she read in his features had her swinging back to study the problem at hand. Seeing no other solution, she stepped off the bank and immediately plunged hip deep into the icy water. She caught her breath and scrambled to reach the other side of the depression.

The saturated woolen tartan about her hips and thighs seemed too heavy a weight as she dragged herself free and stumbled up a knoll of ground to the dock at the back of the castle. She found her way blocked on the left by two clansmen as Alexander stalked toward her from the right.

Mary quickly spanned the crossbow and raised the weapon to ward them off bracing her back against the steps. "Stay back."

He halted only a few paces from her. His wet trews clung to his muscular thighs and calves and outlined the bulge of his manhood.

"I demand to speak to the Laird of this castle!" Her voice, shaking from cold, sounded breathless and weak.

"And what would a lass dressed in such a fashion have to speak of to me?" A deep voice demanded from behind her.

Shifting around the steps to the dock until the stone supports of the structure stood at her back, she glanced at man who had spoken. She caught her breath at the striking resemblance between father and son. Though heavier than Alexander, John Campbell had the same tall, muscular build. His deep chestnut hair, sprinkled liberally at his temples with white, lay in waves against his head and brushed the collar of his shirt. His beard grew thick and red along his jaw. Lines fanned out from the outer corners of his eyes, the same tawny color as his son's.

"I have come from Lochlan to ask for your protection, John Campbell," she said with difficulty for her teeth had begun to chatter.

"Protection from whom?"

"From my father and your son."

His brows rose.

She tugged at the liripipe covering her hair and tossed it to the ground. "'Tis Lady Mary MacLachlan, I am."

"Aye."

"I carry your son's bairn and I ask for your protection and shelter, until the birth."

John Campbell's gaze swung to his son. "Is this so, Alexander?"

"Aye."

Mary leaned back against the stone wall behind her as a wave of nausea rolled over her. She swallowed in an attempt to control it, and pressed a hand, trembling with cold, against her forehead praying it would ease. Her stomach rebelled and she turned aside hating the helplessness of it as she heaved up the small amount of water she had been able to keep down.

Alexander jerked the crossbow from her hand and tossed it to one of the clansmen standing near.

Tears blurred her vision as she accepted defeat. She hugged the stone support too weak from the sickness to fight.

Alexander braced himself for a struggle as he scooped her up and was surprised as she curled against him and buried her face against his shoulder. The fragile feel of her, as he hefted her slight weight, punched fear into his gut. He climbed the steps to the dock and strode past his father.

"You will tell me what this is about, Alexander," John demanded, keeping pace with him as they crossed the courtyard to enter the castle.

"Aye." He gave a short nod. Mary's pale skin and icy legs were more a concern to him than his father's displeasure. "After Mary has been tended."

****

Mary drew the tartan around the bodice of the worn blue surcoat as she went down the stairs from the gallery. The violent shivers that plagued her earlier had subsided. Food and rest had lessened the after effects of the journey as well. Worry over what havoc her father wreaked below had driven her from the comfort of the bed. The tartan that had served her as a kilt now covered the threadbare gown and, she hoped, made her appearance more acceptable. Her stomach felt as though a flock of sparrows fluttered within it as several pairs of male eyes followed her progress down the stairs of the great hall.

John Campbell stepped forward to meet her at the bottom. "'Tis a pleasure to have you here in my home, Mary."

"'Tis pleased I am to be here, Lord Campbell," she said with a curtsy then accepted the hand he offered her as she straightened.

The evening meal is ready. We have been waiting for you." He tucked her hand into the bend of his arm and escorted her to one of the tables.

Collin strode toward her. His cheeks flushed, eyes alight with anger, he lashed out at her with an open palm.

Alexander grasped his arm from behind preventing the blow from landing. "I can not allow you to abuse the lass, Collin. You strike her, you strike the bairn."

"She is my daughter." Collin jerked his arm free. "What right have you to stop me?"

"She is to be my wife, and I do not need a wife unable to do her duty because she has been beaten."

Heart beating high in her throat, Mary faced her father. "Is there any wonder I do not feel secure with you?"

"You are my blood, Mary. That alone should be enough to insure your trust." Collin jaw worked furiously with temper.

"Aye, striking me for certes will inspire my trust," she said, her tone dripping sarcasm. "Hugh Mac Pherson never raised his hand to me or my sister. And I had no such problem feeling safe with him."

Collin's face grew more flushed by the moment. "He was not your father, I am. Do you feel no loyalty for your own kin?"

She raised her chin and fought the urge to spit in his face. "Loyalty is not a birthright, but is earned. You have done nothing to earn or deserve mine." Rage spawned from years of neglect and abuse rose up within her. "My sister and I were beneath your notice until we came of age. You took us to your bosom only long enough to pass us along to those you thought would bring gain to your clan and to yourself. That is why I am here. I will not see you use my child, as you have used my sister and me."

"You are a fool." Collin's his voice sounded hoarse with emotion, his expression a grimace of frustrated rage.

"Not so much a fool to think you followed me here out of concern for my well-being. I will see to myself. You can be on your way now."

"Not until I have been recompensed for the damage done to you and your honor."

She fell silent a moment, too stunned by his audacity to speak. "Do you not mean I shall be recompensed, Collin MacLachlan?" she asked as outrage tightened the muscles of her neck and shoulders.

Something sly flickered behind her father's face. "Aye, that is what I meant."

She studied him, a niggling of distrust and wariness bringing a chill to her skin.

"Speak now and tell us what it is you want."

"'Tis to be spoken in private, before a council of arbitration."

A quiver of fear worked its way through her innards. "Think I will allow you to shame me before this clan, Collin?" She raised her chin and wrapped the tartan more closely about her. "I will not speak before such a council."

"You will daughter." His tone held a threatening note.

"Enough!" John's deep voice traveled the depths of the room. His tawny gaze bore into Collin, and then his son with equal enmity. "I have accepted Mary's request for protection until the meeting of the council. I suggest you both heed that." His features grew more threatening as his eyes settled on her father. "You will not disturb the peace of my table again, Collin, lest you find yourself eating alone outside the gates of the castle."

He guided Mary to the table and seated her at his right then took his place at the head of the table. Alexander took a place next to her as John motioned for the men to sit. Servants appeared with bowls of water for the guests to wash their hands.

After some moments of silence, Mary's interest settled on the only other women present, those few who served the food among the greater number of male servants. Her eyes traveled down the length of the table in search of any others, then settled on her host's face.

"'Tis a household of bachelors you have been brought into, lass," John explained. "My wife died some years ago and I have been reluctant to marry again. 'Tis better to leave such matters to the young."

"Mayhap being older and experienced could bring something worthwhile to a marriage," she offered.

John shook his head and smiled his amusement. "'Tis a kind thought, Lady Mary, but I am too old."

"I did not think men thought themselves too old for anything, lest they were in the grave."

He threw back his head and laughed, and the other men joined him.

"Your chamber was to your liking, I trust?"

"Aye. It has been some time since I have had the luxury of a bath and a bed. I am grateful for your hospitality."

"Did you not sleep upon a bed at the abbey?"

"Nay, a pallet upon the floor. Sister Esther was kind enough to share her small cell with me."

"T'was most fortunate you were able to make your way to the abbey without mishap."

For the first time, she sensed her host had a purpose for questioning her actions. "The priest and the sisters were attending my sister's betrothal. 'Twas an easy thing to join their ranks when they left the next morn. Once there, I convinced Father Patrick to allow me to stay."

He nodded. "'Tis good you were secure."

She studied his features, so similar to Alexander's. The pain of having her honor questioned because of his eldest son's actions made her defensive. "I have not been out of the sister's company since that night, Lord Campbell. The bairn I carry is your son's, no others."

29

A momentary scowl touched his face. "Alexander has already assured me of that, Mary."

A woman appeared at his side with a large tureen of stew. The Laird filled a couple of wooden bowls, first for Mary, then one for himself.

The stew proved rich and well seasoned. Despite her emotional upset, she found the hearty broth soothed her queasiness and warmed her. She looked up to find Alexander's men watching her from farther down the table as she sopped a piece of bread in the gravy and put it to her mouth.

"They are relieved to see you eat so heartily, Mary," Alexander commented from beside her. "All have noticed how little you have eaten these days past."

She stiffened, outraged. How dare he. "I should have known you would stay close enough to spy on me."

"We followed you to offer you protection should you need it."

His quiet tone made her comment seem petty and shrewish. She shifted uncomfortably as her cheeks grew hot with shame. "They should not fash themselves about me." She directed her attention to her food.

Alexander's hand rested against the small of her back in a gesture both comforting and possessive. Straightening her spine, she drew away from his touch.

"'Tis our way to care for each other, Mary. When one member of our clan is ailing, it affects us all."

What cure could he offer her for the things he had done? The touch of his hand made her want to weep. "I am not a member of your clan. You proved that well enough at Lochlan."

Alexander withdrew his hand and cupped the tankard of ale at his elbow, his features set. She felt like weeping all over again.

At the end of the meal, cheese, cakes, and a variety of dried fruits were served. After weeks of nothing but water to drink, she enjoyed the hot aleberry placed before her. She sipped the sweet drink as she listened to Alexander, John, and her father discussing the journey to Loch Awe.

"I did not appreciate having my daughter loose an arrow in my direction," Collin commented.

"My aim is true, Collin. Had I wanted you dead, you

would be."

"'Tis grateful I am you did not mean us any harm then, Lady Mary," a man spoke from across the wide table.

His face thinner and his eyes pale gray, his features still bore an unmistakable resemblance to Alexander. Thick hair the same deep chestnut color waved across his forehead and lay against his collar.

"Mary, this is my brother, Duncan," he introduced her. "And the lad beside him is our younger brother, David."

She studied the youngest brother's features. His resemblance to his father lay in his height and the width of his shoulders; the difference in the curve of his brow and the fullness of his lips. The high structure of his cheekbones gave his face a refined quality. His dark auburn hair, longer than Alexander and Duncan's, hung down his back in soft waves.

David's pale gray eyes studied her face then his lips curved into a smile filled with charm. "'Tis an honor to meet you, Lady Mary."

"I thank you for the use of the tartan." She nodded to Duncan as she wrapped the fabric more closely against her.

"'Twas my pleasure to offer you a gift so well used. It was most becoming as a kilt."

His teasing had her smiling. "I thought 'twould be safer traveling as a lad, than a lass. I did not know I was being protected." Her gaze trailed down the table to the rest of the men. "'Tis grateful I am for that as well," she said by way of an apology.

A wealth of smiles spread across the men's faces.

"I would not be much of a husband, if I did not watch over you, Mary," Alexander said beside her.

She avoided looking at him for fear she might be tempted to soften toward him. Her lingering feelings for him made her wary. "I have no husband. Nor do I want one."

She turned to her host. "T'was a fine meal, Lord Campbell; the best I have had in some time. I find a full stomach has made me sleepy and the journey here has tired me. Might I have your leave to retire?"

He nodded. "Aye, lass. Alexander has told me you have not been well. You must rest."

****

Plagued by gut wrenching frustration, Alexander watched Mary as she mounted the stairs and disappeared down the passageway in the direction of her chamber. If only she would allow him some quarter in conversing with her. Her constant verbal strikes at him were growing hard to tolerate.

"She's a wee lass." John's quiet tone drew his attention back to the table.

"Aye."

For a moment, his father's gaze met his. "And a beauty."

"Aye."

"We will see if a full stomach will lend a more civilized edge to our conversation now." He rose and motioned to Alexander and Collin to follow him.

The three of them made their way down the wide passageway from the great hall to an antechamber. Alexander remembered how as a child he had dreaded being called into his father's presence for any transgression. Being the son of a clan chief had not been easy. He had been expected to be more responsible, more in control, more aware of his duty to his clan than any other.

As a boy, it had been difficult to live up to his father's expectations. As a man, the hard lessons had served him well. He knew his father felt pride in him and his accomplishments. That alone made his present actions all the more difficult to explain.

The chamber they entered was the one in which his father had meted out punishment as a child. Now it was used to settle minor disputes among the people of his clan. Would justice be served for him, or against him?

A large table surrounded by almost twenty chairs dominated the room. His father ignored the massive piece of furniture and moved to stand before the wide stone fireplace.

"I was told by Collin that the lass was resigned to the marriage." John turned to face them.

A brief wry smile touched Alexander's lips. "Mary

knew she had been promised to a Campbell. 'Twas I who told her 'twas me."

His father's features settled into a fierce frown. "Did you not think you should tell the lass yourself, Collin?"

"I saw no reason to, lest the match remain unconsecrated. Alexander has been fighting with the Bruce, and in battle there is always a possibility of injury or death." Collin gave a dismissive shrug.

Alexander continued. "Her sister, Anne, was given a choice, Mary was not. She was less than resigned, when first we met."

"And when did this meeting come about, Alexander?" John asked.

"After the harvest, at her sister's betrothal to Ian MacMillan."

"She was agin you from the beginning?" John encouraged.

"Nay, to her credit, Mary was open to my suit. She said, 'twas not our fathers who had to live together as husband and wife. And 'twas up to us to decide if we could abide together. If we could not do so, 'twould be up to us to speak to the two of you, and see what could be done."

"And you agreed to that?"

"Aye, I believed once we were allowed some time together, she would agree to the match." His attention shifted to the fire for a moment. "Anne decided to accept MacMillan three days later, and Collin extended an invitation for the men and me to stay for the feast to celebrate."

"Aye," Collin interrupted. "'Twas then he sneaked upon her intent on forcing himself upon her."

If he defended himself it would damn Mary, and he had already caused her enough pain.

"She will not even look upon you now, Alexander."

He did not need Collin to point out the obvious. He saw how she struggled not to weep every time he spoke to her. The way she had shifted away from his touch at the evening meal had left a hollow ache beneath his ribs.

"After the bairn is born, Bearach MacDonald may still agree to take her, if she will agree to a handfast," Collin suggested.

The suggestion inspired sharp feelings of rage and

helplessness he could not suppress. "She will never go to Bearach MacDonald," he said, his tone clipped. "She will never agree to leave the bairn. And I will never allow my child to be fostered to a MacDonald."

He stepped closer to Collin, his gaze fastening on the older man's face. "You sought to pit Bearach MacDonald and me against one another at Lochlan, and I would not follow suit. The MacDonalds and Campbells are sworn enemies, for good reason. If you mean to cause further trouble between our clans, Collin, I warn you against it."

Collin's gaze shifted away from Alexander. "'Twas because of your actions Mary was willing to give up the bairn in the place of the contract, not mine," Collin reiterated. "What makes you believe she will change her mind now?"

"Mary told me herself, she was called home only three times in twelve years. She is bitter about being fostered from such an early age. I do not believe she will do the same to her own bairn."

"We but followed custom. We did nothing wrong." Collin's features grew taut with anger.

"She does not feel the same, Collin. That will have a bearing on what she will do."

"Regardless of what she does, you will regret what you have done, Alexander." His blue eyes were cold. "The council will see to that." He stalked from the room having, for once, had the last word.

Alexander searched his father's features for some clue to his feelings, but he turned away to face the fire and gave him no opportunity.

The silence stretched between them. He grew tense as his father shifted and folded his hands behind him.

"There's nothing that brings harm to a woman any more than having her will taken from her in such a way, Alexander. I have seen the grief it caused the women of our clan who have been taken during raids. I have seen the damage wrought before the Bruce, when Prima Notcha was allowed by William Long Stockings, and the English lords took our women on their wedding nights. There are some who never recover from such a thing."

He drew a deep breath and turned more fully to face Alexander. "A lass's body is the only thing that is truly hers to give. It tears her dignity and pride asunder when that choice is taken from her. It breaks something else inside her, we men can not understand."

His father believed him capable of rape. Alexander's mouth went dry and it became difficult for him to draw a full breath "I did not force Mary, Father, she came to me willingly. Collin is hoping she will testify agin me that I did, but she will not do so."

John turned to him a frown drawing his thick brows together as he searched his son's face. "You had better hope that is so, my son."

Silence fell between them.

"You have seen how Mary is with her father."

John's brows rose. "She would have defied him?"

"Mayhap."

"But you were not certes."

"Nay." He raked his fingers through his hair and drew a deep breath. "I was not certes of anything with her. But I was of Collin. I have no proof, but what I heard myself. I know Collin meant to break the betrothal contract by giving her to MacDonald. 'Twas he who was to bed her that night. He was there in the hall outside her chamber when I entered it."

"So you took her so she would have no choice but to accept you." It was a statement not a question.

"With the betrothal broken, there would have been nothing to keep Collin and the MacDonalds from attacking us. I could not put my men at risk, nor could I stand by and see Mary given to Bearach to be used and mistreated."

"Your own actions seem to have accomplished no better, Alexander," John said, his amber gaze intent.

The truth of those words renewed his guilt. He drew a deep breath. He had been gentle. He had given her all the pleasure there had been time for, though she had been denied a woman's fulfillment from their union. If only he had had more time to woo her. If only there had been time to explain his actions. If only Bearach MacDonald had not been waiting to take his place. All the if's ran together in his mind in a useless stream.

"Mayhap the bairn will help heal the wounds," John said after a lengthy pause, his tone lacking conviction.

Alexander did not hold out much hope for that either.

"You will visit with your brothers and me for a short time after the council," John ordered. "I wish to know my new daughter."

Alexander studied his father's stern features. "My men are eager to be home with their families."

"Aye, I know." John shrugged his shoulders, the gesture fraught with tension. "After the council, send those on who wish to go, and my men and I will give you an escort home, when the time comes."

Alexander nodded.

It would give his family time to know his bride. If Mary would not accept him, mayhap she would accept his family, for the bairn's sake.

Chapter Four

Mary paused above the great hall next to John Campbell and looked below at the men below. Her attention focused on Alexander. The muscles of his shoulders, back, and arms stood out like cords as he parried Duncan's maneuver with the heavy broadsword. Both men's chests and shoulders gleamed with sweat, their features set in fierce scowls of concentration as they circled one another.

Duncan thrust forward and Alexander's blade blocked the movement. As the weapons edges met, they screeched as though in pain. Turning his brother's sword aside, Alexander used his greater size to shove Duncan back. With a sudden burst of brutal strength, Alexander seesawed the blade in a lethal combination Duncan was hard pressed to defend. Sparks flew, and the high-pitched ring of metal on metal was nearly deafening. The younger man stumbled under the onslaught and nearly lost his footing. Alexander disengaged, offering his opponent time to recover. At Duncan's signal, they started again.

She recognized the able skill Alexander demonstrated with the sword. His movements had a grace only experience could teach. Her eyes lingered on the strong width of his shoulders and back then dropped to the muscular tautness of his stomach. The masculine beauty of his body inspired a breathless rush of feelings both exciting and disturbing to her. How could she still find him pleasing after he had harmed her so? How could her body betray her with such feelings? She dragged her gaze away.

"What is it you see, Mary?" John asked from beside her as he leaned on the railing of the gallery.

The question threw her into brief confusion. Heat stormed her cheeks and for a moment, she feared her thoughts had been obvious to the Laird of Lorne Castle. A quick glance in his direction eased her discomfort. His attention remained directed at the men below.

She cleared her throat. "David drops the point of his sword before the strike, telling his opponent what is to come. It may leave him open to a thrust above his weapon that will block the blade and keep him from defending himself."

"Aye. And Duncan?"

"He has more grace in his movements than the others, but less strength. He has need of greater stamina because of it."

"And Alexander?"

"His ability as a warrior can not be faulted. He is skillful with the blade and can anticipate his opponent's movements."

John's smile, laced with satisfaction, carved deep groves in his cheeks. "You are quick to find a man's weaknesses and strengths."

Her gaze swung to her father as he stood to one side of the great hall watching the men practice. "'Tis something Collin has taught me. Always be aware of your allies' weaknesses as much as your enemies, lest they change position."

The men opened the door to cool the room. Mary drew the tartan shawl more closely around her as cold air waft upward across the gallery. She looked up to find John frowning at her. "Were my words too direct, my lord?"

"Nay, lass. The truth must always be spoken directly."

She inclined her head in agreement.

"The council will expect such truth as well. They will be here by midday."

A sinking feeling hit the pit of her stomach. "I did not wish this."

"Aye, I know." John said.

She smoothed back the soft wisps of hair from her cheek that had slipped from the braid.

"By Alexander's own admission, you were a virgin, Mary. By papal law, if proven guilty of rape, he may be stripped of his property and—punished in other ways."

Her attention fastened on Alexander's face. As if he

sensed her attention, his pale gold gaze rose to her face and he stepped back from his opponent. He had taken her to him with such tenderness, and then turned against her in the most humiliating way possible. Had she tempted him as the priest had suggested? Was she somehow responsible for what Alexander had done? Guilt warred with her pain. Self-doubt warred with her anger.

She studied the man beside her. In the two days she had resided within the castle, the Campbell laird had sought out her company several times. At first, she had been wary of his interest, but had found his gruff charm hard to resist. She had reminded herself often he was Alexander's father and his loyalty to his son came first.

"The council is meeting here to give you justice, Mary."

She shook her head. "There is no justice to be had." She folded her arms against her midriff.

With the bend of his forefinger, John tipped her face back up to him. "Wed Alexander, Mary. Save yourself the shame of bearing your child out of wedlock. Do not let your bairn be known as a bastard."

If only it was that simple. How could she wed a man whose every touch reminded her of his betrayal?

"Or agree to a hand-fast. If after the year, you still do not wish to wed him, you may be released from the contract with no shame to bear." He placed a large hand on her shoulder. "'Twill secure your child's place within our clan."

Mary's throat ached with the need to vent her grief.

Collin broke into their conversation. "Do not listen to him, Daughter. He is only interested in saving his son from the punishment he deserves."

If only her own father had shown as much interest in her well-being as Alexander's had shown in his. She found Collin's constant hounding impossible to bear. He had done nothing, but taunt and tempt, threaten and cajole, in the hopes she would testify against Alexander. If Collin's reasoning had been to seek justice for her, she may have been persuaded, but she knew he had no such motives at heart.

"Leave me be, Collin," she managed, in a voice she fought hard to control. She ran down the stairs and across the great hall.

****

Alexander breathed an oath as the outer door swung shut behind Mary. He did not trust her not to saddle her horse and flee once again. He hurried to don his shirt and go after her. Heart pounding from the rush as he bounded down the stone steps, he halted in surprise, for she had gone no farther than the dock. The loch behind her traced her slender form with purplish-blue as she stood atop one of the large slabs of rock that edged the water. For a moment, he paused to admire the fragile beauty of her profile before she turned her head. The autumn sun touched her hair with streaks of light as the heavy braid fell from across her shoulder to hang down her back, like a rope, to her waist.

He purposely scraped the soles of his boots on the rocks so she would hear his approach.

"I would ask that you leave me." Her voice husky with emotion, she kept her face averted.

"I can not do that." Careful to keep his distance so she would not feel threatened, he remained just below her.

He dragged his gaze away from her and looked across the loch to the gently rolling hills beyond, while he gave her time to compose herself. Silence stretched between them fraught with such pent emotion the strain settle in his neck and shoulders.

"How long have you been certes about the bairn?" He introduced a subject to which he thought she might respond.

"For more than a month."

"You have grown thin because of the sickness it has brought you." Concern for her plagued him. "Mayhap one of the women can suggest a cure."

Silence settled in again.

He kept his tone soft. "Why did you offer me the bairn, Mary? I know you do not wish to be parted from him."

"'Tis better for him to be accepted into your clan than mine. He'll have the safety of a father to care for him, rather than a grandsire who will use him or abuse him."

"You know Collin well," he said.

"Aye." The huskiness of her tone tinted the word with pain.

Though she kept her head bent, he glimpsed her tear stained cheeks and red nose. He eased closer, driven by a need to comfort her.

She fell silent for a moment then raised her gaze to the stone structure behind him. "He will be a Campbell and he will never have to know what 'tis to have a foot in two clans, and never truly belong to either. He'll know what 'tis to owe his loyalty to only one and be accepted without question."

Something in her expression brought a tightness to Alexander's chest. "I do not wish to raise my son or daughter alone. A bairn needs its mother."

She remained silent.

Grasping her chin with his fingertips, he turned up her face. "Will you allow your hate for me to deprive our child of your care and affection, as you were deprived of your mother's?"

Her blue gaze traced his features with a pain that weighted the pit of his stomach with stones of guilt. "I did not wish to hate you, Alexander. I wanted very much to care for you because you were to be my husband."

The knowledge that she had meant to accept him, struck him with the force of a battle-ax and he drew a deep breath.

She raised her chin. "'Twas a lifetime ago when I was innocent enough to trust you. 'Twill not happen again."

He bit back a curse. "If 'tis any satisfaction to you, your father's revenge was most effective. 'Twas difficult for me to sit, stand, eat, or ride a horse for some days."

"I find no satisfaction in that, Alexander. You are able to walk about your clan, or any other, with your honor whole. Your wounds have healed; mine shall go on for a lifetime." She stalked away from him, the tail of her shawl whipping back and forth behind her.

He watched the sway of her hips. If he could keep her talking and allow her to punish him a bit, mayhap, it would draw some of the poison from the wound.

He caught up to her and matched his long strides to her shorter ones. "Did I not make it plain how much I wanted you, Mary?"

"Aye, just as you made it plain that night you were there to destroy my honor in any way you could." Her voice shook with emotion.

He flinched from the memory her words conjured and reached for her hand in an attempt to comfort her.

She jerked away, her expression defiant. She folded her arms before her in such a way it prevented him from holding her hand again.

In that moment, she reminded him of the wild birds sometimes caught and caged for pleasure. Some could be tamed, but it took great patience and gentleness. Others beat themselves against the bars until they died, no matter how patient or gentle their master. She would continue to fight against him as long as she felt trapped.

"For ten long years I have known little else but fighting, killing, and bloodshed," he said as he followed the path that she traversed close to the water. "First 'twas the feuds between our clan and others, then 'twas the English, then more feuding between those who lust for power and those who have it. 'Twas by spilling the blood of others, that I earned my lands. When The Bruce gave them to me, I thought, at last, I would have something that represented what was good in life to be proud of and to share with the clansmen who have fought at my side."

Folding his hands behind him, he focused his attention on the green rolling hills across the loch and the narrow gullies meandering through them. A breeze holding an autumn chill ruffled the surface of the water, making it glitter in the midday sun.

"You have been a part of that for these two years past, though you were not even aware of it." His gaze swung to her face. "For the first time I allowed myself to think of peace and a wife and children."

Her clear, blue eyes, surrounded by light brown lashes tipped with gold, looked as deep and unfathomable as the loch. The full shape of her lips begged to be traced by a lover's tongue. He caressed the fragile curve of her cheek and jaw with his fingertips, delighting in the softness of her skin.

She stepped back breaking the contact. "You will have your child, your lands, and your clan. Your dream will be fulfilled."

"I want a wife as well." His gaze settled on her so she would know he spoke the truth. "Does the bairn not deserve a father to offer him protection, and a mother to offer him care? Must you punish the child for the sins of his father?"

"Do you wish to wed a lass who can not bear your touch?"

Alexander sucked in a pained breath, her words cutting deep.

David's voice came from atop the battlements. "Father awaits your return, Alexander."

He scowled, resentful of the interruption.

"The council has arrived to meet with you and Mary."

****

The six men that apprized the council had the seasoned appearance of warriors dressed as they were in the full regalia of their stations, their swords at their sides. Gray streaked through their hair and beards, and their faces held the worn lines of time and experience. Their fur-lined cloaks each bore the crest of their clan, three Campbell and three MacLachlan.

Mary found such an awe-inspiring company more than a little frightening. Her eyes sought Alexander's face, but his attention remained fastened on the men as he inclined his head to each.

She focused on the priest who stood beside her father. Father Patrick, his black shrouded figure tall and thin, inclined his head in greeting to her. With his beak-like nose and long neck, he had the look of a large black bird. She studied his expression trying to delve beneath the surface of his features. Would he be ally or enemy in these proceedings?

"In deference to my daughter, I have asked this council of arbitration to meet in private," Collin said.

Rising, his expression grave, John announced, "We will retire to my antechamber." The men rose in force to do as he ordered.

"That will not be necessary, Lord Campbell," she said in a voice she hoped sounded calm though she found herself trembling. "I would ask you to stop these proceedings now. I have not asked for such an intervention between your son and me."

"As Chief of the MacLachlan clan, I can not knowingly ignore a wrong to one of our own, Mary," Collin challenged, before John could speak.

"'This is a private matter between Alexander and me, no one else." She squared her shoulders in determination. She would not have her shame paraded before this clan as it had been before her own and the MacMillans.

"It ceased to be private when you fled from your home to seek refuge from him," Collin said, his features taut. "'Tis my duty to see justice done, Mary."

She folded her arms before her. "'Tis my right to seek justice if I see fit. Not yours." She fought the urge to scream at him that his quest for power and property would shame her just as much as Alexander's actions if he continued.

"'Tis my right being your father and your Laird, lass."

She shook her head. "I will not speak agin him, to you or anyone else."

"If you will not speak, then I will be forced to bring forth witnesses who will testify to what transpired between you."

She stiffened in outrage. "No one, but Alexander and I know the truth. If anyone says otherwise, they speak falsely."

"Do you deny you are with child, Mary?" Collin demanded.

A prickle of fearful wariness ran up the back of her neck. "Nay, I can not deny that."

"Do you admit the child belongs to Alexander?" Collin asked.

"Aye, the bairn is his."

"There are only two ways in which a child may be conceived, Daughter, by consent or against it. By which was your bairn conceived?"

Mary remained silent a moment. She would not lie to seek vengeance and see her bairn deprived of a father. Did Collin truly think she would? Her gaze focused on the priest. "Father Patrick said I tempted Alexander." Her voice shook. "He said 'tis the nature of woman to tempt man, as Eve tempted Adam."

"Nay, Mary." Alexander stepped forward and rested a hand against the small of her back. "You were innocent, lass. "T'was I who—"

"Do not say more, Alexander!" The words were torn from her in panic. She placed a hand against his chest to stay his words.

"'Twould seem the two of them are intent on protecting one another, Collin." One of the men on the council said as he retained his seat at the table close to the fire. "How are we to choose which to punish, when neither will speak agin the other?"

Collin strode forward to face her. "If you will not speak agin him, you must be punished for the part you took in it. Whore!" The word roared through the room as he shouted it at her.

Mary flinched.

Alexander lashed out, striking Collin in the face with such force; it drove him backward into the midst of the cluster of men.

Collin pushed away from them to regain his feet and spat blood from his mouth. His features twisted with rage. He drew his sword.

As Alexander freed his broad sword, she stepped between the two before the first strike could land. Alexander grasped her arm and jerked her back causing her to stagger. He caught her about the waist and held her tight against his side. He turned his body to shield her from her father as he advanced on them.

Campbell and MacLachlan clansmen armed themselves. The chilling sound of weapons being drawn rang out on either side of the room.

"Enough!" John Campbell's shout carried over the din and his fist struck the top of a wide wooden table with the hollowness of a gavel. "There will be no blood-letting here this day." His amber gaze traveled about the room in challenge, then settled on Collin. Campbell's tawny glare held a feral gleam of violence held in check. "'Twas you who ordered this council to settle this dispute peacefully, Collin," he reminded, "You said you would abide by their decision."

"I did not know my daughter would lie to defend him." Collin pointed at Alexander with his sword.

"You have made a charge against your daughter maligning her reputation, Collin MacLachlan. Do you plan to produce witnesses to support such a charge?" One of the MacLachlan chieftains asked.

"Alexander Campbell may witness to her conduct," Collin taunted.

A sound of protest was torn from her.

Alexander's arm tightened around her. "Mary had not been kissed nor touched in any way until I took her to me," he said, his voice carrying throughout the room. "Our union was secured by the betrothal contract and that is as binding as a marriage decree. I mean to wed her whenever she wishes."

"She has refused to accept you because you took her against her will," Collin shouted. "Speak now, Mary, and tell them it is so."

Collin's eyes were a bright burning blue, his cheeks flushed a feverish hue. She felt sick knowing the lengths he would go to gain another's property and undermine their power.

Her attention shifted to the swords drawn and ready. Her answer could cause an outbreak of bloodshed that would only bring pain to the innocent and rekindle a feud that would continue indefinitely. She wanted no such legacy for her child.

She pulled away from Alexander to stand alone.

"Father Patrick." She searched for the priest's habit among the many clansmen.

"Aye, Lady Mary." His voice came from somewhere at the back of the room. Avoiding the drawn swords on every side, he wove his way through the men to come to her.

Her composure nearly deserted her as she looked up into his face. "I would ask that you wed us now, so that peace may be restored."

His relief evident, the priest nodded. "'Twill be my honor, Lady Mary."

****

Dread twisted the muscles between Mary's shoulder blades. Bound to a man who harbored no affection or respect for her, the future stretched like a dark empty abyss before her, frightening and cold. The very thing she had fought against was happening and she was powerless to stop it.

Father Patrick's voice droned on as he expounded on

the sanctity of marriage. A dull ache had settled in the small of her back, and her knees had grown stiff before they rose from their kneeling position and faced one another to exchange the vows.

Her composure uncertain, she avoided looking up as Alexander grasped her cold hands and held them within his.

His deep voice though quiet, filled the room. "I, Alexander, son of John Campbell, take thee, Mary, daughter of Collin MacLachlan, to be my wife. In the presence of God and before these witnesses I promise to be a loving, faithful, and loyal husband to thee, until God shall separate us by death."

Her voice came out just above a whisper as she recited the vows. "I, Mary MacLachlan, daughter of Collin MacLachlan, now take thee, Alexander Campbell, son of John Campbell, to be my husband. In the presence of God and before these witnesses I promise to be a loving, faithful, and loyal wife to thee, until God shall separate us by death."

She finally looked up at him as he drew her close.

"'Twould not be official without a kiss to seal the vows, Mary," he said softly. He brushed her lips gently with his own.

A deafening cheer went up from the Campbell clansmen. She started, thinking violence had broken out despite the occasion.

Alexander's arms tightened around her. "They are voicing their approval of the match, lass," he said against her ear and gave her slender waist a reassuring squeeze.

John rested his hands on her shoulders as he looked down into her face. "'Tis glad I am to claim you as my new daughter." He drew her to him in a hug more fatherly than any Collin had ever offered her.

"You are a fool, Mary," Collin said as he glared down at her. "You could have claimed all he has for the bairn and seen him punished as well."

Mary looked into his face, for the last time she hoped. Never again would she acknowledge him as her sire. The tenuous ties between them were severed by that one word he yelled at her. *Whore.* He had been willing to sacrifice her honor for whatever he could gain for himself.

"Why would you not speak agin him?" he demanded when she remained silent.

She uttered the words most certain to gain for her the only revenge available to her. "Because you wished it."

Collin's head snapped back as though she had struck him. His face grew red, his eyes a glaring blue. The rage evident in his features moved beyond anything she had ever witnessed from him before. He thrust his face close to hers. "You deserve whatever sorrow he brings you, Daughter," he said, the spite in his words intent.

He turned and, signaling his men to follow, left the great hall. The MacLachlan clansmen followed in force, leaving only the Campbells and the few MacLachlan chiefs who had taken part in the arbitration.

"Introduce your wife to our company, Alexander. They shall be staying for the evening meal," John announced.

Chapter Five

Alexander's men were in high spirits at the evening meal. James and Robert Campbell, the two red haired members of the group bore the brunt of the humorous revelry for both were expected to marry soon.

Content to sit and listen to their jests, Mary nibbled sporadically at the food set before her. Roasted fowl and pork, pastries filled with ham and chicken, smoked salmon, cooked vegetables, cheese and flat loaves of bread drizzled with honey, were offered to her, but nerves held her appetite at bay.

Alexander moved the trencher they shared closer to her so she could reach it more easily then frowned when she pushed it back toward him and sipped her drink. "Is the food not to your liking, Mary?"

"'Tis very good, I have eaten my fill."

"There is something to be said for having a good lass to come home to," William said.

"The many wee Campbell's who are running about when I visit your hut is proof enough of that, Willy," Derrick teased, his dark brown eyes alight with humor.

"You're doing your own part to keep the name alive, Derrick. Your brood had swelled to four the last time I counted."

"'Twill be five in not so many months," he boasted with a grin.

"'Twould seem the lot of you have studied but a few scriptures, and only paid service when the words, be fruitful and multiply were mentioned," Duncan teased.

The men all laughed and made comments that had Alexander leaning forward and sweeping them with a look that subdued their rowdy humor.

"Alas, Mary," Duncan said, his tone mournful, "I have a weakness which plaques me greatly." He paused for effect then continued. 'Tis lasses. I like them all. Be they short or tall, stout or slender, fair of face or plain, I find I can not resist any of them."

"Aye. 'Tis the reason the rest of us keep our women folk close by when he is about," Samuel said with a grin.

Alexander had taken little part in their jests and his displeasure was evident in the gaze he fastened on his brother.

"It has been told to me you were raised within the MacPherson Clan, Lady Mary," Shamus Campbell said, introducing a safer topic from across the table.

"Aye. My Aunt Agnes was wed into the clan to the brother of the Laird, Hugh MacPherson. 'Twas the two of them who raised my sister and me from the age of six."

"My wife was a MacPherson. Mayhap you will speak to her about the clan when next we visit."

For the first time all evening, a cautious smile tilted her lips. "I shall look forward to it."

"It has been many years since she has visited her family. Her brother is Robert MacPherson of Cluny."

"My sister and I often played as children with his daughters Edina and Rose. Edina had wed and was expecting her first bairn when we were sent to Collin MacLachlan."

"My wife will be pleased to hear the news. I'll be telling her as soon as I return home."

The next smile came more easily.

"How oft were you called home from the MacPherson Clan, Mary?" David Campbell asked from beside Alexander.

"We were called home thrice in twelve years. Once at Christmastide when my mother still lived. When my mother died, we returned for a week. Then, when Collin decided to find a match for my sister."

"'Tis unusual for a fostered child to remain so long away from home," Lamont Campbell, Alexander's uncle, said from down the table.

"We were treated like daughters of the house by my aunt and uncle. I have no complaints to offer in that."

"I understand your unwillingness to have our children fostered, Mary," Alexander commented. "You should have been welcomed home more oft."

"'Tis not the only reason. Duty and loyalty come more

readily toward those we have lived and worked beside. I but wish to raise my children within the bosom of the clan I would expect them to honor and defend."

He nodded in understanding.

"But your daughters may marry outside the clan," David suggested.

"I pray not. Every child who is sacrificed in the name of harmony or gain means the clan is weakened. You are making a gift of your own strength and courage and honor for 'tis bred into your children just as you breed strength and stamina into your horses."

She focused her attention on the bread she crumbled with restless fingers. "I have always been amazed that men are willing to give away their own flesh and blood to those whom they would not even entrust their sword or shield."

Her gaze rose to find every male eye at the table turned on her. Heat touched her cheeks.

"'Tis fortunate your father has entrusted you to my brother, Mary." Duncan smiled. "'Tis not every day a man gains a sister."

"Aye." David nodded and raised his tankard of ale to her.

The pleasure she felt at their acceptance brought a quick smile, to her lips. "'Tis generous of you to speak so of me."

****

Resentment twisted inside Alexander at the ready smiles Mary offered Duncan and David. It had been some time since she had smiled at him or even looked upon him with anything, but pain or loathing. The words she had spoken to him in the courtyard repeated themselves over and over again in his mind, pricking him each time with new pain. There had to be a way to ease her anger and loathing of him.

Immediately aware of her absence when she slipped away from the table, he watched her climb the stairs to the gallery above and turn in the direction of her chamber. Knowing he would be joining her this night as her husband brought no feelings of the excitement or anticipation to bear. She would not accept him willingly, and he would not force her.

"I wonder, Brother, how long it will be before she forgives you," Duncan said as he took Mary's place beside him.

"My knees will be calloused from begging pardon most likely." It took effort to keep his expression free of the despair plaguing him.

Duncan chuckled in appreciation of his humor. "Do you still believe she is worth it?"

"Aye." He forced a smile to his lips. "Any woman who looks upon her husband as breeding stock has to be admired. You should appreciate that, Brother."

Duncan laughed aloud and slapped him on the back. "At least you have the satisfaction of knowing you have thwarted Collin's plans, whatever they might have been." His tone grew serious. "I wanted to smash his face in myself, in Mary's defense, as did every man here."

"He is gone now." Alexander shrugged. "He will never mistreat Mary again. Whatever kind of father I shall be, I know for certes I shall be well above Collin MacLachlan."

"Aye." Duncan nodded his agreement. "Mayhap that will be the way to prove how good a husband you may be as well."

Alexander studied his brother thoughtfully. Duncan had considerable experience with women. He had witnessed, more than once, the easy way his brother had with them.

"My first duty to my wife will be to warn her about her new brother, Duncan."

Duncan chuckled and slapped him on the back again. "I will not add to your troubles, Alexander. 'Twould seem you already have your fill."

****

"Might I have a wee bit of wine, Cora?" Mary asked. She could not still the trembling afflicting her.

Resting a soothing hand on her shoulder, the gray haired servant set aside the ribbons she held. "Aye, Lady Mary. I'll get it now." The woman hastened from the chamber.

Gunna ran the brush through Mary's hair in a soothing rhythm. She braided the silvery strands at either side of her face then tied them back with a scrap of ribbon. "You're a beauty, Lady Mary. Your bairn will be hearty and handsome, to be sure."

"'Tis my hope, Gunna." Her voice came out breathy and weak and she cleared her throat. "How long has Alexander been a warrior?" Mayhap if she knew more about him, she would be able to reason with him later.

"He fought his first battle at ten and five." The woman's lined face settled into a thoughtful frown as she tucked a stray curl back into place. "It has been that many years since as well. He has fought with the Bruce for some time."

Some of the stories she had heard in her uncle's household came to mind. Stories of battle and bravery and horrible bloodshed. Such experiences could not help but affect a man. Mayhap that was what he had been trying to tell her beside the loch. Mayhap he had never known true affection because all he had experienced, since a lad, was violence and aggression. He cared for his brothers without reservation; perhaps it was only her he could feel nothing for.

"How long have you served the Laird, Gunna?"

"A score of years at least, since I was in my tenth year of marriage. Mistress Kate wished only women already wed to work about the castle. What with three sons and all the men about, she thought 'twas best."

Mary tucked her hands between her knees in effort to still their traitorous twitching. "How long has it been since she died?"

"Five years." The woman moved to the bed, returned with one of the heavy pelts, and draped it around Mary.

Mary pulled the fur close about her, covering her bare arms and hiding from view the soft white muslin shift she wore. She started as a knock sounded at the chamber door.

"'Tis only Cora with the wine," Gunna reassured her as she moved to answer the summons.

Alexander stood outside the portal. In his hands, he bore a tray holding a bottle and two brass goblets.

Gunna stepped back to allow him entrance into the room, her gaze turning to Mary. "Will there be anything more you'll be needing, Lady Mary?" she asked, after a moments pause.

Mary shook her head, unable to draw enough breath

to speak. She followed the woman's progress from the room with a sinking feeling of despair.

Alexander lowered the tray to the table where the washbasin rested. "Cora said you wished a wee drop of wine. 'Twas a good time to slip away from my men before they offered to see me to the chamber door." He uncorked the bottle and filled the brass goblets then brought the drink to her where she sat before the fire.

Unwilling to give up the modesty of the pelt, she tucked it beneath her arms. She cupped the bowl of the goblet with both hands for fear of spilling the liquid. He waited until she took a small sip before raising his own to his lips.

Her eyes sought her husband's face to find his features caught in repose. The light of the fire reflected in the tawny tone of his gaze and played across the strong lean plane of his jaw. His bold features, heavily masculine, held an intimidating gravity. The scar running from his cheek to his jaw made the seriousness of his expression appear formidable.

The strength she had admired so much when first they met remained there, but the light of humor that had tempered it had been lacking all evening. Though he had shown her consideration a number of times after the wedding, he had been stoically silent for much of the evening. His mood made her all the more uncertain of him.

She had never believed herself a coward, but the knowledge that she might have to surrender her body to him again, brought with it a sick feeling of dread. It was not the physical act that frightened her, but the way she might feel after the deed. His gentleness had deceived her. She had believed he held some affection for her. Knowing he had taken what she had to offer in a bid to seek revenge against her father, and her clan, had crushed her pride and shaken her belief in herself. Never again would she trust so readily. If she could not expect him to show her respect, how could she share her body with him?

Aware of Alexander's every move, she watched as he removed the heavy girdle holding his sword and hung it over the post at the head of the bed. Returning to her, he reached to take her goblet and set it aside.

Her breath left her completely as he bent to slide an arm beneath her legs and one behind her, around her waist. He carried her to the bed, and raising a knee on the well-stuffed mattress, lowered her to its center.

Tears burnt her eyes. "I will not allow you to touch me again, Alexander. I will fight you."

His body tensing, he went completely still. She became aware of the heavy beat of his heart throbbing beneath her cheek as his hand moved with gentle pressure to cup the back of her head and hold her. "I do not intend to force you to accept me, Mary."

After several moments she regained her composure and she pulled back to look up at him.

"'Tis a natural thing for a man to want to hold his new wife, lass." He settled himself more comfortably beside her. "'Twas in my thoughts that mayhap if we hold each other long enough and often enough, the pain will ease and other things will come more naturally between us."

Her eyes tracing his features, she wondered if anything could be natural between them after such a beginning. "You do not mean to-to-"

He shook his head.

Relief unwound like a coiled rope inside her. Her trembling eased a bit.

He brushed the soft strands of hair back from her face with a touch carefully gentle, his pale amber eyes intent on her features. "You are my wife now, Mary. No one will dare speak agin you again. 'Twas never my intent to shame you, lass, but to force Collin to abide by the contract."

It was as close to an apology as she could expect from him. It did little to ease the injury to her pride or her heart.

Her gaze shifted downward to the swath of wool material hung over his shoulder. She cautioned herself against the dangers of behaving as a tenderhearted fool. "'Tis in the past now and we cannot change it. 'Tis up to us to learn to live with it, for the bairn's sake."

Silence once again fell between them.

"You speak as though the child will be a boy."

"I hope 'tis."

"I rather fancy a lass with her mother's hair and eyes."

She shrugged aside the compliment. "A boy will never be bartered for what he can bring the clan." She spoke with soft conviction. "Nor will his destiny always be controlled by others. I would have that for my child."

He fell silent for a moment. "Would you wish yourself a lad, Mary?"

Had she been a lad she would never have suffered such indignities. She would have been looked upon with more value. "'Twould do no good to wish for such a thing, but it does no harm to wish better for the bairn."

He frowned. "And what if the bairn is a lass?"

She would grieve for her. "I will stand betwixt her and harm all I can." She turned on her side away from him.

****

Alexander shook his head. What were they to have from the marriage if she could find no pleasure in being a woman, or a wife? He studied her bundled form covered from neck to toe by the pelt. He moved closer to slide an arm around her waist and tuck his legs beneath hers. She stiffened, but did not pull away.

The clean womanly scent of her brought to mind the intimate moments they had shared. His arm tightened around her waist. He savored the feel of her body cradled against his.

He supposed part of his punishment was that he might never know what it was for her to come to him willingly, as she had done the first time. Worse still, he had only himself to blame.

He thought of Duncan's suggestion.

"Might I touch you where the bairn rests, Mary?"

She turned to look at him open suspicion in her gaze. "Why?"

"'Tis my child too. I will not know what 'tis for it to grow inside you lest you allow me to touch you."

He could see the indecision pulling at her as her gaze shifted away from him. He wondered if a sense of duty toward him as her husband played any part in that. "'Tis a small thing to ask in the place of other considerations."

Her movements hesitant, she turned onto her back and opened the cocoon of fur around her. The soft muslin fabric of her shift clung to the slender curves of her body. She was reed thin, but for the generous curve of her breasts and a slight roundness to her lower abdomen. Her body so lightly clad, was completely vulnerable to his gaze. The budding thrust of her nipples against the thin fabric drew his attention. The instant rush of blood to his loins left him hard and aching. He drew a slow steadying breath and placed his palm against the faint protrusion designating where the bairn lay. The soft feel of her beneath his touch intensified his desire.

Mary bent her knees, her legs trembling visibly. Alexander raised his gaze to her face. Her pale blue eyes were anxious and wary, her cheeks flushed with color. He arranged the pelt over her, a painful sense of loss twisting inside him. "I would not have you catch a chill."

He left the bed and turned away to stand at the fireplace. To want her and to see the look of pain and distrust in her gaze was too much for him.

****

Mary studied the broad back he turned to her. His sudden withdrawal though confusing to her, also brought her relief. Her body's response to his touch had surprised her. Her legs felt weak and the tingling heated feeling his touch had inspired still lingered.

Memories of how his beard felt against the bare skin of her breasts played through her thoughts. Her nipples tightened in memory of the wet heat of his mouth. Her heart pounded against her ribs making her breathing ragged.

How could he still have the power to make her feel such things? Her emotions and thoughts spiraling in confusion, she turned her back to the room and burrowed her face into the bed clothes in the hope that, if she blocked out the sight of him, the memories would cease to torment her.

Chapter Six

Alexander studied the village nestled within the narrow valley between the loch and the shoulder of the mountains. The small gathering of stone buildings looked well kept, the yards clean and tended.

Before he and Mary reached the first house, several people came out of their huts.

An ancient woman with a profound limp appeared from the entrance of a small stone cottage. "Have you brought your bride to meet us, Alexander?"

"Aye, Maggie. There'll be a feast to celebrate our marriage before Mary and I take our leave. You must promise me a dance."

The old woman leaned heavily upon a walking stick as she hobbled up the path to the road. Her hair, nearly all white, brushed her bent shoulders. He moved to embrace her with tender care, for she appeared more fragile than the last time he had visited.

"The only lass you should be thinking of dancing with is the one you have wed, Alexander." She shook her finger at him.

He laughed. "Mary this is my grandmother, Maggie," he said by way of introduction as he stepped back.

Her astonishment momentarily evident, she moved forward to greet the woman with a curtsy. "'Tis an honor to meet you." She grasped his grandmother's hands in her own.

He watched the eager way his grandmother studied her features. "'Tis a beauty you have wed, Alexander."

He smiled. "Aye, she is."

"You shall have many handsome children together."

Mary's cheeks grew red and she avoided his gaze.

He gave a brief nod. "God willing."

"Mary Campbell, 'tis glad I am you have come to us. I wish you great happiness with my grandson."

"Thank you, grandmother. I do not think I will mind greatly Alexander dancing with you."

Maggie chuckled. "You mayna feel the same about some of the younger women who have hoped to have him these past years."

"What is in the past, is past. 'Tis what comes from now into the future that is important."

Alexander searched Mary's features, seeking a message in those words for himself, but she did not look his way.

Several people approached to be introduced and to offer small gifts to honor the marriage. Mary exclaimed over each, then placed the tokens in his arms to carry so she could greet each person in turn. He smiled as his grandmother introduced her to several villagers as her new grand daughter. He found it pleasing they should take to one another so easily.

An hour passed. He noticed Mary shivered beneath the meager covering of the wool tartan. "We must go, Mary. You may return to visit again tomorrow if you wish."

Mary embraced Maggie and murmured a word of thanks. She reached to take some of the gifts from Alexander to help him carry them.

"Leave them, lass, I can carry them. You must hold my arm lest you trip along the way."

Calls of farewell followed them down the slope to ground that was more level. He harbored a feeling of pleasure when she continued to hold his arm for she rarely touched him voluntarily.

"How old would your grandmother be, Alexander?"

"Three score and ten at least. She will not tell anyone for certes."

Her soft laughter trickled forth. The first time he had heard her laugh since her sister's betrothal. Alexander relished the sound.

"'Twas very cordial of them all to be so generous," she said.

"Aye, I did not doubt they would accept you, Mary."

"Your father wishes me to take an oath of fealty to him after we have known one another longer."

Unsurprised, he inclined his head. "Was it that you

were talking about earlier this morn?"

"Aye."

"'Twould seal the bonds between you and my family." And perhaps make it more difficult for her to walk away from his clan once the bairn was born.

"Would not a grandchild do as well?"

"Aye, but the other will allow my father, as Chief, to act on your behalf in other matters, should the need ever arise."

"I have thought of that." She drew a deep breath. "I will not do it for that alone, Alexander. 'Twill have to come from the heart or it shan't mean what it should."

Her words had his gaze focusing on her face. Would he ever be able to inspire such consideration from her.

She made certain his clothing stayed mended and clean. She saw the water for his baths warmed and that he wanted for nothing at meals, but she did not approach him for anything for herself.

Her need for clothing was becoming an embarrassment, yet she did not ask him for the coin to purchase the cloth with which to make new garments. They spoke about his family, but she offered him nothing about hers. He knew not how to reach beyond the barrier of her hurt pride and relentless distrust.

****

They entered the castle through the passageway on the west side. Alexander opened a door and led her into a large room furnished only with a long table surrounded by chairs. A fire crackled and popped within the great stone fireplace. He guided her close to the blaze to get warm.

"Will your father not mind that we are here?"

"Nay." He shook his head and laid the gifts in a chair. "To have a moment alone with you between waking and sleep has grown difficult. 'Tis partly his fault I must resort to hiding away with you if only to have an uninterrupted conversation."

His complaint was legitimate. It seemed to Mary that John Campbell meant to keep them apart. For the past fortnight, he had sent Alexander and his brothers hunting or fishing every morning and had kept them late every evening drinking and gaming with his men.

"I'll be going to net salmon early on the morrow with

Duncan and David." A frown worked its way across his brow as he stood beside her before the fire, his hands folded behind him.

"'Twill be a fine dish to serve at the feast."

"Aye." His tone held no enthusiasm.

She focused on the rugged planes of her husband's face as he stared into the fire. Lines about his mouth were more deeply etched than before and he had grown thinner in the past fortnight. They were man and wife, joined in marriage, but so very far apart. She found the thought of spending the rest of her days bound to him in such a cold empty union unbearable. Yet, even if he professed his love on bended knee, would she be able to believe him?

"Alexander—," she began in a tentative tone, uncertain of what to say to lessen the distance between them.

His gaze leaped to her face.

The door behind them opened to admit the Laird of the Campbell clan, his expression grave. "The patrol I sent out earlier has discovered a slaughtered ewe along the loch. There are signs someone has been camping there. Duncan and David will be seeing to it. Will you be going with them?"

Alexander nodded then turned to Mary. "When I return, we will continue our conversation."

Mayhap by then she would know what she wished to say to him.

She reached for the tartan shawl as he left.

"'Tis sorry I am your time together had to be cut short, Mary," John said. His eyes so similar to his son's probed her face.

"Clan property must be defended and recovered."

"Alexander, more than the others, has always had a deep rooted sense of what was expected of him. I was more zealous in my discipline and training with him."

She smoothed the material of the tartan over her arm.

"Mayhap I am partially at fault for his actions, lass."

Her eyes swung to his face.

"If you are to leave the past in the past, you must speak of it to one another. 'Twill take some of the sting from the wound."

61

She found it hard to speak to the back of Alexander's head. "There has been little time of late." Her gaze drifted away from him.

"You are his wife. 'Tis your right to make demands on his time, if you wish."

She bit her bottom lip. She did not feel she had the right to demand anything of him. She was not his wife in any way other than in name.

"I am tired of this hostile silence that grows longer and longer between you, Mary. One of you must end it!" John grasped her chin, his features harsh with a frown. "You have a duty to your husband. 'Tis up to you to abide by the vows you spoke and serve him."

She pulled away from him, angry that he would speak to her of duty when it was his son who had turned away from her. "I do serve him, I carry his son!"

"One of you must bend."

"Aye," she agreed. Surprised to see relief flicker across his face, she continued, "'Twill have to be Alexander. I can not speak of peace to a man who will not even look at me."

A scowl darkened his face. "What do you mean?"

"He stares off into the distance and stands like a stone or turns his back to me in a way that is less than welcoming."

"Nonsense! You are not a weak livered lass. You must be firm." John clenched his fist in emphasis.

She laughed, finding the suggestion amusing. "I shall be firm with a man more than twice my size."

"You are a woman. You may use that to guide him in the direction you wish him to follow."

Her laughter died. Every part of her shrank from the suggestion. "Nay!" To approach him in such a way would be to encourage him. To encourage him would leave her open to hurt once again. "If I can not reason with him then we will continue as we are."

John laid a hand on her shoulder in a gesture of comfort.

She turned her face away as quick tears burnt her eyes.

"You must be willing to try, Mary," John urged. "Or do you wish to be set aside and have another take your place?"

She caught her breath, the idea more painful than she wanted to admit. "If that is what he wishes, there is nothing I can do."

John scowled. "'Twill be you who will have to begin. 'Twill take one small gesture to ease the way," he urged. "I believe my son is waiting for that."

One gesture could lead to more than she felt willing to concede.

"'Tis not only for my son's happiness that I am concerned, but yours as well, lass. 'Tis a hard life and too short to be wed to someone with whom you can not find fulfillment."

She did not understand what he meant by that.

John touched her shoulder again. "Alexander can show you the way to what I speak, if you will allow it."

Silence stretched between them. "'Tis difficult for a man to admit he is in the wrong and twice as hard for him to beg forgiveness, Mary."

She raised her chin. "Mayhap it depends on how much of a man he is, m'lord."

****

Mary lifted the heavy pot from the fire and poured the hot water into the washbasin. She unfastened the sleeves of her kirtle and loosened the drawstring along the neckline to shed the garment. As she soaped a linen cloth, her thoughts dwelt on John's advice and his words of warning. To be set aside would be one more humiliation. She did not think she could face that atop every other blow she had been dealt of late. Just the idea brought an ache to life in the pit of her stomach.

If bruised pride were the only thing keeping her from being a true wife to Alexander, she would seek peace between them now, this moment. But it was not. He had intentionally stripped her honor from her that night, as surely as he had her shift. He had left her naked and vulnerable before her father's men as though she were the whore her father had called her. He had taken her virginity and paraded the proof before all to see, as though she were a thing to be claimed and used like his horse, or his sword, but less. So much less. The fear of being treated without respect, without care, had been beaten into her with every lash she had received. She prayed for the hurt and distrust to leave her each day. And for the broken feeling inside her to heal. Mayhap if he offered her a sincere apology, she could release some of the anger and pain.

Her bath finished, Mary donned her shift then lifted the washbasin to empty it in the chamber pot. A wet patch on the floor caught her unaware and her feet slid across the slick stone. Her arms jerked upward and the crockery bowl she held flew through the air and shattered on the hearth. Twisting, she tried to catch herself. She landed hard on her hip and elbow. Pain shot like an arrow through her arm and she writhed in silent agony as she cradled it against her. Vaguely aware of the door to the chamber being thrust open, she curled in on herself.

"You must show me where you are hurt, Mary," Alexander demanded, his voice penetrating the painful haze. "Is it the bairn?"

Her hand went protectively to the small mound. "Nay. 'Tis my arm."

He helped her sit up. The gravity of what could have happened, what might yet happen, fell on her with the weight of a war axe. In fear, she reached out to him. Alexander's arms went around her in a protective rush.

"All will be well, Mary." He sounded out of breath though his tone was reassuring.

She clung to him, fearful and trembling for some moments.

"You are not in pain?" He rested his hand over hers, cradling the fragile evidence of the life she carried.

"Nay." Her voice, swallowed up by reaction, sounded breathy and weak.

"Or here?" He touched the curve of her lower back.

"Nay."

"'That is good." He gave her back a soothing rub.

"How do you know?" she asked. Desperate to accept his reassurance, her eyes sought his face.

"That is where it brings pain to a woman when she labors."

"How would you know such things?"

His smile was reassuring, though she read concern in his frown. "I've been there when my men's wives were laboring to have their children. I've even birthed one of the babes when the midwife did not arrive in time."

He touched her cheek in a gentle caress. "Do you wish to rise from the floor?

"Aye," she nodded, calmed by his manner. Her legs felt weak as he guided her to the bed. His nearness was comforting as he sat beside her and held her against him. Her trembling eventually ceased and the cold feeling of fear receded.

"You must rest."

Mary nodded in agreement though, for once, she was reluctant for him to move away. She curled on her side and he drew one of the pelts over her. Alexander settled on the edge of the bed beside her. She found his touch warm and reassuring as he held her hand in his. He tucked a wayward strand of hair behind her ear.

"You are sure you feel no pain?"

"My arm."

He turned her arm to view the bruise already forming on her elbow.

"Twill be black by morn." He frowned.

She grimaced as she touched her hip gingerly. "Aye, there'll be one here as well."

"You will not let me see that one."

Mary studied his face intently. Following her earlier thoughts, the concern she read in his face, the gentleness of his touch confounded her. It was difficult, no impossible, to reconcile the man who had turned against her that night, with the one to whom she was now wed. Of course, it was the bairn that concerned him, she told herself. After all, the child would be his heir.

But just once, she wished she could be certain she too, was included in his concern.

Alexander surprised her further by remaining close throughout the remainder of the afternoon. When she retired early after the evening meal, he soon joined her. She found his attentiveness both comforting and disturbing. When he pressed close to hold her in bed, she could not bring herself to turn him aside.

"Cora said you must rest for the next three or four days," he said. "She will stay with you in my stead tomorrow whilst I am away. You must tell her should you have any pain."

She nodded.

His hand found hers and he wove his fingers through hers. "All will be well, Mary."

And if it was not? If they lost the bairn, what then would they have together? The emptiness stretched like a long lonely chasm between them, more painful to her than her distrust of her husband. It was not his duty alone to find peace between them, but hers as well. But how was she to set aside her fears to do it?

Chapter Seven

"Are you warm enough, Mary?" David asked.

She turned to look over her shoulder at him. "Aye." She drew the fur-lined hood of the cloak up over her head to protect her ears from the wind and looked out over the loch. The blue of the water appeared almost purple in spots from so high up. Brownish hills, dusted with snow rolled away into the distance. Being atop the battlements gave her a sense of freedom she had not experienced since leaving her MacPherson kin.

"Which direction is it to MacMillan lands?" she asked.

"South." He raised a hand to point.

She focused her attention in that direction, her eyes following the contours of the land.

"Alexander has told us of your sister. He said she is almost identical to you."

"Aye, 'tis true."

"You have never been apart from her?" David leaned against the stone battlements and looked out over the loch as she did.

"Nay, not until four months ago."

His dark brows drew together above a straight narrow nose. His features were more refined than his brother's, though no less appealing.

"Mayhap she will come to be with you when the bairn arrives." He turned somber gray eyes to her.

Grief rose up to smite her, bringing with it an almost physical pain. That would never happen. Anne's loyalty belonged with her husband now. The past could not be changed.

Her homesickness for her MacPherson kin had been nothing compared to this. In a castle filled with her husband's family and clansmen, she carried an empty ache of loneliness beneath her ribs that never eased.

She changed the subject. "Where do Alexander's

lands lie?"

"North, then west. 'Tis only a two day ride from here." He folded his arms atop the stone wall. "Has he said when you'll be leaving?"

"After the feast your father has arranged. He wishes to arrive home before the weather grows worse."

"'Tis wise. 'Twill snow soon, and the passage will be more difficult. You must have a care for yourself and stay warm, Mary."

"'Twill be easier to do that now with such a fine cloak. Your father's gift was very generous."

David grinned. "I must tell you 'twas Alexander who had it made—and the gowns."

"Aye, I know." She rested her cheek against the cold stone block as she looked below to the group of men on the dock. She did not understand why her husband could not give her the gifts himself. Did he think she would not accept them from him?

Hearing a step behind them, she turned to see Duncan clearing the top of the ladder.

"Alexander will not be pleased you are up here, Mary. He has been looking for you downstairs."

"Nay, I am not pleased."

Her husband's voice had her stomach plummeting. He frowned so oft these days and was nothing like the man who had laughed and smiled with her at Lochlan when first they had met.

"What are you doing up here?"

His clipped tone sounded harsh. She had come at David's invitation, but she would not cause a problem between brothers by admitting to it. "I but wished to view the land around me, Alexander."

"You may do that from the ground, not the battlements of the castle." His masculine features set in lines of displeasure as he held out his hand to her. "Come, I will help you climb down." His stern manner brooked no disobedience.

Mary raised her chin. She would not allow him to cow her before the other men. "I climbed up without assistance, Alexander. For certes I can climb down the same way."

His gaze settled on her face steady and intent. "We

will go down together."

Conscious of her new brothers watching the exchange between them, she could find no merit in refusing. If she persisted, it would only embarrass her further.

With his large frame close behind, his arms on either side, they climbed down together. Surrounded by his strength, his chest firm against her shoulder blades, his thighs cupped beneath hers, feelings of awareness trickled down her slight frame to tempt her. Her breathing grew short and choppy.

"'Tis dangerous, Mary. I do not want you upon anything taller than the bench you sit upon to sup." His breath, warm and moist against her ear, sent shivers down her spine.

Her feet settling on solid ground, she turned and brushed up against his solid length when he did not step back as she expected. Weakness assaulted her limbs, and her hands came up to rest against his chest as she leaned back against the ladder to put some space between them. Her eyes leaped to his face.

"You are pale, Mary. Is all well with you?"

"Aye, all is well, Alexander." The heavy beat of her heart robbed her of breath making her voice sound breathy and weak. "You must trust that I will not do anything to harm the bairn."

"'Tis not only the bairn I am concerned with, but you as well." He tucked a stray curl within her hood.

"Will you not kiss the lass and be done with it so the rest of us may come down, Alexander?" Duncan called from above.

Annoyance flared in Alexander's expression as he looked up at his two brothers, standing above them on the ladder.

Her cheeks grew hot as his gaze dropped to her. Her eyes fastening on the broad expanse of leather-covered chest before her, she prayed he would not humiliate her in such a way. She did not want to be kissed because her husband had to be goaded into it by a jest.

A scowl dark with impatience crossed his face. "When I kiss my wife, Duncan, 'twill be for our pleasure, not for yours." He tucked her hand within the bend of his arm to escort her down the tower steps.

He stood back to allow her to precede him as he swung open the door to their chamber.

"Duncan and I have been netting salmon for the feast," he said as he shed his boots and stockings then moved to the basin and pitcher of water on a table.

Mary perched on the edge of the bed and drew the long braid of blonde hair over her shoulder.

He pulled his shirt over his head and flung it over a chair. "Come wash my back, wife."

She studied his expression as he held out the cloth to her. She had thus far avoided the room when he bathed, she could not avoid it any longer. Her mouth went dry as she looked at him. She tried not to allow her uncertainty to show as she stepped close, but could not control the wave of color that heated her cheeks.

His tawny eyes studied her. "Did you not help with the visitor's baths at your uncle's house, Mary?"

"Nay. Aunt Agnes said men were not trustworthy when they were not properly clothed."

"I must agree with your aunt. It pleases me to know you have not done this for anyone, but me." He bent his head, exposing the nape of his neck as she ran the cloth across the width of his shoulders. Her eyes traced the shape of him as his back tapered downward to his hips. The more heavily muscled areas across the ridge of his shoulders and beneath the flat slope of his shoulder blades bulged as he moved his arms. Growing aware of the strength and size of him in a way she never had before, her hands trembled as she touched him. What would it be like to rub her cheek against the smooth skin of his back and put her arms around him? They were wed, and she had never embraced her husband. Would she ever feel free to do so?

Turning, he took the cloth from her hand and drew her close against him. "Your touch is gentle, wife. Mayhap I should ask you to serve me at all my baths."

The idea seemed both exciting and terrifying. "You are not a child who needs help with your baths, Alexander." She avoided his gaze for fear of what he might read in her expression.

"Nay, I am not a child, but I should like you to touch me and learn you need not be afraid that I'm going to turn on you and do you harm."

She focused her attention on the russet colored hair that blanketed his chest then disappeared in a thin line beneath his trews.

His fingers smoothed her hair as his lips grazed her forehead. "I would like very much to hold you in my arms while you sleep, Mary."

"Is that not what you are doing when I wake each morn?"

"Aye, but 'tis not because you want it," he said, then sighed.

She clenched and unclenched her hands at her sides for she knew not what to do with them. With effort, she held her body stiff within the bend of his arm. Reluctantly she admitted it was not fear of his intent that made her so defensive, but fear of her own response to his gentleness. The desire to give of herself made her feel vulnerable.

"What is it you would ask of me?" she asked, on a husky breath.

"If you truly want to raise the bairn within my clan and you are to stay with me and my kin, I would ask you to think what 'tis we are to have together as man and wife. There's more to marriage than being mother and father to the bairns born from it."

"What other things would you be meaning?" She tilted her head back to look up at him.

"I'm speaking about moments like this one, Mary. Moments of sharing between us, where we are not feuding agin one another."

Fearful of acceding to the reason in his argument, she pulled away from him and strode to the fireplace. A chill hung over the drafty room, for the fire had nearly burnt itself out. She squatted and fed the blaze two long slabs of peat from the wooden box beside the fireplace. "What did I do that made you believe I was not chaste?"

"I have never believed you were not innocent."

She rose, and turned to face him. He was leaning a hip against the table with his arms folded across his bare chest. The muscles in his arms bulged. Her mouth grew dry just looking at him. Perhaps she really was unchaste. "Did I do something to make you believe I would welcome you in my bed, before we were wed?"

"Nay, Mary." He shook his head. "You did nothing wrong."

"Then why did you come to me?" Her voice cracked and she struggled to retain her composure. When he hesitated before answering, her hands fisted at her sides.

His gaze fastened on her face. "You did nothing other than be the woman you are. I wanted you to be my wife because of it, more than the agreement between your clan and mine. But I did not think you would agree to the match, and Collin meant to break the agreement."

So he had come to her.

She swallowed against the painful knot in her throat. Her gaze wavered from his face in an attempt to retain her composure. She had loved him so, the thought of holding back had never occurred to her—but she had never expected him to treat her with anything save respect. Now at least, she understood his motives, but it did not ease the terrible sense of loss the knowledge brought her.

To occupy her hands, and still their trembling, she moved to the washstand to retrieve her brush then sat on the bed to tidy her hair. She started as Alexander unbuckled the girdle from about his waist and allowed his trews to fall to the floor. She stared at the muscular tautness of his buttocks, thighs, and calves, and then quickly looked away. The many hours on horseback and training at the art of war had honed his body to a state of sleek, masculine perfection. The movement, as he bent from the waist to wash his legs and feet, brought into play the muscles of his back and arms and drew her attention despite herself. She forced her eyes away, her face burning at the immodesty of her interest.

"Will you fold my fresh kilt for me Mary? 'Tis in the chest."

Grateful for the distraction, she quickly finished braiding her hair. She rose to find him offering her his girdle. With her gaze carefully averted, she snatched it from his hand. She placed the wide leather belt on the bed and arranged the sheath for his sword and the leather sporran in which he carried his possessions. She spread the kilt over the girdle and folded the pleats in place. She sensed Alexander's movements behind her and straightened.

He moved close beside her, a shirt in his hands. The thick swirls of auburn hair covering his chest tapered into a thin line past his navel, to blossom into a thatch at his groin. His member protruded, long and flaccid, from the center of it. Even as she watched, it grew in size and length, stiffening straight out.

A feeling of helplessness raced through her. She stumbled back surprised, embarrassed ,and turned to flee.

Alexander caught her about the waist, and pulled her back against him.

"'Tis a natural thing, my wanting you, Mary. I can not help the way I feel about you anymore than I can stop breathing, but it does not mean I am going to force you to serve me."

His cheek, cool and beard roughened, pressed to hers. His breath, warm against her ear, sent strange shivers up her spine. "I have not touched you in any way you do not wish, have I, lass?"

"Nay." Fear had nothing to do with the feelings running rampant through her. Her hands ached to stroke the muscular forearms holding her. The feel of his large male body fit so familiarly against hers had her breath coming in ragged gulps. Her body grew weak with longing as he moved against her. She wanted to turn against him and bring his lips to hers. Her body ached to be closer in a way she found both exciting and confusing.

A fist pounded on the door. Duncan's voice came from behind the thick portal. "The MacNaughtens have struck the east pasture and stolen a small flock. I'm going with David to see to it. Will you be coming, Alexander?"

He drew a deep breath. "Do you wish me to go, Mary?"

Possibilities both exciting and frightening stretched before her. Was she brave enough to say nay? Was her pride healed enough to lower the barriers between them?

Chapter Eight

From her seat on a courtyard bench along the castle wall, Mary watched the two grooms' movements. She scanned the small herd of horses penned in a coral at the west side of the stables. Where might the young mare be? Since Collin had reclaimed the gelding, she had no horse, and had been eyeing the mare for days. Waiting for an opportunity to slip inside the stable and find her, Mary leaned back against the wall and pretended an interest in the blacksmith's actions.

The ringing of the smith's hammer clanged against the medal shoe he melded, distracting and loud. She watched as the sparks flew from the blows and nearly missed the young groom's passage across the courtyard to the gate. She looked about for the other man, but could not see him.

Rising slowly from her seat, she circled the stable's perimeter seeking the back entrance. She ducked through the railing of the coral and wove her way around the horses penned there to the opening.

Once inside, she rested back against a stall door and breathed in the scent of hay, leather, and horses while her eyes adjusted to the dim light. Something tugged at the hood of her cloak. She turned to find a horse nibbling playfully on the fabric. She stroked the animal's forehead and nose then moved down the center aisle.

The sounds of movement alerted her to the groom's presence. Occupied with shoveling out the stall, his back to her, he remained unaware of her presence as she eased past the open door.

She found the mare in one of the stalls closest to the courtyard. Clicking her tongue to gain the animal's attention, she withdrew small bits of dried apple from the deep pocket of her surcoat. The mare nuzzled her neck, breathing in her scent, then took the offered treat from her palm.

Looking about for the necessary bridle and saddle, she crept to a sturdy wooden door along the south wall and pressed her ear to the panel. Hearing no movement within, she eased it open. The light of a dully-burning torch illuminated the bridles hung on one wall. Saddles draped across narrow wooden benches lay in rows the length of the room. Closing the door behind her, she plucked a bridle from its hook, then wove her way through the organized clutter until she spied a woman's sidesaddle. She rested her hand against her stomach and sighed. She would not chance harming her child to lift it. She thought about riding bareback and shook her head.

"Do you wish a horse saddled, Lady Mary?"

She started violently and smothered a gasp as she turned to face the groom, a slightly built gray haired man.

"Aye, I would."

The man nodded and scooped up the bothersome sidesaddle and carried it out of the tack room. He wiped the leather of the saddle down with a rag. "'Tis been some time since this has been used. 'Twas Lady Isobel's."

"My husband's mother's?"

"Aye."

She watched as he checked the leather girth and stirrup straps.

"The Laird will not mind my using it?" she asked.

"Nay," The man glanced at her. "I'd say he would make a gift of it, had it occurred to him you needed it. 'Tis plain he is taken with you."

Mary smiled. Her father-in-law's open acceptance of her had smoothed the way with his people. But what trials might she face with Alexander's people?

There was time enough to worry about that at *Caisteal Sith*. She turned the thoughts aside. "And what of Lady Isobel?"

A smile played about the man's lips. "She had a temper as hot as a forge and a heart as big as all of Scotland. She would welcome your use of the saddle."

She watched as he made quick work of readying the horse for her. As he guided the mare out of the barn, he looked about him. "Have you no escort?"

"I am only going to the village."

He nodded. He steadied the horse then bent to offer her a boost into the saddle. She felt foolish for having sneaked about when Alexander had not forbidden her use of a horse, as she had expected. For days, she had felt a prisoner behind the walls of the castle when in actuality she had never been one at all.

A smile sprang to her lips as she accepted the reins from the groom.

"Have a care, m'lady," he cautioned, "There be strangers trespassing upon the Laird's land."

"'Tis grateful I am for the warning. I shall take care." She kicked the horse sending it forward.

As she rode through the castle gate, she experienced a wondrous sense of freedom. She had a horse beneath her and could go wherever she might. Should she wish to ride away from Lorne Castle forever, she could do so. Her gaze fastened on the distant hills across the loch. Now wed, she could go to her sister, or mayhap to her MacPherson kin.

She had ridden only a short distance when her exuberance began to falter. The Loch beckoned a deep purplish blue. She guided the mare through a stand of trees and down the slope. Remaining mounted, she was content to sit on the horse and stare into the depths of the water, peaceful and calming.

Thoughts of Alexander intruded. Her cheeks burned as she thought of those moments in their bedchamber. He had believed her afraid of the changes in his body, and she had allowed him to think that.

Mary covered her face with her hands and drew a deep breath. They could not go on as they were. She could not go on causing him pain, punishing him for something that could not be changed. She could not go on punishing herself.

She lowered her hands and studied the sparkle of light on the water. The wind lanced off its surface chilling her as it hit her in the face. Shivering, she drew the cloak more securely around her. Mayhap it would be best for them both if she left and went to live with her MacPherson kin.

She turned, her gaze seeking the distant turrets of the castle. She thought of what it would be like to be parted from her new Campbell kin. It had been only a short time, but she had grown fond of her new brothers, and John Campbell treated her with an open affection of which her own father was incapable. She longed for a place to call home, a family that could embrace her as one of their own. They had offered her that without hesitation.

And what of Alexander? He too had embraced her as his wife in every way, though she had offered him nothing in return. Guilt swelled in the pit of her stomach. His care and patience deserved better from her than she had offered him. Should he finally become tired of the strife between them and take another in her place, she would be relegated to the position of a nursemaid and a servant in his castle. She did not want that. She drew a deep breath.

It suddenly grew clear to her she had more to lose now than ever before. And it occurred to her as well, what a dishonorable coward she had become. She had been throwing what her husband offered her back in his face at every turn, using it against him, and allowing him to think her frightened of him, besides. She had behaved as badly as he, or worse, but no more. Mary turned her mount for home.

****

Alexander reined in his horse as he topped the rise of the east pasture. David and Duncan followed close behind and they raced downward toward more level terrain. Small groups of sheep dotted the verdant landscape. As they approached, the nearest herd raised their heads, then scattered to join a cluster grazing at a safer distance.

He halted his mount to study the depressions in the soft turf to discover which direction the thieves had traveled.

"They're going east and taking their time about it," he announced to his brothers and the three accompanying Campbell clansmen. Flicking the horse's haunches with the end of the reins, he spurred the animal forward.

They crossed the open field to a wooded copse then slowed to a more cautious pace. The sodden ground made it easy to follow the trail of hoof prints. It also made the horses' footing uncertain as the grade grew steeper.

They immediately spied the offending reivers some

distance away. The thieves drove a small flock of fifteen fat Campbell sheep before them wielding sticks to hurry the animals.

At Alexander's silent signal, Duncan and two others broke away to circle around in front and intercept the thieves, while he and David pursued them at a less frantic pace from behind.

As he and David rounded a bend in the trail, the trio, turned in unison to look over their shoulders. The three men abandoned their stolen bounty and kicked their mounts into action.

Alexander whooped a war cry, and quickened the pace of pursuit. The raiders broke free of the trees and headed for open ground just as Duncan and the clansmen with him cut ahead right in front of them.

His horse galloping full out, he closed to within a stone's throw of the lad bringing up the rear when his horse fell from beneath him. He flipped over the animal's head and landed heavily on his shoulder. Stunned, he lay still as the world spun then righted itself.

The agonized screams of his mount brought him staggering to his feet. He looked about for any threat, but found no sign of his brothers or the men they pursued.

The horse struggled to rise as the bone protruded from its lower leg, a devastating injury. He ignored the pain in his shoulder as he stooped to comfort the animal. Bracing a knee against the gelding's neck, he forced it to remain on its side, as he drew his dagger and quickly slit its juggler. Warm blood spurted from the wound and the animal grew still almost immediately as blood streamed onto the ground.

He swore at the loss of the valued steed as he straightened to his feet. Too late, he heard the warning hiss of an arrow. The deadly missile plowed into his thigh and sent him staggering back. He dove behind his dead mount and drew his sword as the horses thundered past his position.

"Alexander!" David shouted his name as he leaped from his horse almost before the animal had come to a stop.

Placing his sword close to his side, Alexander drew his dagger. He slit the fabric of his kilt to expose the injury.

David's face paled and his eyes grew round as he viewed the wooden stave.

"Has it gone through to the back, David?" He turned gingerly exposing the back of his leg.

"Nay."

Alexander drew deep breaths to control the pain beginning to surface. "Ride back to the castle, David. Tell Mary and father what has happened. You must prepare them. Duncan will be back for me."

"Nay! I will not leave you!"

The horse's blood covered the front of his kilt making it next to useless in controlling the flow of blood from his leg. "Give me a scrap of your kilt. 'Tis cleaner than mine."

David cut away a wide strip from the fabric draped over his shoulder and tucked the rest back in place beneath his girdle.

Folding the wool around the hilt of the arrow, Alexander pressed it against the injury to staunch the trickle of blood.

Duncan and the others returned a short time later, the three offending thieves not with them.

"Go now, David. Take Gabe with you." He slapped his brother's shoulder in encouragement for his worried countenance offered him no comfort.

David raced to his horse and heaved himself into the saddle.

****

"God's Blood, Duncan! Do not touch it!" Alexander swore as his brother accidentally brushed his arm against the shortened shaft of the arrow. Blood ran in a thin rivulet down his leg to his knee, but he couldn't staunch it and retain his seat behind his brother at the same time.

"I did not know you could speak so colorfully, Brother. You have not used the same blessing twice since we lifted you upon my horse," Duncan spoke over his shoulder.

"I do not fancy losing my life over a flock of sheep. I can not believe the lad shot me."

"Reiving was only a game to us. 'Tis taken more seriously these days."

Alexander grunted in pain as the horse's

hindquarters bunched beneath him. They climbed upward, crested the rise, and then started down into the valley. Every movement jarred the arrow embedded in the muscle as he tried to retain his position atop the horse's haunches. He gritted his teeth against the pain and swore silently at his own carelessness.

"I can not believe you allowed yourself to be caught in so unprotected a position, Alexander. Mayhap your mind was not on the task at hand but on some other problem," Duncan quizzed, laughter in his tone.

Alexander breathed an oath. He did not appreciate his brother's humor when his blood slowly seeped out.

"Mayhap I can offer a suggestion or two. I have some small experience with women."

"I am not interested, Duncan."

"Sickness brings out the mother in all women, Alexander. If I were you, I would allow Mary to do a bit of mothering. A warm breast is a better place to rest your head than a pillow, is it not?"

The idea had more than a little appeal. "She has threatened to pierce me herself. She will probably be glad someone has finally done so in her place."

"Threatening is not the same as doing, Alexander. I do not see her seeking revenge in any manner. Does she harp at you in private?"

"Nay." She had so little to say to him of late he found it difficult to approach her.

"'Tis a woman's purpose to be needed. A well placed arrow could prove very useful."

"You are devious, Brother," Alexander accused. The idea was a good one. He gritted his teeth again as the shaft of the arrow was jarred. "By the time we arrive I shall be so weak from loss of blood 'twill be easy to act helpless."

****

A crowd of servants and clansmen had gathered outside the castle awaiting their arrival. His father stood outside the heavy hall door, but Mary was not present.

Two men rushed forward to help Alexander dismount. "Where is Mary?" he ground out through teeth clenched against the pain.

"She rode out about an hour ago and has not

returned yet," John answered.

Alexander swore and attempted to pull away from the two supporting him. He had frightened her with his manly display, and she had fled. To where? He pivoted on his good foot intent on mounting Duncan's horse and going after her.

The sound of an approaching horse had the group turning toward the main gate. Mary appeared atop a small mare, her cheeks red from the cold air, her hair flying in a tangled mass.

One of the men ran forward to grasp the reigns of her horse and she dismounted. "What has happened?"

"Alexander has been pierced by an arrow," David explained.

Alexander gritted his teeth against the pain as they carried him into the great hall. He sighed in relief when they lowered him on to the table before the fire. The pain eased to a dull ache, as long as he did not move.

"Would you loan me your dagger, Gabriel?" She asked the large bearded man who had helped him inside. She shook free of the cloak and tossed it across a bench close by.

He presented the knife to her, handle first.

Alexander eyed Mary warily as she studied the hole in his kilt. "There are no pieces missing from the cloth," she said, relief in her tone. She folded back the garment to examine the wound. Blood oozed from around the injury, but the bleeding was not as serious as he had thought. He relaxed beneath the gentleness of her touch as she probed the abused flesh. Her hand gently guided him to turn on his side so she could view the depth of the arrow.

"Cora, please bring some wine," she said as she positioned a basin of water and some clean strips of cloth close beside her. Her eyes looked a clear, glorious blue against the whiteness of her skin. Though her demeanor remained calm, he could read the fear and worry behind the composure of her features. She folded her cloak and placed it beneath his head. "'Twill have to come out, Alexander."

"Aye," he agreed.

"'Twill have to go the rest of the way through first," she said softly as she bathed away the blood turning his skin a pinkish hue.

He swallowed, sickened by the thought.

"The head of the arrow is just beneath the skin. I will prick the skin at the point of the arrow and push it forward just enough to cut the head off the arrow. Then the shaft may be drawn out more easily and with less pain."

He nodded.

Mary went to the fire to thrust the blade of the dagger into the flames then set it aside. She bathed his bloodstained hands while they waited for it to cool.

"David said you had to kill your horse."

"Aye."

"I am sorry. I know how valuable he was to you."

"He did not suffer long."

Her touch soothed him, though the pain had grown worse again.

She set aside the pinkish water and accepted a fresh bowl from Cora.

"I am sorry for any pain I may bring you, Alexander." Her gaze steady, she smoothed his hair back in a gesture of comfort.

"I forgive you any pain you may bring me, Wife." He attempted to summon a smile for her.

"I will push the arrow forward, Mary," John said as she moved around behind Alexander.

His gaze settled on his father, grim with concern. David's hands came to rest on his shoulders.

"Duncan, will you cut off the head of the arrow?"

"Aye." He stepped beside her immediately.

She cut the back of his leg and the pain pricked him. The arrow popped through the skin easily. With two swift slices of the blade, Duncan used his sword to free the head of the arrow from the shaft.

Alexander's eyes met hers as she circled the table to stand before him. He felt his father grasp the wooden shaft. He focused on Mary's face rather than the men surrounding him. The pain, sharp and deep, sliced through him as the shaft drew free with one sure tug.

He sucked in his breath and held it against the worst of the agony. He nearly came off the table though when she poured the wine over the wound. The pain radiated up into his groin and ran down to his knee. Some moments passed before his vision cleared and he was able to breathe again.

She applied pressure to both wounds with a cloth until the bleeding had stopped. Her touch soothing, she bathed away the blood that had streaked across his legs. After carefully applying a balm to the injury, she pressed a clean folded cloth across it.

"You have had much experience tending such wounds, Mary?" He watched as she tore strips of muslin with which to bind the injury. Weak and shaky, Alexander relished the time to rest.

"Aye. My aunt and uncle have nine children. Six of them are lads. There was always someone who needed tending."

He had never known a woman to hold her own council half so well. He was discovering her a small piece at a time, like pealing away the petals of a flower to uncover the heart.

She finished tearing the strips. "Has the pain eased now?"

"Aye, some. You did not warn me about the wine."

"The dread of it would have made it worse." She caressed his cheek in a gesture of comfort. Her gentle touch filled him with a gnawing hunger that rivaled the pain in his leg.

"You may have some wine to drink while you rest after I have bound the wound, Alexander."

He wanted more than that. Duncan's suggestions ran through his mind with greater appreciation.

David and Duncan lowered him into a chair before the fire where she could more easily bind the injury. She cleared away the basin and cloths and left the room.

His father moved to stand before the fire "She did well," he said.

"Aye," Alexander agreed.

"'Tis of value having a wife who can tend you when you are ailing." John braced a foot on the hearth and eyed his eldest son with a frown.

"Aye."

"'Tis of value to a woman to have a husband who can do the same," he suggested.

Resting his head against the high back of the chair, Alexander studied his father's features without comment. It seemed his entire family had advice on how he could win favor with his wife. He felt light headed.

David moved to his father's side and Alexander's attention rested on him.

"'Twould not go amiss should you smile at her now and again and speak to her as a lady instead of a servant."

His resentment flared and he stiffened. "I did not speak to her in such a way."

"You did on the allure today," David said as he folded his arms against his chest. "'Twas by my invitation she was there, though she did not say when you ordered her down."

"'Twas not a proper place for you to escort her," John said, scowling at his youngest son.

"She wished to see the lay of the land."

"Aye, probably to plan her escape," Alexander said. With freedom before her, why she had returned?

"She is your wife, Alexander. She proved she would stand by you at the council meeting. You should be searching for peace between you," John said, his tone stern.

Alexander clenched his fists atop the chair arms. His thigh ached like a worrisome tooth. He did not need his father taking him to task for his behavior. He sipped more of the wine allowing it to dull his temper.

"What is and has been between us is our own affair," Alexander said, his tone laced with resentment as his attention settled on his father's features.

Setting aside the stein, he struggled to rise from his seat. The room spun in a sickening circle and he caught himself as he fell back into the chair. The scabbard of his sword thumped against the wooden seat with a loud hollow sound. He swore against the pain.

"You must not try to rise on your own, Alexander." Mary rushed to his side from the stairs. "You have lost much blood and will need to rest."

His insides churning, he struggled to control the wave of sickness. She bathed his face with a cool moist cloth, and the feeling eased.

"'Twill pass after a moment," she reassured him.

He hoped it would not if it encouraged her to continue touching him. Once again, he thought of Duncan's suggestion. It could do no harm.

****

"You weigh as much as a full grown ox, Alexander," Duncan complained as he and David negotiated the stairs, supporting most of Alexander's weight between them.

"Mayhap your excessive activity with the lasses has weakened you," Alexander retorted through gritted teeth.

"Are you jealous, brother, that you can not claim the same?" Duncan snapped, his usual good-humor absent.

"Should you learn to speak with greater care, Alexander, mayhap things would change," David said as he glanced over his shoulder at Mary.

"I do not need more advice from you, David."

Mary eyed the three large men with wary confusion. They had snapped and snarled at each other all the way up the stairs. She wondered if their aggressions would have taken a more physical turn if Alexander had been able to fight.

Once they lifted him on the bed, Duncan and David removed Alexander's boots then beat a hasty retreat.

"Should you wish to heap revenge upon him while he is at your mercy, Mary, we will turn a deaf ear to his cries for assistance," Duncan quipped as he reached the door.

She stifled the quick laughter inspired by the remark, but she could not hide the smile. She hung the heavy sword, by the girdle, on the bedpost next to Alexander, where he placed them each night, and fought the urge to smile again.

She moved back to the bed after they had gone. "Do you wish to shed your kilt , Alexander?"

"Aye," he answered in a growl and unbuckled the girdle holding his kilt in place.

Mary tugged the fabric from beneath him as he held himself up with his arms. She studied the fabric already stiff with blood then folded the item and set it aside to be washed and mended.

He didn't attempt to cover himself, but rested back against the pillow naked except for his stockings and the garters holding them in place just beneath his knees. He flaunted his maleness like a challenge to her.

She calmly spread a tartan from the foot of the bed over his lap then sat on the edge of the bed to untie his garters.

"I will not allow you to leave, Mary."

Her eyes leaped to his face in surprise. His jaw clenched, his features were set in a forbidding scowl.

"Why would you think that?" She rolled the bloody stockings together.

His expression relaxed somewhat. "You rode out alone. I could not think of any other reason you would wish to see the lay of the land earlier."

She rose to set aside the stockings.

"Your place is with me and my clan." Alexander spoke in a quieter tone, though it remained no less stern.

She returned to the bed with a basin filled with water and a cloth and bathed away the blood on his legs. "Ordering me about is not the way to convince me of that."

His frown turned to a scowl and his jaw tensed as she met his gaze. She understood how hard it was for such a proud man to bend. It was proving more than difficult for her as well.

"We will talk of this later, Alexander. You must rest now."

He tucked a curling tendril of hair behind her ear. "Will you lie beside me for a time?"

She stared at him, surprised by the request. Now was the time to follow her earlier decisions. She drew the layer of pelts over his legs to insure his warmth then rose to set aside the damp cloth. Her heart beat an unsteady rhythm as she moved around the end of the bed to the other side and lay down beside him.

"'Twould please me if you would stroke my cheek as you did before."

Her limbs grew weak. Seeing him injured had frightened her badly. For a short time, her defenses had been completely lowered, bringing out something fiercely protective in her.

Her fingers grazed his forehead, smoothing back the thick auburn hair that waved there. She traced the strong curve of his cheek and jaw.

Alexander closed his eyes. Deep auburn lashes fanned out against his pale cheeks. Pain had left its mark on his face. Loss of blood had weakened him. She smoothed the lines around his mouth and across his forehead.

It seemed completely natural for him to draw her closer and rest his cheek against her breasts. An unexpected rush of tenderness had her cradling him against her and caressing the bruised slope of his shoulder.

For long sweet moments, she continued to hold him even after he had fallen asleep. For the first time she allowed herself to know what it was for her husband to hold her without strife between them, and for the first time she felt like a wife.

Chapter Nine

Alexander watched Mary's every movement. Too modest, or too wary, to bathe in front of him, she had kept on her shift. Unlacing the garment to the waist, she had managed to soap every inch of covered flesh without his catching even a glimpse of what lay beneath. Each time she raised her arm it pulled the fabric of the garment taut, outlining the curve of her buttocks. The tantalizing distraction was a true test of his self-control. In fact, being confined to the bed and the room with her was proving to be both a heaven and a hell. The roiling need twisting in his gut each time she came near proved almost painful. The only thing that held it in check was the trust he was attempting to build between them.

A sigh of half pain-half relief, escaped him as she donned her kirtle.

"How does your leg fair, Alexander?" she asked as she turned to look over her shoulder at him.

"'Twould ease if I could rise and walk about a wee bit, lass."

She emptied the washbasin then set it a side. "Mayhap 'twould not harm you to walk about the room," she agreed, her attention directed at the tiny row of buttons down each sleeve of the kirtle.

Alexander dragged his gaze away from her and swung his legs over the side of the bed. He grabbed the pelts to cover the evidence of his discomfort as she approached the bed. "A shirt would not be amiss, lass, and a fresh kilt."

Mary nodded, and moving to the trunk at the foot of the bed, retrieved the items. She laid the shirt next to him, and stretching his girdle on the bed, bent to spread the fabric of the kilt and fold the pleats.

Alexander watched her hands move with practiced skill, smoothing the wool into place. "'Tis well you do that,

Mary?"

"'Twas good practice folding the wee ones' kilts at my aunt and uncles."

She so seldom spoke of her family, her words caught his interest immediately. "How many of them did you speak of before?" he asked, encouraging her to continue.

"Nine all together, six lads and three lasses. Anne and I made eleven."

"Were they a hardy lot?"

"Aye." She nodded. Sadness flickered across her features.

Alexander grasped her wrist to draw her between his legs. "Mayhap your aunt may come for a visit at *Caisteal Sith*. Would that please you?"

She nodded, her eyes carefully averted. "Aye, very much."

"Because you are wed within another clan, it does not mean you must give up your affiliation to the clan you were raised in."

"'Tis not that I wish to do that."

"Then what is it, lass?"

She ran an unsteady hand over the front of the kirtle. "I do not wish to be shamed before my aunt as I have been before the others."

Alexander felt as though he had received a kick to the belly. He drew a deep breath. "You are wed now, Mary."

Her eyes finally rose to his face. "T'was I who accepted you in my bed that night. My aunt would not have approved." She turned away to don her surcoat.

Alexander bit back an oath. Just when he thought her anger toward him seemed to be easing, her pain rose up to smite him with guilt. There were times he wished she would scream at him or beat him with her fists, just so her anger would be out in the open between them and not held so deeply inside her.

"'Twas I who accepted you" the words played through his mind. With those words, she accepted partial responsibility for what had happened. He wished she had no reason to regret that decision so thoroughly.

He donned his shirt and folded the kilt and girdle around his waist. His nudity covered to put her more at ease, Alexander rose. Each movement of his thigh brought him twinges of pain as he limped toward her.

"I must bind your wound more tightly, Alexander," she cautioned.

"Nay, lass. 'Twill do." Though capable of standing alone, he rested an arm across her shoulders as though depending on her support to retain his balance. Together they paced about the room.

"Mayhap we may make our way downstairs together to break the fast," he suggested.

Mary looked up at him, her head barely reaching his shoulder. "I will summon some servants to help you downstairs or mayhap Duncan and David may assist you."

"I must shave first."

She wandered about the room putting the chamber to rights while he lathered his whiskers. He watched her blurred image in the metal disk as he shaved and cleaned his teeth. When he would have emptied the washbasin himself, she was there to see to it for him.

She replaced the crockery bowl. Alexander placed his hands on either side of her, his body pressing close against her from behind. He rubbed his freshly shaven cheek against her smooth one in a playful caress.

She stiffened within the circle of his arms. He wondered if she would ever welcome him being close. "'Tis better without the beard, eh lass?"

He felt the obvious effort she made to relax. "Aye." She turned to look up at him, her gaze falling on his scarred cheek.

"Does this distress you, Mary?" He touched it.

"Nay. How...How did you come by it?"

It was the first time she had asked him anything about his life as a warrior since their meeting in Lochlan. "'Twas in one of the first battles I fought with the Bruce. I was grazed by a sword and did not know I was cut until the battle ended. Derrick's tender care pricked me more than the blade."

She raised a hand to trace the smooth texture of the healed skin. "'Tis only a wee mark."

Her touch as well as her attempt to spare his feelings gave him some hope she might harbor some small affection for him. Mayhap if he told her of her father's plan at Lochlan, she would believe him.

"Mary, you know the Campbell and MacDonald clans are grave enemies."

"Aye." She studied him attentively.

"Why do you suppose your father invited Bearach MacDonald to your sister's betrothal, knowing I would be there?"

"I do not know, Alexander. Collin oft did things I did not understand."

"How long before we arrived was he there?"

"Mayhap a week."

"Did Bearach attend you before my arrival?"

"Aye. Collin insisted I sit with him at the evening meal two nights. I did not care for his manners at table or otherwise." Her gaze probed his expression.

A fist pounded on the door. He sighed in frustration as Mary slipped away to answer the summons. He should have been more straightforward with his questions instead of trying to lead up to them.

Duncan stood outside the door. "Do you mean to break the fast with us, lass, or will you be eating in your chamber again this morn?" he asked with a smile.

Mary's smile, laced with warmth, flashed forth. "Alexander has decided to venture below."

"Good. It has been three days since your presence has graced our table. Father grows vexed at your absence—and yours of course, Brother."

Alexander experienced a twinge of jealous resentment toward his brother. Duncan's easy manner with Mary only pointed out the constraints within his own behavior with her. She appeared withdrawn and careful about him, fearful of provoking either his anger or his passion, and he maintained a tight control over his own responses to her, to try to put her at ease. How long could they continue in such a vein, before the strain grew too much for them both?

"Can you walk down the stairs, Alexander, or do you need to be carried?" A teasing smile played about Duncan's features.

Alexander scowled at him. Should Mary discover he was not as helpless as he pretended, all would be ruined.

"I shall make it below with your help, Brother, and Mary's."

****

Mary gave a sigh of relief once Alexander was seated at the end of the bench to the left of his father. She checked the bandage about her husband's thigh to reassure herself his injury had not broken open from the strain of coming down the stairs. Alexander slid down the bench, making room for her next to his father. She settled there with a smile in his direction.

"I too would lie abed all day if I had a lass such as Mary to wait upon me, Brother," Duncan said from across the table.

"'Tis unfortunate her sister is already wed. It could have been arranged, Duncan," Alexander replied easily. "Anne is very much like Mary in looks, but different in temperament. There were those at Lochlan who could not tell the two of them apart, though I had no difficulty doing so."

"You once said your horse knew my scent as well as you did. Mayhap I should have bathed more oft," Mary said.

A heartbeat of silence followed, then the men down the table roared with laughter.

David's voice rose above the melee of comments that followed. "I apologize for my brother's choice of words, Mary. I am certes Alexander did not mean them as anything, but a compliment." He shot Alexander a frown.

"At the time the words were spoken, you had just coaxed my horse to come to you, lass. 'Twas you who wondered why he came so easily." Alexander reminded her playfully. "'Tis true enough that each lass has her own scent. Yours is like sunshine and woman, with a hint of spring flowers beneath."

Mary found her face growing hot with a blush, the intimacy of the comment, spoken before such company, throwing her into confusion. She kept her gaze lowered to the wooden bowl Alexander had filled with porridge for her.

John changed the subject. "One of the stable lads brought to me this morn a weapon you had left in the stables, Alexander. 'Tis a crossbow. Where did you come by it?"

"'Tis Mary's, not mine, Father."

John's brows rose and his gaze turned to her.

"'Twas a gift from my uncle, Hugh MacPherson, my lord. He fashioned it for me. 'Tis lighter in weight and easier to span."

"'Tis an unusual weapon for a woman."

"Aye. But more accurate than the long bow at a distance and more deadly."

"You shall show me how skilled you are, after the meal," John said in his usual brusque manner.

She gave a brief nod. "If it pleases you."

"Mary will not span the bow, Father, David will do it for her," Alexander stated.

She looked up, surprised by his objection. 'Tis not difficult."

"'Tis not good for you, or the bairn, to strain yourself spanning the weapon."

She tried to ignore the feeling of pleasure his concern brought her.

Her gaze moved about the table to each of the men's faces. She could live amongst them for the rest of her days and never truly be a member of their clan, unless accepted by John Campbell. What price would she have to pay for that acceptance? Submission to his son?

Alexander place a chunk of bread spread with butter next to her. Her eyes rose to his face. How could he have harmed her so? Why? The questions ran over and over again in her mind. There had to be a reason. She believed him sincere in his regret for what had happened. But why would he risk her father's wrath by openly declaring they had been together?

"What is amiss, lass?" Alexander asked.

She shook her head and brushed aside the fine wisps of hair curled against her forehead. Her appetite gone, she pushed away the bowl of porridge.

"Will you have a bit of honey on your bread then, Mary?" he asked.

"Aye."

She could ask Alexander about that night, but every time she started to speak about it, fear of what he might say overwhelmed her. To shame her so, must mean he held no affection for her, and if he spoke those words aloud, she could not continue living with him. If she was to remain with him for the rest of her days, she had to hope that one day he would care for her in some way.

She had seen what a marriage devoid of caring had done to her mother. It had drained the life from her and made of her a shadow within the landscape of the castle. Looked upon as breeding stock by her husband, she had lost the will to live, long before the last babe's birth had taken her life. She had to hope for something better.

She followed Alexander's uneven progress from the steps of the great hall to the side courtyard. After watching him lower himself into a chair two of the men brought out for him, she turned her attention below.

She surveyed the makeshift practice field John had ordered organized during the meal. A straw dummy hung from a pole suspended from the west wall. A quintain, its arms outstretched, had been erected near the loch. In between, targets stationed in staggered rows zigzagged across the courtyard at farther and farther distances.

"Is it a warrior you are hoping to make of my wife, Father?" Alexander asked, frowning.

"Nay, I thought 'twould do the men no harm to practice a bit after Mary is finished."

She studied the field as she accepted the loaded bow from David. She remembered her uncle's patient presence beside her and the many hours of practice he had encouraged. He had meant for her to be able to protect herself, if need be. Perhaps he should have counseled her on the merits of caution and patience as well.

The men's laughter rang out behind her, loud and irritating. Anger surged through her. She nodded to the lad who stood next to the dummy, and he set it to swinging and backed out of range. Bracing her feet apart, she raised the bow to her shoulder and loosed the bolt. The arrow stuck the stuffed form in the chest, dead center, setting it to dancing wildly.

With David spanning the crossbow and returning it to her each time, she sighted the targets one by one, piercing the wood time and again with the wooden shafts. With each heavy hiss and thump of an arrow, some of the pent anger and pain released from her. She barely noticed the men growing silent behind her.

She turned her attention to the quintain planted a farther distance away than the other targets. The mechanism had a stuffed sack representing an outstretched hand mounted on one end of a pole and a shield fastened to the other. The same lad as before set the figure to spinning. She raised the stock of the crossbow to her shoulder, and focused on the stuffed cushion representing a clenched fist as it rotated. She held her breath and squeezed the trigger. The bolt struck the weighted end of the quintain, its force not enough to spin it around as a lance would have done, but enough to make it wobble and jerk.

Mary dropped the weapon to her side. Her muscles felt weak, but for the first time, the rage and pain plaguing her had drained away. She turned to face the men behind her. Alexander had risen to his feet. His gaze searched her face intently, his expression forbidding, his brows drawn together in a harsh frown. Conscious of the other men's gazes as they waited for their leader's reaction to such a display, she turned her attention to John for the first time anxious about his response.

"Well done, lass," John praised as he stepped forward to take the bow from her, his pale amber gaze steady. He squeezed her shoulder. "'Tis a fine Campbell warrior you are."

Fighting a sudden need to weep, she swallowed against the knot in her throat.

"Alexander, Mary has grown chilled despite her labors. You must see her inside."

She tried to still the trembling besetting her as Alexander limped forward to take her arm.

As he guided her up the stairs of the great hall, he paused to look down at her. "You could have killed me anytime at the cave. What stayed you?"

She debated her answer for several moments in silence. Why had she been reluctant to pull the trigger? Because she still cared for him.

"Killing and violence come more easily to men. Only to protect myself, or those who belong to me, could I raise my hand, or a weapon, agin another."

"'Tis oft been those same reasons behind what I have

95

done," he said, his expression grave.

She remembered how he had protected her in route to Castle Lorne. Why could he not have ministered those protective urges upon her and protected her honor with as great a zeal as he had taken it? Why was she driven to find a reason for his actions? The answer came to her with little surprise. Because she wanted to find some redeeming answer to his actions. And even if she did, what then? Would it make her love for him any more or less?

"Will you kiss me, Alexander?" she asked.

He stared at her, open surprise in his expression. He cupped her face in his hands, his tawny gaze trailing over her features with a look in their depths that caused her throat to grow tight with emotion. He lowered his lips to hers, their pressure at first careful then hungry with need.

Tears coursed down her temples as her hands grasped the leather girdle about his waist, and she clung to him. A sob rose up inside her, and she turned her face against his chest.

Alexander held her while her grief spilled out in great heaving sobs that shook her entire body. "I am sorry, Mary. So sorry," he said.

Chapter Ten

The high sweet notes of a flute and fiddle flowed on the gentle evening breeze as Alexander guided Mary to a spot close to the open doorway. The aroma of roasting meat mingled with the straw and animal smells drifting from the stables in a reassuring blend that spoke of prosperity and well-being. Light streamed from the open doorway of the great hall, where dancers swung and twirled in hearty abandon to the music.

The room had grown stuffy with the movement of the dancers and the fires built in the two huge fireplaces at either side of the great hall.

"Might I get you something else to eat, Mary?" David asked from beside her as he placed a heavy wooden chair behind her.

"Nay, I have eaten my fill."

"Mayhap a tankard of ale then?"

"'Twould be welcome, thank you," she agreed with a smile.

Alexander raised a brow as he listened to their conversation. "'Tis I who am injured, David."

David grinned at him. "Would you be needing anything, Alexander?"

"Aye, a tankard of ale would be fine."

Alexander's attention turned to Mary as she watched the dancer's fancy footwork. Stamping their feet, they swung around each other, the women twisting the long tails of their skirts back and forth in rhythm to the music.

David returned with the ale and she murmured a word of thanks as she accepted it.

"Would you wish me to take your place and partner Mary in a dance, Alexander?" David asked.

Alexander's brows rose as he turned to Mary.

"I am content to watch, Alexander." Her eyes rose to David's face. A faint smile touched her lips. "There are more than a few bonny lasses awaiting your invitation, David. Do not fash yourself about me."

David flashed her a smile then bowed away to do as she suggested.

Searching her features in hopes of discovering what she was thinking, he finally shrugged his shoulders. "Why do you not wish to dance?"

Soft color touched her face. "'Tis too soon after I have supped."

He bit back a sigh of frustration. "Might a stroll be safe enough then?"

"Aye." she agreed readily.

"'Twill be cold outside, and you will need your cloak."

'Twill only take a short time for me to get it." Mary rose and strode through the crowd to the staircase.

He slouched against the chair's high back and watched her disappear up the stairwell. A memory of the uninhibited joy she had taken in dancing at her sister's betrothal feast came back to him. A smile laced with pleasure had played about her features as she had followed his steps, her movements graceful and skilled. Was she reluctance to dance because it reminded her of that night? His eyes moved around the crowded hall. Mayhap everything about the feast reminded her.

"Greetings, Alexander. 'Tis been a long time past since last we saw each other," a husky female voice said from beside him.

He looked up into a pair of emerald green eyes surrounded by thick black lashes. A smile curved his lips at the saucy grin before him. "'Twas not me you have not seen that should distress you, Nessa."

"And who would it be then, Alexander?" She flipped a cloud of dark hair over her shoulder and turned a perfect profile to him in spirited arrogance.

He raised a mocking auburn brow. "Duncan is doing his duty on the dance floor."

"Duncan is always doing his duty." She rested her hands on her hips in challenge.

"Aye," He agreed in a solemn tone. "It grows tiresome even for us at times."

She stared at him her expression reflecting surprise until he smiled. "I did not appreciate an arrow in the leg for retrieving sheep."

Nessa laughed. "Father spoke of what happened. The wound is healing well, I hope."

"Aye."

Her eyes dropped to the area of his kilt where the heavy binding around his thigh bulged. "'Twas lucky the arrow did not go any further astray," she commented, her eyes dancing with merriment.

He laughed aloud. His eyes followed Mary's progress as she hurried toward them through the crowd. Would she one day feel the same? Her steps slowed as she noticed Nessa.

Alexander stood. "Come Mary and meet my cousin, Nessa," he said as he motioned to her to join them. "'Tis difficult to explain, but Nessa is a cousin, though distant kin. She is Ian Campbell's youngest daughter."

Mary nodded her understanding. "'Tis pleased I am to meet you, Nessa."

"And I you, Lady Mary. 'Tis a great inconvenience for Alexander to be injured so soon after you have wed. I am sure it has not been pleasant caring for a wolf with a sore paw."

A rare smile of amusement played about Mary's features, and he drank in the sight as her gaze wandered to him.

"He has tried to behave tamely, though I have seen him snap his teeth in frustration at the inactivity forced upon him."

"Aye, he would. If he does not have a sword in his hand, he is not happy," Nessa agreed.

"Of late I have been eager to spend my time seeking some peace, cousin. I will be content to continue to do that, if others will allow it."

Nessa's brows rose, her surprise evident. "'Twould please more than a few lasses of our clan for their husbands to follow your lead, Alexander," she said earnestly. "I'd wager 'twould take a miracle from God to work such a change though."

"Aye, for some," he agreed. "And it will not come easily. Change never comes with easy grace."

"Nay, it does not," Nessa agreed, her features grim. "Especially when men have a part in it."

The trace of bitterness in Nessa's tone made Alexander frown. Was the lass's patience with Duncan finally at an end?

Nessa's chin rose and her gaze swung toward the other end of the hall. "I must greet your father, Alexander."

"Aye, he will be pleased you are here."

"If 'tis peace you wish, 'tis also my wish for you Alexander, and you Lady Mary." Nessa excused herself.

Alexander reached for one of the cloaks Mary held and draped it over her shoulders then donned his own.

"She is more than a distant cousin." Mary stated as they went out into the cold night air. They walked deeper into the courtyard.

"Aye. It has been suggested a betrothal could be possible between Nessa and Duncan."

Her silence stretched for a long moment. "'Twould be difficult to be bound to a man who enjoys other lasses so very much."

She had gone to the heart of the matter between his brother and Nessa with unerring directness.

"I have enjoyed the lasses as well as he," Alexander stated deliberately and felt Mary's hand tightened around his arm. "The difference is I have not bragged about it." He stopped beneath the boughs of a large oak where a wooden bench was set against the outside wall of the fortress. He drew Mary down on it and leaned against the stone wall behind him to stretch out his leg. The injury didn't pain him so much now, but his leg had grown stiff from disuse.

"'Tis a need like any other, Mary." He wished he could see her expression. "Why do you not wish to dance?" he asked when she remained silent.

"'Tis because of the bairn."

"'Tis not because it reminds you of that night?"

Mary drew the hood of her cloak over her head covering the pale gleam of her hair. He experienced the disturbing feeling he talked with a shadow. It was not the first time he had felt that way since they had been wed.

"Why do you blame yourself for what happened that night?"

She remained so still for such a lengthy time he

began to wonder if she had slipped away into the night. He placed an arm around her to insure she didn't.

"The priest said I tempted you," she admitted softly.

The thought of the clergyman's judgmental posturing when faced with the grief of a frightened, hurt young lass had anger clenching in his gut. "He does not know what he is about."

"He is a man of the cloth, Alexander."

"Which does not excuse him from being a fool," he said, his voice harsh with feeling. He tugged the hood of her cloak down and ran his fingers through the heavy weight of her hair. "If you tempted me, 'twas with your spirit and your innocence. 'Twas not through any deed."

Her hair clung to his fingers like heavy silk and smelled of soap and sunshine. He breathed in the scent. "Will you tell me one thing I did, if you can, that brought you pleasure."

Her silence stretched for a lengthy time. He felt the heat of her blush as he caressed the curve of her cheek.

"'Tis not proper to speak of such things, Alexander."

He wanted to laugh aloud. So, there had been something, something intimate, she found too embarrassing to speak about. "How else is a wife to get what she wants if she does not demand it?"

"Men seldom agree to anything unless it serves their own purposes, my lord," Mary said with spirit.

"My only purpose is to serve you, dear wife."

"When it pleases you."

"Aye, 'twould please me very much to serve you as a husband, Mary." He felt her catch her breath and smiled again.

She had begun to accept his touch with less distrust in the last week. She was growing to enjoy these moments of sharing between them, he was certain. "I would serve you with a kiss if 'twould please you," he suggested and waited for any resistance as he raised her face to him. He felt the conflict in her as his lips found hers. Her lips remained passive beneath his—at first uncertain—but he persisted, and after a moment, her lips grew soft and pliant. He tasted the contours of her lips with the tip of his tongue, and they parted to accept him. Her tongue moved shyly to meet his in a response new and tempting.

He wanted to groan aloud in frustration, his desire for her a burning heat in the pit of his belly. His lips left hers to explore the safer territory of her ear. She shivered and he breathed in the womanly scent of her.

His hand trailed down the slender column of her throat. He longed to cup the tender weight of her breast, and barely stopped himself from doing so. To always have her within reach yet be unable to touch, kiss, or caress her was torture.

His hand cupped her cheek, and his lips found hers once again for one last lingering kiss before they had to return to the hall.

Mary's hand came to rest against his chest as she leaned against him, her breathing as affected as his.

He drew her to her feet for it was safer to rise and walk than to sit and feel her soft curves so close against him and not continue to touch and caress her. He had to progress slowly with her, but God's Blood it was difficult!

Duncan stepped from the side entrance as they reached the door. "Father asked that you and Mary come to the hall." Alexander took her cloak from her and removed his own as they passed through the crowd. At one of the fireplaces, surrounded by clansmen, John waited for them. The heads of all the clan families stood with him.

Mary looked small and fragile in the midst of all the men. Alexander stepped closer to her side in a protective gesture, drawing his father's attention. A smile flashed across his father's face.

Agatha stepped in to take their cloaks as his father raised a hand to silence the merriment around them. The room quietened in a ripple starting with those closest and moving along the walls of the room.

"We have all come together to celebrate the marriage of my oldest son, Alexander, and to welcome into our clan my new daughter, Mary." John's voice carried easily around the large room. "But we are here for more than that alone." He paused, his eyes moving around the room. "Mary embraces our clan as her own and wishes to take an oath of fealty to me and our clan. You are here to witness that oath." He drew Mary forward. Duncan appeared at his father's side with a Bible and held it while John guided her hand on it and placed his hand over hers.

"Repeat these words Mary Campbell."

Pride swelled within him as she repeated the oath without faltering, her eyes focused intent and sincere on his father's face. The memory of their wedding day intruded. Her voice had trembled, as had the rest of her as she spoke her vows. She had not looked at him once throughout the ceremony and she had been stiff when he kissed her to seal the vows.

But she had not been so when he had kissed her this night.

Chapter Eleven

Mary sat on a chair before the fire, and ran the brush in long even strokes through the heavy mass of pale gold hair hanging over her shoulder. Aware of Alexander's attention, her stomach fluttered with nerves as she braided the thick strands into a tail then secured it with a scrap of yellow ribbon.

Her thoughts dwelt on the kiss they had shared in the garden. Just the memory of it made her feel weak and breathless. The tingling between her thighs brought heat to her cheeks. Surely, it was sinful to feel this way.

"Your grandmother has spoken about coming to *Caisteal Sith* for the bairn's birth," she said turning on the chair to face him.

"So has half the clan here. I fear we may not have a bed for you to lie on to give birth nor a crumb of bread to eat afterwards." Alexander said from the bed.

She chuckled at his jest and tossed the braid over her shoulder.

"I had not seen my father dance in some years," He bent the knee of his injured leg beneath the covers and adjusted the pillow at his back against the heavy headboard of the bed.

A smile tilted her lips. "He did not wish to dance, but felt 'twould insult me if he did not offer the invitation." She rose and laid the brush on the table.

"'Twas clever of you to choose a tune that was not too demanding."

"'Twas not for him I did so, Alexander, but myself." Her eyes wanted to linger on his broad muscular chest and the red-cast hair covering it in swirls. Of late, she had longed to run her hand over that thick pelt.

He drew down the layered animal skins beside him before she could do so for herself. "You are not ill so often as before."

"Nay, thank God!"

The dim light of the candles flickered and cast uncertain patches of light across the bed. Mary watched the flames' fleeting dance as she curled on her side next to Alexander. Music muted by the thickness of the castle walls remained discernable, though she could not distinguish the tune.

"Come closer so we might share each others warmth, Mary," he suggested.

She wiggled closer until her bent knees almost touched his thigh. She jumped when he rested his hand on her leg. His touch burnt through the thin fabric of her shift.

"Will you never put your trust in me again?" he asked, his voice quiet, his expression serious in the dim light.

"Trust does not come easily to me anymore," she admitted.

"I could not behave the husband, injured as I am."

"'Tis your leg that is hurt. There is nothing wrong with the rest of you," she replied in a wry tone.

His smile flashed forth showing off to perfection the deep creases in his cheeks she found so appealing. "I would have to have your help in order to consummate the deed. 'Tis still painful for me to move."

His claims sounded reasonable. Sliding closer, she lessened the distance between them and straightened her legs.

"Will you not rest your head on my shoulder, Mary, and let me hold you?"

She shifted closer and did as he wanted. His skin felt cool to the touch. Mary drew the layered bedclothes up to insure his warmth, though it was she who shivered.

He held her carefully for several moments, and her anxiety eased. She wondered how she could want this and be afraid of it at the same time.

"'Tis a cold bed we have lain upon these weeks past, Mary."

She hated her own timidity, but could not voice an opinion.

"You did not seem to notice or care."

"I could not speak of such things to you," she

admitted, her voice whisper soft.

Alexander drew a deep breath. He guided her hand to his cheek and turned his lips against her palm. "Mayhap 'twould be a good time to try."

A tingling heat raced down Mary's arm. His gentleness brought a weakness to her limbs. This was how she had expected him to be on their wedding night. An ache of loss squeezed her throat together.

He held her hand atop his chest. The thick blanket of hair there felt soft and springy against her skin. Her entire body grew shaky with longings new and pleasurable.

"It should have been our wedding feast tonight," he said in a subdued tone.

So, he too, recognized the loss of so much that could not be replaced. "'Twas like a wedding feast," she said, her tone hesitant. She ran her hand over the heavy blanket of hair on his chest in a slow heady exploration she had never attempted before. He felt warm and woolly, and she longed to rub her cheek against the texture of the hair there.

His lips brushed her forehead. His fingertips ran up and down her forearm.

Her mouth went dry. His hands so calloused by the practices of war, felt good on her skin. Visions of his long fingers caressing her breasts were a tempting torment tracing their way through her thoughts.

"Might I touch you where the bairn rests, Mary?"

Of late, he asked her that as though he were measuring how much the babe was growing. "Aye." Her voice did not wish to work and the word came out little more than a whisper. She turned on her back. His large hand covered the curve of her stomach exploring the resting place of his child.

"Have you felt him move yet?" His voice grew hushed as though he feared he might disturb the babe, his eyes resting on the small roundness.

"Aye." A tempting emptiness ached between her legs.

"Why did you not speak of it to me?"

Surprised by the question, she studied his face. "I-I did not know you wished to know."

"There is nothing I do not wish to know about you

and the bairn."

A sweet feeling of pleasure swept through her. She covered his hand with hers. "'Tis like capturing a moth within your hands and feeling its wings beat against your skin but 'tis deep inside," she offered in a soft tone. "Mayhap in another month you will be able to feel it too."

He grew silent. His hand continued to cup her belly.

He would not turn against her again. She had to believe that. She could not live with him, if she had to wonder if his every show of interest was sparked by lust or true affection. "I will see to your leg before we seek our rest, Alexander," she said to distract herself.

Alexander pushed himself up into a sitting position and leaned back against the headboard. He bared his wrapped thigh for her as she rose from the bed but kept the bedclothes spread over his lap. Of late, he had become less blatant about his displays of nudity, and she realized she felt less pressured because of it.

Mary unwrapped the heavy bindings from his thigh then removed the cloth pad with which she had cushioned the wound. The injury, scabbed over and bright pink around the edges, looked to be healing well.

"You did not have to bind it. 'Tis almost healed."

"'Twould not close so well again should it break open, Alexander. 'Tis not knitted completely." She rolled the bandages neatly then handed them to him to set aside on a small table next to the bed.

"It has been a long while since I have been cared for with such diligence," he said as he twisted a stray curl that had escaped her braid about his finger.

For half his life, he had been a warrior. How often during that time had he had known the tenderness of a woman's touch? "Is that not what wives do, care for their husbands?"

"Aye." Alexander leaned forward to brush her cheek with his lips.

Mary found it hard to draw a full breath for the harsh beat of her heart drummed against her ribs prevented it.

"What would you have me do to care for you, Mary?" He rubbed his beard-roughened cheek against her soft one.

"I am well cared for, Alexander."

He smiled as he drew back to look down at her. He cupped her face in his hands, his pale amber eyes alight with pleasure. His mouth, moist and parted, molded to hers. The soft coaxing movement of his lips against hers drained the strength from her limbs and her lips parted to taste and feel his.

She wanted to hold his mouth to hers for a longer time. As if Alexander sensed that, his lips settled over hers. The slow gentle thrust of his tongue between her lips brought heat to the most intimate parts of her body. His tongue coaxed hers into a wet slithering dance that went on and on. He tasted of wine, and his skin had a clean musky scent all his own. A strange emptiness found its way between her thighs.

The warm touch of his large hand cupping her breast brought with it a pleasurable feeling, then a wave of guilt and anxiety. She grasped his wrist and turned her lips from his to murmur his name.

"Look at me, Mary," Alexander urged.

His cheeks were flushed and his eyes held a gleam she had not seen since they had first met. "I'm eager to be a husband to you. 'Tis a natural thing for a husband to touch his wife."

She did not know what was natural, only that it made her feel vulnerable and uncertain. She struggled to ignore the pleasure his touch brought her.

"'Twill never be as 'twas before, Mary. I swear it." His tone laced with urgency, his hands moved in restless caresses up and down her arms. "You've accepted my clan as your own, but what of your husband?"

Something in his face brought a breathless feeling beneath her ribs. He was right. She could not live her life forever distrusting him. She had to try to put the hurt behind her and forgive him.

"'Tis a beginning we are speaking of, Alexander," she warned him.

"Touching you, kissing you, holding you is all a beginning, Mary."

The idea felt both thrilling and frightening to her. "'Twould be the holding I would be asking you to do first."

A smile spread across his face causing a tide of color

to storm her cheeks with heat. "Come to bed," he invited.

She was not sure she trusted the gleam that lit his amber eyes. Had she agreed to more than just a touch, a kiss, and his arm about her?

She blew out the candles. The flickering light of the fire cast wavering shadows across the foot of the bed where its meager light penetrated the darkness. She slipped beneath the pelts. Alexander gave her no time to agonize over her decision, but gathered her close against him and drew the covers over her shoulder.

She grew weak at the intimacy of his touch as his hand followed the curve of her spine and ran over the rounded curve of her buttocks pressing her closer. Her heart beat against her ribs as his body fit against hers.

"I have wanted to hold you like this since we were first wed."

He seemed content with only holding her so she relaxed somewhat.

"Will you not tell me what 'twas I did that pleased you, Mary?" Alexander coaxed.

She turned her face against his chest though he could not see the hot color flooding it.

"How am I to please you if you do not tell me what gives you pleasure?"

She found that an intriguing idea. "I did not think it mattered as long as you were served."

"Men are easily pleased, 'tis more of a challenge for a man to please his lass."

His lass. Those two words sounded very possessive. "It pleases me when you are gentle," she said decisively. "And when you are not barking orders at me." She sensed his smile.

His hand moved with restless intent up and down her back, molding her closer still. "Do you like to be kissed?"

"Aye." Her voice sounded breathy and soft for she felt as though she had run a long way and could not catch her breath. The heated maleness of his body brought a lethargy to her lower limbs.

His lips brushed feather light against her forehead, her eyelids, her cheeks, her chin, making her aware of the areas he avoided. She grew weak with longing as his lips brushed hers in a teasing caress so light his mouth barely touched hers. Mary placed a hand against his chest, too shy to guide his lips to hers though she craved it.

Alexander's tongue traced the curve of her bottom lip then touched the parted surface between, and her lips opened to him. Her arms went around his neck to urge him closer as his tongue thrust into her mouth with an easy push. Their tongues intertwined in a slow sensuous meeting.

His hand explored the shape of her breasts through the linen fabric covering them. Her nipples grew taut beneath his touch. Heat consumed her.

She did not protest when he untied the drawstring of her shift and reached beneath the fabric to cup her breast in his hand. His fingers felt so natural touching her skin.

"'Tis wicked, Alexander," she murmured as his lips left hers to caress her throat.

"Nay, Mary, 'tis right and good." His tongue traced the fragile edge of her collarbone then moved lower.

Mary caught her breath in shock as his tongue circled her nipple. His mouth, hot and wet, latched onto it. Pleasure flowed down her body in rivulets to settle at her very core. She murmured his name as her fingers combed through the thick hair at the back of his head. Her hands moved restlessly across the broad width of his shoulders as he paid similar homage to the other breast.

His lips came back to hers and instinctively she turned against him. Her breasts nestled against the furry warmth of his chest. The texture of the hair there felt rough against her sensitive nipples.

"'Tis a dream to feel your skin against mine." Alexander groaned as he buried his face against her throat. His skin felt feverish. The hard heat of his manhood pressed into her thigh through the fabric of the shift. She was trembling, though she could not decide whether it was with longing or fear.

"Touch me, Mary, as I have touched you," he murmured huskily as he drew back.

Mary cupped his face in her hands and drew his lips to hers. She pressed soft, inexperienced kisses to his lips then hesitantly pushed her tongue into his mouth.

He made a sound deep in his throat like a groan and

his hands molded her closer as his tongue moved in eager response to hers.

Her hands followed the shape of his face, his shoulders, then found the woolly breadth of his chest. The hair there, though not as thick, felt like lambs wool. Her lips tasted the warmth of his throat. She slid downward and rubbed her cheek against the thick pelt of hair on his chest, as she had wanted to do earlier. She explored the texture of his nipples with her fingertips. Alexander shuddered as she touched her tongue to one of them. He pulled her upward and caught her lips with his. She was surprised to find he was trembling as badly as she was.

His hand followed the curve of her hip easing the fabric of the shift farther down. He caressed the rounded curve of her stomach exploring with tender attention the small ripening of her shape. He guided Mary onto her back and slid downward to press soft kisses on her stomach.

Mary sensed a change in the feverish passion he displayed as he touched her. The empty ache between her thighs grew rampant as the moist heat of his lips and tongue lathed her skin. His hand slid up the inside of her thigh beneath the useless fabric still encasing her legs.

As he approached the most intimate areas of her body, she grew suddenly fearful of taking that last irrevocable step, and clamped her legs together around his hand and caught his wrist.

Alexander slid upward, his lips finding hers. His breathing ragged, he cupped her cheek.

"'Tis only my intent to give you pleasure." He drew her against him, his hand tracing a searing path down her back to mold her tightly against him once again. His fingers followed the curve of her spine then stopped, his body going still as his fingertips brushed over her skin.

He withdrew so suddenly, Mary shivered from the loss of heat. "What is it, Alexander?" Confused, disoriented, she sat up and followed his progress to the fire.

He lit a tallow candle and approached the bed.

The closer the light got the more exposed she felt. She grasped the fabric of the shift and held it against her.

His features appeared harsh in the dull glow of the

light, his gaze a pale wolfish gold. "Come here, Mary." Her heart skipped a beat as he grasped her wrist and pulled her to the edge of the bed then to her feet. He turned her back to the light and lifted her hair over her shoulder.

Aware of his intent, Mary attempted to twist away.

"I must see, Mary." Never before had he used such a tone, nor looked at her with such fierceness. She suddenly knew what he looked like on the battlefield with the blood lust riding him.

His fingers found the flat ridges where each lash had fallen laying open her skin, ten of them, because Collin had not wanted to damage her worth over much. Mary suddenly felt sick with shame and jerked away. She sought the shadows to pull the shift up and cover herself.

"Mary—" He squeezed her shoulder. "I did not know he would punish you in such a way."

The regret she heard in his voice brought an ache to her throat. "What did you expect that he would do?"

"I expected he would focus his rage upon me, not you."

"You are speaking of a man who looks at his women folk as property to barter, Alexander. You damaged my value. Had I not left that night, he would have sold me to whomever he could, just to see your claim denied." For a moment, Bearach McDonald came to mind and a tremor worked its way through her limbs. "Had it not been for the nuns, I might have died. I was sick with fever for nearly a fortnight and 'twas more than a month that every breath I drew did not bring me pain." She allowed him to draw her close again. His hand stroked her back with soothing caresses as he rested his chin atop her head.

****

Back in bed, a hard knot of pain and regret wedged beneath Alexander's ribs as he continued to hold her. After a time, Mary fell asleep. But even with her head resting on his shoulder and her body pressed against his side, he could not relax.

He had behaved dishonorably toward her and to himself, as well. He had been so hungry for her. Seeing family, a future in her had made him too eager and Collin MacLachlan had—He could no longer blame Collin for his actions. Nor could he make excuses. He should have guarded her against Bearach MacDonald, not forced the issue and taken her. He could have taken her away from the castle, an action that would have caused some uproar, but would have kept her safe, until they wed. He could have taken her into his confidence that night instead of rushing to seal their connection.

Her pride had been ground into the dirt before his men and her father's. She had been brutally beaten, and atop it all, the priest had drummed into her a sense of shame and responsibility for what had happened. It was a miracle she would even allow him to touch her.

Her response to him earlier came to mind. Even though she had allowed him to caress her so intimately, he had sensed her reservations. She had been so innocently sensuous it had set him aflame. He had gone too far too quickly. It would be better to ease her into their marriage bed a little at a time and make her as hungry for him as he was for her.

His thought turned to Collin. Rage as hot as a smith's forge flared within him. If ever the MacLachlan chief came within striking distance, he would pay for what he had done. It would not be clan to clan, but man to man. The scars marring Mary's back could not be erased, but Collin would beg her forgiveness if he had to beat it out of him.

Chapter Twelve

The group rode in single file along the narrow rutted path. Mary caught a glimpse of Alexander and Duncan in the lead now and then when the column curved along the trail. Alexander had placed her in the center of the troop so she could more easily be protected should their company be attacked.

They had traveled the distance of three leagues when snow began to fall. It came down in large fat flakes that powdered the men's fur robes and bare heads. They looked like great hulking bears atop their horses' backs.

Mary arranged the dark tartan shawl beneath her cloak to cover the lower half of her face then drew the hood of her cloak over her head. The leather gloves David had given her, as a parting gift, were fur lined and protected her hands. She felt reasonably warm though the wind whipped the flakes about in a wild dance and made visibility difficult.

When they stopped, she was stiff from the hours on horseback and welcomed Alexander's help as she dismounted.

"How do you fare, Mary?" he asked, his amber gaze running up and down her bundled form.

"I am faring well, Alexander," she replied at once from behind her tartan mask.

"'Tis good. Should your hands and feet become chilled you must send Gabe to me at once. I do not fancy a wife without her fingers or toes."

"The highland clime I am used to is colder than this. You forget I have been raised farther north with my MacPherson kin."

He guided her close to the meager fire Derek had started. The men parted to make room for her and Alexander. Offered a ration of bread, cheese, and meat by one of the men, she tucked into the food hungrily.

Noticing her husband's attention, she paused to offer him a questioning look.

"'Tis better than the first journey we made together despite the weather, eh lass," he observed.

"Aye," she agreed, remembering the long ride from Lochlan and how sick she had been.

After the meal, Mary wandered behind some brush, away from the men, to see to her personal needs. Stepping from the yew bush's cover, she found Alexander leaning back beneath the sheltering boughs of a large hemlock a short distance away.

He grasped her wrist and drew her between his feet to rest against him. She found herself enveloped in the warmth beneath his robes as he folded them around her.

"You look chilled, lass."

"Aye," she agreed. "'Twould suit me to wear trews as you have."

"Then you would be lowering them instead of raising them."

She shivered then snuggled closer to the heat he exuded. The call of nature had forced her to readjust the layers of clothing she wore and exposed her most tender spots to the icy air.

"Would you have me rub some warmth into the parts that have grown cold?" Alexander asked, laughter in his tone.

Mary poked him in the ribs in warning, but was at once reminded of how his hands had felt on her bare skin.

Her head finding a place within the hollow of his shoulder, she rested against him more heavily and slipped her arms around his waist.

"Have you finally found a use for your husband, lass?" he teased huskily.

"Aye." Mary tilted her head back to look up at him. "To keep my feet warm at night," she retorted.

"And what about the rest of you?" he asked, his gaze intent.

She pressed close again, cutting off his view of her hot face. His fingers cupped her head.

"That too," she finally admitted.

Alexander gave her a gentle squeeze and murmured, "Stubborn."

That he was trying to make amends for what he had done was plain. Though his eyes often rested on her in the evenings, he had not tried to press her into intimacy again, but seemed content to hold her within their marriage bed.

He had become curious about her family. The darkness made it easier to talk about the MacPherson kin she had lived with, before Collin had betrothed her. Sharing such knowledge with him made her feel vulnerable, yet she could not withhold things from him, he was her husband. Each time she did so, she felt guilty.

She drew back to look up at him. "How much longer before we reach your land?"

He turned her to walk back to the company of men. "Tomorrow, by midday."

"I am anxious to see my new home."

"The castle is not finished yet, but our chambers will be secure."

She smiled. "'Twill be no worse than sleeping on a cold stone floor upon a reed pallet."

"Nay, lass. We'll share a bed bigger than the one at Lorne."

The snow fell more heavily as the afternoon wore on. Mary was chilled by the time they stopped for the night. They sought shelter against a stone outcropping at the base of one of the hills that hugged the loch. The natural depression folded around the group, blocking off the worst of the wind and snow.

She watched with interest as the men broke into groups to organize the camp without an order being spoken. The horses were loosed to be fed grain close by, while some of the men gathered wood for a fire. Duncan unwrapped peat from the packhorses to feed the blaze while Alexander hung one of the water bags on a low-lying branch for all to use. The rest of the bags remained on the horse carrying them allowing their body heat to keep the liquid from freezing.

Two of the men passed bread, meat, and cheese around. The cold kept the group from socializing for very long after the meal. Alexander posted the watch. The rest of the company retired to wrap themselves in the thick animal skin robes to keep warm.

Using a saddle for a pillow, Alexander folded his robes around her and drew a thick pelt up over their heads to seal out the cold. "I do not like being unable to feel you against me, Mary," he grumbled after a moments silence.

"'Twould be too cold if you could," she replied.

He opened his robes and drew her within the folds of wool and fur. He wedged his knee between her thighs and hugged her close against him.

Mary turned her hot cheek against the coolness of the saddle. His thigh pressed against her intimately through the layers of their clothing sparking a sensation of pleasure she found wickedly tempting.

"How does your leg fare?" she asked.

"'Tis stiff, but will do," he answered. "How fares the bairn?"

"I have not felt him move today. 'Tis a comfort when he does."

"Do not fret, lass. You are young and hearty and the bairn will be strong." He gave her a reassuring squeeze.

She wiggled around until her back rested against his chest and drew his arm around her waist.

****

Alexander smiled as he pressed close against her and curved his legs beneath hers. He breathed in the soft scent of soap and flowers lingering in her hair. He found her innocence a torment for she had no idea what she did to him as she wiggled back against him. Visions of how many ways their bodies might fit together ran through his mind to make his discomfort worse. He speculated for every time he wanted her, and did not have her, he perhaps paid atonement for what he had done. As his need gnawed and burnt deep within the pit of his belly, he wondered if the end of his penance was anywhere in sight.

****

Dawn broke clear and cold and saw the men hastening to break camp while the weather remained clear. They continued down the valley close to the loch. By midmorning, they rode into a wooded copse and stopped to eat a hasty meal of bread and cheese.

Mary found a place to settle against a large oak. Alexander and Duncan joined her there. Duncan passed her a tied cloth. She opened it, and then smiled as she offered him some of the dried apples he had given her.

He shook his head. "'Tis for you, little sister."

His gaze went to Alexander. "Do you mean to share the tidings about the bairn with the rest of the clan?" he asked.

"They already know, Duncan," Alexander said as he accepted some of Mary's apples.

"Do you not wish to strut about like a proud cock crowing about it as the other men do about theirs?" he asked.

Alexander's gaze settled on Mary.

"Tis your first born, Alexander," Duncan reminded.

"Do you wish to share the tidings?" she asked, her voice soft.

He gave her a wry smile.

Warmth and pleasure curled up inside her. "They will know soon in any case," she reminded him. "Twill be best such news comes from you."

Alexander's smile brought an airless feeling beneath her ribs.

"I will try not to crow too loudly," he teased.

She found him so appealing in that moment she could not hold back a smile. She wanted to lean against him and feel his arms about her. The heat of a blush stormed her cheeks. She rose to her feet and excused herself.

****

"You are making progress, Brother," Duncan observed as they watched Mary slip discreetly behind some nearby brush.

"Mayhap." Alexander rubbed his thigh for it had begun to ache. "'Tis a double-edged sword I find myself astride. And the worst part is knowing 'tis my own fault I am there."

Duncan chuckled. "Mayhap you are making atonement for your sins." He got to his feet and stretched. "She is a sweet-natured lass."

For the first time Alexander saw a question in Duncan's eyes as he looked down at him. "Aye, sweet-natured and too precious to be sacrificed to the likes of Bearach MacDonald."

Duncan's features hardened. "'Twas in my thoughts there had to be more to your reasoning than desire."

Alexander drew a deep breath. "'Tis a reason, but not an excuse for what I did. I did not know the damage I would cause by traveling such a path. She is not the same lass she was before, nor I the same man."

"Mayhap 'tis good. You have finally fallen to earth to join the rest of us sinners," Duncan said, his expression serious.

Alexander studied his brother in surprise. "I have never considered myself above any man."

"Nay, 'twas what you expected of yourself."

Mary returned and he rose. As though signaled, the men prepared to remount. Mary pulled her gloves from within her surcoat and one dropped to the ground. Alexander bent to retrieve it as she did the same. The unmistakable hiss of an arrow sped just over their heads to land just behind them.

Alexander grasped Mary's arm and dragged her unceremoniously behind a clump of brush for cover.

"Where did it come from?" she whispered.

"The trees above," he answered. "Stay here." He looked up in surprise as her hand latched onto his arm, preventing him from leaving her.

"Take heart, lass. I do not intend to make you a widow at such a tender age."

****

Mary's insides grew liquid with fear as he circled around behind the men and signaled to them.

Those with bows began to return the sporadic fire of the hidden archers. Though their aim focused in the right direction, their arrows could not penetrate the thick branches of the pines in which their attackers had taken refuge. Some bounced away to land in the snow beneath the trees while others found purchase out of sight.

A lull came in the firing of the arrows by both parties and a horrible gut wrenching silence ensued.

Mary looked away from Alexander's progress then back to find him gone from sight. She shivered and huddled beneath the branches of the small evergreen, as fear for his safety twisted inside her.

A strange sound cut through the silence. Like a wave,

it built to a horrible roar that grew as the pounding of horses hooves sped closer. The men drew their swords and readied themselves.

****

Alexander broke from behind the horses and raced to Mary's mount. Using the animal as cover, he retrieved her crossbow and quiver of arrows. Arrows hissed through the air, their venomous strike deadly and quick as they hit the small mare along the shoulders and haunches. The horse went down screaming in pain. Alexander leaped away, his tracks in the snow hounded by arrows loosed on his heels as he ran for cover.

The lead horse appeared through the trees with several others close behind. Another battle cry rent the air as the warriors bore down upon them.

Alexander stepped from behind the trees and released the arrow in the crossbow. The dart split the air and found its mark in the chest of the animal in the lead. It dropped like a stone from beneath his rider, sending the man sailing through the air in an arc to land against a tree with a fleshy thud. The riders and horses close behind reached the fallen animal without warning. Several others went down causing those behind to either pull up or leap over to keep from trampling their fallen comrades.

****

Mary started as the Campbell war cry filled the air and the men surged forward. The crashing of metal against metal thundered loud in the clear cold air as the two forces met in a violent clash of arms and wills.

Duncan staggered through the brush falling back beneath an onslaught of weighty swordplay. She rolled to her feet and stumbled back out of the way.

Two men broke through the underbrush to her right. Their immediate surprise at finding her there gave them pause, then they leaped forward. Mary darted around Duncan. She hiked her skirt above her ankles and raced uphill. Her breathing grew harsh as she struggled against the uncertain footing, the snow and mud making her slip. Her muscles burned with the effort, as the sound of the men's pursuit behind her drew closer.

She cut back through the trees circling the camp to

120

where she had last seen Alexander. The sounds of battle increased in intensity.

She broke through the stand of trees, to find herself in the thick of the fray, and ducked as a blade swung dangerously close over her head. She leaped over a man in her path, his throat slit, the snow bloody from his wound.

She reached the horses and ran around them seeking a place to hide. A yelp of fear tore from her as someone grabbed her from behind and knocked her to the ground. She turned onto her back to face the threat, and was immediately pinned to the ground by the weight of one of the men. The other stood over her.

Straddling her, her captor grinned. She had only time to experience a momentary rush of dread when an arrow caught him in the throat obliterating his smile and splattering blood in her face and across the snow. He toppled and fell forward on top of her.

The other man wheeled to face the threat. Alexander swung the empty crossbow hitting him in the face. Lifted clear of his feet by the force of the blow, the man landed flat on his back in the snow. He lay motionless, his body twisted at an awkward angle.

Mary wiggled to free herself from the dead weight of the man's body as his blood leaked out to run beneath her. She avoided looking at him.

Alexander flipped him off her. Grasping her arm, he lifted her to her feet. He urged her into the cover of the trees a small distance from the fighting and turned to give her a searching once over to check her for injuries. "Are you whole, Mary? Did they hurt you?" he demanded.

"Nay." She ripped a piece of fabric from her kirtle to wipe the blood from her face. "Tis his blood not mine," she assured him, her voice shaky.

Alexander bent to scoop some snow in his hand and rub it over her cheeks to clean it away. "Come, lass." He looked about for a place of safety for her. He led her to a sturdy pine, the branches thick with needles. "Have you ever climbed a tree?"

"It has been some time, but aye."

"I need you to climb this one, lass, and stay here until I come for you."

She nodded.

He bent and gave her a boost. Reaching one of the lower branches, she hastened to secure purchase on some of the larger branches to push herself upward. Her assent awkward, she settled on a branch a safe distance above the ground. She offered Alexander a smile, though she had never felt less like smiling. Fear for him and the others had her heart pounding so hard it was almost painful to breathe. Sounds of the battle still raging carried easily to them.

Alexander loaded the crossbow and stretched for her to grasp it, then reached up the quiver of arrows. "Do not hesitate to use it, Mary."

She nodded. "Have a care for yourself, Alexander."

Flashing her a smile, he drew his sword then turned and ran back to the fighting.

Chapter Thirteen

"'Tis a bird," Alexander said, as he looked up at Mary perched high above them.

"Nay, what kind of bird would perch in such weather? 'Tis a wee beastie," Gabriel said.

Mary smiled down at the two men and wanted to laugh from sheer joy. The sounds of fighting had gone on for an endless time. Now that it was finally over, she felt weak with relief.

"Is all well with Duncan and the others, Alexander?" she asked as a fresh wave of anxiety struck her.

"Aye, lass," he said with a grin. "Do you not wish to come down now?"

"Aye," she breathed, eager to have her feet on solid ground.

She tossed down the crossbow and the quiver of arrows. Her skirts continually caught on the many twigs and needles of the tree and she had to free herself several times. "'Twould have been easier dressed in trews as you are," she complained. Alexander grasped her about the waist to steady her as she dropped to the ground.

"I do not believe I would approve your climbing about in trees often, Mary," he teased then frowned as she turned to face him. "Are you hurt, lass?"

She touched the spot along her neck where dried blood left a grainy residue on her skin. "Nay,'tis that man's blood, not mine. I could not get it off. I'll see to it when we return to camp."

The men exchanged a look.

"You must prepare yourself, lass," Alexander said.

A feeling of fear curled around her insides, leaving a hollow sensation in its wake.

"'Tis a bloody mess you'll be seeing. Do not dwell on the men's faces. T'will stay with you if you do."

Mary nodded. "How many of the men have been

hurt?"

"Three," he answered, his expression grave. "Derrick, our healer, is one of them and can not help the others. Do you think you can do something for them?"

"We will see." She prayed she would be able to care for them.

The camp lay in shambles, the snow trampled to mud in spots where the heaviest fighting had occurred. Blood mixed with snow tinged the ground pink in several places.

The men had cleared the area of bodies and were gathering the weapons of the fallen warriors they had battled. The bodies lay in a row at one end of the camp far away from the injured Campbell clansmen.

"They will return for their dead once we are gone," Alexander said as he guided her to the fire.

Mary searched for Duncan and drew a relieved breath when her gaze found him among the men moving the dead.

Her eyes traveled to the row of eight bodies he stood beside and a shudder of revulsion shook her. She could do nothing for them. She quickly turned back to the three men lying close to the fire.

Drawing a deep breath in an attempt to steady herself, she straightened her shoulders and turned to Alexander. "I will need water heated and, if my things are still about, I will need scissors, and the muslin you purchased for me before we left Lorne."

Mary kneeled beside the first man. She peeled back the fabric of a hastily fashioned bandage to find a gapping sword wound traveling the length of his arm that laid bare the muscle beneath. She swallowed as nausea rose up and she closed her eyes for a moment feeling light headed. It was a moment before she trusted she would not bock. She schooled her features into a calm expression and forced her gaze upward to the man's face. His gray hair, wet with sweat, lay plastered to his head. His jaw harshly clenched against the pain.

"It cannot be left open, Artair. I will have to draw it closed somehow."

He nodded.

Mary laid a hand on his uninjured arm. "'Twill be well, as soon as I may make it so."

She started to kneel beside the next man, but he shook his head as he held a cloth against a wound in his thigh.

"'Tis only a cut and not as bad as Artair's. See to Derrick first. He has more need of your services than I do, Lady Mary."

She moved to Derrick. He lay propped against a saddle, an arrow protruding from his chest. He tried to offer Mary a smile though it was obvious every breath he drew caused him pain. One of the men cut his shirt away to bare the injury. The sight of the shaft protruding from his flesh had her swallowing against the sickness again. She studied the depth of the arrow for a few moments. "Twill be difficult," she said.

"Aye," he agreed. "Let us do it and put it behind us both, lass."

She nodded then looked around . "Have my things been found?"

"Aye, Mary." Alexander stepped forward to place the items she needed close beside her.

"Have two of the men scrub their hands then tear the muslin into strips for bandages. Is the water heated yet?"

"Aye, lass."

She laid a muslin cloth, scissors, and needle and thread out on a flat piece of fabric then turned to scrub her hands thoroughly.

"Gabriel?"

"Aye, Lady Mary."

"I would ask you to hold him steady while Alexander draws the arrow free."

The burley clansman moved around behind Derrick and looped a muscular arm around his chest above the arrow. Alexander did not delay, but jerked the arrow free with a quick heave. Mary applied pressure to the wound, holding back the flow of blood. When she cautiously eased the fabric back to view the wound, she breathed a sigh of relief. The blood did not spurt and there were no air bubbles escaping from the wound. She cleaned the torn flesh then padded the injury and bound it tightly.

Aware of the possibility the men who had attacked them could return, she rushed to see to the other two clansmen. She found her sewing ability more handy than she had ever thought as she drew the gapping sides of Artair's wound back together. Her hands grew slick with blood and the sweet smell of it forced her to draw deep breaths to control the nausea plaguing her. She bound the thigh injury of the last man then scrubbed her hands one last time.

She saw the three men were given something to drink, then stepped away from the fire for a breath of air untainted by the smell of blood. Absently, she wiped at the rusty stains marring her surcoat.

Alexander placed her cloak, crusty with dried blood, around her shoulders. She looked up at him. "How much farther to the castle?"

"A few more hours."

"Have Gabriel ride with Derrick so he is well supported."

He nodded.

"Artair's arm is the worst I have seen. If it does not fester he may yet keep it."

She studied her husband's face. To know this was the kind of life he had known for nearly half his years had an almost physical ache settling inside her. She wanted to comfort him in some way, but the men were all around them. She was not sure he would understand even if she did. She slid her hand into his larger one melding her palm to his.

Alexander's attention swung to her face, and for a moment, their gazes met and held.

"'Tis a warrior's wife you have become this day, Mary," he said his voice soft.

His words following the same vein as her thoughts had her swallowing against a knot of tears that suddenly rose to block her throat.

"I was a warrior's wife the day we wed, Alexander." She rested her hand against his shoulder for a moment then turned back to the fire to gather her belongings.

Alexander saddled one of the horses seized after the battle to replace her dead mare. The black gelding had three white stockings and a blaze down his forehead. Mary studied the animal thoughtfully. She had seen the horse before, but could not place where.

Her gaze moved to the row of bodies laying a short

distance away. She stepped in that direction, but two Campbell clansmen blocked her way.

"You do not wish to see such things, Lady Mary," one of the men said. "'Twould not be good for the bairn."

Could anything be worse than the injury she had stitched? "What clan are the men from?" she asked.

"'Tis not known for certes."

Her gaze moved back to the horse.

"Is there something amiss, Mary?" Alexander asked. He stood by her mount, ready to give her a boost.

Aware of the company's eagerness to be away, Mary crossed to him. "You do not know what clan the men hail from?"

"Nay, they have taken pains with their dress to ensure we do not know."

He boosted her into the saddle.

"Why would they attack so far inside Campbell land?" she asked.

He handed her the reins. "I do not know, lass. I'll be riding beside you the rest of the way, lest there be trouble ahead."

She nodded and reached for her gloves tucked within her surcoat. She looked down at the leather and noticed her hands were shaking. "The first arrow was meant for you, Alexander." She tugged on the gloves.

"Aye," he acknowledged. "'Tis a fact of warfare you take out the commander of the company first to throw the men into confusion."

Her gaze rose to his face. "How did they know you were the leader?"

His gaze rested on her for a moment. "There are times you are too quick, Mary."

She swallowed. Her father's threats after the council came back to her. She was afraid to voice her fears, afraid to dwell on the possibility that her father wished her and her husband harm.

As they rode past the row of dead men, her eyes were once again drawn to them. "Mayhap I could—-"

"Nay," he cut her off shortly.

For the remainder of the journey Mary concentrated on the three injured men. The task left her little time to brood over her fears.

The valley widened at the end of the loch. The rugged craggy hills encircling the land looked cold and forbidding in the weakening light. Snow began to fall again.

The village spread around the hulking form of the castle lying close against the loch. The stone structure appeared gray and forlorn, its crest misshapen. One side was finished the other was not.

Mary viewed her new home with mixed feelings of relief and anxiety. It would be up to her to do her husband and herself proud, to run his household and care for the people beneath his roof. She prayed her aunt had trained her well enough.

As they passed through the village, Alexander dismissed the men to go to their homes. Their party quickly dwindled to ten.

They entered the castle courtyard and stable lads ran forth to grasp the reins of their horses and hold them steady. Men appeared to help lift the injured from their mounts and take them into the castle.

Alexander dismounted and reached up to help her down from her horse. He guided her inside out of the cold. They stood close to one of the fireplaces at either side of the great hall. The room looked similar to the great hall at Lorne except the gallery above projected over nearly half the room holding the heat of the fireplaces closer to the floor.

Alexander took her cloak from her shoulders and handed it to one of the servants. "Mary, this is Fergus, my steward. He will see to whatever you need."

She nodded to the stoop shouldered man who greeted her. He had a thatch of gray hair curly and thick and bushy brows. He focused moss green eyes on her, studying her openly.

"The men will need a chamber in which to rest and some brewed sorrel bark to ward off fever. I will also need thyme and some salt brewed to clean their wounds, and more bandages. Some broth would not go amiss once they have been settled and are in less pain."

She turned to Alexander. "Have you sent word to Derrick's wife so she may know he is hurt?"

"Aye. 'Tis done."

Mary saw the two men with sword wounds settled in

a chamber together. She had Derrick placed in a room alone. A manservant soon appeared to help her rid all three of their muddy boots and bloody clothes. She bathed away the dried blood and cleaned their wounds. Fergus sent a soothing balm to apply to the injuries, to keep the bandages from sticking. She lathed it on generously.

She decided, as she put a fresh bandage around Artair's arm, the violence she had witnessed until that day had not prepared her for the realities of war and what men were capable of doing to one another. If the wound healed, Artair would carry the scar with him for the rest of his days. Her thoughts brought her husband's scars to mind for he had several marring his body due to injuries he had suffered through the years.

With the help of the manservant, she fed the men and offered them each some wine. It had grown late and a servant appeared to light the torches mounted in the walls of the passageway. She leaned wearily against the stone wall outside the sick rooms, her muscles aching with fatigue.

"Mary?" Alexander's deep voice came from down the wide corridor and she looked up. "Are you ill, lass?"

"Nay, mayhap a wee bit weary."

Alexander grasped her hand. He drew her down the corridor and up a spiral staircase. He paused outside a room furnished with several tables and chairs. A window seat constructed in an alcove before one of the tall narrow windows, offered a place in which to sit as well. Rush mats covered the wooden floor. "'Tis the solar," he explained.

He continued upward to another doorway. "This is our chamber."

He drew her into the room. She noticed at once the bed dominating the space, much larger than the one they had shared at Lorne. Thick woven mats covered the floor beside the bed and before the hearth. A pitcher and washbowl set atop a table near the fireplace. Her brush and comb rested there beside Alexander's shaving things. The blazing fire, lit candles, and the wooden shutters closed against the cold, combined to lend a cozy intimacy to the room.

"I have had your clothing placed here with mine," he

said as he raised the lid of the chest at the foot of the bed. She stepped close to peer inside and found her clothing neatly folded away.

"Your sewing things are here within the bedside table." He opened the doors of the small chest to show her the cloth and her basket.

"The garderobe is there," he pointed out to her an alcove covered by a heavy drape.

Mary offered him a smile. His eagerness for her to be pleased with the room gave her a warm feeling of belonging, of homecoming. "'Tis a fine room for us to share." She perched on the edge of the bed.

"Aye," he agreed as he looked around the room. He moved to sit beside her and placed an arm around her waist. His amber eyes focused on her face, the irises appearing a tawny gold surrounded by a ring of brown. "You have done well this day, Mary," he said huskily.

A rush of tenderness for him made her chest feel tight and full. She raised a hand to caress his scarred cheek.

His lips brushed her forehead and his arm tightened about her. "I have ordered a meal brought to us here and water for a bath."

"I am in great need of both at the moment," she said with a smile.

"As am I, my lady."

"Your leg, how has it fared the day?" she asked, laying her palm flat on his thigh where she knew the injury to be.

"'Tis close to being completely healed," he said his voice growing huskier.

Color stained his cheeks and she stared at him in surprise. He had never responded to her touch in such a way before.

The meal arrived and the water placed on the hearth in a heavy kettle so it would stay hot. Alexander hastened to move a small table before the fire so they could eat. He held her chair for her, then took a place opposite her.

"You will have time to meet all the servants and men tomorrow," he said as he served her from the tureen of stew. He placed the wooden bowl before her then broke apart a loaf of bread to share with her.

"If the men should grow worse in the night I have asked that I be awakened." Suddenly famished, she lifted her spoon to her lips.

"Aye." He served her a slice of the meat pie and poured her a glass of ale.

"The food is very good," she said as she pushed her bowl away and sipped her drink. The warmth of the room and her full stomach made her drowsy and she covered a yawn. Exhaustion pressed down on her and she longed to lie down.

Openly watching her, Alexander smiled. "I will pour the water for your bath whenever you are ready," he suggested. "'Twill be I who will have to act as lady's maid until you choose who you will have."

"I have never had a maid."

"You may wish to meet with some of the women and ponder it for a time," he said with a shrug. He offered her some of the cheese and dried fruit on the tray.

Mary shook her head and rose from her seat. She made quick use of the gardrobe then moved about the room to study her surroundings. She plucked the scrap of ribbon from the end of her braid and ran restless fingers through to unweave it. She stopped by the large metal disk hanging over the washbasin to study her image. She reached for her brush and ran it through the twisted strands of hair with long deep strokes until it lay in soft waves across her shoulder.

"You look as though you, too, have done battle," he said from behind her, his fingers touching a stain on the shoulder of her gown.

"A battle of a different kind. I hope the stains can be cleaned from my cloak and surcoat." She unfastened the wooden buttons at the front of the garment and it parted to the waist. She shed the outer gown and draped it over the back of a chair.

Alexander lifted the heavy kettle of water and filled the basin for her. Aware of him watching, she shed her shoes, stockings and garters. After washing her face and hands, she unfastened the sleeves of her kirtle and untied the drawstring at her neck to pull her arms free. A wave of nervous shyness made her fingers clumsy as she shed the garment and stood before the basin in her shift. She pulled the lace that held the garment closed and wet a cloth. Dried remnants of blood still flecked her neck and she wiped it away.

Alexander's reflection joined hers in the metal disk. His hands lightly messaged her bare shoulders, slid gently over her skin to her arms, then around her waist to draw her back against him. He bent his head, his lips, parted and moist, finding the sensitive area between her neck and shoulder. Delightful shivers raced down Mary's spine. Her knees grew weak and her nipples tingled and grew taut beneath the fabric of the shift. She leaned back against him welcoming his support and his closeness.

A knock at the door had them both turning. Alexander murmured an impatient oath at the interruption and strode to the door to answer the summons.

"Alexander—you are home," a husky feminine voice came from the open door. Slender arms slid around his neck and a supple body clothed in a deep green surcoat molded to his tall frame. The woman, her face obscured, drew his head down and offered him a kiss openly passionate and inviting.

A dropping sensation struck Mary's midriff, her legs going weak with shock.

Alexander worked the woman's arms from around his neck and quickly set her aside.

"I'm sure you knew, as did the rest of the clan, that I was returning with my wife this day, Tira," he said dryly, his expression stony. "You will apologize to my wife for your intrusion on our homecoming then you will leave the castle and take yourself back to where you belong." He grasped the woman's arm none too gently and brought her to stand before Mary.

Tira's emerald green eyes surrounded by sooty lashes glared in open hostility as they ran down Mary's scantily clad figure. She had lush lips and a slender nose. Her hair hung dark as night, along either side of her oval shaped face. She easily topped Mary's height by an intimidating measure.

Mary's heart sank, a feeling of despair knotting beneath her ribs. The enmity in the woman's gaze had the hair rising on the back of her neck.

"You will beg my wife's pardon for your intrusion, Tira." Alexander's masculine features grew harsh with anger.

"I beg your pardon for intruding on your homecoming," Tira parroted without expression.

The woman's insolence had Mary stiffening her spine. She raised her chin and tried to speak with more confidence than she felt. "'Tis of little consequence."

Dark color stormed the woman's cheeks, and her eyes glittered with anger. "He has not told you about me, has he?" the woman taunted. "'Twas I who filled his bed and his needs for more than half a year."

Alexander breathed an oath. "What we had has long since passed, Tira. This is my wife and you will show her respect or you will find yourself banished from our village."

The woman's features stiffened.

"You have trespassed where you have not been invited. Do not do so again."

Tira tossed the thick blanket of blue-black hair over her shoulder and her expression grew vicious as she swung back to Mary. "You will always know 'twas I who was with him first."

Mary flinched inwardly, her anger rising from the fog of shock and pain like an erupting volcano. "I am sorry for your loss, Tira," she said with exaggerated kindness. "'Tis a pity such a bonnie lass would settle for being less than a wife to any man. Mayhap you should have had more pride than that."

Her features flushing red, Tira took a threatening step toward her. Alexander grasped her arm anew and marched her from the room.

Mary drew a deep breath and wrapped her arms against her waist. Shivering with reaction, her eyes roamed about the room, all the pleasure she had felt in her surroundings draining away. Visions of her husband and his mistress sharing their bed had her stomach pitching, and bile rose in her throat. What more could she be expected to endure to be wife to Alexander Campbell?

****

Alexander climbed the stairs to their bedchamber his steps heavy with reluctance. He did not relish facing

133

Mary's wrath after such a scene. He had planned a different sort of homecoming, one where they could start their life together here on more fertile ground. He no longer held out much hope for that now. It had shriveled away the moment Tira had appeared.

His steps flagged and he drew a deep breath before opening the oak door to their chamber. His gaze swept the room and found his wife perched on a stool near the fire. Her hair looked like spun gold against the dark pelt from the bed she had wrapped about her. She did not rise to rant and rage at him as he had expected, but continued to gaze into the fire in silence.

He strode forward to stand before the fire beside her and folded his hands behind him. The silence stretched for several minutes. He frowned, reminded of the first weeks of their marriage. Her eyes were large and dark in a face still pale with shock. The anger he glimpsed in her features was all too familiar. With a sigh, he sat on the mat at her feet and leaned back against the hearth behind him.

"I will not be taken to task for what has passed before we were wed, Mary."

She was silent for a moment. "Did you wish to wed her?"

"Nay, lass," he rushed to assure her. She did not understand passion for passion's sake, for her own was steeped in only what she had experienced thus far. It would do more harm than good to try to explain.

"Why did you not warn me of her?"

"It has been months since I have seen her." He drew a deep breath. "Tira is a widow. Her husband was one of my men. He was killed while fighting for the Bruce. 'Twas only a passing fancy, though she would wish it otherwise."

"Your father once told me if I sought to avoid my duty to you, you would set me aside and take another. Would that not make me a passing fancy as well?"

Alexander's shoulders tensed with resentment. He understood why his father would council her so, but he did not appreciate his interference. "'Tis not my father you are wed to, Mary. He had no right to suggest such a thing to you."

"He spoke the truth," she said in a flat tone, her blue

gaze intent.

It seemed she would damn him for things not done as well as those past. "Then mayhap you should do your duty," he snapped, his patience at an end. He would not allow her to make him feel guilty for the past. He rose to his feet and went to retrieve the tankard of ale he had been drinking with his meal. The brew was bitter and warm and he set it aside then reached for an apple slice soaked in cinnamon and honey to suck on and clear the taste from his mouth.

His gaze swept the room as he sought to keep his attention away from her until his temper cooled. Her movement behind him had him turning. He watched as she donned her kirtle and the stained surcoat again. "Where are you going, Mary?"

"To do my duty, as you bid me, my lord," she said her tone strangely muffled. "I am going to see the men are comfortable."

Catching a glimpse of her tear wet cheeks, Alexander swore harshly beneath his breath. The door clicked shut behind her.

****

After checking the men, Mary settled in the solar, for she knew not where else to go. The fire had burnt low and the room, now drafty and cool, offered little comfort. Wedging herself into the window seat and bracing her back against the stone, she tucked her feet beneath her gown attempting to keep them warm.

Why was it each time she thought they had reached a measure of peace between them, something rose up to thrust them apart? Resting her head against the back of the wooden bench, she drew a deep breath and fought against the tears that clogged her throat and stung her eyes.

He had said he enjoyed the lasses as much as his brother. As long as they had remained nameless, faceless entities, she had been able to ignore the other women Alexander had known. Confronted by his mistress, the images that had thrust into her mind, ate at her heart like a hungry wolf. She could no longer consign such images to the back of her mind. Knowing he had enjoyed Tira's tall shapely body was like a knife sharp and twisting beneath her ribs. His reminding her of her duty to him, on top of it, had been too much.

Trying to console herself with thoughts of the tender moments they had shared in the past weeks, did no good. She could run his household and care for the people of his clan, she could bear his children and his name, but the fact remained, she had never served him in the way he wanted her to, and his mistress had.

****

Alexander left a single candle burning, then stretching out beneath the pelts on the bed, he waited for Mary to return. The time passed slowly. He would not go in search for her. It would do no good anyway; he could not change what had been done before they were wed, and he would not apologize for it. He had been telling himself that ever since she had left.

Moments passed, the silence of the room broken only by the crackle of the fire and the distant moan of the wind outside the drawn shutters. The bed felt empty without her. He moved restlessly, unable to get comfortable.

He heard Mary at the door and closed his eyes, feigning sleep. He heard the rustle as she removed her clothing and expected her to slip beneath the pelts beside him. One of the pelts was dragged away and he opened his eyes to spy her spreading it on the matt before the hearth and lying down.

At first stunned, he lay still, and then anger surged at her stubbornness. He flipped back the pelts and padded silently to the fireplace. Squatting next to her, he grasped her arm to turn her toward him. He swallowed back his temper with an effort and tried to use reason.

"The floor is cold and no place for you to be sleeping, Mary. If you have no care for yourself, you should think of the bairn." He pulled her to her feet, but when he tried to draw her to the bed, she dug in her heels and jerked away from him.

"I will not share a bed or a chamber with you that you have shared with her," she said, her body stiff. "I will have a place of my own where only memories of what we might have together may be built."

Studying her more closely, he read pain behind her careful composure, and was moved to comfort her. "Tira has never been within this chamber until this night, Mary. Everything here was chosen anew for when we wed."

Her throat worked as she swallowed. Her gaze dropped to his chest.

"Come to bed," he urged.

She moved to the bed and climbed beneath the pelts. Turning her back to him, she curled on her side.

After a long silence, he asked, "What memories may we have with you on one side of the bed and me on the other?"

"The only thing between us is an empty space," she countered. "You may fill it if you wish."

Her willfulness stirred his impatience again, and he eyed her slender back with a frown. He folded his arms beneath his head. He would not bend. It was she who would have to come to him this time.

Again, silence settled between them. His hope began to flag.

Mary turned to look over her shoulder at him then rolled to face him but her silence dragged on.

Disappointment settled like a stone in the pit of Alexander's stomach. Suddenly, she wiggled across the space between them and curled against his side to rest her head on his shoulder. Relief brought a welcome release of tension from his body and he drew a deep breath. As he slipped an arm along her back to cradle her close, a rueful smile tugged at his lips. This small upset had made him aware of how deep his feelings ran and how vulnerable it made him. But as much as he disliked such a weakness, he knew no way of preventing it.

He breathed in Mary's sweet musky scent and fought the instant desire to crush her to him and taste the soft fragrant skin of her neck and shoulder. She would probably punch him if he did. He sighed.

"There is one thing I would discuss with you, Alexander." She rose up to look down at him, the reflective light of the fire etching her features with pale yellow.

"Aye."

"Should you ever betray my trust with another, now we have spoken the vows, I will cut out your liver and serve it up to break the fast."

Alexander started to laugh, but something in her expression strangled the urge. Studying her features more closely, he recognized the same level, iron hard resolve in her face she had displayed while holding a crossbow aimed at his chest. It was no jest; she meant every word.

She was jealous of Tira. The realization shot a heady feeling of surprise and pleasure through him. That she would attempt to rule his actions with a threat though, had him frowning.

"'Tis unseemly for a lass to tell her husband what he can or can not do," he said in a stern tone.

"You once told me a wife should tell her husband what she wants. I am doing as you suggested."

It was more than that, much more, but he had no desire to further the argument. He struggled against the desire to smile like a fool for fear of sparking another. "You have told me, and we will say no more about the matter."

She gave a brief nod then turned aside to lay with her back against his side .

Long, slow minutes passed, followed only by the snap of the smoking fire.

With frustrated desire still roiling deep inside, Alexander could not settle. "Are we to end our first night together here on a note of anger then?"

Mary's silence had him turning to confront her. She lay curled on her side, her hands tucked beneath her cheek. Her breasts rose and fell with the slow, steady rhythm of a deep exhausted sleep.

As he leaned over her, a humph of self-deprecating irritation escaped Alexander. With a murmured oath, he rolled onto his back and closed his eyes.

Chapter Fourteen

Mary rushed down the wide passageway to the landing above the great hall. For the third time in as many days, she was late for the morning meal. It had once again taken longer than she had expected to bathe the men's wounds and see them fed. She hesitated at the top of the stairs to draw a deep calming breath in preparation of joining the company of men filling the tables below. Brushing back the wisps of hair that had escaped her braid, she descended the stairs.

"So brother, the bairn has served as a bridge between you as I suggested," Duncan said as she approached the table. She paused, her attention arrested. The realization that Alexander had sought his brother's advice on a private matter between them hit her like a slap.

"Aye," Alexander agreed. "A womanly breast did prove most comfortable to rest my head on whilst my hurts healed as well."

"Having your *coileapach* near to spark a bit of competition will do no harm either," Duncan said. "Women, though they would not admit it, are as territorial as the rest of us. I will wager you will reap rewards from that, if you have not already."

"And what sort of rewards would you be speaking of, Duncan?" Mary asked, unable to hold her silence any longer.

The men stiffened then turned to look over their shoulders at her. Their identical expressions of guilt did nothing to sooth the hollow ache in the pit of her stomach.

Her gaze focused on Alexander and she searched for some form of reassurance in his expression that would ease the outrage and hurt bubbling inside her. He had tricked her to get his way. Shaking her head, she backed away toward the stairs from which she had just come.

Alexander rose, alarm in his expression. "Mary__"

Mary spied the aumry against the wall close to the stairs, its shelves stacked with wooden platters, bowls, and brass tankards and pitchers.

She armed herself with a wooden platter as rage rose up overtaking her pain. "Knave!" She spun the wooden disk.

Alexander ducked beneath the edge of the table at which he and Duncan sat. It struck the wooden planks of the top, bounced upward, and struck the stone wall behind them with a dull thud.

Clansmen at neighboring tables looked up at the disturbance then dove for cover as a large wooden bowl spun wildly across the room out of control.

"Judas!" Mary yelled, her pain and outrage affecting her tone. She threw another platter in Alexander's direction, but it sailed off harmlessly to turn on its face then slide across the floor.

"Deceitful, swine!" A platter that took her both hands to heave, crashed into the midst of a wooden bowl of eel porridge. It splattered across the table sending a large glob across the side of Duncan's face from his ear to his nose. His laughter nipped at her raw feelings and spurred her on.

She saw Alexander punch Duncan in the stomach, driving the breath from him, cutting off his sounds of mirth. "Damn you, Duncan for the advice you offered me! And damn you for speaking of it!" His voice carried to her.

"I was not to know Mary was behind us," he wheezed as he held his middle.

"Ham-handed, rogue!" She spun another platter in Alexander's direction. His quick jerk to the side saved him from being hit in the head.

"'Tis your bairn you've been using agin me for your own purposes," Mary cried, her voice beginning to shake as tears rose up clog her throat. She threw a tankard with better aim and nicked his ear before he could duck.

Unable to catch her breath and shout at the same time, she ceased calling him names and took closer aim instead. A brass pitcher made a hollow clanging sound as it stuck the edge of the table close to his head and ricocheted striking his shoulder giving her only a momentary satisfaction.

Tears broke forth, blurring her vision and she threw the next wooden disk with only a half-hearted aim. The platter spun in a graceful wobbling curve landing flat on the table.

Silence settled over the great hall. When nothing else followed, Alexander eased upward to see what Mary was about. His stomach plummeted with anxiety. She was gone.

Heads appeared from other areas about the large chamber. The men rose from their places of cover like so many phoenixes rising from the ashes of the mid-morning meal. A servant ran forth to right a pitcher and blot up the milk that had pooled beneath the table.

Duncan accepted a damp cloth and wiped the remnants of porridge from his face.

"'Twould seem you have done something to displease the mistress of the house, Alexander," Tobias, one of the older men commented, as he picked up a wooden platter from the floor. 'Tis grateful you should be no true weapon was at hand."

"Aye, I am. Her aim is as good as yours with a bow and quiver, Tobias," Alexander quipped with greater levity than he felt and brushed past him. He had to find Mary. His heart beat in a sickening rhythm.

He took the stairs to their chamber two at a time. The room stood empty though a young chambermaid swept the corridor outside. "Have you seen Lady Mary, lass?" he demanded.

"Aye. She took her cloak and ran back down the stairs, m'lord," she answered.

With every overheard word racing through his mind, Alexander bound down the steps. He cursed Duncan's loose tongue again. She would never understand what had driven him to trick her, nor would she forgive it. But he had to find her and try to explain.

He ran across the courtyard to the stable built against the east wall and saw the head groom shoveling up a clump of manure. "Cory have you seen, Lady Mary?" he asked the head groom.

"Aye, m'lord, but I can not be sure which direction she took from here." The gray haired man pointed upward. His gaze shifted to the ladder leading to the loft.

Alexander nodded as relief steadied his racing pulse. At least she hadn't had time to escape. "I shall look about," he said, his tone loud.

****

Mary leaned back against the stable wall behind the mounds of hay and folded her arms against her waist. Her anger simmered as pain at Alexander's deception rushed in to squeeze her heart. She turned at the sound of someone climbing the ladder.

"You're causing your own pain by believing the worst of me, Mary," Alexander said as soon as he reached the top. He squatted down blocking her only escape route from the loft.

She raised her gaze to his face though it was hard to do so without crying. She searched his expression seeking reassurance, even as she damned herself for a fool. Her voice shook when she spoke. "I do not know what has been truth and what has been trickery. Am I to believe in anything that has passed between us, Alexander?"

He rose in one slow graceful movement. "'Twas not for the purpose of tricking you that I favored the injury to my leg. I but acted a wee bit more helpless than I was, so you would not be so wary of me. That was all."

Mary probed his expression for several moments. Her anger and distrust began to drain from her when he continued to meet her gaze unflinchingly. Then Tira came to mind and her anger surged again.

"What gains did you hope for by parading your *coileapach* before me? Did you mean for me to compete against her for your attentions?"

Alexander's features stiffened, anger and impatience easy to read in his expression as he stalked toward her. Catching her about the waist and bringing her against him, he grasped her hand and guided it beneath his kilt. "Does this not feel as though I have made my choice between you, Mary?" he demanded, his amber eyes pale gold with heat.

Mary jerked, shocked by the feel of his warm distended flesh. She might have pulled her hand away had his not held it.

"I have done all I can to earn your trust and end this damnable wait! I can do no more! 'Tis you who will have to make a choice, or live with the consequences!" His mouth descended on hers, anger and desire making the pressure of his lips hard and his tongue swept her mouth with possessive thoroughness.

The raging heat of the kiss stole the strength from Mary's limbs and blazed a path of sensation down her body to the center of her being. He released her so suddenly she staggered and had to brace an arm against the rough wooden wall of the stable to retain her balance. Her legs felt as wobbly as spun yarn.

Alexander's angry strides took him to the ladder. With one final glare in her direction, he descended the ladder.

****

The men still lingered over their meal when he entered the great hall. Alexander strode to the table and took a seat next to his brother.

"You do not mean to be harsh with the lass?" Duncan asked as Alexander reached for a boiled egg.

Alexander bit back an impatient retort.

"'Twas my fault Mary believed herself wronged, Alexander."

He glared at Duncan in mute warning.

"You said 'twas my words that caused her anger."

"I will not allow my wife to challenge my authority, Duncan. She is mine to do with as I see fit. You'll be offering me no more advice about how she is to be treated."

Conversation among the men momentarily lulled alerting him to Mary's entrance. He followed her progress across the hall his thoughts dwelling on how her hand had felt wrapped around him. He grew hard as stone. As she gained the stairs, she glanced in his direction. Alexander knew some of his feelings were evident on his face when her cheeks blossomed with color. She quickly lowered her eyes and continued up the stairs in the direction of their chamber.

"She is my sister. 'Tis my duty to see to her well-being as well as I would see to yours," Duncan argued.

Jealousy and frustrated desire rekindled Alexander's anger. "I have never known you to be so protective of a woman, Duncan." He searched his brother's features.

143

"You have been my brother for a good many years. 'Twould grieve me sorely should I have to split your skull over this one."

Duncan's gray eyes turned the color of lead, his features hardening. "Do not let the fact that I am your brother keep you from trying," he retorted, his voice flat and his gray gaze steady. He rose to his feet. "Mayhap Mary is wise to be wary of such a fool." He stalked out of the great hall.

Swearing beneath his breath, Alexander set aside the boiled egg. He could no longer allow Mary to bewitch him so. When with her, his body craved the taste and feel of hers as surely as it craved food and drink. He could not sleep for wanting her. He could not be apart from her without wondering what she was about. The time had come for her to face her responsibilities and serve him as a wife.

His hastily spoken words rose up to plague him for they taunted him with a threat he had not intended. He had no intension of seeking out another. No other woman could fill her place.

His absence over the past two months had left too many clan problems unsolved. Now they demanded his attention. He weighed the possibility that she might take advantage of his distraction and attempt to leave him, as she had a want to do in the past. He motioned to a servant and sent word to Grace, Mary's maidservant, to join him in his antechamber.

Once he had given his instructions to the maid, he felt more certain he had the situation in hand. Mary would not be pleased with being confined to her room, but his concerns were temporarily eased that she would not leave the castle.

****

Mary thrust her feet into her slippers and moved to the door of the chamber. Her anger over being ordered to stay in her room had long since cooled. The punishment was less harsh than she could have expected. She had embarrassed Alexander before his men and it was within his rights to choose a more severe reprisal.

As she opened the door, her maid, Grace, bobbed up from the chair where she sat just outside the portal.

"Would you be needing something, Lady Mary?" The girl, little more than a child, shifted nervously from foot to foot. Her light brown hair, hanging in stringy strands on either side of her small face, swayed back and forth with the movement. The smattering of freckles adorning her upturned nose, lent her features an elfish charm that had Mary smiling at her reassuringly.

"Aye. You may bring me some bread and cheese and dried apples for the noon meal," she said.

The girl's expression grew anxious at the prospect of leaving her post.

"If my lord wishes me to remain in my chamber, I will do so, Grace," she promised with a sigh. She had allowed her temper to dictate her actions and she had only herself to blame for the consequences.

Being confined had given her some time to rest and to think. Knowing he had deceived her, still hurt, no matter what reason he gave for the deception. Did he not understand that every time he sought to manipulate her it made her doubt him? Yet, he said he had done it to ease her distrust. The way he had held her hand around him, his tawny gaze hot with anger and desire, stole her breath every time she thought about it.

She settled before the fire with her sewing things as she awaited Grace's return from the kitchen. She smoothed the wrinkles from the shirt she stitched. The russet cloth would go well with Alexander's auburn hair and tawny eyes. She straightened the laces picturing the fabric stretched across the muscular width of his shoulders and chest.

She noticed, with surprise, how often of late her thoughts dwelt on her husband's body. His nudity at night as they lay in bed together had become more disturbing. There had been times she had wanted to press back against him and align her body to his. She wanted, but did not understand what it was she wanted. She often felt hot and restless, but did not know why. How could she crave the feel of his hands on her body, the brush of his bare skin against hers, yet wish to avoid the joining of their flesh? Or did she?

Memories of how close they had come to mating after the feast at Lorne brought a fine mist of sweat to her brow and a heated ache to intimate areas of her body. She rose to dampen a cloth and hold it to her hot cheeks. It was sinful to feel this way; it had to be.

They had more between them than the bairn now, she felt certain. If she allowed Alexander to use her body to serve his needs, would it strengthen the bond? She prayed it would. Perhaps, the small glimmer of affection she sometimes spied when he looked at her, would grow to more if she gave him what he wanted.

Grace returned with her food, but Mary felt too restless to do anything, but nibble at it.

The day dragged on. For every stitch she made, her emotions swung between uncertainty and excitement, hope and dread.

Alexander came to their chamber before the evening meal. Mary watched him surreptitiously from her seat on the bed as he went to stand at the fireplace and brace a booted foot on the hearth.

She freed her hair from the braid and drew it over her shoulder to smooth the heavy mass into soft waves with a comb. She became aware of his interest as he moved to hang his sword on the bedpost. She grew still as he plucked a long silvery strand from her shoulder and smoothed it into place in a possessive gesture.

"Will there be anythin' else you'll be needing, m'lady?" Grace asked as she finished filling the pot at the fireplace with water.

"I will help with Lady Mary's bath this eventide, Grace. She will not need you again this night," he said.

Mary looked up at him. The steadiness of his pale amber gaze brought the heat of a blush to her face and an airless feeling beneath her ribs. Raising his hand, he caressed the curve of her cheek with calloused fingers.

The door clicked shut behind the girl and silence settled between them.

"I could not overlook your taking me to task before the men, Mary," he said.

Her gaze dropped to the pelt beneath her and she ran her fingers over the soft fur. "I could not overlook your deception either."

She avoided looking at him, for if she gazed into those amber depths she would forgive him his trickery.

She could not continue doing that without an end to them. "Good can never come of anything, but the truth, Alexander."

He folded his hands behind him. "'Tis true I chose such a path, but 'twas because I thought to end your distrust of me." His gaze moved over her face. "Once you began to care for my wounds and touch me without hesitation, I could not tell you and see you withdraw from me again."

Her anger melted away beneath the weight of his confession. The realization came to her that her wariness had been in itself a punishment to him.

"I am told, 'tis making up that is the best thing that comes from fighting with one's wife," he said as he sat down beside her.

"Who told you that?"

"'Twas Derrick. He has been wed for some time and thinks he knows a thing or two about lasses."

"Does he, now," she said, her brows raised, her heart growing lighter with his teasing.

"Nay. He is as big a fool as the rest of us."

She laughed then grew thoughtful. "Have you been seeking anyone else's council about us besides Duncan and Derrick?"

He shook his head.

"Mayhap you should have asked a woman's advice instead," she said.

"Who would you suggest I ask, lass?"

"Me."

He studied her for a long silent moment. "How do I earn your trust, Mary?"

"By always placing truth before all else, and by dealing with me with as much respect and honor as you would one of your men."

Alexander nodded. He lapsed into a thoughtful silence. "I once traded my honor and another's for something I thought more important. I have since learned to regret it quite bitterly."

He looked so gravely serious Mary found she was holding her breath as she waited for him to continue.

"Would you have left with me, had I asked you to do so the night of Anne's betrothal?" he asked.

She was silent as she thought about the question. She had loved him so she had given her body to him. She would not have denied him that either, had he asked. But would it ease his guilt and regret to know that, or would it only make it worse?

"Who's to know what might have been, Alexander? Thinking back will not make it so. 'Tis better to look forward than play what if with what has already passed."

Chapter Fifteen

The men had gathered in the great hall by the time Alexander guided Mary downstairs for the evening meal. He had already braced himself for a round of jests. The opportunity for the men to taunt him was too ripe to ignore. At his place at the table sat a metal helmet and shield, and he studied them with some interest.

"'Tis to offer you protection should your lady be angered during the meal, Alexander," Tobias said. The cluster of men nearby broke into grins of mischief.

Alexander smiled, seeing the humor in the gesture. "'Tis grateful I am for the thought, Tobias, but what of the rest of you?"

"They are so well trained they have no need of such protection, Alexander," Mary assured him. "'Twas truly quick they were to take cover this morn."

Tobias laughed aloud as did several of the others. "Mayhap after we sup you may give us all instruction in the use of such weaponry, m'lady," Tobias suggested, his blue eyes alight with humor beneath thick gray brows.

"'Twill be my honor, Tobias," she said with a nod. "Though 'twas not a good choice of weapon and I fear my temper affected my aim."

The men's laughter became a roar, and even Alexander had to join in.

"I am truly sorry for my show of anger earlier," she apologized in a quieter moment when they were seated. "'Tis a fault for which I have often been chastised."

"'Tis a sin we have all been guilty of, Lady Mary," Gabriel said from down the table.

Alexander frowned at the quick way the man came to her defense and the smile with which she graced him. More than one of the men seemed taken with his wife, including his brother. Their interest tweaked a jealousy that had never troubled him before.

"'Tis sorry I am if my behavior caused you embarrassment before your men, Alexander," she offered quietly.

"A bit of spirit in a lass does no harm," he said with a shrug. He ran a hand down her back to her hip.

He could not seem to keep his hands from roaming whenever she was near. It was a relief that she no longer pulled away or avoided his touch, but it also bred a hunger for more that taunted and teased him beyond measure.

Would she accept him soon? Her eagerness to seek peace between them offered a measure of encouragement. If she wouldn't, what then would he do?

His gaze returned to her face to find her attention focused on one of the men as he spoke. Mary's presence at the table at mealtime had been unobtrusive, until this morn. The men had begun to take more care with the language they used and the ribald humor they sometimes shared.

His gaze traveled around the great hall. Of late, the floors had been swept each day and the rushes changed. The food was more lightly seasoned and cooked while it was fresher. Even Fergus had voiced approval of the changes in the running of the castle she had made.

Just as the meal was being served a metallic clanging sounded from outside. Alexander froze in the midst of filling the trencher before him, as did the other men. Pandemonium broke out as everyone surged to their feet at once then rushed for the doors.

"Stay in the castle, Mary," he ordered.

"Fire-Fire in the village!" came a cry from atop the battlements.

The men crowded forward as they drew their swords. Alexander spared only a moment to prepare himself. Whatever threat lay beyond the gates, he would strike it down. He nodded and the heavy bars were lifted. In a wave, the men rushed forward, parting the gate and swarming up the hillside to the village. The thatched roof of one hut was aflame, but no enemy was visible.

The villagers had already begun to battle the blaze, filling every available vessel with water from the well and slapping at the burning thatch with wet cloths. The houses were built close together and the sparks rising on the cold December air threatened to set them all aflame.

"Take the villagers in hand," Alexander yelled to Duncan, "I'll be back." He sheathed his sword then gathered a group of six men. They raced back down the hill to the castle.

It took precious moments to harness horses to two carts in the stable and load the barrels of water used there. The quick pace of the horses over the rutted path made the carts movements bone jarring despite the weight it carried. He barely had time to pull the horses to a stop when men ran forward to dip the water from the barrels and rush away again to throw it on the blaze and douse the small sparks peppering the other roofs. The water was soon gone and he pulled away to return for more.

In his absence, a row of torches had been stuck in the ground from the loch to the top of the rise. In the light they provided, servants from the castle stood ready with buckets. They formed lines from the water to the road above. He pulled the horses to a halt. Vessels already filled were passed up the line to empty into the barrels.

He spied his wife in the blaze of a torch where she stood in line with the others hefting the heavy buckets of water. His stomach clenched in concern. He swore and passed the reins to one of the men.

"Mary!" His voice carried across the distance, his tone sharp as he leaped from his seat. He bound down the hill to her. "What are you about here, lass?"

"'Tis my place to be here, Alexander," she answered.

"'Tis your place to carry my son and take care while you're about it! The buckets are too heavy, Mary. 'Tis a danger to you and the bairn." He softened his tone mindful of the servants. "'Twould be a help if you would ready your things to care for the injured. There will be burns to see to."

He motioned to a man to take her place in line and grasped her arm to help her up the slippery bank.

"How does the battle go?" she asked.

"With enough water, we will save the village."

They topped the rise and she pulled away from him to go back to the castle. He ran to jump aboard the cart as it lurched forward to travel the distance back up the hill.

The men had managed to beat out the smaller fires, but the larger one still blazed. Duncan and two other clansmen had armed themselves with pollarms and were trying to break loose the burning thatch with the spears. If they could encourage it to fall into the protective walls of the hut, it would contain it.

A loud agonizing moan of wood under too much pressure came from inside the structure Alexander yelled a warning to the men and they scrambled back out of the way. One of the rafters broke loose and the roof fell inward with a crash that sent hot air, ash, and sparks flying upward.

Ladders were set into place against the walls and water poured down onto the rubble while others doused the flames through window and door openings blackened by soot and flame. Hissing steam billowed forth in misty clouds to climb into the sky. Its appearance inspired a cheer of relief from the villagers who stood watching.

He took in the smoke blackened faces around him in search of his brother. He crossed to where Duncan stood armed with a lance.

"Well done, Brother!" he exclaimed, pounding Duncan on the back with exuberance.

Duncan's smile was white against the background of soot-blackened skin. "'Twas good you brought water in such abundance. 'Twas that which saved the other huts."

For some moments, they watched as the remaining flames and embers were doused with water.

"There is one more problem to be dealt with brother," Duncan said.

"What is that?"

"'Tis Tira's hut that has burned."

Alexander drew a deep breath. "Aye."

"'Twill be interesting having the two of them beneath one roof while Tira's hut is repaired."

"I do not see a problem, Duncan."

Duncan shook his head as he studied his brother. "You, brother, have a lot to learn about lasses."

****

Mary's gaze traveled the length of the great hall then back again. Servants served the men a hastily reheated meal while others replaced the borrowed items in which the water had been transported. The men were in good spirits, now the threat to the village had been overcome. Their laughter flowed as freely as the ale in which they imbibed even though the smell of smoke lingered about them.

Tira sat at the end of one of the tables, her hair dark as pitch against the pale blue of her gown. A boy of seven sat beside her, his red hair and freckles a startling contrast to her dusky coloring. The child's features were obviously similar to his sires, Mary surmised, for he looked nothing like his mother.

Her attention came back to the task at hand, as Duncan sat on the bench before her and bared his arm for her inspection. A large blister had formed on his forearm and the hair had been burnt away around it.

She cleaned away the black smoke stain from the burn with gentle stokes of a sponge, taking care not to tear away the skin.

"'Tis a soothing touch you have, Mary," Duncan said.

She looked up into his smoke darkened face for a moment.

"Are you still angry with me, lass?" he asked.

She blotted the burn dry with a linen cloth then dipped her fingers into the salve in a crockery bowl beside her. "Nay," she answered with a shake of her head. She smeared the salve on liberally. "I can not fault you for wanting your brother to be happy in our marriage."

"'Tis for you I want that as well, Mary," he said, his gray gaze serious.

She wrapped a clean strip of linen around Duncan's arm, covering the burn.

"Do not fash yourself about, Tira. She is nothing to Alexander."

"If she was so little to him, you would not feel the need to offer me comfort." Her attention returned to him once she had secured the bandage. "Will not her presence encourage me to defend the boundaries of my territory?" she repeated his words.

Duncan's features settled into an expression of sheepish regret. "At times my wit overrules my reason, little sister. 'Twas only a jest, though a thoughtless one. I

153

beg pardon for any pain it has caused you."

"You may earn my forgiveness by seeing Tira's hut is repaired quickly," she said.

Duncan flashed her a smile. "'Twill be so, Mary."

"Do not get the bandages wet when you bathe, Duncan. I'll be sending water to your chamber to be heated. One of the maids will mend your shirt where it was burned."

"Thank you, lass." He flashed her another smile as he rose to join the other men.

Mary emptied the water into a bucket then cleared away the pile of discarded cloths she had used to clean the men's injuries. Thankfully, there had been few. Only a few villagers had sought her out for salve and dressings. They had come, she was sure, out of curiosity more than need. She would venture up to the village the next morning to see if they were in need of anything.

The large wooden door of the great hall opened allowing an icy blast of wind to accompany the men entering. As he crossed the distance between them, Alexander's gaze raked her from head to toe. "I see we have both fared well, despite weather and fire."

"Aye, Alexander." A smile touched her lips. "You look cold, husband. Come closer to the fire."

He sat on the bench at the table, his back to the fire. Mary motioned to one of the women serving. Water, with which to wash his hands, was brought at once while the table was cleared and cleaned. The trencher filled with meat and vegetables set before him brought a smile to his lips.

"Will you not join me, Mary?" he asked.

She sealed the crockery bowl of salve with a scrap of linen and a strip of rawhide. "Aye." She sat next to him.

"I had not thought to announce the news of the bairn in such a manner," Alexander said as he sliced the meat and offered her a piece.

"'Tis probably been spoken of by the men already, Alexander."

"Aye. I had hoped to speak of it myself in a more festive way."

Her gaze swung to the men eating and laughing. "They are far into their cups with celebration."

Alexander chuckled. "To fight and win against a challenge brings with it a joy that must be celebrated, Mary."

"'Tis a joy to be sure that no one was harmed greatly," she agreed. "I have given Tira and the lad a chamber in the west wing."

"Good. We will start tomorrow repairing her hut."

Her gaze returned to her husband's features again and again as they shared the meal. Her fear of having Alexander turn away from her was greater than any other. Duncan's jest of protecting her territory carried a bit of truth. She would do whatever she had to keep Alexander by her side.

The servants began to clear away the debris of the meal. Her eyes moved over his face and a quick blush warmed her cheeks as he turned his head and captured her gaze with his own. A breathless weakness invaded her limbs, and her heart began to beat like a drum beneath her breast.

Shaken by the depth of her emotions, she rose to her feet. "I must see that Derrick's and Artair's bandages have been changed." She excused herself.

****

Alexander watched Mary climb the stairs to the gallery above. There were times he found her pale blue gaze as mysterious as the depths of the loch. He turned to join the men and found himself confronted by Tira.

"Aye," he encouraged as she stood close.

"'Tis a kindness for you to take me and Cassidy in, Alexander." She touched his arm. "'Tis grateful I am to you."

"You may thank Mary as well," he returned. "We will start on the morrow repairing your hut." He folded his arms across his chest keeping a distance between them for all to see. "How was it the blaze started?" he asked, curious.

"I do not know. Cassidy and I were not there. One of the men in the village gathered some of our belongings and threw them out a window or we would have lost everything."

"Mayhap the rest of us may share with you. If there be anything you need tell Fergus or Mary."

Tira shifted closer, her breast brushing his arm. "You did not treat me with such coldness when you wished a woman to ease your needs," she reminded him softly, her hand resting on his forearm.

"'Twas not only my needs that were served," he said with a shrug. "I was not wed then either, Tira."

"She was bairned before you wed," she accused.

"'Twas a blessing and a joy Mary conceived so easily," he said, his tone flat.

A sly look tinted her eyes with black. "If the bairn be yours," she challenged.

Rage flared through him and his arms fell to his sides.

Tira's gaze went from sly to fearful and she retreated as he stepped forward.

Alexander forced a control over his anger that he was hard pressed to retain. "The bairn is mine, Tira. Do not question it again. Should you speak agin my wife to anyone, you will regret it." He brushed past her to join his men.

Duncan joined him as he accepted a drink of ale from one of the men. "Did I not tell you 'twould be interesting to have them both beneath the same roof, Brother?" he questioned.

Alexander flashed him a look meant to silence him, but Duncan only grinned.

Chapter Sixteen

The wooly brown hide of the slaughtered cow blended well with the dull umber of the rocky terrain around it. Frozen beneath the layer of white, the remains were not completely hidden by the snow. The white blanket lay around it unblemished by the tracks of man or beast. Gently rolling hillsides stretched onward to meet the snow topped mountains in the distance along one side of the valley. On the other, the glittering ice against the banks of the loch sparkled in the early morning light.

"Which way should we search, Alexander?" Duncan asked.

Alexander remained silent, his eyes roving over the area. He sought the telling smoke of a peat fire or the plume of steam from a man's breath. No sign of the butchers disturbed the brae.

His gaze moved over the terrain for a likely place for the horses to have been tied. He spied a small crop of brush in the open space and strode forward, leaving deep tracks in his wake.

He brushed aside the snow with his hands, seeking the imprint in the ground of a foot or hoof. After several minutes, he was rewarded by hoof-shaped depressions turned in a northeasterly direction.

Choosing two to ride ahead as scouts, he signaled the men to mount, and the patrol rode in single file in that direction. The men were silent, alert to possible trouble at every turn. They had been trained well in the art of war and fought well together in the past.

A feeling of unease had taunted him at Lorne because of the butchered sheep on his father's land. For days, his instincts had been telling him danger was nearby. The attack against them in route to *Caisteal Sith* proved his feelings were well founded. Where were they? He was being challenged, but by whom? Collin

MacLachlan was only one possibility. There were always those who were discontent with what they did or didn't have. Neighboring clans were always hungry for more land and the power it gave them. Whoever it was, he wanted an end to it now.

Nearly an hour passed before he discovered evidence of horses passing into one of the narrow valleys at the edge of the loch. Within minutes, one of the men he sent ahead returned with word of a group of fifteen or twenty camping nearby.

The smell of peat fire reached them before the smoke became evident. A goodly distance from the camp, Alexander raised a hand to halt the men and dismounted.

"I wish to know from which clan they hail so I might seek restitution for the suffering they have inflicted. The food they have stolen from our clan must be replaced as well," Alexander said. "Do not hesitate to spill blood, should they press the matter."

His orders given, the group armed themselves and each man covered his mouth and nose with the wool of their kilts to prevent the mist of their breath from rising in the cold air. Swiftly, their footsteps muffled by the snow, the men fanned out in a sweep up the hillside.

The high-pitched warbling of a bird had them all crouching and going still. James Campbell showed himself from above the rise.

"They have camped here more than once, I'd wager," he announced when he reached them "They're almost thirty in number, for there were others here waiting."

Alexander studied his men's faces. They were outnumbered by eight. He could send for more men, but it would take until midday for the others to reach them. He had no wish to endanger his men, but if they did not take a stand now, the thieves might escape to threaten them with further trouble. Three butchered cows discovered in as many days and evidence of trespass on their land was enough. The fire in the village could have been caused by them as well, though he had no true proof of it.

"How many look outs, James?"

"One at the north entrance, one at the south, and two on the rise above."

He nodded. "Could you tell how well they are

armed?" he asked.

"Swords and daggers and long bows, but I saw no pollarms or crossbows. I could not get close enough to their camp to tell for certes they do not have more."

He nodded again. "We must take out the lookouts. 'Twill lower the number they have greater than we to two instead of six. 'Twill also allow us to survey the camp without threat of an alarm. We must know for certes what we face before we face it."

The men nodded.

"This is what must be done—"

Alexander flexed the muscles of his shoulders to ease their tension. Hugh and Douglas would have worked their way to the north entrance by now. He watched William and Bruce ease their way beneath the two men posted on the rise. Only moments before, James and Robert had taken position at the south entrance.

The twittering of a bird signaled the men at the north entrance were ready. Seconds passed as Alexander focused on the shaggy pelts the lookouts wore as protection from the cold. It made it impossible for them to identify clan affiliation.

He raised the spanned crossbow to his shoulder, aware of Duncan crouching at his side in readiness. He trusted his brother's skill as well as he did his own. They rose as one, sighted the men, and loosed the bolts. The quick hiss of the arrows was the only sound. They struck their targets. The men toppled toward one another. Bruce and William quickly dragged them from the knoll and took their places.

No hue and cry split the air and Alexander drew a deep breath of relief. He and Duncan moved forward to just below the men.

"Hugh and Douglas are in place," William said at once.

"There are thirty horses and five pack animals," Bruce added. "They are roasting meat and preparing weapons."

"'Tis twenty-five men I reckon, but I can not see beneath the edge of the creag," William said.

He and Duncan turned their attention to the two dead guards. They searched the bodies. Duncan held out a leather cord with a metal disk suspended from it. Etched into the medallion was a fist grasping a sword above a three-tiered castle.

"'Tis a MacDonald crest!" Alexander exclaimed.

"Aye," Duncan agreed.

Alexander's jaw clenched with anger, his uneasiness increasing. He tucked the medallion away then motioned to one of the men to signal them below in case the company of men mounted to leave the valley.

He and Duncan worked their way down to the rest of the men below.

"They will change the look outs soon," Duncan said.

"Aye, and be four more men short," Alexander nodded. "'Twill be then we will have to attack."

No fires could be lit so the men clumped together in small groups to share their warmth. They talked softly among themselves to pass the time though the tension of the coming confrontation did not lend itself to levity.

"I do not care for this waiting," Duncan complained after a slow hour had passed. He shifted impatiently against the rock he leaned on.

"Father once told me 'tis not strength or skill that makes a good warrior but the patience to know when to use them."

"For your patience alone, you deserve whatever makes you content, Brother," Duncan said, his gray gazed focused on him.

Aware Duncan spoke of more personal matters, Alexander remained silent though his thoughts turned to Mary as she had been earlier that morn. She had sought his touch in rubbing the ache in her lower back. She had nearly purred with pleasure beneath his administrations though she had blushed when she realized what she was doing.

The startled look in her blue eyes had both thrilled and amused him. His wife was beginning to awaken to being a woman. He believed it would not be much longer before she accepted him as a lover.

"To earn what one desires, brings with it a respect and regard that would be difficult to attain if 'twas achieved without effort," he said with conviction.

The twittering of a bird, their signal, had him tensing

and rising to his feet. "'Tis time."

The archers worked their way up to the top of the rise and took position. The rest of the men mounted.

The three men captured during the changing of the guard were bound and gagged, bruised and battered, but otherwise unhurt. The company of twenty Campbells rode past them to the entrance.

"Did they claim their clan, Gabriel?" Alexander asked as the large man rode up to join them.

"Nay. One wore a tartan much like those worn at Lochlan," he answered.

Alexander's uneasiness increased. "MacLachlan or MacDonald, whichever they be, they will no longer be stealing our live stock, nor trespassing upon our land."

"We will not be warning them we are coming," Alexander cautioned the men. "Let us attack before they know we are here." He drew his sword then signaled them forward.

The narrow neck of the canyon required them to ride through two at a time. The hillside curved around blocking the view of the camp until they were upon it.

Mayhem broke out among the trespassers as the alarm came too late. The men drew their weapons and raced for their horses. Arrows from above gave them pause until Alexander's men had blocked off access to their mounts and crowded in around the camp. The men froze weapons in hand.

"Let him who leads you step forward," Alexander commanded, in a tone that carried well around the site.

A single pelt-draped figure stepped forward, sword in hand. Stone gray eyes glared at him out of a narrow face marred by a livid scar that ran from cheekbone to jaw.

"For nigh a week you have trespassed upon my land and slaughtered my livestock. 'Twould please me to know what clan you hail from, before we exact payment for such thievery," Alexander said.

"It does not matter what clan we be from. We will still send you to hell." The man's signal sent his men forward, their battle cry rending the air. Five men fell beneath the aim of Campbell bows above on the hillside. The other eighteen men swarmed the Campbell forces.

Still astride his horse, Alexander blocked the

thrusting sword of the man on the ground. The other's gray gaze burned with hatred as he chopped and thrust from below.

"You will be buried upon Campbell soil without benefit of your MacDonald kin," Alexander taunted as he parried a thrust.

A growl of rage emitted from the other man's throat as he swung his sword wildly. Alexander blocked the blow before his horse could be injured. His patience at an end, he rode away a short distance and dismounted to face his adversary on foot.

A shout arose and Alexander found himself facing three adversaries instead of one. He parried the first blow then swung the flat side of his sword against the other man's head knocking him unconscious. The man crumpled to the ground. The other two attacked. Alexander found Gabriel at his side engaging the one while he concentrated on the leader.

"You can not win the day. Do not spill the blood of your men without need, MacDonald," Alexander urged. He would spare the men if possible.

"Have you lost your stomach for killing, Alexander Campbell, or have you turned coward," the other man taunted.

Alexander shook his head wondering how the man knew his name. "'Tis your choice to die then?"

The man attacked with a ferocity that taxed Alexander's skill, and had him falling back a pace. Having given him as much leeway as he intended, Alexander returned the volley of strokes with a swift combination of his own. The man staggered back beneath the barrage.

The sound of metal crashing against metal all around them echoed throughout the canyon, as did the cries of the injured and the dying. Angered by the foolish waste of the other leaders actions, Alexander beat the man back, seeking to throw him off balance and end the conflict.

A movement to the right drew Alexander's attention. He grabbed the wrist of his adversary and jerked him forward in front of him. An arrow caught the man in the middle of his chest and he crumpled to the ground. From above, a hail of arrows struck the archer.

Their leader dead, the remaining men paused. A lone

cry of rage rent the air and a single man raised his sword and charged Alexander.

He turned to face the threat, his sword swinging to knock the warrior's blade aside. Alexander punched the man in the jaw, knocking him to the ground. The pressure of heel to wrist pried the assailant's hand open and Alexander kicked away the sword.

He looked down at the lad at his feet, instant recognition giving him pause.

"What is afoot, Alexander?" Gabriel asked.

"'Tis the lad who's arrow pierced me at Lorne."

Chapter Seventeen

Alexander swung open the chamber door without knocking and dropped the heavy wooden bar in place to lock the portal. His eyes searched the room for his wife and settled on Mary curled on the large bed, her back turned toward him. He approached her with long quick strides and paused to look down at her.

Light brown lashes tipped with gold formed crescents of soft color beneath her eyes. The hushed sound of her breathing, slow and deep, was barely discernable. Alexander's gaze traced the sleep-flushed curve of her cheek and the rose tinted shape of her lips.

Desire settled like a stone in the pit of his stomach. A wry smile curved his lips. The shedding of blood had made him hungry for other things. He wanted to thrust himself into her sweet body and reaffirm the life that pulsed in his veins by claiming her as his in every way. He ran his fingers through his hair and drew deep breaths to ease the need.

His foot nudged Mary's sewing basket next to the bed and he noticed the partially stitched baby gown draped over it. He lifted the basket atop the chest to prevent her from tripping over it when she arose. His fingers brushed the soft cloth of the gown then his gaze swung to the distended roundness visible through the linen shift she wore. A bit more than four months would see her delivered of their child. He looked forward to, yet dreaded the event. She looked too fragile to bear the strain of labor. What if the bairn was too big, or turned wrong in the womb? He had seen it happen in the past. She could die having the babe. He turned his mind from the thought, unprepared for the hollow feeling it brought to his chest. She was a strong lass, all would be well, he reassured himself.

Moving to the other side of the bed, he hung his

scabbard on the bedpost then withdrew his sword to clean the blade and inspect its surface for nicks. Finding the edge unmarred, he wiped the blade clean with a cloth and returned it to its sheath.

A pot of water, still warm on the hearth, awaited him and he shed his clothing to bathe. He took some time to wash his hair and body to rid himself of the blood tainting his skin. He sensed, rather than saw movement behind him and turned as Mary stepped to his side to take the wet cloth from him. She washed his back then dried it with a cloth.

He looped an arm about her waist and brushed a soft kiss across her cheek then trailed his lips over her brow.

"I tried to wait for you," she said, her voice soft and breathy as her eyes traced his features. "Come to bed and seek your rest."

"Aye." He brushed her lips with his own, finding her too tempting to resist. "The room is cool, Mary. You will take a chill."

He watched as she wiggled beneath the pelts offering him an uninhibited view of well-shaped legs and dainty feet before she covered them with the thick fur.

An appreciative smile lingered on his lips as he blew out the candles and found his place beside her. Her head settled in its customary place in the hollow of his shoulder. Her hand moved over his chest in restless caresses warming him and bringing him pleasure. She bent a knee across his thighs and pressed closer.

The velvety softness of her bare skin rubbed against his bringing a hectic beat to Alexander's heart and instant heat to his loins.

"There has been more trouble?" she asked.

"Aye, we will speak of it on the morrow," he answered. His hand found her knee then glided up her bare thigh, pushing the fabric of the shift higher as he rubbed her skin to bring it warmth.

He turned, displacing her so he could look down into her face. He had a driving need to feel her skin beneath his touch, to feel the movements of their child beneath the palm of his hand without barriers between them. He ran his hand beneath the shift and traced the rounded curve of her stomach raising the fabric.

Mary did not protest. She caressed his cheek, her touch making him ache for more. "My belly grows rounder every day," she complained. He watched her throat work as she swallowed, the movement fraught with tension. "Can you still want me like this?"

The import of her words struck Alexander with the force of a battle-axe. Grasping her hand, he pressed a kiss within her palm then guided it to the evidence of his desire for her. "Seeing my seed growing inside you feeds my need, Mary."

Instead of jerking her hand away, as he expected her to do, she ran her fingers over the long length of him in exploration. Her touch, gentle and hesitant, brought him near to trembling. His earlier hunger for her returned with a vengeance.

His gaze dropped to her mouth. The generous curve of her bottom lip beckoned. He lowered his lips to hers to taste it with his tongue and draw it into his mouth. He tried not to rush her into a passionate embrace, but the fluttering caress of her tongue against his had him growing painfully hard. He sucked on the tip of her tongue as though it were a piece of black truckle candy. His hunger for her was a raging fire he fought hard to control as he pressed her back on the bed.

The kiss ended, and he rubbed his cheek against hers as he gave her time to catch her breath. Mary's arms slid upward around his neck to hold him closer. She followed the trail of the scar across his cheek with a fingertip then with her lips.

Alexander found it hard to remain acquiescent beneath her attentions. He had been starved for her kisses and her touch. Now that she seemed intent on showering him with such gifts, it was difficult for him to control the responses that leaped to meet her every advance.

He turned his mouth to hers. The kiss went on and on, their tongues meshing in slow sensuous movements that probed and tempted in a parody of lovemaking.

He tightened his hold bringing her against him. The pebble hard nubs of her nipples pressed into his chest. The hard heat of his manhood thrust like a blade between them against her bare stomach.

The kiss grew languid and hot. Her hands caressed him moving in a slow exploration over his shoulders, down his chest and ribs. She wiggled closer, her bare skin brushing against his. Raising her knee along his hip, she opened herself to the lusty friction as he thrust against her, tempting and teasing her with his body.

He groaned beneath the pressure of the kiss. He craved the warm moist heat of her body, but the distrust that had once held their intimacy at bay demanded he proceed with caution.

Breathing as hard as she was, he broke the kiss and slid downward to nuzzle her breasts through the fabric of her shift. Her fingers stroked his hair and cradled his head against her. He peeled the shift over her head and tossed it aside, baring the velvety soft warmth of her flesh.

In the meager light of the fire, his eyes took in the changes her pregnancy had wrought. Her rose tipped breasts looked round and full, their crowns darker. Her abdomen, slightly distended with their child, gave her a ripe womanly look that brought feelings of possessive tenderness into play.

He traced a dusky nipple with a fingertip causing it to pucker and harden. His gaze rose to her face as he continued to toy with the tender peaks. He guided her arm around his neck. "Put your arms around me, Mary. I've longed to feel your bare skin against my own."

With kisses, he drank of the budding passion she offered him as his hand kneaded the tender flesh of her breasts. She pressed against his touch with an unmistakable eagerness. He followed the rounded curve of her belly then moved lower to stroke the soft skin of her thighs.

"Open to me, Mary," he urged. "'Twill give you pleasure."

Joy swelled within him as she parted her legs, for in doing so she offered him a trust she had thus far denied. He rested his hand on the soft hair covering her Mons as his lips and tongue explored the curvature of her ear.

She shivered in response and turned her lips to his. She whispered his name again, as his fingertips delved between her thighs parting the lightly furred flesh. Her body quivered as his touch settled on the sensitive little nub he encountered. Her thighs inched apart as her hips began to undulate in response to the careful pressure he applied.

Tracing the intimate opening of her body with a fingertip, he found her hot and wet, ready for him. He pushed a single finger inside her by slow degrees. The warm moist heat of her taunted him with the pleasure awaiting him. He moved his finger in a flickering movement to tempt her further. Mary caught her breath and her hand grasped his wrist though her body arched in response.

"'Tis how it shall feel when I come inside you, Mary," He murmured as his lips sought her throat then her shoulder. His mouth latched onto one of the dark rose peaks and he sucked on it. His finger matched a rhythm she began to catch as he probed and caressed.

She opened herself wider and pushed into his hand, his name a plea of passion he had never thought to hear. She raked her fingers through his hair.

He slid downward to position himself between her legs. He ran his tongue down the outer crevice of her Mons. Her hand grasped his where it curved around her thigh and she gasped his name in shocked surprise. He parted the tender folds and ran his tongue over the tiny bud he encountered, tasting the salty, sweet heat of her.

She began to relax and melt into the caress of his tongue and push against his lips. He settled to his work more intently. His tongue flickered and writhed inside her making her moan as her fingers gripped his hand tightly. Her muscles tensed, her hips tilted beneath the probing depth of his tongue, straining toward a deeper penetration.

Mary was panting when he covered her body with his own. His gaze focused on the passion flushed features of her face as the tip of his manhood slipped inside her. He eased forward slowly for she was small and tight and his need was great. The sweet, tender intimacy between them, when he settled deep inside her, was like nothing he had ever experienced before.

Looking down into her eyes was like gazing into a hot summer sky. His lips covered hers, joyful relief in the kiss they shared. "I could not wait any longer, Mary," he said huskily.

"You have waited long enough." Her hands ran in restless caresses up and down his back.

His lips settled over hers in a long lingering kiss. He rocked forward then back, his movements slow and careful giving her time to grow accustomed to the feel of him moving inside her. Gradually, her body began to relax and accept each easy thrust. She melted around him, warm and wet.

His movements grew more definite though he kept the same slow pace. Mary began to respond to the rhythm with movements of her own, drawing on him with delicious heat. He whispered fevered words of encouragement as his quest for release became a compulsive need that stripped away some of the careful control he had exerted earlier.

Her lips sought his throat as her hands caressed him. She spoke his name in ragged tones spurring him on. Their bodies strained against one another, burrowing closer and closer, craving more as their pace increased.

She ran questing hands down his back cupping his buttocks, as the moist heat of her palpitated around him building and building toward release. His name became a whispered incantation rising in strength as she arched beneath him, her body clenching around him as fulfillment found them both. Alexander's body bucked and heaved as his seed pulsed forth, the power of his release making him groan aloud.

It was some moments before he risked disturbing the closeness they had found, for fear it would disappear. Slowly, he raised his head to look down at her. He smoothed back the silvery strands of hair from her face and viewed her flushed cheeks and dark glittering eyes with a smile. "Is all well with you, sweet wife?"

A slow smile, warm and alluring curved her lips banishing his concern. Her laughter bubbled forth. "Aye, all is wondrous, my husband."

****

For long moments, the only sound in the room was the heavy sound of their breathing. Mary ran restless hands up and down Alexander's back until the heavy beat of their hearts settled to a steadier rhythm.

His hands had often been restless when he touched her of late, but there had been something more tonight in the way he had reached for her, the way he had looked at her. She had not thought to be afraid, only to offer him what he needed. She had not expected to feel such pleasure in the giving. The wonder of it settled inside her more light and joyous than anything she had ever known. She smiled again.

He started to ease from atop her. "Do not part from me yet awhile, Alexander," she urged softly, her arms tightening around him holding him in place. Now that she had discovered such a feeling of closeness with him, she wanted him to stay inside her as long as he could.

"Mayhap the bairn will not be pleased by such an intrusion," he teased.

"I am told 'twill not bring him harm to share my attentions," she said with a smile.

His brows rose in surprise. "And who was it you sought out to ask such advice, Mary?"

"Derrick's wife, Anabal is a midwife. She comes each day to see him." Just the memory of their conversation caused her face to burn.

Chuckling, he brushed her lips with such tender attention her heart seemed to melt with love.

"When was it you spoke to her?" he asked.

"'Twas a few morns past." She wondered at how easily he had stirred the embers of her feelings with such a gentle caress. Once again aching with a glorious feeling of need, she felt ready for the thrust of his body all over again.

"The priest told me such acts are only practiced in the hope of begetting children, but Anabal and Derrick are most—affectionate though she is bairned."

He drew back to look down at her. "If God had not meant for husband and wife to seek such comfort and pleasure with each other, he would not have given us such a gift, Mary. 'Tis right and good and meant to breed affection and loyalty, as well as children," he said, his tone and features intent.

"You are late in offering me such assurances, Alexander. We have already done the deed."

His smile reminded her of a mischievous lad. "Aye, we did very well."

It thrilled her to know she had brought him pleasure for he had certainly brought it to her. Mary trailed her fingertips up and down his back. "'Tis a wicked thing."

Alexander frowned. "'Tis not a wicked thing to share yourself with your husband, Mary."

"Nay, not that. 'Tis a wicked thing to be shamed for doing what is natural with one's husband." With the act, she had shed some of the guilt instilled in her by the priest during her stay at the abbey. Her husband's willingness to share himself, his gentleness, had eased her fears and made it a natural thing to give herself to him. "'Tis a wondrous gift you have given me, Alexander."

His lips brushed her cheek, her brow then settled over hers once again. "'Tis a gift we have given each other."

"The way it was before—- "she stopped. "I did not expect to receive pleasure in our marriage bed, only to accept my duty," she explained.

"Duty is a cold master, Mary, and has no place in our bed," he said, his features tense. He started to say something more then nuzzled her neck instead.

She worked her hands upward to encircle his neck. Her lips sought his throat where the warm blood throbbed beneath his skin. She tilted her hips upward seating him deeper inside her. "Does this feel like duty, Alexander?"

"Nay," he murmured, "It feels like heaven."

"How oft might we appreciate such a gift together?" she asked. She nibbled at his earlobe and she felt him shiver in response and the swelling fullness of him growing hard inside her.

"As oft as we wish." He turned his lips to hers and his tongue taught hers a flickering dance that tempted and teased and set a titillating ache of need throbbing within her.

"If you are not too tired from your labors, 'twould please me to taste such joy again," she said, her tone breathy and soft.

"I will never be too tired to serve you, Mary," he promised, as he began to move inside her.

Chapter Eighteen

The quick beat of the music being played in the great hall above penetrated the thick stone walls as Mary followed Alexander down the stairs. The air felt damp and cold, permeated with a musty scent of dust and dirt mixed with a foul stench. The pitch torches on either side of the stairwell cast eerie shadows on the gray stone. The booted steps of the men behind her sounded loud in the confined space.

The smell of sweat and human excrement became almost overpowering as they reached the base of the steps. Feeling nauseous, she covered her nose and mouth with the tartan shawl draped about her shoulders, to try to dull the stench. How did the men who resided here, and the ones who stood guard, bear it?

The chamber was little more than a wide passageway. The cell's wide oak doors were slatted with thick lengths of wood barring the prisoners from escape. Alexander led her to one of the compartments. At his nod, the man who stood guard lifted the heavy bar.

Alexander stepped through the portal first, holding the torch aloft. A man lay on a pallet on the floor, his eyes glassy with the fever shaking his body. The dull light reflected off the sheen of sweat bathing his pale face.

Setting the basket she carried to one side, she kneeled on the cold stone floor beside him.

"I will not have any Campbell bitch laying hands upon me," the prisoner said in a slurred tone around the chattering of his teeth.

Alexander stepped forward at the man's words.

Mary rose to stay him. "Nay, Alexander." She shook her head. Her gaze returned to the man's face half covered by a scruffy beard and streaked with sweat and dirt. "Is it your wish then to lose your arm or your life for the sake of your pride?" Mary asked.

A struggle ensued behind the man's gaze then his features settled into stubborn lines.

"I will leave you to it then," she said with a nod and turned to retrieve her basket.

"Wait—" he croaked as they reached the doorway. "I would be grateful for your care," he said, his tone less than gracious.

"I will not be insulted for my trouble," she warned.

He nodded, his movements weak. "I will not again offer you insult."

Her gaze rose to Alexander's face. One heavy brow rose, leaving the decision to her. She turned back to the prisoner to kneel beside him once again. She laid bare the arm streaked with red. The injury was not a bad one, but the color around it had her frowning in concern. "I will need him moved upstairs, Alexander," she said as she looked over her shoulder at him.

His features settled into a frown. "If we must. He will have to be guarded and I will not allow you to remain alone with him."

"She nodded and rose to her feet. "Now, there must be something done about the smell of this place," she said. "The air is not fit for beast or man."

"'Tis they who have fouled it. One of them may be chosen to empty the buckets they are using."

'Twould do no harm to bring them out one at a time for me to tend their hurts."

"Would you kill them all with kindness, wife?"

"If MacLachlan clansmen are amongst them I have met, we will know for certes one way or another."

Alexander was silent and a frown drew his auburn brows together. "Their hands will be secured first."

"If a small table may be brought down, I will see to them after I have cared for this man."

"There is no hurry for you to tend them. They are not going anywhere. You may see them tomorrow, after the air has had time to sweeten."

He turned and motioned to the men who stood at the wide entrance. The men stepped forward to lift the man to his feet. In his weakened condition, the prisoner swayed unsteadily. The brawnier of the two clansmen swung him over his shoulder and carried him out of the cell. The other followed close behind.

Alexander's hand rested against the small of her back as he urged her out of the dank chamber. He paused to order that one of the prisoners empty the buckets.

Mary preceded him up the stairs.

"Derrick is almost healed. Mayhap he can see to them," he suggested as they came out of the stairwell into a large storage room.

"All will be well, Alexander. I will not lower my guard about them."

His frown darkened into a scowl. "If I can not be here, Gabriel is to be with you at all times."

She nodded, well pleased by his concern for her safety, or was it the bairns? There had been times of late she had felt closer to her husband, yet he did not speak words of affection even in the throws of passion. She knew he desired her, but what of affections? Would it bring him pleasure to know of her love? Would he treasure it as something precious, or would he accept it as his due? Would he return her feelings in some way?

Mary drew a deep breath. Sharing her body with him had narrowed the distance between them in some ways. It had partially healed the hurt inflicted five months before, as well. His gentleness over the past months had done more. If only she could be certain of his feelings for her. Why did men think it unmanly to show their emotions, yet think women cold if they did not?

The great hall was filled with men and servants celebrating the sixth day of the Twelfth Night feast. Mistletoe hung in every doorway and sprigs of holly decorated the windowsills. Huge Yule logs burned in each fireplace at the ends of the room. Candelabrums, twelve candles full, had been lit and placed on the tables. The carved Yule candle she and Alexander had lit the first night burned on the head table.

Servants carried in great steaming kettles of wassail and placed them atop braziers on a table against one wall, where the heated brew would be safe from mishap. Barrels of ale and honeyed mead lined the back wall away from the fire.

The men were in high spirits, their laughter loud and raucous as they ate and drank. Musicians, hired for the celebration, played lively tunes between courses. The music and voices reverberated in the room.

As soon as Mary entered the hall, Fergus sought her out. "I have placed the man in the chamber Artair was in, Lady Mary."

She nodded. "Please send my things. I will have a need for some salt, water, and willow bark and a brazier on which to keep the water hot."

Fergus nodded and left to do her bidding.

Alexander grasped her arm. "You will share a meal with me first, Mary."

His tone had a wry smile curving her lips. He sounded very much like his father when he ordered her about. "'Twould please me to be asked, my lord husband."

His tawny gaze fastened on her face. "Will you not share a meal with me, my lady?" he asked, his manners at their most courtly.

She smiled and curtsied. "'Twould please me well, my lord."

"'Tis the finest feast I have celebrated in some time, Mary," Duncan commented as they joined him at the head table. "You have done well."

"'Tis grateful for your praise I am, Duncan, but I could not have done it without Fergus and the others. 'Twas their willingness to do their part that has made it a fine celebration." She washed her hands in the basin a servant brought to their table. She watched as Alexander filled the trencher placed between them with smoked venison, meat pastries, and boiled vegetables.

The day had been hectic and Mary had found little time to rest. A nagging pain had settled in the small of her back. Straightened in her seat to ease the ache, she brushed at the fine wisps of hair teasing her forehead. The noise and heat of the room pressed in around her and she longed for a quiet moment in their chamber.

Her gaze rose to Alexander's face to find him watching her. She noticed, not for the first time, how the lighter tawny gold of his irises were ringed by a darker tan and how his thick dark auburn lashes made them appear even lighter. His hand came to rest against the small of her back as though he would draw her close. "Is all well with you, Mary?" he asked his brows drawing

175

together in a frown.

Her gaze dropped to the dark patch of auburn hair visible in the open neckline of his shirt. "Aye, I am well, Alexander."

His fingers caressed her cheek drawing her attention to his face again. "Look up, lass." He pointed toward the ceiling.

She tipped her head back and spied a large cluster of mistletoe tied to a thin rope left to dangle directly over them from the oak rafters above. "How did that come to be there?"

"I climbed up this morn and hung it there."

She laughed, delighted by the gesture.

"'Twill give me leave to kiss you anytime I wish," he teased. He cupped her cheek and tilted her face up to him. His lips were tender as they caressed her own.

She found her face growing hot, not with embarrassment, but a desire to press closer to him and further the contact.

"I may leave it there until it crumbles away," he said, his gaze alight with similar feelings.

He didn't need mistletoe to claim her kisses. Every time he drew near, she felt a bone weakening rush of desire. With it came a need to hold him, to smooth the lines of responsibility from his face and give him ease. Sometimes, she longed for him to do the same for her. Yet, there were times she held back from him, fearful of the power he had over her body and her emotions.

"How fares the prisoner?" Duncan asked, making her aware of where they were.

"His arm is festering and he is feverish," she answered.

"Let us hope he does not die. We do not wish to foul Campbell soil with the likes of his MacDonald carcass," one of the men commented from down the table.

They would feel the same if the man proved to be of the MacLachlan clan. Her father had done little to endear himself to Alexander's people. Being his kin, she was judged for his actions. The coolness of some of the women of the village gave testament to the length of the feud between their clans. The fact she had been a part of the MacPherson clan at the time, meant little. She still had

MacLachlan blood.

Mary's gaze wandered about the room as she nibbled at the choice samples of food Alexander offered her and listened to the conversation around her.

Her attention was captured as she noticed Tira's interest directed at their table. The repairs to her hut were nearly complete. She would be glad to see her leave the castle.

The woman's insolent green stare settled on Mary's growing belly and a smile, almost threatening, curved her lips. Fear and anxiety twisted inside Mary. The woman was a danger to her and the bairn. Gossip could harm the bairn's place in the clan if doubts were cast on his parentage, and she was certain the woman meant to do everything she could to harm her and her babe. Worry pressed like a relentless weight on her shoulders.

Mary shifted in her seat once again, this time to ease closer to her husband and seek comfort from his nearness. Alexander placed a hand against the curve of her spine and rubbed with nimble fingers against the spot that ached. Her eyes rose to his face and she forced a smile to her lips. "Your training as a husband is going well, Alexander."

His brows rose as his amber gaze looked down into hers. "I have only begun yours, lass."

Heat flared in her cheeks and settled in more intimate areas of her body. Even with the threat Tira represented, marriage to Alexander was proving a great deal more pleasurable than she had thought it would be months before.

****

"The lass looks a wee bit worn, Alexander," Duncan observed after Mary left the table.

"Aye," he agreed as he watched her climb the stairs to the chambers above. "She is working hard to be accepted as one of us." How would his men react should the prisoners they held prove to be MacLachlan clansmen? Would they blame Mary for their trespass? Surely not. He would stand by her and offer her at least as much loyalty as she had given him. After all, she had done to prove herself, his men would stand with her too. He had to believe they would.

"Is something amiss with her?" Duncan asked.

"Nay. She seems content enough here."

"Is she?"

Alexander's gaze rose to his brother's face, anxiety tightening his stomach muscles. Did Duncan know of some doubt voiced by the men?

"She is alone here, Alexander," Duncan said. "Just as she was at Lorne."

Understanding his brother meaning, Alexander breathed a sigh of relief then frowned. How was he to ease her situation?

"There has been no word from her sister since you were wed?" Duncan asked.

"Nay."

"Do you not think that strange, Brother?"

"Aye," he agreed. "Mary has not written to her either, though I know she can read and write."

"Did they have words then, mayhap about the bairn?"

"I do not know. Mary does not speak of her sister to me." She seldom spoke of her family at all.

"'Twas in my thoughts to send an invitation to Anne to visit in the spring. For certes 'twould please Mary for her to be here when the bairn comes," Alexander said. "Grandmother wishes to be here as well."

"Father has already stated his intent to be here too," Duncan added. "'Twill be his first grandchild. He will not wish to miss such an event."

"Aye. In truth, I believe he is anxious about the lass giving birth."

"Not so, her own father. 'Tis doubtful he will wish tidings sent about the birth," Duncan commented.

Alexander's jaw tightened as anger surged within him. "Mary has renounced him and does not wish further contact between them. She fears he may betray her again in some way."

Duncan nodded.

"Has there been talk amongst the men?" Alexander asked.

"Aye, all thus far are showing loyalty to the lass because of her stand agin her father on your behalf."

The tight feeling in the pit of his stomach eased somewhat. "Good."

"It could change," Duncan warned, his gaze wandering to Tira where she sat at a table with several village women talking and laughing.

Alexander followed Duncan's interest. "I have warned her to hold her tongue."

"She has been here for some time. There are those who are loyal to her."

"They owe their first loyalty to me, Brother."

Duncan shook his head, his expression grave. "You have much to learn about women, Alexander."

"Mary has more than proven her loyalty to the clan with the care she gives our people. Artair would not have regained the use of his arm had she not given him such care. Derrick may not have lived. It angers me that she will have to continue to prove her loyalty again and again when she has done nothing to deserve suspicion."

"You do not have to defend her to me, Brother," Duncan said with a grin.

Alexander gave a wry smile. "I will not see her harmed by gossip mongers. She has borne enough."

"For all you would spare her, there are some battles Mary will have to fight on her own," Duncan warned.

"Aye, but those I have brought her are the ones I would fight for her."

"There will be none left," Duncan teased.

A presence at Alexander's side drew both their attention. Tira stood close to Alexander's shoulder. "'Tis a word I would like to have with you, Alexander."

"What would you be speaking to me about, Tira?"

"'Tis about Cassidy," she said.

He frowned. "Is the lad ailing?"

"Nay, 'tis about something else."

His responsibility lay in serving as a guide to his people and settling their disputes Tira was one of his people. He rose, with some reluctance, to his feet and led the way to the antechamber just off the great hall.

"And what is it that can not wait until the morrow for you to discuss with me?" he asked as he closed the door and turned to face the woman.

Tira's emerald gaze settled on his face and a pout ripened her full lips, drawing attention to their lush shape and color. "'Twas for nearly a year I served you as a wife, Alexander. 'Tis cold you have become to treat me as though I have never been anything to you."

He kept his tone even. "I am wed now, lass. You do not expect to continue as we were after I brought my wife to *Caisteal Sith*, did you now?"

Tira's eyes narrowed. "Had she proven less fertile, you would not have wed her."

Her insolent tone sparked his anger and his jaw tightened. "Fertile or not, Tira, she was two years betrothed to me. I meant to wed her."

Her lips grew thin as her mouth tightened.

"You spoke of Cassidy," he reminded her, hoping to finish the conversation and escape the room.

"Aye." Her gaze dropped. "'Tis my wish for him to be fostered with a clan where he might gain some advantage."

Surprised, Alexander's brows rose, his gaze probing her expression. The sons of a yeoman were rarely fostered. Only those with royal ties were normally done so.

"You owe me some recompense for the service I gave you, Alexander." She raised her chin in a haughty gesture.

He remained silent a moment. Would this then satisfy the woman and end her enmity toward Mary? "Do you not have kin of your own with whom you would see him fostered?"

"Nay." She shook her head.

"You may wed again, lass, and have no need to foster the lad," he suggested.

"Nay, I do not wish to wed," she said her words quick and emphatic.

"Very well. I will think for a time on the matter," he said with a nod. He would think on what clansman would make a strong husband for the lass, as well.

Her quick smile gave him pause, he searched her expression once again.

"'Twould be better for him to be accepted in a household where he might find his place as a warrior like his father, Alexander."

"Aye, but you do not have to be separated from the lad for him to do so. He is but a wee lad yet. You may be with him, if you wish it."

"Has she succeeded in turning you agin your own traditions, Alexander?"

His anger flared anew. "'Tis not for you to question what I do, Tira."

Mayhap Mary had changed his reasoning about some of their customs. He could not deny he had a desire to guide his son into manhood, just at his father had him. He had wed a woman who would fight him should he try to separate her from her child, be it lad or lass. Why was the woman who stood before him so eager to rid herself of her son?

"I will speak with you again on the matter in a few days. 'Twould do you well to think about such a decision for a time."

"I will not change my mind."

He urged her toward the door and opened it. They stepped into the passageway in plain view of the company in the hall.

"'Tis grateful I am to you, Alexander," she murmured and rose on tiptoe to press an unexpected kiss on his cheek.

He frowned after her as she made her way back across the great hall to her place at one of the tables. His gaze circled the chamber then rose to the staircase above to see Mary standing on the steps midway down, her pale blue gaze locked on him. Her expression remained composed though two bright spots of color stained her cheeks.

Alexander bit back an angry oath and stepped to the base of the stairs to offer her a hand.

She stopped, one step above him, and her eyes looked directly into his, their color so pale a blue they looked almost white around the darkness of her pupils. "Is there some problem you would share with me, Alexander?"

"'Tis a matter spoken to me in confidence, Mary," he said with a shrug.

Mary's features went still.

He wished he could read what lay behind the careful stillness of her features.

"We must begin the dancing," she said, her tone short. Placing her hand on his sleeve, she allowed him to draw her forward to the center of the floor.

The mandolin player strummed a chord, then the flute and fiddle started a moderate, lively tune. Mary turned in his arms to face him, her palms melding to his as her feet caught the beat of the music. The plaid skirt of her wool surcoat fanned out, brushing his legs as she spun in a graceful turn. The loud cadence of voices died as the crowd's attention came to rest on the two of them.

Alexander rested his hand against her waist, and his other grasped hers as they promenaded the circle, their feet stomping an intricate rhythmic pattern in beat to the music. She turned before him over and over again, the golden length of her hair swinging free, mimicking the movement of her skirt. As the music ended and they halted. Her pale gold tresses clung to the sleeve of his russet shirt, spilling like liquid moonlight over his arm.

The men pounded on the wooden tables and clapped their hands in approval.

The noise died down and a female voice carried well above the crowd. "'Tis shamed she should be to be barely wed and five months bairned."

Alexander's anger flared hot at the insolent remark. His gaze focused on Mary's features in time to see the dark color creep upward into her face and her hand moved defensively to the front of her gown. He turned to face his people and his gaze circled the room traveling to each table, seeing speculation tainting the women's expressions seated with Tira, but outrage and anger directed at their table from others.

"Fergus." He motioned to the steward where he stood near the barrels of ale. "Bring us each a cup so we may share a toast."

The man rushed to do his bidding and brought them both a stein filled with the brew.

Alexander lifted his tankard aloft and raised his voice so all would hear his words. "To my first born, and to my wife, Mary, the woman who carries him. May this child be the first of many we will have together. I would ask you all to drink a toast to them and their continued health."

A rowdy cry of agreement came from the tables where his men sat. The villagers followed suit. Gazing directly at the women at Tira's table, Alexander waited for each of them to raise her tankard before he tipped his head back and drank his fill.

He guided Mary to their table. He noticed how her hands shook as she set aside the stein, smoothed her skirt then clasped them in her lap. He bit back an oath.

His gaze settled on Tira once again. As Duncan said, she had been a member of their clan for some time and the loyalties she had secured could prove a problem if left unchecked. His resolve hardened. He would find a mate for the woman as soon as possible. He would see her out of the castle and back into her own hut before the week passed.

"'Twill take some time, Mary," Duncan said, his tone soothing.

"Aye," she agreed. She directed her attention on the stein before her. The color having faded from her cheeks, she now appeared pale. She raised a hand to once again brush back the feathery curls from her forehead.

Alexander placed a palm against her back in a gesture of comfort and her eyes rose. "All will be well, Mary." She did not look as though she believed him.

Chapter Nineteen

Mary eyed the reddened flesh of the man's arm in hopes of seeing some improvement. For hours, she had applied warm compresses laced with salt and oak bark to clean the injury and sooth the inflammation around it. The wound seemed less angry now. She spooned tea made from dried sorrel leaves and willow bark into his mouth to cool his fever.

"You must seek your rest, Lady Mary," Grace urged. "'Tis not good for you or the bairn to go without."

Brushing the curling twigs of hair from about her face and brow, Mary straightened, so stiff from bending it was painful. She rubbed her back to ease the ache. Studying her fingers, she grimaced at their pruned appearance.

"He does not deserve such care, Lady Mary," Gabriel said, his displeasure palpable. "He would kill you if he had the chance."

Her eyes focused on Gabriel's face. "Aye, and he would have to live with that." Her attention shifted to the man on the bed. "'Twould pain me much more should I turn my back on a man who asked for my care." Her attention returned to Gabriel. "Every life is a precious thing, Gabriel. I do not begrudge the effort it takes to preserve it."

She rested a hand on Graces shoulder. "'Tis to your care I shall leave him, Grace. I will seek my rest for a short time."

Her steps heavy, Mary climbed the stairs to their chamber. She eased the door open so as not to wake Alexander then secured it behind her.

A single candle on the bedside table lit the room. She shed her clothing then slipped beneath the pelts beside her husband. She caught her breath as Alexander's warm body pressed close to her from behind. An arm snaked around her waist to pull her more firmly back against him. His knees followed the bent posture of hers, and his manhood rested with bold familiarity against her buttocks. The stark intimacy of his maleness brought Mary no fear, but a shocking sense of comfort.

"Our bed has been empty without your presence, Mary," he complained in a voice gravely with sleep.

As tired as she was, the comment brought her quick pleasure and a smile sprang to her lips. "'Tis a relief to seek my rest, Alexander."

His lips found her shoulder, making her shiver.

"Sleep, lass. You need your rest."

She would have been more than happy to do that, but worrisome thoughts plagued her, making it impossible for her to close her eyes. She drew Alexander's arm more tightly about her and tucked his hand beneath her cheek.

"Do not fash yourself about the pettiness of a few lasses, Mary," he soothed.

"Gossip is like a festering wound, Alexander. It spreads and eats into the flesh until it can not be healed." She drew a deep breath and turned her face against the pillow in an effort to hold back her tears.

He withdrew his hand from her grasp to run his palm over the protruding roundness of her belly. "'Tis my bairn too. I will not allow anyone to harm him or you."

"If he is not born with the look of you upon him, they will always doubt me."

"I do not doubt 'tis my bairn, Mary." His arms tightened around her. "I am certes I am the only man you have ever lain with."

She turned to face him. The fire had died down and the darkness of the room prevented her from being able to read his expression. "How do you know that, Alexander?"

He fell silent a moment. "There is honor in you, an honor that runs bone deep. You would not promise another man's child to me. You would not have stood by me before the council and claimed me as a husband otherwise." His hand found her cheek. "I have never doubted you, lass."

Overwhelmed with relief, she felt the sting of tears burn her eyes.

"Sleep now. There is much to do on the morrow and

you are tired," he said as he rubbed her back and eased her close against him.

****

Mary woke to the feel of Alexander's warm body pressed close to her from behind. One of his arms lay beneath her head then folded down across her breasts, the other lay about her waist. For sleep-dulled moments, she remained content in the security of his embrace.

"Did you know your ear is the color of the inside of a shell where the light touches it?" he asked, his voice husky. "The curve of your cheek is touched by the same color." His fingers trailed against her cheek.

She turned onto her back to look up at him as he braced an elbow on the bed and rose above her. Early morning sunlight filtering through the shutters high in the east wall played along his features and bathed his skin with gold. "Have you become a poet now, Alexander?" The strong curve of his jaw appeared more boldly masculine darkened by the stubble of beard.

"A lover, lass." His pale amber gaze settled on her. "It has oft been my wish to hold you like this and know I could gaze upon you at my leisure."

She caught her breath with the piercing pleasure the admission brought her. She had never dreamed he had felt like that about her, or ever could.

She raised her hand to his cheek testing the texture of his beard. Alexander's eyes turned a wolfish gold and he brushed his lips against her palm. A wondrous tempting feeling raced through her, sparked as much by the way he looked at her as the touch of his lips against her skin. She wondered if he could recognize those feelings in her face as easily as she could read them in his. Could he see her love for him?

The bairn moved between them and Alexander changed his position so he could rest a hand against her abdomen. The instant eruption of movement beneath his touch had his gaze rising to her face.

"Does it bring you pain when he behaves as though he will kick his way out?"

She smiled. "Nay, 'tis not painful. He is just stretching a wee bit just as you or I do when first we awake."

Alexander slid downward, his gaze intent on the movements. He whispered soft Gaelic words against her skin. His whiskers tickled and Mary giggled and wriggled away.

His grin grew devilish as he looked up at her. "I was having a serious word with the bairn on your behalf, Mary."

She laughed again. "About what, my lord?"

"About treating you kindly along the journey the two of you are traveling together."

His gaze settled on the darkened peaks of her breasts and his expression grew more intent. He dipped his head and latched onto one of the nipples with gentle suction.

The rasp of his tongue against the tender peak made her catch her breath as instant pleasure trickled down her body to settle in the center of her being. His fingers took the place of his mouth as he raised his head to look down at her, his tawny gaze gold with heat.

"I can not touch you enough, nor ease my hunger for the taste of you, nor ease my need to be inside you, Mary."

His words sparked feelings within her making her hot and wet with wanting him. She ran her palms over his broad chest and slipped her arms around his neck to draw him down to her. "Come break the fast and we will find our ease together, Alexander," she invited.

His lips captured hers with a tempting sensuality that danced down her body, leaving a delicious lassitude in its wake. She captured the hungry thrust of his tongue within her mouth and sucked on it. He eased closer and his erect manhood brushed her thigh.

Alexander's hand settled on the lightly furred curve of her Mons, tempting but not touching. Her thighs fell apart and her body rose toward the pressure of his hand, seeking his caresses. The feather light touch of his fingertips found the sensitive jewel, sparking a sensation that made her hungry for the thrust of his body.

He turned bringing her atop him. His palms rubbed, restless and eager, up and down her back. She smoothed the rumpled thickness of his hair back from his forehead as she looked down into his face. She traced each rugged feature and gazed into the pale gold of his eyes searching his expression for more than the desire that awakened his body. The tender smile playing about his lips reassured her.

Her thighs hugged his hips, the most vulnerable heart of her poised above him. She touched her lips to his briefly, drew back, and then returned to trace the parting of his lips with her tongue. His lips parted and her tongue delved forward to meet his.

His hands gently cupped and squeezed her buttocks as his tongue slithered and danced with hers for endless moments. Mary's hand moved between them to grasp the tempting length of his manhood. She ran her fingers up and down as her lips found his earlobe and she sucked on it.

"Mary—", Alexander whispered her name, a tremor racing through his body.

She eased downward, guiding him to nest deep inside her. The closeness she felt to him in those moments, when their bodies met and became one, was like nothing else she had ever known. It happened every time they made love. The joining of their flesh and the giving of her heart were the same. She hoped it was so for him.

Her lips sought the strong pulse in his throat. She began to move up and down in a slow steady rhythm. Thrusting upward beneath her, Alexander deepened the contact and her pleasure. The titillating torment began to build. She felt him in and around her. The brush of his skin, the taste of his lips, the musky male scent of his body, fed her desire. The feverish need for fulfillment drove her to quicken her pace. The ragged sound of their breathing remained the only sound in the room as they labored toward completion.

Mary tilted her hips forward deepening the contact, pressing down on him. The sweet pleasure of her release taunted her, making her catch her breath as she hung on the edge for countless moments. The wave of sensation overtook her, rising to a peak, rushing like wildfire through her body. The answering throb of Alexander's response heightened the feeling of completion.

After a time, she moved to lie beside him. She rested her head on his shoulder and pressed close against his side. The longing to hear him speak some word of affection in the moments following their lovemaking, lay like a knot of tears in her chest.

"Do you know if you have sired any other children, Alexander?" she asked, the question springing from her feelings of insecurity.

"Nay, lass. There are no others."

"With all the lasses you have known, how can you be certes?"

"Would they not have bid me claim them if I had?" he reasoned.

"'Tis a wonder that you gave me a bairn so easily then."

He turned to look down at her, his brows drawn together in a frown. "'Twas conceived because 'twas meant to be," he said.

Her gaze rose to his face. "In truth you believe that?"

"Aye, I do, Mary." He nodded. His tawny eyes swept her face with a look of possessive pride.

She fell silent for a moment, her thoughts returning to the first time they met. He had ridden through the gates with his men during the start of a hunt. Amid the noise and confusion of the event, she had felt the strange prickling sensation of being watched. She had turned to look into the face of a man on horseback only a short distance from the steps. The hard masculinity of his features had been almost beautiful to her. She had felt both excited and frightened by the way he had looked at her. Just the way he was now. His body, large and muscular, had moved with the easy grace of a warrior as he had dismounted and climbed the steps of the hall to join her.

Mary drew her attention back to the present for she found a certain sadness in looking back at a past that could never be recaptured. "'Tis seldom a lass may claim ownership of her guidesman in the way men claim your wives, Alexander. You may only be owned if you wish to be, and rarely as completely as are we."

He raised one brow and shrugged his broad shoulders. "'Tis the way of it, lass."

Her gaze narrowed. "One would wonder if you would feel so complacent if the tide was turned, my lord."

A wicked grin split his face with the gleam of teeth, even and strong. "'Twould not be such a hardship, I'd wager, my lady. I would still find great pleasure in serving you. " He drew her close against him, his hand trailing with slow attention down her spine to her buttocks.

"'Twould seem you are destined to have what you will, one way or another," she complained though she leaned into him of her own accord as tendrils of desire nipped at her.

"Aye." He nodded with exaggerated satisfaction. "'Tis grand, indeed."

****

"Take care, Mary. 'Tis two steps down now," Alexander said as he guided her down the front stairs from the great hall. "Do not open your eyes yet." He grasped her hands and held them firmly lest she trip.

A smile worked its way across her lips tempting him to stop and sample the taste and feel of her lush mouth.

"Where are you taking me?" she asked, her eyes remaining closed.

"'Twill only be a league or two we must travel," he teased.

"Would we not be able to cover the distance more quickly if I opened my eyes?"

"Nay, lass. 'Tis not necessary." He settled his hands on her shoulders. "You must stand very still."

She nodded. He marveled at the trust she showed him now, when before she would hardly turn her back on him. He motioned for Cory to bring forward the gift from the stables.

"Open your eyes, lass," he murmured close to her ear.

"Oh–" With surprise and confusion evident in her expression, she extended her hand to the black mare before her and allowed her to nuzzle her glove. Though nearly as tall as his own gelding, the horse had a lighter build. She stood proud and still as Mary stroked her forehead.

"We shall ride slowly about the village and outlying areas of the glen. 'Twill give you ample time to get acquainted with your new mount."

Her brows rose and her lips once again shaped a surprised oh as she eyed the horse with greater interest. She ran a hand down the animal's glossy black neck. The mare nuzzled the edge of her cloak and nibbled at it.

Mary laughed and drew the fabric away from her. She spoke softly to her as she circled the animal.

"She be a bonnie, lass, eh, Lady Mary?" Cory said, smiling as he watched her.

"Aye, Cory, she is," she agreed as she stoked the diamond shaped white spot on the mare's wide brow.

"The Laird himself has been training her for you."

Mary's gaze returned to Alexander.

"'Tis important she be well behaved if you are to be riding her," he said. Would he soon grow used to the smiles she gave him each time he did something that pleased her? He hoped not.

"Will you give me your hand, so I might mount, Alexander?" she asked.

He cupped his hands and gave her a boost into the saddle. Watchful of the mares every move, he stepped back as Mary accepted the reins Cory handed her and set her foot in the side saddle's stirrup.

"Take a turn about the stable yard for a wee time, Mary. I would see how she rides beneath your touch instead of mine," he instructed.

She nodded and kicked the animal lightly sending her forward. He watched the horse's response to her every move.

"She be a good rider, for a woman, eh m'lord?" Cory said from beside him.

"Better than you know. Put her astride a horse in a man's saddle, and she'll best even some of the men," he said, remembering the mad race to Lorne Castle.

One of the stable lads brought forth his horse saddled and ready. Mounting the gelding, he rode forward and joined Mary. "We will stay close to the castle. There has not been anymore trouble, but I will not risk going further a field."

She nodded. Her nose and cheeks were already red from the cold, but her blue eyes sparkled with excitement, and she flashed him a smile.

They rode along the uneven path uphill to the village. The smell of baking bread mingled with the aroma other foods on the cold air. The day was too chilly to encourage outside activity and few of the villagers were about. Snow, dusted with the soot of peat fires, lay heavy on the rooftops of the dwellings and shops. Patches of ice scattered across the rock-strewn path made the horses footing uncertain and they picked their way cautiously over the terrain.

"Lord Campbell," a voice shouted from above the tavern drawing their attention to one of the shuttered windows opened on the second floor of the dwelling. The man's bald head popped out like the cork from a bottle. "Would you bring your lady in to warm herself and share a cup with us?" he invited.

Alexander waved. "Aye, I will." He urged his mount toward the railing before the structure.

"We just began, Alexander," Mary said in a soft tone as he dismounted and reached up to help her down.

"Aye, 'tis important for you to meet some of the clan face to face," he explained. "Sharing a meal or a hot drink can go a long way in winning them over, Mary."

She dropped her gaze, but not before he saw a flash of uncertainty in her expression. A young boy came out to take charge of their mounts, preventing him from offering her reassurance.

The room, permeated with the smell of ale, bread, and roasting meat, harbored an atmosphere of warmth and welcome. There were more people about than he had expected so early in the day.

The proprietor and his wife stepped forward from the crowd to greet them. "Mary, this is Akira and Callum, he introduced the two."

"'Tis honored we are to welcome you, your Ladyship," Callum said as he offered them a seat at one of the biggest tables. He wiped his bald brow with the sleeve of his shirt. "'Twas a generous thing you and the Laird did for the wee ones of the village."

"'Twas a custom of my MacPherson kin to see the little ones had a gift from the Laird, every Christmas Tide. Alexander and I wished to continue the custom here at Gleann Sith," Mary answered with a smile, her gaze swinging to Alexander's face.

Surprised, for he had known nothing about it, Alexander's studied her for a moment before he returned his attention to the innkeeper. "There were none neglected, were there Callum?" he asked.

"Nay, m'lord," the man shook his head. "Her ladyship saw to it."

Alexander leaned back in his chair and watched as soft color tinged Mary's cheeks and she focused her attention on the wooden cup of mulled wine Akira set before her. "'Twas offered in honor of our own bairn due about May Day or there abouts, Callum," he announced, aware that all who were present listened to their conversation.

"I had heard her ladyship was bairned. 'Tis a grand happening, to be sure," Akira offered. She folded her arms over her broad waist.

"Aye, 'tis." Alexander agreed. "'Tis a blessing I have oft longed for and have finally found with Mary." Those clansmen at the tables nearby raised their cups in salute. Several others came forward to offer their well wishes.

An hour or more passed before Alexander rose and pulled Mary's chair back. Amidst greetings of farewell, they took their leave.

"You did not speak to me of the gifts given to the wee ones," Alexander said as he bent to give her a boost into the saddle.

"You did not tell me you were so well versed in the art of persuasion. Where did you learn such things?" She accepted the reins from him and settled herself on the sidesaddle.

"At court, lass. It does no harm for a leader to know when to lead and when to persuade." He placed a possessive hand on her thigh.

Mary rested her hand atop his and the smile she offered him he found both soft and alluring. "I know well how you practice those arts, my lord."

****

For most of the morning, Alexander guided their visits to the clan people who farmed the flat areas of the valley. The cold winter sun was directly overhead, by the time he finally turned for home. When they arrived at the castle, the inner courtyard was empty but for the guards posted atop the battlements. The stables were deserted except for two young lads who ran forward to grasp the bridles of their mounts.

"'Tis time for the noon meal," Mary observed as Alexander grasped her about the waist and lifted her down.

"Aye. 'Twill only take a few moments to unsaddle the horses and rub them down. You may go to the great hall and join the rest," he suggested.

"I do not care to wait for you, Alexander."

Her willingness to remain with him brought a smile to his lips. Being alone with her, but for the time they spent in their chamber, had become a rarity. He missed having her near to speak of the mundane happenings of the day.

"'Twas not the ordeal you were expecting, eh lass?" he asked as they followed the horses into the stable.

"Nay."

His open support of her made it more difficult for anyone to doubt her or at least to give vent to such thoughts. Once the bairn was born, there would be no more opportunity for them to cause her grief.

Mary stood outside the stall while he instructed the lads how the horses were to be rubbed down and covered with wool blankets until their coats dried. The mare came to the door of the stall and poked her head out to nuzzle Mary's arm for attention.

"What do you have a mind to name her?" he asked as he stepped from the stall to join her and rested an arm atop the door.

"I shall call her Breandan, for it means little raven."

He nodded in agreement. "'Tis good."

The sound of feminine laughter came from the end of the stable. Slender feet incased in black leather shoes and white stockings showed themselves at the top of the ladder. The rounded shape of a skirt-covered buttocks came through the loft opening as the woman descended. Alexander recognized Tira's black tresses immediately.

A male voice came from above though his words were indistinct. Long legs clothed in trews and boots followed the path Tira had taken. Until the man leaped to the bottom of the ladder, Alexander did not recognize him. As they watched, Gabriel caught Tira about the waist and bent his head to kiss her in a passionate fashion, his hand cupping her hip to press her against his tall frame.

Mary's eyes rose to Alexander's face, her eyes round with surprise. He placed a finger to his lips and caught her hand to draw her out the side door of the stable. He did not miss the surreptitious glances she cast his way on their way to great hall.

"Do you not think you must speak to Gabriel about her, Alexander?"

Surprised, he stared at her. He had thought she would be pleased Tira's attention rested on another man and not on him. "Why should I do that, lass?"

"Gabriel is not—he seems—he does not know the way's of women." she said. He read the uneasiness in her expression quite easily.

"He's a man full grown, Mary. He knows the ways as well as any of the rest of us. He would not care for my interference." He stopped. "Why do you question their being together, if 'tis what they wish?"

She fell silent for a moment, her brows drawn together in a frown. "'Tis just—he seems just a lad."

For a full minute, he gazed down at her in stunned surprise, then a niggling feeling of jealousy and suspicion began to take hold. Why should she be concerned for Gabriel's well being? What was he to her? "That lad is half a score older than you, Mary."

"But he is tender of heart, and I do not trust her to care for him. 'Twould suit him better to wed someone like Grace."

Alexander snorted. Compared to what Tira could offer him, the idea of the man marrying a child such as Grace was ridiculous.

"Grace is but a year younger than I, Alexander."

He halted in surprise.

"She would treat him with care," Mary said decisively with a nod

Jealous anger rose up like a flaming torch within him and he struggled to control the angry words that leaped to his lips. "'Twould serve you well to fash yourself with the care of the man you're wed to and no other, Mary," he said, his voice taut with as much control as he could muster. He shoved open the great hall door with enough angry force the wooden portal banged against the wall.

****

Mary crossed her arms as she pondered the many shifts of humor men seemed to go through. One moment they were laughing, the next snarling and snapping. Since returning from their ride, Alexander's demeanor had become so cranky and out of sorts, she wondered if he were growing ill. Her whispered inquiry about his health earned her such a terse reply, she decided she would part from him before he tried her patience further.

"I must see how Grace is faring with the prisoner, Alexander," she said when she had finished her meal. Though few of the men remained to see it, the dismissive gesture he gave her set her cheeks to burning. She climbed the stairs to the landing, giving vent to her temper beneath her breath with each step.

Had her prying aggravated feelings of jealousy over Tira now he had seen her and Gabriel together? She should be relieved the woman had found someone else on whom to focus her affections. But she did not truly believe she had. She did not trust Tira's motives and she didn't want to see Gabriel hurt. He had watched over her and her bairn and had protected her from harm. She felt a need to do the same for him, just as she would the others who had protected her.

The quiet eased her temper as she made her way down the many passageways working her way toward the prisoner's chamber. Pausing outside the room, she drew a deep breath to compose herself lest the servants noticed her upset. The door stood ajar and she pushed against it. The heavy portal swung open with barely a sound.

Just inside the chamber, lay a clansman face down on the floor in a pool of water. Two overturned buckets rested on their side next to him. With a gasp, Mary rushed to him and placed a hand on his back. The slow rise and fall of his breathing had her drawing a relieved breath. She ran a hand over the wet matted hair at the back of his head and felt an egg shaped lump there. Her fingers came away bloody.

She shook him calling to him to awaken. The man groaned but did not rouse. Her eyes moved belatedly around the room. Gabriel's comment the night before about the man's intent to do harm ran through her mind. Instant concern for Grace raced through her. So slight of build, the girl would be easily controlled, even for a man as ill as the prisoner.

She had to get help and raise the alarm. She looked about the room for a weapon. Finding only the unconscious clansman's dagger and her own at hand, she drew her blade, gripping it tightly as she crossed to the door.

Her heart pounding, she surveyed the empty corridor before running down the passageway in the direction of the great hall. Pausing at each turn, she peered cautiously down the many corridors before moving on. A maid appeared unexpectedly from around a corner, and she yelped in surprise as they almost collided.

"The prisoner has escaped, are there any weapons stored in any of the chambers on this floor?" she asked the woman.

"Aye, m'lady. Come this way."

She followed the woman to a chamber just a few doors further along the passageway. The servant pushed the door of the chamber wide and stood back. Her gaze traversed the narrow storage room.

"There are many such rooms throughout the castle, m'lady," the woman explained. "But what good will they be to us?"

Mary sheathed her dagger then crossed the room to a wooden rack on which bows were stored. She ran her hand over the slender length of a bow and lifted it from its position. She looked about for the arrows. She tiptoed to lift down a quiver hung on the side of a heavy wooden wardrobe. She chose two arrows then turned back to the woman. "Lock yourself inside the chamber and stay here until I send someone for you," she ordered.

"You must do the same, Lady Mary," she urged.

Mary shook her head. "Nay, I am well armed and must raise the alarm. "Do it now."

Holding the bow in her hand for reassurance, Mary hastened down the corridor. As she paused above the gallery, she was struck by the unnatural quiet of the great hall below. Her gaze swung downward. A few men remained seated on the benches, the tables before them partially cleared. Every eye below seemed focused on the stairs and a stillness hung over the room. Mary moved with stealth to the railing.

The prisoner stood on the stairs, his arm lodged beneath Grace's chin. He held the girl before him, a blade pressed against her midriff. Her cornflower blue eyes were wide and glistened with frightened tears, but she made no sound. The man forced her down several more steps, their staggering progress unbalanced.

The man's eyes, glassy and glazed, looked wild. His fever-flushed face burned a hectic red. He stumbled nearly falling on top of Grace and the dagger pricked the girl's side. Blood, bright red, stained the gray wool of her gown and she whimpered in pain. Pushing back against him, she attempted to support his weight to prevent the blade from going deeper.

"'Tis plain to see you are not strong enough to seat a horse, nor ride for any distance," Alexander said as he stepped forward. Two men eased forward on either side. "The lass has done naught but care for your wounds and ease your pain. Is this how you would repay her kindness?"

"'Tis enemies that surround me. I would leave this place," the prisoner said.

Grace's face turned dark red with the effort to breath and her hands clawed at the man's arm as it tightened against her throat.

"Aye, MacDonald. Once you are strong enough to make the journey, you and all the others shall leave my land."

The man laughed, the sound hoarse. His throat worked as he swallowed. "We are all dead men, lest you be dead too. We can not return until the deed is done."

"Return to Lochlan or MacDonald Glenn?" Alexander asked.

"Think me a coward that I would betray my men, Campbell?" His fever glaze gaze narrowed. "A horse, bring me one now!"

"Look about you, Man." Alexander raised his hand to motion to the men seated and standing around the room. "How far will you ride before you will be hunted down and captured anew?"

The prisoner's gaze swept the room then returned to Alexander. A smile more like a grimace bared his teeth.

"There is nothing to lose then."

"Only your life," Alexander said.

"My own will not be the only one lost this day," he threatened, his arm tightening across Grace's throat once again.

The girl's struggles to breath grew audible in the silence of the room as she twisted against the pressure.

Her hands shaking, Mary armed and raised the bow. She sighted the man. Grace's body blocked his, leaving only his head as a target.

"She is but a servant and of little value as a hostage," Alexander said.

Grace sagged, her legs crumpling beneath her.

"What value do you hold, Campbell?" the man jeered at Alexander below him. He flipped the dagger into the air, its blade turning in the light.

Fear for her husband lanced through Mary . She loosed the arrow. The barb struck the man's wrist traveled through and lodged deep into his throat pinning his hand into an upraised position. The force of the shot thrust him sideways. Grace's loose-limbed form fell on top of him as he slumped backwards onto the steps. The two slid down almost to the bottom. The dagger dropped to the stairs and bounced between the wooden banister and landed harmlessly on the floor below.

For several moments all remained still then Alexander turned to look upward.

Lowering the bow to her side, Mary grasped the oak railing to steady herself as her limbs grew tremulous and weak with reaction. She had shot a man. The enormity of what she had done struck her and, as her ears filled with a horrible hollow ringing, her legs gave way. The world spun about her and she closed her eyes against the sensation. Blackness closed about her.

When next she opened her eyes, she lay in the comfort of her own bed, a heavy pelt drawn up over her to her neck. Alexander shifted beside her his tawny eyes grave with concern. Tears burnt her eyes and immediately he leaned down to gather her to him and hold her close. Mary clung to him and breathed in the familiar musky scent of horses, peat smoke, and the man himself. He was whole and safe.

"Grace?" she managed after a few moments.

"She is alive, though her throat is bruised."

"He meant to kill you both."

"Aye," he agreed.

Her arms tightened about him.

He shushed her, as he cupped the back of her head and held her close. "Be at ease, Mary. All is well."

Chapter Twenty

Mary ran a steadying hand along the wall as she descended the steep stone steps to the dungeon. The smell had improved somewhat, but dampness permeated the walls, and a chill hung over the dimly lit passageway. She shivered, reminded of the cave and the many miserable days she had stayed there. It seemed a lifetime had passed since then.

Setting her basket of herbs atop the small table just outside the cells, she stepped aside as one of the men placed a brazier filled with hot coals on the table. Another man set a pot of water on it and, at her direction, positioned a wooden bench against the wall.

"Alexander said the men's hands were to be bound behind them before you would be permitted to see them, Mary," Duncan said as he came to stand beside her.

"Aye."

"Are you certes you wish to do this?"

She raised her gaze to his face. His open concern brought a smile to her lips. The bonds of kinship she felt toward him were growing. "Aye, Duncan, I am certes." She laid out the herbs and dried barks she might need. "You may bring out the first of them."

An hour passed while she bathed and bound minor wounds. She studied each man's face carefully, relieved when she did not recognize any of them. The taut dread she had carried inside her began to ease. If none were familiar to her, then perhaps her suspicions of her father were wrong.

The next man balked at being led from the cell and a scuffle broke out. Duncan stepped between her and the clansmen dragging him forward, blocking Mary's view.

"I do not need the services of a healer," the man protested.

The sound of a meaty fist landing with a solid impact

made Mary flinch.

"You do now." One of the men muttered as they dragged him forward and hefted him none too gently onto the bench.

Wondering at the men's senseless violence, she drew a deep breath.

"'Tis the man who's arrow pierced Alexander's leg at Lorne, Mary," Duncan explained as he stepped from in front of her.

The man held his stomach, bent over in pain from the blow. When he straightened, pain-filled eyes, as bright blue as her own, settled on her face. Grimy hair streaked with pale gold hung limply on either side of his face, the strands following the curve of a cheekbone marred by a purple bruise that had turned green and yellow along the edges. A light brown beard darkened the lower half of his jaw.

Shock drained the strength from Mary's legs and forced her to brace a hand on the table. She caught back a groan of disbelief.

"Do you know him, Mary?" Duncan asked, his gray gaze fixed on her face.

"Aye," she managed, her mouth dry with dread. Tears blurred her vision. Her hopes of being accepted by Alexander's clan dwindled away like so much dust in the wind. "Why have you done this thing, Gavin?"

"Do you not know why, Mary? He destroyed your honor and brought you harm! 'Tis my duty as your brother to seek revenge for what he did." His cheeks, flushed with outrage, caused the bruise to stand out all the more.

"Brother!" Duncan exclamation sounded more like an oath.

Mary ignored him, her attention focused on Gavin's face. "He is my husband, Gavin. He is the father of my bairn. Would you make me a widow and my child an orphan?"

Gavin's features grew tense, his blue eyes flared with rage. "Better a widow than to be forced to serve him after what he did."

Drawing a deep breath to steady herself, Mary stepped forward to lay a hand on his shoulder. Her gaze settled on his and she swallowed against the tears clogging her throat. "I do not need you to seek revenge on my behalf. I do not wish that for myself or my child."

"How can you defend him, Mary? He shamed you!" He clenched his hands, his frustration palpable.

Mary flinched, and her temper finally erupted. His presence put her place in the clan at risk and put her child's future in jeopardy. "Where would you have it end, Brother? If you strike him down then his brothers will strike you, then our father will strike back, and the bloodshed will go on and on. What will be left for my son? What will be left for me? Would you have me return to our father to be bartered to the next man. And the next. She slammed both her fist down on the table. "And the next. If you are here to serve his purposes 'tis you," she pointed her finger at him, "who are the fool, Gavin. He will use you, and use you, until your heart will be as hard as his, and you will be as hungry for power as he, because that is all you will have left."

She rose to her full height, her body trembling with passion and anger. "How many husbands do we bury in the name of revenge, Gavin. How many sons? Do I allow it to go on and on until my own sons are laid at my feet in the name of honor?" She shook her head. 'Twould be better to be dead myself than to leave that legacy for my children." Her voice cracked on the last word and her composure wavered.

Gavin's scowl set in stubborn lines. "'Tis better for you to be dead than forced to live with a man who would dishonor you."

His words had Duncan and the other men stepping toward him threateningly.

Mary raised her hand to ward them off, resenting their interference and their presence. "Do you think our father honored your mother or mine, Gavin?" she asked, her voice growing softer as she calmed. She shook her head. "Marriage to him is little but the begetting of heirs and has nothing to do with the honor or the care of the woman with whom he chooses to beget them. That is why both his women are dead."

"Can you say the man you are wed to is any better?" he demanded.

"Aye, I can. He is not harsh with me in his word or deed. What has passed between us is for us to settle, no one else."

"Can you forgive the harm he has done you so easily?" Gavin asked obviously amazed.

She could not say it had come easily to her. "You have spilled his blood, you have pricked his pride, and wounded him. What more would you have him suffer in the name of my honor?"

"He has killed my men," Gavin shouted.

"In defense of his own life and that of his men. Indeed, he has done so in defense of me as well. Or would you have your men abuse me in the name of revenge?"

"Nay, Sister. Never!"

She placed her hands on her hips. "Then mayhap you should have spoken more plainly of your wishes before you ordered them to attack us on the way to *Caisteal Sith*."

His brows furrowed, "My men and I were at Lorne and here as well, Mary, but we did not attack anyone along the way."

Her gaze searched his face in surprise. "Then whose men was it that did so, if not yours, Gavin?"

He shook his head. "I do not know, Mary." His gaze dropped to her thickening waist. "I would not risk you or your bairn, Sister."

She did not know whether to believe him or not. She did not know how much influence Collin had on him. All she did know for certain, was she did not want to lose any more of her kin. Anne was lost to her now she had wed. Because of Collin's actions, she would probably never see her younger brother Kenneth again. Gavin, her half brother, was the only blood kin she had left with whom she had hope of retaining contact, and that hope was slowly melting away.

"Will you give me your oath 'twas not your men who attacked us?" she asked, working against the knot of tears rising again in her throat.

"I give you my oath, Mary, 'twas not me or my men," he answered, his pale blue gaze steady on her face. His sudden smile laced with mischief and satisfaction. "But I have bedeviled his cattle and I did pierce him with an arrow."

Mary found no humor in the situation. "I too have killed one of your men, Gavin. Would you wish to take my life in revenge for that as well?"

His smile quickly died.

"He tried to strangle my maidservant. It could have as easily been me, had I arrived at the chamber in which he slept a few moments before. He sought to kill Alexander with a dagger and claimed he could not return home lest my husband was dead first. I loosed the arrow and I killed him. I will have to live with his blood upon my hands because of you, dear Brother. That is what has come from your quest for revenge."

****

The unusually quiet of the Great hall greeted Alexander when he returned from the evening patrols with his men. Just inside the door, he shrugged off the heavy fur robes that covered him from neck to mid calf and handed them over to one of the servants. His eyes went to Mary's empty place as he crossed the distance to where Duncan sat at the head table. With every step he took, he sensed an unsettling tension in the air. He became aware of the men's interest in his progress and heard the lull in their conversation.

"Is something amiss with, Mary, Duncan?" he asked, concern bringing a sharpness to his tone.

"Nay, Alexander." Duncan shook his head. "The lass is well. Though—Mayhap 'twould serve you well to go up and speak with her."

Alexander's brows drew together, and his gaze settled on his brother's grim expression. With a brief nod, he turned toward the stairs.

Concern for her quickened his pace, and he took the stairs to their chamber two at a time. All was quiet as he shoved open the door. His eyes swept the room until they fell on Mary's small figure before the fire. His heart beat a rapid rhythm against his ribs as he strode forward into the room. Searching for some injury, his eyes raked her from head to toe. He breathed a sigh of relief when he saw none.

She rose to her feet as he approached, but there was something tentative and uncertain in her expression as she turned to face him. He kept his tone even, though her anxious gaze did not ease the feeling of foreboding plaguing him.

"What is amiss, lass?"

"'Tis about the men you captured, Alexander. I saw them today."

"Aye, and did you recognize any of them?"

She drew a deep breath. 'Twas my brother who pierced your leg with an arrow, Alexander. 'Twas he who has been killing your cattle and sheep," she said with a bluntness that had him staring at her. 'Tis he who is leader to the men you have imprisoned downstairs in the dungeon."

He shook his head. "Your brother is but a wee lad, Mary."

"Aye, Kenneth is but a lad." Her blue eyes were clouded with worry. "'Tis my half brother Gavin you have captured and imprisoned."

"Half brother...Half brother," he repeated taking it in slowly, his gaze locked on her. Her brother had pierced him with an arrow and had stolen his cattle and sheep. "'Twas he who attacked us between Lorne and here?"

"He says, nay, Alexander. He gave me his oath it was not he, and I believe him."

She instantly believed her half brother who had tried to murder him, but it had taken him, her own husband, months to earn her trust. Or had he? If her trust was his, why had he not heard of this half brother before? Rising anger brought heat to his cheeks, and he clenched his hands at his sides.

"From where does this half brother hail?" he asked.

"He was fostered by the Frasers. Gavin oft came to see us, for he was close by when we lived with my aunt and uncle." She swallowed. "He is all the kin I have now, Alexander. You do not mean to harm him, do you?"

"Nay, I do not harm men that are intent on murdering me," he said with biting sarcasm.

Mary flinched. "'Twas on my behalf he was acting, Alexander. He...he felt 'twas his duty to seek revenge for...for what happened. If you had a sister and she—"

"I have no sister," He cut her off. He was tired of paying for his actions those many months ago. He would have an end to it. "The man tried to murder me, Mary. Had his aim been true, you would have been a widow, before you became a wife. Only days ago, had I not defended myself, he would have struck me down."

"He is my brother, Alexander," she reminded him, her gaze pleading.

"Aye, and I am your husband and your loyalty belongs to me!" His temper flared anew making his tone harsh. "'Tis the second time in as many days I have reminded you of that!"

Mary caught her breath and outrage crossed her features. "And would you have me remind you of your loyalty to our bairn?" She demanded her cheeks growing flushed and her eyes alight with temper. "Will you spill the blood of his uncle and start anew the feud we hoped to settle? Is that the legacy you intend for our son? Would you have the two of us torn asunder beneath the bloodlust the two of you are intent upon?"

"Whatever I decide 'twill be my decision, wife, and you will abide by it."

"You have denied me my sister and Collin my brother, is it to be that I am to lose all my kin?"

He caught back the angry tide of words that leaped to his lips. "How have I denied you your sister?" he demanded.

"Because of what happened at Lochlan, Ian MacMillan has forbidden Anne to consort with me. He believes me to be unfit for her to—" Her words dwindled away to silence. One hand clenched against her breast as though pain struck her there.

He swore. What else had she withheld from him? He raked his fingers through his hair and drew a deep breath to cool his temper. He did not know which enraged him more, Ian's injustice toward her or Mary taking her brother's side against him.

"Mayhap 'twould have suited you for him to strike me down. 'Twould have finally given you the justice you were denied," he accused.

"Had I wanted you dead, I would have killed you myself," she shouted at him.

His fist slammed down on the table in frustration. "You do not have to; you have a brother to do it for you."

Her eyes flashed blue fire at him. "After all I have borne on your behalf, after all the suspicion and doubt that has been heaped upon me because of what you did those months past—" She fought with obvious effort to rein in her temper. "If you believe I have conspired with him, Alexander, you are a fool!" Her voice cracked beneath an ire that brought a hoarseness to it. "Had I wished you harm, I'd have given testament agin you at Lorne and ended it there! Had I wished you harm, I would not have..."

"'Twould be my wish to know why you did not," he stated, his gaze probing her face. "Why did you choose to wed me?"

"Why does any lass wed?. 'Twas for a roof over my head and over my babe's, and I preferred yours to the threat of Bearach MacDonald's," she said, a wry twist to her lips.

The name coming from her lips was like slap across the face. The confession that would release some of the bitterness between them was there wrapped beneath a tongue that begged to speak it. The open hostility he read in her gaze offered him little hope she would believe him if he did.How many times had he wished he could tell her? He sighed in frustration and raked his fingers through his hair with a distracted hand. It would be better to speak of it at a calmer time.

"'Tis an honor to know you preferred me to a MacDonald," he said in a quieter tone.

"Mayhap I should not have been so quick to decide to wed. Mayhap a hand-fast would have been better."

He studied the defensive way she folded her arms against her waist and averted her face. He did not hear conviction in her tone, but something else.

For the first time in months, she was stiff and wary as he grasped her arm above the elbow and drew her against him. Alexander tilted her face up to meet his gaze. "We are wed, Mary, and only death shall part us." He attempted to soften his tone. "In truth, I do not doubt you. My words were thoughtless and spoken in anger. How can I doubt you when you have borne arms to defend me?"

For long silent moments, she searched his face for

reassurance. "If I do not have your trust, Alexander, there is no place for me here. If I can not depend upon your faith in me, then how am I to earn it from your people?"

"'Tis you who have seen fit to withhold things from me," he reminded her. "I have not heard of this brother, Gavin, until now, nor have you seen fit to speak of Ian MacMillan and your sister to me."

She lowered her face from his gaze. "I could not speak of Anne," she said so softly, he would not have heard her had he not held her near.

He gathered her closer as reaction brought a tremor to her limbs. After a few moments, her arms crept about his waist and her head found its familiar spot against his chest.

He drew a deep breath as he felt her relax against him. His hand lingered in the silver streaked softness of her hair as he cupped the back of her head. He ran his fingers through the pale tresses at the nape of her neck and let it spill over his palm like spun moonlight. It seemed the peace between them was like moonlight as well. It was destined to shine brightly in the distance and no matter how close they came, it remained stubbornly out of reach.

Chapter Twenty-one

Alexander's men, heavily armed, mounted in preparation for the journey to Lorne. With their faces partially covered by tartan scarves, and each man covered from head to mid-calf by a thick fur robe, they appeared menacing. Mary shivered as she watched Alexander give the order for them to spread out and surround the prisoners. With practiced precision, they positioned themselves at equal distances around the men, guarding them from escape. The horses danced with nervous energy, eager to be off, their breath billowing out in steamy plumes.

"Take heart, Mary, we will not have to feed them throughout the winter if we rid ourselves of them now," Duncan said from beside her.

She attempted to control her expression though worry twisted inside her. "'Tis the weather that concerns me, Duncan. 'Twill not be fit for man nor beast should it begin to snow."

"Aye," he agreed, "but Alexander knows the dangers. All will be well."

Her gaze focused on her husband as he spoke to Gabriel. Alexander's large frame was covered from neck to calf in fur; his hands protected by leather gloves and his feet by knee high boots. He appeared well prepared for whatever the heavens decided to offer, but even the furs he wore would not keep the cold from penetrating should a blizzard strike.

His tawny gaze touched her as he strode to where she and Duncan stood on the steps of the great hall.

"We will ride hard and hope to see Lorne before dawn tomorrow," he said. "'Twill be at least three days before we return."

Duncan nodded.

"If the weather turns, we will seek shelter at Lorne

until it clears." His gaze dropped to her face. "You will have a care for yourself while I am away, Mary."

Though they had set aside their anger, the harsh words they had spoken only days before still hung heavily between them. Driven by a need to touch him before he left, Mary unwound the tartan scarf she wore about her throat beneath her cloak. She stepped close to him, looped it around his neck, and tucked it beneath his robe. "I do not fancy a husband without his fingers or toes," she warned in much the same bossy tone he used with her. "You will have a care for yourself, as well."

His wolfish gaze turned to pure gold and a devilish smile touched his lips. "And will you offer me a kiss, wife, to warm me along the way?" he asked, a challenge in his gaze.

Her eyes never left his face though she was aware of the men behind him waiting for him to mount his horse and lead them forward. She stepped close to slide her arms about Alexander's neck and draw his lips to her own. The kiss she offered him was not one of passion, but of tenderness. When she drew back, his tawny eyes traced her features with such intensity it brought an airless feeling beneath her ribs and a weakness to her legs. His lips brushed her forehead before he released her and stepped away.

"Safe journey, Brother," Duncan bid him as the men exchanged a glance.

Alexander nodded. He strode to his horse and mounted. At his signal, the men rode forward.

"'Tis good to see the Lord and his lady so openly affectionate, Mary," Duncan commented. "'Twill show a united front to all, in spite of what has happened between Alexander and your brother."

She drew a deep breath. Despite her worry for his safety during the journey, she felt relieved by Alexander's decision to escort the prisoners off Campbell land. His decision to continue holding her brother prisoner dismayed her. As much as she loved her brother, his presence continued to cause her trouble with the Campbell clan at a time when she could ill afford it. They had not fully accepted her yet, despite the fact that she had killed to defend her husband. Their acceptance would certainly be slower in coming as long as hostilities continued between her husband and her brother. Because the two men were too proud to bend, neither would admit to any wrong.

"'Tis between them I am caught with little to do to ease their differences," she said with a sigh.

"Let us hope you will not have to make a choice between them, Mary," Duncan said, his expression grave.

"There can be no choice, Duncan. Alexander is my husband. My place is with him." She drew the hood of her fur-lined cloak up over her head.

Duncan fell into step with her as she strode across the courtyard to the gate. "Where might we be going, Mary?" he asked.

"To the weaving shed. Alexander has need of a new kilt."

They climbed the hillside to the village in silence. Mary stopped to rest as they reached the top of the rise.

"Does it not please you that Gavin has been moved from the dungeon to a chamber?" he asked.

"Aye. I am grateful Alexander has relented enough to allow him to be moved. And as much as Gavin has complained about being confined to his chambers and guarded, he is pleased to be clean and comfortable again." A wry grimace thinned her lips momentarily. "I believe 'twould break off his tongue to speak a word of thanks to Alexander for his treatment though."

Duncan nodded. "He believes he is right in seeking revenge for your honor, Mary. I can understand his position. You are my sister now and 'twould be my duty to retaliate agin anyone who would bring you harm." His gray gaze fastened on her face as he drew a deep breath. "I can understand my brother's position too. Alexander would have what happened be, if not forgotten, at least left undisturbed, now you have accepted him as your husband. He is concerned your brother will find some way to turn you away from him by sparking anew feelings of hurt and bitterness over the incident."

Mary realized Duncan was trying to be helpful, but she could not speak of anything to him. To do so would be disloyal to Alexander. Her gaze turned from his face to the distant snow topped hills beyond. "What is in the past can not be changed. It does no good to dwell on it."

She continued down the rough-hewn road to the weaving shed. The scent of the dyes used to color the wool hung strong within the enclosed area of the room. The women's laughter sounded pleasant and happy as she and Duncan entered the structure. Seven looms, and the women who worked at them, filled the cramped space.

Tira was the first to look up and see them. Her expression grew cool, and her gaze flat and unfriendly. Silence fell over the room. The other women's expressions grew shuttered as they focused on Mary. After a lengthy pause, one woman rose from her seat and approached them. Her auburn hair, plaited in a long tail, hung down her back. Her youthful features were marred by lines at the corners of her eyes and around her mouth.

"My name is Mai, m'lady. What may I do for you this morn?" she asked.

"I have come to purchase a length of wool," Mary explained, offering her a smile the woman did not return.

Duncan wandered restlessly about the room while they spoke. The woman proceeded to show her several bolts of tartan fabric already woven. Mary frowned as she tested the quality of the wool between her fingers. "I would have the best for my lord," Mary stressed. "'Tis for him a new kilt."

Mai led the way to a wooden table stacked high with more bolts of cloth.

Mary ran her hand over a soft wool tartan of blue, green, and black and nodded. "This one I think, do you not agree?" she asked, trying to draw the woman out of her hostility.

"The men have gone this morn to take the prisoners away?" Tira asked as she sauntered up to them.

Mary's gaze rose to the taller woman's face. "Aye."

"If not for you, they would not have to risk their lives to do so," Tira accused.

Mary's chin rose though a sick feeling settled in the pit of her stomach. She did not appreciate having Tira challenge her with the very thoughts that riddled her with guilt and worry. "I did not invite the men upon Campbell soil, Tira. Nor did I council their attacks on the livestock."

"'Tis because of you that they were here." Her eyes glittered green malice. "'Tis because of you, our men must risk their lives to protect us."

"'Tis my husband's life that is at risk as well, Tira. Have you forgotten that?" Mary asked.

"A husband you do not want or deserve."

Mary felt helpless not defending herself against the statement. She could no more change the past than Alexander could. "Women of my station seldom choose the men they wed, Tira. 'Tis the men that choose them. 'Tis I, Alexander chose and 'tis I, whom he wed. He is my husband and I will serve him in whatever way he asks of me. I will honor him with my respect and my loyalty." Mary stepped closer to the woman meeting her emerald gaze with unwavering regard. "He deserves at least as much from the people he leads and defends. You are offering him none of that by questioning his judgment. Think well on that, Tira."

Her attention turned to the other women in the room, moving from one to the other to find none would now meet her gaze. She reached for the purse at her waist for the coins to pay for the wool, but Duncan was already counting out the necessary amount. Whether by chance or on purpose, his large frame stepped between Tira and herself.

Her expression mirroring her fury, Tira stalked away to her place before one of the looms.

Duncan accepted from Mai, the bundled wool secured by a scrap of fabric. Guiding Mary to the door, he escorted her from the hut.

Mary kept her face carefully averted from him as reaction brought tears to her eyes and a tremor to her limbs. She drew the cold air deep into her lungs then released it slowly as she struggled to retain her composure.

"Well done, lass," Duncan praised her.

"What she said was true, Duncan. 'Twas because of me, Gavin and his men were here. 'Twill be my fault should Alexander be harmed on this journey."

"Nay, lass. Men will do as they will without regard for their women, Mary."

A wry chuckle forced its way past her worry. Mary

raised her gaze to his face and offered him a smile. "'Tis grateful I am to you, Brother, for reminding me of a lesson that I should have indeed learned by now."

****

The heavy fur robe draping his body succeeded in keeping most of Alexander warm, but the wind's deep bite penetrated his woolen breeches between knee and boot. He rubbed the spot periodically to warm it. The tartan scarf Mary had looped around his neck protected the lower half of his face, though ice crystals formed at regular intervals on his brows and lashes. Brushing them away with a gloved hand, he cleared his vision.

Pale moonlight bathed the snow-covered hills, illuminating the path ahead. Lorne and warmth beckoned only an hour away. Though his fingers and toes had long since gone numb, he was reluctant to stop so close to their destination. The suns slow rise over the edge of the hills to the east firmed his decision. Its rays would warm his men and him enough for them to continue.

Snow laden trees shimmered in the early morning sunlight as they approached the castle an hour later. Ice coated one side of the tall walls giving a metallic sheen to the stone blocks from which it was constructed. The formidable beauty of the place never failed to impress him. Though no longer his home, the memories the castle evoked offered him feelings of belonging.

He remembered the day Mary had spoken of being part of two clans, but never truly belonging to either. After all, she had endured, she deserved to be accepted by his clan.

The gates opened before them, allowing them entry. Men rushed forward to take control of their mounts as Campbell clansmen and their prisoners dismounted in the courtyard. The group moved in force to seek shelter within the great hall.

"Alexander, welcome!" John approached as soon as they entered the hall, his deep voice carrying easily across the hall. "Is Mary well?"

His father's inquiry about her, before Duncan or himself, was proof enough of his affection for the lass. Alexander smiled despite his cold stiffened cheeks. "The bairn is growing and she is well."

Campbell clansmen clustered at one fireplace while the prisoners sought the warmth of the other. Servants hastened to offer both groups warm drinks, bread, and meat.

"Come to my antechamber where you may warm yourself and we may talk in private," the Campbell Laird suggested. He called to a servant to bring mulled wine and food.

His feet feeling like blocks of wood, his steps deliberate, Alexander followed in his father's wake to the large room off the great hall.

"Sit before the fire and warm yourself, Alexander," John ordered, his brows drawn together in a frown of concern. He pushed a chair closer to the huge fireplace. "You should not have pushed yourself and the men so harshly."

"'Tis important I return home as soon as I might." Alexander offered a booted foot to his father and John deftly gripped the shoe and pulled it off. 'Tis my belief there are MacDonald or MacLachlan forces hiding there."

John's brows rose then he nodded, his expression grave. "My patrols found evidence of two camps here, one to the east just beneath the outcropping that boarders MacNaughten land and the other to the south. After you departed, no more were found."

Alexander extended the other foot and grunted in pain as his father jerked the boot free. He rubbed through the heavy stockings he wore to warm some feeling into one foot then the other. "We were attacked on the way to *Caisteal Sith*, and some of the men were injured."

"The lass?" John asked immediately.

"Mary was not harmed. Derrick was pierced in the chest by an arrow and Artair's arm was nearly sliced through. Mary's care saw them through."

"The men you have with you?" John urged.

"They are MacLachlan or MacDonald or both. They were brought upon my land by Mary's brother, Gavin. He has been wreaking havoc with our herds and stirring up mischief trying to draw me out in order to revenge Mary's honor for what happened at Lochlan. I can not be certes Collin is not responsible for his presence."

"Where is this brother?" John demanded. "I would

speak with him."

"He is still at *Caisteal Sith*."

John's brows rose again.

"He is the only family Mary has left." Alexander quickly explained about Ian MacMillan forbidding Anne to consort with Mary.

John's scowl grew darker.

Interrupted by a servant with a tray laden with mulled wine, meat, cheese, and bread, they fell silent.

"I am willing to try and make peace with Gavin—if he does not force me to kill him first," Alexander said when they were once again alone. "I have pledged I will try to heal the breach between Mary and the MacMillan's as well." He freed himself from the fur robe and stretched out his long legs, positioning his feet closer to the fire. Exhaustion weighed heavily on him as the fire warmed away the chill. He leaned back in his chair.

"You have found some peace together?" John asked as he poured mulled wine into a brass tankard and handed it to Alexander.

"Aye." Silent for a moment, he stared into the fire and sipped the brew. His thoughts returned to the kiss Mary had given him before they had parted. To offer him such sweetness, she must surely have forgiven him.

"Eat, Alexander," John urged.

He turned his attention to the food his father offered him. They spoke of the journey the next day and his return to *Caisteal Sith*. Alexander raked his fingers through his hair and yawned widely, his body demanding sleep.

"A fire has been built in your chamber," John said. "You must rest. We will speak again at the evening meal."

Alexander passed through the great hall en route to his chamber. The prisoners, guarded by several of his father's men, lay on the floor before one of the fireplaces. Snores erupted from the group here and there, but otherwise the men were quiet. His men had obviously sought the barracks to sleep in preparation for the journey on the morrow.

With slow steps, he climbed the stairs and made his way to the chamber he and Mary had shared well over a month before. He shed his weapons and clothing and sought his rest on the fur-covered bed. The silence closed around him. The emptiness of the room and the bed struck him and he opened his eyes. For a moment, Alexander experienced the familiar loneliness and separation that had plagued him during his many years of fighting. In the past, he assuaged those feelings by seeking out some willing wench to fill his bed and distract his thoughts. That comfort held no appeal for him now.

His eyes settled on a stool close to the fire. In his minds eye, he saw Mary as she sat there mending his clothes. In the months they had been wed, she had begun to fill the void inside him. Her smiles, while still rare, warmed him, her touch offered him comfort and ignited his desire, her body fulfilled his passion and nurtured his future. His need of her grew each day and, with it, his vulnerability. By allowing her entry into his heart, he had opened himself to a pain more lethal than any battle-ax or arrow could deal him. But because of her, he had also experienced the most satisfying moments of pleasure and contentment he had ever known.

The worry he had glimpsed in her expression when they had bid each other farewell surely meant she harbored some small affection for him. Her reticence about her feelings and her family continued to confound him and make him uncertain. Her reminder that she had wed him for a roof over her head and her bairn's still stung. Surely, they had come farther than that.

Alexander turned on his back and drew a deep frustrated breath. He had prided himself on being decisive and confident in his dealings with women, but when it came to his wife, he found himself behaving like a besotted fool. Mayhap, if he were firmer with her in future...then again, when he was gentle, she let down her guard and allowed herself to respond without reserve. The thought stirred his body and he quickly turned his attention to other concerns.

If he could find a way to settle the hostilities between her brother and himself without bloodshed, he might yet win her heart. Her love was what he wanted—to hear her speak the words and see the feelings open and alive on her face as her eyes looked into his. He would be satisfied with nothing less.

What if she could not feel such affection for him because of what he had done? The thought brought with it a hollowness beneath his ribs. He would have to learn to live with that, but he would not give up.

Chapter Twenty-two

"Alexander, welcome," David greeted him from one of the tables as he descended the stairs to the great hall that evening. The younger man grasped his forearm and slapped his shoulder in greeting. "The prisoners have been secured below for the night."

Alexander nodded. "Is all well with you, Brother?"

"Aye." David's expression grew sober. "Father has spoken to me of your trouble. If you have need of me, I am ready."

He studied his younger brother's features with a smile. "I would not wish to deprive Father of both his right arm and his left, but I am grateful for the offer, David."

David's grin was laced with something Alexander could not quite decipher. "You may yet change your mind," he said with a shrug. He urged Alexander toward a group of men where a mug of ale was pressed into his one hand and a pair of dice was thrust into the other.

Alexander threw the dice on the table and watched them spin. His gaze drifted upward as his father appeared on the stairs above, but his attention turned immediately to the woman whose hand rested on his arm. She appeared so eerily similar to Mary, Alexander blinked to clear his vision. "Anne," he breathed the name as realization dawned.

"She arrived a little over a week ago, half frozen and less than gracious. She has been most insistent she be taken to Mary as soon as the weather clears."

"Where is Ian?"

"He was killed a month ago."

His gaze flashed to David's face for a moment then returned to settle on Anne as she approached with his father. Her features set in an expression of controlled anger, she acknowledged him with a brief narrowing of her lips. He had endured that look often when first he and Mary had wed, and though it did not carry the same impact from the eyes of this woman, he found himself tensing defensively in preparation for whatever might follow.

"Anne, I bid you welcome. Mary will be pleased you have come to be with her," he said before she could speak. "She has missed you sorely."

Her blue gaze icy, Anne inclined her head. "I have missed her as well. I trust she is in better health than last I saw her?" she asked, her tone accusatory.

"Aye, in good health and nearing the end of her sixth month."

He and David fell in behind his father as the older man escorted Anne to the table. John seated her to one side of him then took his place at the head of the table. Alexander sat on the opposite bench, where he might look directly into his sister-in-law's face, while David seated himself beside her.

The clansmen began to take their places at the other tables lining the room. Servants passed from person to person with bowls of scented water with which to cleanse their hands while others set out trenchers of bread.

"Your sister oft spoke of your uncle, Hugh MacPherson, Lady Anne," David said as he dried his hands on the linen towel draped over a servants arm. "Did he train you, as he did Mary, in the use of the crossbow?"

"Aye," she answered. "Our uncle thought it wise to train us to defend ourselves agin those who would bring us harm." Her attention focused on Alexander. "Of course with such a weapon one must be aware the enemy is afoot in time to ready the bow. It does no good agin those who would sneak upon you in the dead of night lest you are warned."

He remained reticent beneath the barb and placed his attention on filling the trencher set before him with meat and vegetables.

"Mayhap you would show us how good an archer you are after the meal," David suggested. "Your sister's skill has been recognized by all the men.

"If 'twould please my host I would not mind," she answered. "'Tis a skill best honed with much practice."

Alexander's gaze rose to her face to find her blue eyes settled on him like chips of ice. She would no doubt prefer to practice on him.

"Your sister has spent much time practicing the art of healing instead, Lady Anne," he said. "She has saved no less than four Campbell lives since we wed, one of which was my own."

Anne's brows rose. "'Tis fortunate for you her sense of duty was encouraged by my aunt as well."

Alexander controlled his expression with effort. Her knowledge of her sister gave Anne a wealth of weapons with which to prick him. Her anger and desire for revenge on Mary's behalf, were just as intense, it seemed, as Gavin's.

"Your leg shows no weakness?" John asked.

"Nay. It grows stiff now and then, but serves me well."

"How did you happen to become injured?" Anne asked.

Surprised by her interest he looked at her. "I was struck in the leg by an arrow while defending Campbell herds agin thieves."

"Mayhap they did not recognize one of their own," she said sweetly.

David covered his mouth to hide the smile of amusement tempting it, and Alexander fixed him with a warning stare.

"Nay, 'twas kin of yours who pricked my leg. 'Twas your brother, Gavin."

Two spots of hot color touched her cheeks as her eyes grew wide with shock. "Gavin!"

"Aye. He followed us to *Caisteal Sith*, trespassed upon my land, slaughtered my livestock and sought to do further harm to me and my men."

"If he did such deeds, 'twas to avenge my sister," Anne said, her chin rising in challenge.

The gesture and her words were so much like Mary's, Alexander found himself staring at her. "His reasons do not concern me."

"Where is he?" she demanded.

He has been confined to a chamber at *Caisteal Sith* whilst I escort the rest of his company from Campbell holdings."

Her pale blue eyes fastened on him with open hostility. "What do you intend to do with him?"

"I intend to hold him until your father may journey and claim him."

"'Twill be spring before 'twill thaw enough for that," she protested.

"Aye. 'Tis at Mary's request I have not punished him further, as would be my right."

"Have you not caused my sister enough pain?" she demanded, her cheeks flushed with color.

After her attacks on him, Alexander had only a brief compunction in using the knowledge Mary had given him against her sister. "Your concern is late in coming, Anne. It has been many months since you wed Ian MacMillan. Mary has received no words of comfort from you hence."

Her gaze dropped away.

"Mary honors me as her husband. That should be enough for you and your brother."

"I will ask her myself how that came about, after everything she has endured because of you," she proclaimed her eyes blazing with temper.

"That is enough!" John slapped a heavy hand down on the table. His gaze traveled from Anne to Alexander then back again. "As you have said, Mary has endured enough. If the two of you can not find peace between you, Anne will remain here at Lorne until the spring and her father may come for her as well."

She paled, her lips tightening. "It is not my intent to cause my sister any more pain, Lord Campbell."

John's attention focused on her. "You are her sister, but you have no right to question the choices she has made." His gaze swung to Alexander. "She is my daughter now and I will not stand by and see her torn apart by the two of you fighting over her like a joint between two hounds."

Alexander frowned, but held his tongue.

"David, will you be joining us on the journey?" she asked, jumping into the silence that followed.

David's gaze turned to Alexander.

"Aye, he will," he said, his tone short.

David grinned.

Alexander pushed the trencher away, his appetite waning beneath the prospect of more of his in-laws presence about the castle. They would do all they could to turn Mary against him, he was certain.

****

Snow mixed with tiny pellets of ice powdered the horse's mane and lay in a thin coating on the sleeves of Alexander's thick fur robe. He squinted against the sting of the frozen mixture blowing directly in his face, his eyes watering.

The sky had been clear when they left Lorne, but the icy chill in the air had offered the possibility of bad weather. He chastened himself for ignoring those inner feelings of unease rather than allowing the desire to return home to sway him.

The well warn path covered by a layer of ice and snow made progress slow and dangerous. Alexander's mount stumbled and instinctively his thighs tightened to retain his seat while the animal regained its footing. They had to find shelter to wait out the storm.

His gaze searched the snow-dimmed hills for any possible cover. His attention returned again and again to the woman behind him. She huddled beneath the layer of her fur-lined cloak, head down, her body balled against the elements. As though in challenge the wind whipped more snow into the air and flung its icy breath against her with renewed effort.

Alexander brushed the cold-stung tears from his eyes and surveyed the surrounding timberland that followed the edge of the loch. A narrow icy projection of stone and earth forked upward onto a higher portion of the bank. The structure of the land caught his attention and He turned his mount in that direction.

The rocky ground slick, his vision obstructed by snow, he gave his mount its lead to pick the way forward. The hillside opened up into a hollowed out area with an overhanging projection of rock and vegetation. Beneath the outcropping shelter, he pulled the animal to a halt and dismounted. His leg had stiffened and he limped forward to grasp the reins of Anne's horse and lead it inside the alcove.

"David, see to the lass," he ordered as soon as his

brother came near.

The men did not have to be encouraged to set up camp. Some gathered the horses at one end of the depression while others laid and lit peat fires. The hillside curved around protecting the group from the full force of the wind. Snow lay in heavy banks against the rocks, shoring up one end and making it more impervious to the elements.

David, take the lass to that end," he ordered pointing to the far section. "'Tis more protected." He rubbed his thigh absently as he watched Anne's progress to the far end.

Guilt tweaked him. He should have waited to leave Lorne. This obsession with his own wife had led him to put himself and his men in danger. It was time he learned to control the feelings that clouded his judgment. It was a weakness.

He turned aside to help with the horses. He was responsible for the safety of his men; they had always been tantamount in his thoughts in the past. He would not allow this to happen again.

Chapter Twenty-three

"I do not wish her here, Gabriel!" Tira snarled from the open door of her hut. "Why have you brought her here?"

"The lad is ailing fiercely, Tira." The large man tried to push past her into the structure, but she resisted. "Lady Mary can help him, lass. Do you not ken that?"

"She will not help him, she will bring harm to him because of what Alexander and I shared," she accused, glaring at Mary.

"'Twould take a heartless beast to reap petty jealousies upon a helpless child, Tira." Mary said, anger at the woman bringing a surge of warmth to her cold face. "You and Gabriel will be here to see I do not do such a thing."

The wind thrust hard against them whipping snow and ice into the air and forcing itself beneath Mary's skirts and cloak. She sucked in her breath and turned her back to the gale.

"I do not know of cures and such. You could poison my son and I would not know what you were about."

Mary sucked in her breath again, this time against the blow of such an insult. She turned away, but Gabriel grasped her arm drawing her back. "I will be the first to drink of any cures she offers him. Would that ease your fears, Tira?"

Tira's green gaze went from his face to Mary's once again. "If my son dies because of her, 'twill be you and her I will hold at fault, Gabriel."

Anger hardened the man's features making him appear dangerous as his brown eyes went dark with emotion. "He may yet die because of your own stubborn pride, woman. Is that what you wish?"

"Nay!" she denied, her voice sharp. A sudden round of harsh coughing drew her attention. "Enter if you will, I must go to him." She stepped aside, leaving the door open behind her.

Gabriel urged Mary inside then shut and secured the door, sealing out the elements. The heat of the fire provided a welcome relief against the harsh breath of icy wind. Evidence of the fire that had burnt the interior of the room still blackened the stones of the hearth, but the walls had been plastered with a fresh layer of mortar and the log beams that held the roof put out a faint scent of freshly cut wood. A table with two chairs, a stool, a narrow bed, and a small wooden trunk were the only furnishings in the room along with an assortment of sundry housekeeping articles.

Shedding her outer layer of wrappings, Mary set aside the basket she carried. She strode forward to stand on the opposite side of the bed from Tira. Her attention focused on Cassidy as he wiggled fitfully beneath the pelts covering him trying to kick them away. His skin was flushed a fiery red, his eyes glassy and bright as he looked up for a moment then went back to his restless rocking.

"We must get his fever down," she said, urgency in her tone. "Gabriel, go outside and fill two buckets with snow and bring them in."

Her instructions were barely voiced before he rushed to do her biding.

Her attention focused on Tira. Have you any tartans about?"

"Aye. The woman moved to the chest and returned with the woolen blankets.

Mary threw back the heavy pelts and quickly encased the child in the wraps. Frightened by his sluggish movements and the heat emanating from his small body, she laid a soothing hand against his brow and murmured a few words of comfort as much to control her own racing heart as to ease the child.

"Spread it over the tartans then refill the buckets," she instructed when Gabriel returned. "I need a brazier with which to heat water and herbs. Once we have covered him with snow you must ride to the castle and return with one."

"Aye."

The three of them covered the restless child with a

layer of snow then Mary covered the bed with a heavy pelt. Within minutes, the child's cheeks became a less vivid color of red as his temperature lowered.

"Hurry now, Gabriel, the brazier."

He crossed the room with long quick strides slamming the door behind him.

Cassidy began to shiver beneath the weight of snow.

"He is too cold. We must take the snow off of him," Tira said, throwing back the pelt.

"Nay, not yet. We must first brew some willow bark to keep his fever down lest he become over-hot again," Mary said.

The boy began to cry. Tira turned to comfort her child.

Mary crossed to the hearth and dipped some water into a small pot there. She retrieved her basket and sorted through the contents setting several bundles on the hearth. She ground willow bark with a mortar and pestle then emptied the powder into a small square of fabric and bound the top. Dropping the pouch into the water, she set it over the fire to steep. In another vessel, she poured vinegar and ground licorice, setting it close to the flames to melt. She returned to the bed and placed a soothing hand on Cassidy's forehead to find him cooler to the touch. "We may remove the snow now," she said as she reached for the wooden bucket and began scooping snow off the cocooned child.

The sodden tartans replaced with dry ones, Cassidy seemed more comfortable. Mary poured the liquid over the fire into a wooden cup and set aside to cool. "'Tis willow bark tea. 'Twill help keep his fever from burning so hotly." She poured the melted licorice concoction into a similar vessel and put it on the table. "'Twill ease the cough and sooth his throat."

She drew a chair to take a closer look at the boy now his fever appeared temporarily under control. The freckles across his nose stood out against the paleness of his skin. His throat looked red and raw, his cough harsh and deep. Mary propped him up with pillows to make it easier for him to breath.

"Gabriel said you killed a man," Tira said. "A prisoner. One of your brother's men."

Mary flinched inwardly and remained silent for a moment, her attention focused on the child. "Aye."

"'Twill take more than that for you to be one of us."

Mary drew a deep breath and reminded herself she was here for the child's sake, not his mother's. "I did not do it to be one of you, Tira. I did it to protect Alexander and Grace from harm." She finally turned her head to look at the woman, but found only skepticism in Tira's green eyes.

They both turned as Gabriel entered the hut without knocking. He shook the snow from his hair and strode to Mary with a cloth sack. "Frazier sent a poultice he thought would do the lad good. 'Tis to be put on his chest."

Mary withdrew the metal brazier from the sack and a crockery jar sealed with a cloth.

"I will get the coals from the fire for you, Lady Mary," Gabriel said. He shook free of the heavy fur robe then reached for the metal disk fashioned to hold the coals. Mary rose to get water from the hearth. She ground more herbs and sprinkled them into the water then set it atop the brazier. Steam soon rose in the air close to the bed and a pungent smell filled the room.

She handed Gabriel the cup of willow bark tea. "'Tis to cool the lad's fever. Will you taste the brew?"

Gabriel didn't hesitate though he grimaced at the taste of the liquid. She repeated her request with the licorice laced cough remedy and he complied.

"If you are satisfied I am not trying to harm the lad, you may spoon both into his mouth, a few spoonfuls at a time," she said to Tira.

Gabriel lifted a heavy pot of water onto the hearth and hung it over the flame. Mary added more herbs to the water. The air in the room soon became muggy with moisture and heat.

She loosened the neckline of her surcoat as sweat beaded her skin. "'Twill be many hours before we may see a change. We must wait."

****

Alexander surveyed the camp from his perch on a rock ledge just above the camp. Snow coated the blankets of fur covering every man and beast. The animal's body heat offered them warmth and they in turn kept their mounts from freezing by sharing the protection of the pelts.

Though the worst of the storm had passed, the wind still blew quite fiercely. Early morning sunlight bathed the fresh banks of white with a reddish hue and the hillside cast purple shadows across the pristine surface.

Hugh arose and began rebuilding the fire. Soon others began to stir then wandered away from camp a short distance, seeking privacy to relieve themselves away from Anne. Derrick and Douglas passed out shares of bread and meat.

One after another, the horses were urged to their feet. The animals shook themselves then stomped their hooves as though to relieve cramped muscles from being forced to recline on the ground.

Alexander straightened from his position against one of the larger oaks and turned his attention to the north. Light reflected off something in the distance. He squinted against the sun's glare on the snow to focus on the area. Movement, faint and indistinct, brought tension to his muscles. He covered his mouth with the wool scarf about his neck and waited.

A shadow cast on the snow had him jerking the scarf down, cupping his hands around his mouth, and whistling a bird's call down toward the camp below him. The men moved quickly to arm themselves with swords and bows. With some difficulty, a group of six archers climbed the hill behind him. Alexander pointed northward and motioned for them to spread out and seek cover.

"'Tis the ones that attacked us," Derrick said in a whisper from beside him.

"Aye," he agreed, having recognized several of the horses. He weighed the wisdom of attacking in retaliation or letting the troop pass. Only three extra pack animals trailed behind them. They carried no extra bounty just water and food, thus there was no evidence they had attacked the village in their absence.

The band of men had become a distant ribbon of movement to the south before Alexander gave the signal to regroup below.

"I will not order any two of you to follow, but would ask for two to volunteer. I would know once and for all what clan 'tis that threatens us. We'll be prepared to deliver retribution to the ones responsible, when next we meet."

"I'll follow them, Alexander," James, one of the youngest clansmen, spoke.

"I suppose I too will have to go, to see he does not get captured," Robert, his brother, said.

Alexander eyed the two. Neither had a wife or children to consider. "I do not wish either of you to risk yourselves. You are to follow them, nothing more. You will return as soon as you might with word of where they go and who they meet."

The brothers nodded.

"'Tis I who will see to the care of your mother until your return," he assured them.

James grinned.

"Keep your hair covered lest they think you are some kin of mine," he teased, breaking the tension of the group.

He listened to the cautious advice offered by the other men as the two prepared to leave. Two of the men loaded a packhorse with provisions and extra pelts for them.

Once the two were mounted, Alexander tossed Robert a money pouch. "Lest you need food or shelter along the way."

"Where are they going?" Anne asked as the two rode out.

"To visit your father mayhap," he replied, "if 'tis where the clan they follow leads them."

"What reason would my father have to send men here?" Anne asked.

"Mary would not speak agin me so he could claim my lands and take my life in retribution. He challenged her good name and called her a whore." He acknowledged the shock that crossed her features with a nod. "Mary has broken her ties with him and no longer calls him father." He focused on the men as they readied the horses to leave.

"Should I be killed, Collin would not gain my land, but control of your sister once again. Mayhap to wed to Bearach MacDonald as he wished to do before." He turned his head just in time to catch a fleeting look on Anne's face that sparked an instant suspicion. Why *had* she arrived in so secret a manner? Her skin looked pale in the new morning light, her nose bright red from the cold.

"We will arrive at *Caisteal Sith* by midday," he relented then strode away to saddle his mount.

If he did not want to distance Mary, he would have to learn to control his resentment toward her sister and half-brother.

****

The heat in the room was stifling, the moisture thick. Cassidy heaved once again with a fit of coughing and spat into the cloth his mother held for him. The cough was no longer tight and unproductive, but loose and rattling.

"He is worse," Tira accused.

"Nay." Mary shook her head. "He is no longer drowning, but coughing the poisons up. His fever is down as well. We must continue until the coughing eases and the fever is gone."

"How long will that take, Lady Mary?" Gabriel asked.

"Mayhap three or four days." Mary stretched to ease the cramp in the small of her back and kneaded the tired muscles. They had all dozed in short intervals throughout the night, but not enough to bring them any rest. "You and Tira must sleep. I will stay with him and will wake her to take my place once you are both rested. You may take the night watch, Gabriel."

"Nay," Tira said in a harsh tone. "I do not wish her to be alone with him."

"Tira—" Gabriel began, his expression weary.

Mary shook her head. The fractious insult no longer stung, but sounded spiteful and foolish. "He is her child and she may choose whomever she likes to take my place. I will grind the herbs and show you what to do."

The storm had passed leaving a blanket of pristine white atop every surface. When they left Tira's hut, the evening shadows had already begun to lengthen and cast purple blotches across the new fallen snow. Mary covered her mouth with a tartan scarf to block the icy air for it almost hurt to breathe it. Had Gabriel not held her arm, she would have fallen several times along the way.

"'Tis sorry I am that Tira could not offer you thanks for what you have done for Cassidy, Lady Mary," he said.

"My thanks will come when he is well once again.

Take care he does not get chilled."

"Aye, I will."

At the muffled sound of horse's approaching behind them, they turned. She smiled as she recognized Alexander's mount, sweet relief sweeping through her in a rush. She and Gabriel stopped and waited for the column of men to reach them.

"What is amiss that you are out in such weather, Mary?" Alexander demanded as soon as he reached them.

"Tira's son, Cassidy, has been ailing fiercely, my lord. The three of us have been with him since yesterday morn," she explained.

A horse farther down the line moved forward. Her attention turned to it, then its rider. Shock held her immobile as Anne brought her mount to a halt before her and dismounted.

"Mary—"

Anne's voice broke the spell. Dropping her basket, Mary stepped forward to embrace her sister. Tears of pain and joy sprung to her eyes and ran unheeded down her cheeks. The two clung together for several moments.

"Is Ian with you?" Mary asked as they drew back to look into each other's faces.

Pain flickered across Anne's features. "He was killed a month ago."

"Oh, Anne." She embraced her sister again.

"Come, lasses. The castle is near and a warm hearth and meal beckons to us all," Alexander urged. "'Twill be easier to ride through the snow than to walk through it, Mary." He motioned for her to come to him.

Gabriel lifted Mary quite easily atop the horse in front of Alexander then helped Anne to remount.

Mary raised a hand in farewell to him. "Come for me should the lad grow worse," she called.

"Aye, my lady."

Mary's gaze returned to her husband's face as he kicked his mount forward. Darkness smudged the skin beneath his eyes and lines of exhaustion bracketed his mouth.

"It has been a hard journey for you. How did you find shelter during the storm?" she asked.

"'Twas luck that led us to an outcrop that offered

some shelter. We had to lie among the horses to keep warm."

"Was anyone hurt?" she asked.

"Nay, God smiled on us."

A relieved smile tugged at her lips. "And Anne?" she asked, curious as to how her sister had come to be with them.

"She was at Lorne when we arrived."

"How was Ian killed?"

"She has spoken of it only to say it was an accident. Mayhap she will tell you more." He changed the subject. "Has all been well with you, Mary?"

"Aye, but—my feet have been fiercely cold since you have been away," she teased.

His deep chuckle rumbled against her back and his arm tightened around her.

"I will see what might be done to warm them later, *leannan*."

Mary caught her breath at his use of the Gaelic endearment. He had called her "Wife" and "Lass", but never "Sweetheart". Pleasure bubbled forth and with it, the fragile hope, that he cared for her in some special way, rose up to warm her and bring a smile to her lips.

****

Alexander lifted Mary from the horse's back and set her on her feet. As he looked down into her face, it seemed he could see all the way to heaven in the depths of her pale blue eyes. She smiled and an instant hunger for the taste and feel of her slashed through him like a blade. He wanted to gather her up and carry her upstairs to their room. A sigh of exasperation escaped him. He had resolved to control his cravings for her and the moment he saw her, his will crumbled beneath the sweet feeling of homecoming he found in her smile, her presence.

"Welcome home, my lord," she said, her voice husky and soft. She surprised him by rising on tiptoe to place a sweet kiss on his lips.

He crushed her to him and slanted his mouth against hers with eager heat. Aye, he was home.

Chapter Twenty-four

Mary watched Gavin's swaggering progress down the wide stone steps of the great hall. He had been allowed to join them for meals in deference to Anne's presence, but his habit of baiting Alexander at every opportunity was growing tiresome. Thus far, her husband had shown restraint, but she was uncertain how much longer his patience would last. She prayed that, for once, her brother would forgo such sport and the evening would be a pleasant one for all.

Anne stepped forward to greet their brother bringing a smile to Mary's lips. They were together as a family as they had once been on MacPherson land. She gave Alexander's arm a squeeze and looked up at him with a smile. "Thank you for bringing my sister to me, Alexander."

"She is as stubborn as you. She would have journeyed here on her own had I not," he said dryly, a wry twist to his lips.

She laughed, the dull ache of fatigue plaguing her lower back, nearly forgotten in the pleasure of the moment.

"'Tis good to see you in such fine spirits, little sister," David said as he joined them.

"Aye, I am pleased to have family about me, David," she answered with a smile.

"That is good, Mary," Gavin said as he joined them. "The weather is not hearty enough to kick us out."

She chuckled at the quip.

"'Twould be a difficult task for me to leave through a locked door anyway," he dug, flashing Alexander a resentful look. Duncan appeared at the top of the stairs and lazily descended the stairs to join them.

Mary looked across the width of the table at Gavin as Alexander guided her to a seat on his right. Anne had sat at her hosts left since her arrival and the change drew Mary's immediate attention.

"I have no dagger with which to cut my meat, sweet Sister. Mayhap our host will serve us with his," Gavin said to Anne.

A sense of foreboding struck her at the gleam in her brother's blue eyes.

"'Tis a host's duty to see to his guest's comfort. 'Twill be no hardship to cut your meat, Gavin," Alexander said with easy grace.

Mary's gaze moved about the room in search of Fergus. The steward stood nearby observing the servant's progress as the meal was served, and at her signal, came forward.

"Is there something you wish, Lady Mary?"

"Fergus, may I use your dagger to sup?" she asked.

"For certes, my lady." He drew the knife and presented it to her handle first.

"Thank you, Fergus, I will see it returned to you."

He nodded and moved away to continue with his duties.

She placed the blade beside her and rose to withdraw her own dagger. "My dagger will serve you well, Gavin." She slid it across the table, giving him little choice but to accept it.

He raised his blond brows at the dainty blade clearly made for a woman's hand. "My thanks, Mary," he said after only a momentary pause. "Is it your custom then, to lock your guests within their chamber?" he asked, turning to Alexander.

"Nay, nor am I accustomed to being attacked by those who share my table and my food," he returned, his gaze level and sharp. "If such aggressions may be avoided between us, I see no reason why you can not move about the castle as the others do."

Gavin's gaze became speculative. "And if I choose to leave?"

"'Twill be your choice, but I would warn you the weather has turned vicious and your return to your clan, be it MacLachlan, MacPherson, MacDonald, or Fraser, would be a difficult journey."

Gavin's jaw tensed at Alexander's comment. He

236

turned away to say something to Anne.

Mary drew a relieved breath.

Alexander offered her a slight smile as his hand covered hers clenched on the table. He released it as a servant paused by his chair with a laden platter sporting a roasted leg of lamb. He cut a healthy portion of meat to share with Mary then another for both Gavin and Anne.

Gavin inclined his head at Alexander as he speared the slab with the dainty dagger and placed it in the trencher setting between him and his sister.

Mary relaxed a bit more when it seemed he was going to cease his tiresome behavior and extend some courtesy to her husband. Now that his position had changed from prisoner to guest, she hoped his disposition would be more amiable. She turned her attention to Alexander and offered him a smile.

"I know it has distressed you for your brother to be locked away, Mary. My men will still be watching him, but until he proves himself unworthy, I am willing to extend him his freedom."

"I will pray he does nothing to deny himself that privilege, but he is hot tempered and does not forgive easily."

"Aye," he agreed. "'Tis to my great, good fortune his sister is not so hard of heart." His amber gaze rested on her face for a long moment before he once again turned away to heap a healthy portion of vegetables atop the meat.

Had she indeed finally forgiven her husband? Learning to accept her feelings for him, had forced her to acknowledge that she had felt desire for Alexander from the moment they met. That admission had caused her more guilt and self-doubt. Had he somehow sensed her feelings and come to her that night because of them?

She wished she could stop seeking the answer to his actions and forget about it, but the need inside her persisted. There had to be a reason for his actions at Lochlan. She was determined to discover what it could have been.

"How fares the lad, Cassidy, Mary?" Duncan asked from beside her, distracting her from her thoughts.

She leaned aside as a servant brought the heavy

wooden platter of meat to the head table and left it there should anyone wish more. "He is much improved. Mayhap he will be healed completely in another week."

"I do not ken why you tend every lad and lass here, Mary," Gavin said, his frown fierce. "Do they not have another healer to seek in your stead?"

"As Lady of the castle, 'tis my duty, Gavin. You know well 'tis so," she answered, confused by his obvious anger.

"You have spent days nursing the son of your husband's whore, Mary. Where is your pride, lass?" he demanded, his cheeks flushed with ire.

Mary stiffened, caught off guard by both his knowledge of Tira's past with her husband, and his criticism.

Alexander grasped the thin end of the joint of mutton before him and swung it. The greasy limb struck Gavin squarely in the mouth sending him backward off the bench. He hit the stone floor with a meaty thump and lay momentarily stunned.

Alexander lunged to his feet, sending the heavy chair he sat in crashing to the floor. He stood over Gavin and pointed the roast at him like a club. "For your sister's sake, I have ignored the feeble barbs with which you have attempted to prick me, MacLachlan, but I will not abide you turning them agin your sister. I will warn you now, you will keep a civil tongue in your head when you address my wife, or you will be gumming your food for the rest of your days."

Gavin rolled to his feet, spitting blood from his mouth and taking on a fighting stance. The lower portion of his face shone greasy and red from the blow. A steady stream of blood trickled from his nose and he wiped it away with the sleeve of his shirt. "You have insulted my sister by having her care for the likes of them, for even allowing the woman to remain in your village. Or is it you have not set her aside?"

The room behind them, having at once grown quiet at the disruption, came alive with hurried sounds as the men abandoned their meal and began to crowd around the two.

Mary hastened from her seat to try to get between the men and prevent further aggressions. She found her way barred by Duncan and shoved ineffectually against her brother-in-law's broad chest as he attempted to hold her back.

"'Tis a danger to you and the bairn to come between the two of them, Mary," he warned.

"Mary chooses who she will tend, not I," Alexander said as the two began to circle each other. "I do not force her to do anything."

"For certes you put an end to that when you forced your bairn upon her," Gavin taunted. "The child is the only reason Mary serves you now, Campbell. She will abide any insult to remain with it, as well you know. "

Alexander's features took on a hard look; his gold eyes gleamed with rage. "Enough!" He tossed the joint of meat back onto the table. It landed with a soft thump amidst the partially filled trenchers. "You have wanted a fight since first we met, MacLachlan, you may have it." He flicked his fingers motioning for Gavin to attack if he dared.

Gavin though smaller in stature, was agile and quick, but he lacked the experience of a seasoned warrior. Alexander, taller and heavier, and with much more fighting experience, easily had the advantage. The blood lust Mary read in both their faces promised only grief for all. She wiggled and twisted against Duncan's restraining grip and finally raised her arm where he grasped it and sank her teeth into his wrist. He jerked his hand back with an oath, releasing her.

Just as the two opponents tensed to spring forward at each other, Mary stepped between them. "Cease," she shouted loud enough to be heard above the taunting chorus of encouragement the men had begun to call out.

"Mary!" Anne's voice, raised in anxious warning, came from behind her.

"Move, Woman!" Alexander roared.

"Do you mean to hide behind a woman's skirts, Campbell?" Gavin sneered.

"'Tis you she's protecting, fool," Alexander said.

Badly frightened by how close she had come to being crushed by the two of them, Mary's brow grew moist with sweat and her heart beat heavily against her ribs. She clenched the fabric of her surcoat to still the trembling of her hands. "If 'tis in defense of my honor the two of you will fight, 'tis I who deserve the right to choose the weapons, and the place at which the battle will be fought."

Alexander's gaze leaped to her face in surprise. Gavin straightened from his half-crouched stance, his expression a mirror of his opponents.

Mary's gaze moved from Alexander's features to her brother's then back again. "Will you agree to my wish?"

Alexander folded his arms before him, his gaze locked on her, unreadable and still.

She prayed he would agree. She could not prevent them from fighting, but she could possibly prevent them from damaging each other overmuch. Her gaze met her husband's.

"Aye," Alexander said, his tone flat.

Gavin nodded reluctantly.

"Since the two of you have already seen fit to disrupt our meal, you may prepare to fight as soon as we have finished eating. A full belly will not hinder either of you, will it?"

"Nay," Gavin answered.

She nodded. "Since 'twas you who has persisted in causing strife at our table, I would ask you to finish your meal elsewhere, Gavin."

His features tightened in renewed rage, his hands fisting at his sides. "How much more are you willing to abide to keep the peace, Mary? Will you allow him to rob you of your pride as well as your honor?"

She flinched from the words as quick tears burnt her eyes.

She held Alexander back when he stepped forward intent on coming to her defense in a more physical manner.

"Enough, Gavin," Anne stepped forward. "'Tis you, now, who dishonors Mary by attacking her before this company."

"Will you too be taking his side agin me, Anne?" he demanded.

"'Tis Mary's side I will be standing on, Gavin," she retorted. "Agin the both of you."

He backed away with a snort and stormed back up

the stairs of the great hall.

After a lengthy pause, the men began to return to their seats. Uncertain of her composure, Mary avoided looking directly at anyone as she returned to her place at the head table. When she could bring herself to look at Alexander, it was to find him studying her, his features harsh, his amber gaze alight with some emotion she could not decipher.

They finished the meal in silence.

****

Alexander focused his attention on his men as they positioned the tables in the great hall along the walls of the structure leaving the central part of the floor open for the fight that would soon ensue.

He had been stunned at Mary's desire to see them do battle. Did she still harbor some need for revenge against him? Was that the reason she had proclaimed the right to choose the place and the weapons for such an event? He felt as though he had been kicked in the chest by a horse, so deep was the pain of her betrayal. He had thought himself forgiven, accepted, no matter how uncertain he had been of the depth of her affections. He had been wrong.

If he were forced to kill her brother, how then would she feel about him? Or did she believe Gavin had a chance to defeat him? Which one of them did she hope would survive?

His gaze traveled restlessly about the room. His attention fell on Gavin as he stood by the fireplace at one end of the room. The lad looked pale, but composed, his features under careful control. His lips looked swollen and red and his chin misshapen and blue with a bruise.

He did not doubt Gavin had courage, but he allowed his anger and pride to rule his actions. He had yet to acquire the patience or the prudence of a seasoned warrior. It would be a shame to see his young life end after only a score of years.

Fergus appeared from the back entrance of the room. With a lump of charcoal, he drew two lines on the stone floor. The black marks traveled from one end of the room to the other a fair distance apart.

Alexander had only time to wonder what he was

about when Duncan strode forward to stand at the center of the room. His features set in somber lines, he motioned for Alexander and Gavin to join him.

"Alexander Campbell, you have come before this company to fight in defense of your honor and the honor of Mary Campbell, your wife."

Surprised by the formality of the proceedings he nodded. "Aye, I have."

"Gavin MacLachlan, you have come before this company to fight in defense of your sister's honor and your own."

"Aye, I have."

"The rules of engagement shall be—"

The men who lined the room drew closer.

"You may not cross the lines drawn at the center of the floor. All weapons must be used only once and cannot be retrieved to be used again. The first to draw blood will be declared the winner and all hostilities shall cease betwixt you." Duncan's gaze traveled from one man's face to the other. "Will you agree to this and speak an oath to that before this company?"

So, this one battle was to bring an end their differences. Alexander looked to the younger man. He could not see the hatred the lad held for him ending so easily. If he lived.

"Aye," he nodded, "I will pledge my oath."

"Aye," Gavin said impatiently, his pale blue eyes, so much like his sisters, gleaming with excitement. "I too will pledge."

"The weapon Lady Mary has chosen shall be—" Duncan paused for effect, "platters."

A deafening silence fell across the crowd, then a roar of laughter echoed through the chamber as the men gave vent to their amusement.

"What jest is this? Platters!" Gavin exclaimed. "They are not weapons."

"Aye, they are in your sister's hands," Alexander said, fighting the urge to grin.

Gavin turned away with a look of disgust.

Several servants converged on the hall laden with stacks of wooden platters and bowls.

Alexander watched as Mary entered the room behind

them. She crossed the hall and made her way to the stairway leading to the gallery above. She took cover behind the banister railing, one step above her sister.

Alexander stepped to the stack of wooden platters of all shapes and sizes. He chose a small oval, on which butter was usually served and hefted it in his hand. The men scattered for cover behind the tables that lined the walls.

"Let us see if we may have better aim than your sister, Gavin," he challenged. With a graceful flip of his wrist, the platter flew across the room with the speed of an arrow.

Gavin jerked to one side avoiding being hit by a narrow margin. A smile twisted his lips and he laughed. "If that is the best you may offer, 'twill be a short fight, Campbell." He wasted no time arming himself with one of the wooden disks.

The two began to throw the unlikely weapons at one another with dizzying speed. The force at which the wood struck the stone walls of the hall sent splinters flying in all directions, peppering the floor and the men's clothing and hair.

Alexander hurled a large meat tray with a spinning fling. It sailed through the air to collide in mid-flight with a lighter weight bowl. Chunks of wood from the smaller vessel bombarded the group of men behind one of the large tables. A brief cry of pain and an oath followed. The tray landed with a heavy thump on the table then slid off one side striking something with a meaty whack.

"Take greater care Alexander lest we have nothing to eat our hodge-podge from on the morrow, nor anyone left to eat it," Tobias called out.

Gavin spun another bowl in his direction. Alexander batted it away with a large serving bowl he held like a shield. He cast a small vessel in retaliation. The dish struck Gavin in the top of the head with a loud pop and a brief exclamation of pain escaped him.

"From the sound of it, there may be nothing betwixt your ears, but a hollow skull," Alexander taunted, then quickly danced out of the way of a rectangular tray that spun a wobbly path past him to strike the wall. A corner broke off, flipping through the air dangerously close to his face.

Momentarily distracted by the flying debris, he did not see, but heard the whirl of the large platter just before it struck the floor at his feet. He leaped in an attempt to avoid it, but the momentum of the disk thrust his feet from beneath him. He twisted and fell, hitting the stone floor buttocks first with a jarring impact, his teeth snapping shut with a loud click.

"I can see 'twas not for your grace my sister wed you, Campbell," Gavin said, laughing openly.

His backside numb from the blow, Alexander reached for the first weapon at hand and slung it backhanded as he attempted to get to his feet.

The small round dish caught Gavin squarely on the knee and he yelped in pain and grabbed the injury as he hopped on one foot.

"I do not know you were a dancer, Gavin. 'Twill impress the lasses at the next feast," Alexander quipped through gritted teeth as he regained his feet. He felt the after effects of the fall from his backside to the top of his head. Turning his pain aside, he reached for a large bowl.

Gavin, red of face and favoring his leg, armed himself with one as well. Hampered by his injured knee, he could not move as quickly as before and thus was an easier target. Alexander managed to clip his arm with the weighty container then dodged away when Gavin retaliated with his own. They exchanged several throws that missed. Alexander loosed a thin wooden platter skimming Gavin's brow before he could duck away. A fine stream of blood poured forth down the lad's cheek to his chin.

Mary was on her feet at once crying, "Cease! Blood has been struck."

Alexander strode toward his opponent and guiding his arm over the back of his neck, he offered the other man support.

"I do not know if I could be so gracious a winner, Campbell," Gavin said, accepting his help. "But I have given my oath and I'll abide by it, for Mary's sake."

The men rose and came forth in mass to thump the two of them on the back and congratulate them both on a battle well fought.

Mary and Anne thrust their way to the center of the crowd bearing basins and cloths to tend Gavin's injures as a chair was brought forth for him to sit.

"How do you fare, Alexander?" Mary asked. Anne began wiping away the blood on Gavin's cheek.

"I am no worse than I deserve to be, for letting my guard down," he said with a rueful grin as he rubbed his bruised backside.

She brushed away the splinters of wood from his shoulders and hair.

"I fear my injuries may have to be tended in private, Mary," he murmured close to her ear. A bright blush stained her cheeks.

****

"Ah, lass, your hands truly have magic within them," Alexander sighed in pleasure as Mary's fingers found the spot along his spine where a dull ache continued to plague him. The fall that evening had left him feeling sore in places he tried hard not to notice.

"You have more than a few bruises, my lord," she observed, her fingers lightly touching a blue mark along the top of his shoulder.

"'Twas from flying bits of wood. I have bruises in places rubbing will do no good."

She chuckled. "I did not think harm could be caused by the service in the aumry."

"Aye, I know." Alexander rolled over to look up at her. The sense of betrayal he had felt earlier had faded away. She had chosen the weapons to try to spare them both. That had become clear to him the moment Duncan had made the announcement. Her tender heart made her too vulnerable to hurt. He could no more protect her from that, than she could protect herself.

"'Tis the nature of man to destroy himself, Mary. You can not prevent it."

"Aye, I know," she said with a sigh.

The wistful look in her pale blue eyes drew him to a seated position to brush back the silvery blond strands from her shoulder. Light from the fire brought sparks of life to the wavy tresses. The white shift she wore skimmed her body, outlining the generous thrust of her breasts and the swollen distention of her belly. Every time he looked at her he felt moved by both tenderness and passion. Never had a woman made him feel so much.

"'Twould seem 'tis the nature of man to show trust to their women only within their bedchamber," she said softly.

He hesitated. "'Tis because 'tis hard for me to believe you have truly forgiven me, Mary."

She fell silent for a moment. "At first I did not believe I could." Her throat worked as she swallowed.

The pain she experienced each time they spoke of it stilled the words he wanted to say. If only he could explain to her—He slipped an arm about her to draw her close and hold her. He stroked the shining hair at the back of her head, his lips brushing her temple. The babe moved between them with surprising strength. She drew back allowing him to rest a hand on her abdomen, to feel a tiny limb press outward toward his touch. The emotions rising within him in that moment were a jumble of tenderness and wonder. If this fragile life they had made together was the only reason she served him, it was good as any. He could learn to live with that. Or could he?

Mary leaned forward to brush his lips with her own. Her mouth moist and parted, she found the bruise she had discovered earlier. With delicate pressure to his chest, she urged him to lie back. She found another mark on his ribs and treated it to the same caress. Her tongue sought his button flat nipples, sending a lancing heat down to his groin leaving him hard and aching.

Thus far, he had always been the aggressor in their lovemaking. The fact that she was taking the initiative excited him beyond measure. The silken length of her hair lay against his skin, pale and soft, against the darker matt on his chest. Her tongue followed a straight path down the center of his belly to his navel, delving within, and then circling it.

She dipped lower, and her mouth, wet and warm, closed around him, and a raw wild pleasure lanced through him. The act of drawing breath became difficult. A groan of arousal worked its way up from his very depths. He could not bear such sensual torture for long and also retain control. His hands reached for her, guiding her upward so his mouth could claim hers. The frantic, beat of his heart settled over hers as he turned, shifting her beneath him. Unable to wait, he thrust deep then drew back to looked down into her face. "A man could die from such pleasures," he complained through breathless tones.

"I will remember that," she threatened raising her hips in challenge, spurring him on.

A blessed time later, their passion spent, they held each other as sleep hovered.

"How now does your injury feel, Alexander?" she asked, her hand caressing one cheek of his buttocks.

He laughed. "'Tis cured, lass. 'Tis cured."

Chapter Twenty-five

Alexander's gaze followed David, Duncan, and Gavin as they rode across the glen from the east. From where he stood atop the battlements, he could see at least two red deer hung across the backs of the horses. His eyes swept the verdant landscape. After a long tedious winter, spring had blossomed with a vengeance. The May Day feast was almost upon them.

He turned, intent on making his way down to the solar where he had seen Mary and Anne sewing earlier. As he descended the stairs the women's laughter, high and sweet, reached him, and he smiled. Mary laughed more oft since her sister's arrival, and her smiles came more easily. After nearly three month's beneath his roof, Anne seemed to have lost some of her enmity for him as well. They had been so graced with good fortune, he felt almost wary that some pestilence might befall them to end it.

His gaze sought Mary as soon as he entered the solar. She sat in a high backed wooden chair, her feet propped on a small stool. She had blossomed as the snows had begun to melt and small flowers had made their appearance across the hills. Another two weeks would see her delivered of their child.

Anne rose from her seat, opposite Mary, and poured a tankard of ale and brought it to him.

He murmured his thanks with a smile. "Tis good to hear such laughter, lasses. Will you share the jest?"

"'Twas Tobias," Mary explained, then began to smile. "He has made the bairn a wee gift. She offered him the small object wrapped in bit of cloth. Alexander folded back the fabric then chuckled. Within his palm rested a small wooden oblong shaped disk. A platter in miniature.

"He said 'twas for the bairn to practice with, so he might become more able than his father or uncle."

248

"Twill be used for him to teethe upon most likely," he commented.

"Or her," Anne pressed.

"'Twould please me to have a daughter with her mother's eyes and hair," he said.

Mary looked up at him in surprise. "I thought you wished a son, Alexander."

"Nay, lass. I wish a healthy bairn, be it a lad or a lass does not matter. If you are not pleased with what you are given, mayhap we may try again for another." He smiled at the blush that tinted her cheeks.

"Mayhap Mary will have something more to say on the matter after birthing this one," Anne suggested.

He frowned. That was something that had not occurred to him. Curbing his needs, for a short time before the birth, had thus far, not been too difficult. Being denied her sweet body for a lengthy a time, after the birth, brought him real concern.

His gaze went to Mary to find her fighting a smile. His expression must have been easily read for the two women laughed aloud.

The fact that she jested about the subject brought a smile to his lips. Aye, they had traveled a long journey together and had found some contentment with one another.

He took his leave of the women a few moments later and made his way down to the stables. Waving to Corey, busy trimming a horse's hooves, he entered the stables. He paused at the stall and lifted the slat that held the door closed.

"Greetings, Alexander," Tira murmured softly. Her musky scent teased his nostrils as she came to stand close beside him.

He found himself stepping away a pace. "What are you about, lass?" he asked.

"'Tis been some months, since we last spoke. 'Twas my hope you had made some decision about Cassidy."

He relaxed somewhat, though a frown worked its way across his brow. "'Twas my hope you would change your mind about sending the lad away, Tira."

"Does he not deserve to be rewarded for his father's service to you. And my own?" she asked, her green eyes focused on his face intently.

He nodded, the movement abrupt. "The Mayday feast is, but a week hence. I will see to it then." He began to turn away only to feel her hand grasp his arm.

"Lady Mary has grown large with child. 'Tis difficult for a lass so well bairned to see to her husband's needs." Tira grasped his hands and stepping forward she guided his arms about her waist. Pressing her full breasts against him, she slid her arms about his neck. "'Twould not be a hardship for me to serve you once again, Alexander. Remember how good 'twas before." Her lips found his throat.

Surprise held Alexander still beneath the woman's blatant invitation. Her hand snaked downward to his groin. A feeling akin to revulsion rushed over him, and he grasped her wrist. She clung to him like a vine, cloying and obstinate. With greater force, he grasped her upper arms and set her away for him. "Nay, Tira." His voice was sharp. "I do not need, nor want your attentions. I do not want any woman, but Mary."

Tira staggered back a few paces as though he had struck her. At first, her features started to crumble, then her anger flared and her lips twisted in a spiteful grimace. "She will not ever love you, as I have. May God strike her dead before she does." She shoved past him to the open doorway of the stables.

Her steps faltered, and Alexander looked up to see Gavin, Duncan, and David behind her in the doorway. And still worse, behind them stood Gabriel, his features slack with shock. With a sound somewhere between a shriek and a sob, she thrust between the men and ran away from them all.

Silence followed her departure, broken by the hollow rasp of Corey still working on the horse's hooves outside. Alexander's gaze moved past his brother's and Gavin to the large man behind them. "Gabriel—" he began only to cut himself off as the man raised a hand.

"'Twould be a service to us all, and to her, if you would send her back to her own kin, Alexander." He turned abruptly and walked away.

Alexander slammed the heel of hand against the stall door, rattling it on its hinges and startling the horse within.

"He is right, Alexander," Duncan said, his tone grave. She will not forget or forgive you for spurning her. Nor us for hearing and seeing you do so."

****

Mary tapped her foot to the lively tune being played by flute and fiddle as she watched the dancers weave in and out around the maypole. The graceful, light bands of color they held fluttered up and down with their movements. Sunlight reflected off the ribbons and dappled the women's faces and clothing with color. Their skirts bounced about their ankles, and the green sashes about their waists swung merrily with their steps.

When they could weave the pole no farther, they turned and began to unwind their handiwork, their movements practiced and sure. As the long streamers straightened completely from the pole, the music ended and the dancers kneeled. The crowd of onlookers clapped and cheered their appreciation, as did Mary and Duncan.

Mary wiggled on her seat to lean back a little as a tiny foot seemed to wedge itself beneath her ribs and push downward. She absently rubbed the spot until the babe eased its painful stretch and curled into a more comfortable position.

"You are not growing tired, are you, lass?" Duncan asked from beside her.

She grimaced. "Nay, I have not done enough to grow tired. I have barely had my feet on the ground this week past."

"I have warned Alexander of the dangers of encouraging a lazy wife but he will not heed them," he said, his features stern.

She smiled at Duncan's teasing and wriggled forward to the edge of the wooden bench. "I should like to walk about and enjoy the festivities for a wee bit, Duncan."

He chuckled and offered her a hand to rise.

They wandered down a meandering path through the village and paused beside a field where a group of young men played a game. The large stone they threw landed dangerously close to one of them, but he seemed not to notice. Mary shook her head at the folly of manhood. Even in play, they courted danger. Worry over Alexander's continued absence plagued her. He had ridden out with twenty of the men soon after the morning meal. There were riders on their way to the castle.

Recognizing one of the men in the game, Mary said, "'Tis good that James and Robert are back among us. It has been a lonely winter for their mother without them."

"Aye. They could not make the journey back until the snows ended."

"Where did they journey that it took so long a time to return?" she asked, curious. They began to stroll once again.

"Mayhap you should ask Alexander, Mary. 'Tis he who sent them."

His unwillingness to answer her question surprised her. "The day after they arrived home, they spent a long while with Alexander. Mayhap they brought news of your father, though Alexander did not speak of it."

"He will be journeying here within the week. He is anxious to be here for the birth of the bairn, as is Grandmother."

Mary gave a sigh. "I feel a wee bit like a pot everyone is watching in hope that 'twill soon boil."

Duncan laughed aloud.

She looked forward to the birth with a combination of eagerness and fear. It would be a relief to be able to walk with grace once again, or to lie or sit without discomfort. It had been two weeks since she and Alexander had made love. Though he continued to hold her at night, she missed the special closeness of their bodies blending. She worried that now she could no longer serve him, he would seek another to fill his needs.

As she and Duncan wound their way through the village, Mary found herself searching for a glimpse of Tira. Though she knew he had ridden out with his men, if she could see the woman, it would put her fears to rest.

Only a few moments had passed when she spied Tira's dark hair and dusky skin through the crowd. She stood before an open fire in the village square sampling the roasted joint of meat for the feast. The May Queen crown of woven vines and leaves suited her well. She had fashioned her hair atop her head, and because of the heat, had loosened the laces at the front of her gown, baring the scooped neckline of her kirtle. The heat from the fire had brought a fine mist of sweat to her skin. She looked beautiful and pagan. Mary noticed several men watching her with open interest. Even Duncan's attention wandered to her and paused for a moment, a frown creasing his brow.

As though she felt their attention on her, Tira raised her head and looked up. Her gaze skittered away from Duncan to rest on Mary with open enmity for a brief moment. Her chin rose and she gave a gloating smile. She had been chosen May Queen by the men and villagers early that morn. Mary wondered if her eminent departure from their midst might have guided the choice. She would be relieved to see the back of the woman.

The sound of approaching horses proved a welcome distraction from her thoughts. She turned to look up the village street. Alexander's mount rounded the bend and her smile broke forth at sight of him, then died as shock overwhelmed her relief. Beside him, on the chestnut gelding she had once stolen, rode Collin and next to him, riding a black horse with white stockings, was Bearach MacDonald.

Alexander reined to a halt beside her and Duncan, and the rest of the men, about fifty in all, did as well. Mary's gaze sought her husband's. His expression appeared bland enough, but a warning glint shown from his tawny eyes.

"Greetings, Daughter," Collin said, nodding to her.

Mary turned her attention to him, her features stiff. Distrust and wariness rose like a shield within her. "Why are you here, Collin?" The bluntness of her tone held no welcome.

"I have come for the birth of my grandchild."

"Why?" she asked again, her mind seeking an answer before he could reply.

"You are one of my only daughters, Mary. I wished to be here with you at such a time."

She no more believed that, than she believed the sky was brown and the earth blue. Her gaze went to Bearach MacDonald. His barrel shaped body looked clumsy on a horse. A beard, as shaggy as his black hair, covered most of his heavy, round jaws. His small, close-set eyes focused

253

on her belly with blatant interest and his ugly features settled into a smile just short of a leer.

"Why have you brought a MacDonald here for such an event?" she asked. "'Tis certes, I am, that he would have no interest."

"On the contrary, Lady Mary. Since I was at Lochlan the night the seed was planted, it seems fitting I should be here for the harvest as well."

Though his choice of words were spoken in a jesting tone, there seemed an implication of something more behind them. Her cheeks grew hot with color and her temper flared. Alexander's features looked carved from stone when she glanced in his direction.

"Duncan, return with Mary to the castle. We will have company for the feast," he said, his tone curt. He kicked his mount forward, leading the way.

"Collin would not be here lest he had something to gain from it," She said before the troop had even disappeared from sight. She walked quickly back the way they had strolled."He is not to be alone with my sister or me, Duncan. Nor is Bearach. Will you guard Anne whilst he is here?"

"Aye, if 'tis what you wish."

"Aye, 'tis." Her gaze swung upward to his face. "'Tis for Anne he has journeyed here. He will try to force her to accept Bearach, if he can. I must go to her and warn her."

Out of breath by the time they reached the cart, she paused to rub at the painful stitch in her lower abdomen. She breathed a sigh of relief as Duncan helped her atop the seat of the small conveyance. Anxious for her sister, for the first time, she resented Alexander's insistence she not ride horseback.

"Anne went riding with David, Mary." Duncan settled on the seat beside her. "They are probably at the castle awaiting our return by now."

"We will look in the stables to see if their horses are there. If not, you must send one of the men to warn her." A feeling of urgency made her impatient to be there. She gripped the seat as Duncan clicked to the small pony and shook the reins, sending him forward.

****

Mary drew several deep breaths to still her racing

heart and trembling limbs. She composed herself with an effort.

"Are you ready, lass?" Duncan asked as he grasped the handle of the heavy door to the great hall.

She gave a nod. Straightening her spine and raising her chin, she entered the chamber. Her gaze swept over the many servants hanging the greenery, gathered that morn, about the hall, to settle on the three men who stood before one of the huge fireplaces. Anne was not among them and she breathed a sigh of relief. Mayhap she was in her chamber changing after her ride.

The light pressure of his hand against the small of her back urged her forward. With leaden feet, she moved toward the group. The three held tankards of ale, and as they drew near, a servant brought meat pies, bread, and cheese to a table nearby.

"I would hope for a more cordial greeting now, Mary," Collin said, his tone stern. "'Tis certes, I am, your aunt trained you in the ways of making a guest welcome."

Alexander laid a hand against her waist at the same time Duncan stepped next to her. Comforted by their support, she drew another steadying breath.

"'Twould seem you have already had your needs seen to, Collin. What more do you wish?" she asked in a bland tone.

Though his jaw tensed, he conceded the point.

"I will see to having your chambers readied then."

Bearach drank deeply from the tankard he held then wiped his mouth with the back of his sleeve. "Where is your sister? I would greet Anne, were she here."

"She has gone riding and will be back shortly." The lie came easily. With a brief glance up at Alexander and Duncan and a nod to the two other men, she excused herself.

She climbed the stairs as quickly as her bulky condition would allow. A cramp once again settled in her lower abdomen as she reached the passageway to Anne's chamber. She paused to catch her breath and let it ease then moved on. Giving the door a cursory knock, she opened the portal and slipped into the room. A movement from the bed drew her attention, and she strode toward it. Shock halted her steps in mid stride then held her frozen.

Her cheeks flushing a hectic red, Anne held a pelt high against her bare breasts. Ignoring his own nudity, David placed a comforting hand on her bare shoulder, the gesture protective. His features settled into a frown so much like his brother's, Mary felt her shock ease. She knew well the Campbell charm, and the passion it could inspire.

Her attention returned to Anne. "Collin has arrived and awaits you in the great hall, Anne. Bearach is with him."

Anne jerked as though stung by some unseen wasp.

"Be at ease, lass," David soothed. "He will not take you from me."

His tone brought a smile to Mary's lips. She turned away to give them the privacy they needed to rise.

"Mary," Anne's voice, tentative and soft, followed her to the door.

She turned to look over her shoulder. Her sister's anxious expression had her smiling. "'Twould be a good time to announce a betrothal," she said and left the room, shutting the door behind her.

Chapter Twenty-six

Alexander's gaze circled the great hall. Though the May Day feast represented a time of celebration, the men were quiet and subdued, as were the many villagers present. Mary signaled for the music to begin in order to fill in for the lack of revelry. Food was abundant and as the many dishes were served, the act of eating gradually helped to relax the tension between Campbell and MacLachlan clansmen at some of the outer tables. The low rumble of voices grew audible.

"How did you journey here to *Caisteal Sith*, Lady Anne?" Bearach asked. "My men and I came to pay our respects after Ian's death and you had already left the MacMillan stronghold."

"Ian's men brought me to Castle Lorne and Alexander brought me to Mary," she answered, her attention on the food she shared with David. Her features though composed, looked pale, and she did not readily meet Bearach's gaze.

"Nor did I get to offer you my comfort for more than a day, Daughter," Collin added. "'Twould seem you and your sister have no trouble stealing away whenever you wish."

"Mayhap the comfort you offered was not what I needed, Collin," Anne said, her gaze hostile. "I wished to be with my sister."

"There is something unnatural in the need the two of you have to always be about one another."

"'Tis called love, Collin," Mary said, her voice quiet and even. Her eyes remained on his face for a moment. "Had you not fostered us so young, you may have learned to feel more affection for us. If you had, you would not have to question us about our need of one another."

For once, he seemed at a loss for a reply. "When we journey home, Anne, you will be accompanying me," Collin said, "You must know your place is there, now you are widowed."

"My place is where I might choose it to be, Father. Mary wishes me to stay, and I shall."

Collin's features grew red at her defiance.

Alexander broke in before the older man could vent his spleen, "You are here for the birth of your grandchild, and that may take several days yet. There is time to discuss this further later."

"'Twill be time soon enough, Collin," Bearach said from beside him.

A servant began to refill the tankards around the table. "Did you have any trouble along the way to *Caisteal Sith*, Collin?" Alexander asked, changing the subject, "'Twould seem there are men about bent upon mischief and thievery. My men and I killed eight of them whilst journeying from Lorne with Mary. She came close to injury because of them." His gaze settled on Collin's face probing the older man's features.

"'Twas a blessing the lass was not harmed," Collin said as he took a sip of the brew.

"Aye, 'twas. We saw another band crossing Campbell holdings just after the winter snows set in. They wore no clan markings, but journeyed in the direction of Lochlan."

Anne head went up and she frowned, her blue eyes going to her father's face, with open interest.

"We had no such trouble, Alexander." Collin's attention fastened on him. "How do you know they were bound for Lochlan?"

Alexander studied him a moment longer. "I sent two men to follow them from afar. 'Twould seem a group broke away to visit Lochlan Castle, whilst the rest traveled on to MacDonald land." He raised one brow in inquiry.

"I remember no such visitors arriving at the castle, Alexander. Mayhap they sought shelter from the snow until the weather improved." Collin said, his features bland.

"The rest traveled on to your land, Bearach," Alexander continued, his gaze going to MacDonald.

The man shrugged his broad shoulders. "My men did not report such trespassers to me."

"Mayhap you should both take more care in offering shelter to strangers," Alexander suggested. He took a bite of venison then chewed it slowly. "'Tis of interest that Gavin's men journeyed the same route. Once they arrived, they did not travel on, but seemed at home amongst your clans."

A beat of silence followed his words. Gavin's gaze rose to Alexander's face then went to his father's.

Collin's blue gaze remained bland. "Of course I could not turn away my son's men to freeze in the snow, Alexander, nor would Bearach."

Alexander chose his words carefully. "Having so great an understanding of duty, you will respect the oath I have given to Anne that she shall remain under my protection until she decides to take her leave."

Mary's hand rested on his thigh beneath the table in silent communication. Anne's gaze moved to Alexander's face and a look of relief swept her features though she appeared pale.

Collin's brows drew together in a frown. "Her place is at Lochlan now she has no guidesman."

"As she has mentioned herself, now she is a widow, she has no duty to anyone, but herself," Alexander said with a shrug. "I have a duty to protect and provide for her now she is part of my clan, as Mary's sister. But of course, you may be able to persuade her differently."

Collin turned red in the face. "'Twas not your place to give such an oath."

His patience at an end with bating the older man, Alexander suppressed his irritation with an effort. "Once an oath is given, 'tis difficult to rescind. Mayhap you will have better luck persuading Anne to change her mind, than you did Mary. In any case, I have given my pledge and only Anne may release me from it," he repeated, his tone even.

****

Servants cleared the tables at the meals conclusion. The music became more exuberant as the dancing began. Mary grew restless as the ache in her back intensified and her chair became more and more uncomfortable.

"'Tis grateful I am, Alexander," Anne offered from close beside her. "Ian was a good man and a kind husband, but I will not be bartered into marriage again," she declared, her tone adamant as her gaze fastened on her father.

Collin's gaze narrowed. "'Tis a woman's place to wed and bring bairns into the world."

"Aye," Anne agreed. "And I shall wed again and have many bairns, Collin, with whomever I choose. I have done my duty by you, and your clan. I owe you nothing more." She turned away and stalked away from the table to be swallowed up by the crowd.

Mary bowed her back, her fingers kneading the taunt muscles to ease her discomfort. Alexander turned to her, concern in his expression. Mary offered him a reassuring smile. "'Tis but a wee ache from walking about too much. I must go to our chamber for a short while." He rose to accompany her, but Mary waved him back down. "You must stay and watch over Collin and Bearach. I do not trust them."

The pain had eased by the time she reached her chamber. Of late, she had experienced so many odd discomforts, she shrugged this current one aside. It would do her no harm to lie down for a few moments. Removing her shoes, she stretched out and covered herself with the tartan fabric at the foot of the bed. The music below, though barely discernable, provided a comforting beat as she drew deep breaths to relax the tension from her body.

****

"Anne will not be pleased with Bearach's efforts, I am certes," Duncan said dryly.

Alexander's attention fell on the rotund man speaking with her, his lips curling as Anne shook her head in an adamant gesture.

"Nor will David," Alexander commented. He grew more serious. "The men have been warned to keep watch over the MacLachlan clansmen's movements as well as Collin's and Bearach's. "Collin will not be content to use persuasion now she has openly defied him. We must all keep watch over her."

His gaze moved to Tira as she joined one of the village men in a dance. The May Queen crown of interwoven branches and leaves perched on her dark head, had his jaw tightening. Because she would be leaving soon, the villagers had shown their appreciation of her by crowning her May Queen. Her dark hair swung

free about her hips as she circled her partner, her feet
beating a feverish rhythm. Gabriel leaned against one
wall watching her, his expression harsh with a frown.

Alexander's attention returned to Anne as she
purposely avoided Bearach MacDonald's grasp on her arm
and turned toward David to accept his hand instead. Her
father's frown boded ill for both her and David, as he led
her forward in the dance. Thus far, neither Collin nor
Bearach had managed to corner her, though both had
attempted to several times. Alexander had become almost
amused at their efforts.

Bearach's attention focused on Tira and he moved in
her direction inspiring another of the MacLachlan Chief's
frowns. Collin started forward, then pausing, he moved to
one side of the room where large casks of ale had been
aligned along the wall. A servant dipped him a tankard of
the brew and he sipped it as he watched the dancers in
the center of the floor, his expression sour.

Alexander's gaze searched the room once again for
Mary. Concerned by her continued absence, he wound his
way through the crowd of villagers and clansmen to the
stairs. The passageway felt blessedly cool after the heated
press of the great hall and the quiet, a restful respite from
the festive music below. Opening the door to the chamber,
his gaze settled on his sleeping wife. Relief brought a
smile to his lips and an easing of the anxious tension
along his shoulders and neck.

Of late, he had noticed how easily she seemed to tire
and how often she sought the comfort of a chair to ease
her swollen feet and legs. His gaze followed the rounded
protrusion of her belly outlined by her gown. Her father's
presence had upset her. She needed her rest. He slipped
from the room careful not to wake her.

As he returned to the hall, he noticed Gavin standing
to one side watching the dancers, his arms folded before
him, his expression closed. He had been strangely quiet
all evening. Alexander crossed the room to stand next to
him.

"Is Mary ailing?" Gavin asked.

"Nay. Your father's arrival has tired her, and she has
fallen asleep in our chamber."

Gavin nodded.

"'Twould seem Collin intends to press the lass." Alexander nodded toward Anne.

"Aye," Gavin agreed, his tone short.

"Ian was killed at a most opportune time, was he not?"

Gavin's attention did not sway from his sister, but his jaw tightened.

He wondered if the man was content with his father's plans or if he even suspected them. "Is Bearach who you would have for your sister, Gavin?"

"Nay," he answered. "You were not who I wished for Mary, either."

"Aye, I ken that." Alexander folded his hands behind him. "Does she seem unhappy to be with me?"

Gavin remained silent a moment. "I do not understand it, but nay, she does not."

Alexander studied the younger man's face. "Do you believe she would have been as content with Bearach?"

For the first time, Gavin turned his head to look at him, his gaze searching. "Nay."

Alexander focused on the lad, his expression purposely serious. "Having a MacDonald ally has made your father as arrogant now as he was at Lochlan when last I was there. I would watch over Anne, as well as I tried to Mary, Gavin."

The lad remained silent a moment, his gaze once again intent on Alexander's face. "Aye, I will."

****

Mary sat up on the side of the bed, shaking and panting, as a wave of pain rolled from her back around her mid-section. The muscles tensed to a tight peak then gradually eased. She waited several minutes, in suspended anxiety, for another contraction to come. When nothing happened, she drew a deep breath and clasped her trembling hands between her knees. The beginning of her labor had started. She had to remain calm.

The distant sound of music below in the great hall became audible to her. It was late. The candle on the bedside table had melted down to a stub and the red coals gleamed hot in the fireplace, but no flames were evident.

She rose, put several chunks of peat on the coals, and watched as it caught. Moving to the chest at the foot of the bed, she removed several clean sheets and laid them atop the tartan blanket. It would be many hours before they would be needed. She drew several breaths to calm herself again.

A tap on the heavy wooden door of the chamber had her moving in relief to answer it. Just knowing someone was close by eased her fears.

Grace stood outside in the passageway, her hair in disarray, her surcoat half buttoned. "I told her nay, Lady Mary, but she says 'tis important."

Tira stepped forward from behind Grace. "'Tis Cassidy. He fell into a blaze and has been burned badly. Will you come?"

Tira's green gaze held a frantic look and the anxious demand in her tone had Mary biting her lip. The child had to be grievously hurt for Tira to come to her for help. Her labor was just beginning and there would be time for her to tend him until Derek could arrive and take her place.

"Grace, send for Derek and Anabal. I have need of them both." She paused, her gaze resting on the girl until the importance of her words became evident in Grace's expression.

"You should wait for Derek to come to tend the lad," Grace said, her young face creased in a worried frown.

"There is time for him and Anabal to arrive. Send Derek to Tira's hut when he arrives. I will return to the castle then."

Grace curtsied hurriedly and rushed down the passageway.

"Is Cassidy in great pain?" Mary asked as she threw a tartan shawl about her shoulders and retrieved her basket of herbs and salves from the bedside table.

"Aye."

Instead of moving down the passageway toward the hall as Grace had done, Tira turned in the opposite direction. Mary was once again reminded of the woman's familiarity with the castle and her husband. To know the passageways so well, she must have often slipped unnoticed into his chamber. Attempting to ignore the thoughts, she drew comfort from the knowledge Tira would soon be gone.

Mary halted halfway down a flight of stairs as another contraction struck her. "I must catch my breath, for a moment," she managed. Tira stopped several steps below her, her movements impatient. The pain passed quickly, and she gestured to the woman to continue.

Through a back entrance unfamiliar to Mary, they exited the castle. The early summer air, damp with frost, felt chilly. A new moon, bright and round, shown down on them, elongating their shadows as they crossed the courtyard to the gate. The music from the hall, lively and rhythmic, traveled on the breeze. Deep masculine laughter came from close by as they followed several villagers from the castle courtyard.

"We must hurry," Tira urged.

Mary found matching the woman's pace difficult.

"'Tis this way," Tira said before they reached the village. She turned off the well-worn path to one that was smaller and harder to follow.

Mary's steps flagged and she stopped only a few paces from the road. Derek would not know where to find them. A startled squeak of protest broke from her as something black was thrust down over her head and she was grasped around the waist. Panicked, she twisted and kicked at her attackers. Another contraction struck her and she had to stop to wait out the pain.

"Tira, what have you done?" a familiar voice demanded from close by. The sound of a scuffle erupted from behind her and the meaty thud of blows being struck against flesh made her flinch and cringe away from the person holding her arms.

"Walk," a masculine voice ordered close to her ear. She was forced forward, away from the sounds of fighting, by the painful grip on her arms.

Chapter Twenty-seven

"You whore!" Collin exclaimed. He dealt Tira a vicious backhand across the face sending her reeling. She fell heavily on the ground and curled into a defensive posture as he stood over her. "'Twas Anne I told you to bring, not Mary."

Despite her anger toward the woman, Mary flinched at the violence directed at her. She tugged at the bindings around her wrists with steady pressure, trying to loosen them.

"I could not seek her out. They are watching her too closely," Tira protested.

"Mary is of no use to me," he spat.

"Hold, Collin," Bearach said, grasping the other man's arm, his eyes on Mary as she sat on the ground before the fire. "If we can put some distance between the Campbell forces and yours, and join with my men, we can force Alexander to exchange Anne for Mary and be gone from here."

"I am laboring, Bearach. I cannot ride a horse. If the babe and I should die because of this, there is no place in Scotland you or Collin will be able to hide from Alexander."

Collin took a threatening step toward her. "Had you not taken that devil to your bed there would not have been a need for any of this." He pointed his finger in her face. "'Tis your fault your sister's husband is dead."

She gasped in outraged dismay. Her suspicions had been true.

Collin's features appeared gaunt in the firelight. He drew himself up. "Call the men together. We are taking our leave of this Glen of Peace."

"You will not ride without me, will you, Father?" Gavin asked as he stepped into the light of the fire.

Mary reeled beneath the crushing blow of betrayal,

her gaze seeking her brother's face. How could he be a party to this?

****

Alexander covered a yawn and stretched. Duncan chuckled beside him drawing his attention.

"'Tis a wonder to watch you, Brother. 'Tis with Mary you wish to be, why are you not there?" he asked.

He frowned. "Are you claiming to be able to read thoughts now, Duncan?"

"It does not take a seer's gift to know you wish to go upstairs to your chamber, Alexander. Your eyes have strewn to the stairs more times than I can count in the last hour. You may take your leave of us and seek your rest. Anne has retired and Collin and Bearach have retired to the camp with Collin's men."

"Aye, that is what keeps me here. Mary has readied chambers for them here at the castle and they chose to sleep at the camp with Collin's men. There is something afoot."

Derek and Anabal entered the hall with Grace and wove their way through the sleeping men littering the hall. "There is no one at Tira's hut in the village, Alexander. Are they here?" Derek asked.

"Who do you seek, Derek?" he asked, confused.

"Grace said Cassidy had been badly burned and Tira sought Mary to tend him. Mary sent Grace to bring me to tend the boy and Anabal to tend her. She was laboring."

In shocked surprise, Alexander's gaze swung to Duncan and the two gazed at each other. Why had she not sent Grace to tell him? He leaped to his feet and ran to the stairs. He took the steps two at a time then raced down the many corridors. Breathing heavily, he rounded the passageway to their chamber and flung open the door. Mary's name broke from his lips as his gaze searched the room. He strode forward to the gardrobe and jerked aside the curtain. The room was empty.

As he returned to the hall, Duncan met him at the top of the stairs. "Gabriel has been found outside the village, he has been beaten. The MacLachlans have left their camp and the horses are gone."

Alexander swore. "They've taken Mary and are on the run."

266

Guilt crashed down on him with brutal weight and he raked his hands through his hair. Why had he not guarded his wife as closely as he had her sister? "Wake the men. We will ride to cut them off before they reach the borders of our land and escape." His gaze moved about the hall. "Where is Gavin?" he demanded.

Duncan hesitated. "I do not know. He may have ridden with them."

****

"Stay close to me, Mary. I will not allow him to harm you," Gavin soothed. He bent to boost her into the saddle.

Unable to raise her leg, Mary gripped the horn of the saddle as another contraction had its way with her. They were growing stronger and coming with more frequency.

"If you can not get her astride that horse, I'll have her thrown across one," Collin snarled. "We do not have time to waste."

Mary sensed Gavin's anger though his features were indiscernible in the shadowed darkness beneath the trees.

"Come, Mary," he urged.

She fit her foot into his cupped hands and he boosted her upward. As she settled into the saddle, her thoughts turned to Alexander. He had been wary of her being on horseback lest she fall off and injure herself or the bairn. She wondered how close his men might be. "Hurry Alexander," she murmured as another contraction struck.

Gavin swung himself astride the animal behind her. "Try to rest between the pains."

"'Tis difficult," She managed.

Tira's shriek of distress made her cringe. Bearach had dragged her from the back of his horse moments after they had halted and disappeared into the brush with her. The heavy grunts coming from just beyond the bushes left little doubt what he was about. She felt sick for Tira. The woman had more than paid for her trickery with the abuse her father and Bearach heaped on her.

The MacLachlan clansmen, mounted and ready, held a silence that seemed as filled with disgust as she felt.

"Mayhap you should call your pig to mount his horse, Collin. 'Tis he who keeps us waiting now," she taunted, hoping to cut short the woman's ordeal. "How can you wish to wed your own flesh and blood to such as he?"

Collin did not answer, but roared Bearach's name.

He appeared from the shadows. Tira's shoulder showed pale and smooth through a rent in her clothing, and her mouth was dark with blood as he dragged her forward by the wrist. "This Campbell whore tempts me sorely, Collin."

"After we are away you may do whatever you wish with her, but for now, get on your horse." Collin snapped, his tone strained.

The night air held a chill. Sweat beaded Mary's forehead and wet the hair at her nape making her shiver. Trickles of moisture ran between her breasts and she longed for a cloth to wipe them away. The jarring movement of the horse beneath her, made every contraction seem endless.

The sky became a milky blue as the sun appeared over the horizon. She turned her face from its glow as once again, a grip of agonizing pain seized her. A cry rose in her throat she refused to voice, though her body arched against the hurt. She gripped Gavin's forearm hard. She did not know how much longer she could bear this.

****

Alexander leaned forward, his mount stretching out once again into a full gallop as the path became flat and wide. Urgency clawed at him talon sharp. Mary and the bairn could be killed by such a ride. They had to overtake them.

To his left, Duncan and David kept pace with him. To his right, Anne eased her mount further forward. The usual single file formation had been cast aside by them all. The fifty Campbell clansmen rode behind them four deep as well.

The early morning light eased their way down the valley to the rocky burn leading upward. Thick clumps of trees embraced the mouth of the valley, lending cover to any who would lay in wait. Alexander slowed the pace, his gaze raking the area for any threat. If Collin were fool enough to abduct Mary and run, he could be bold enough to try to attack as well. Alexander felt certain Bearach's men were close by. Rage fired within him spurring him forward. He would no longer temper his dealings with Collin with mercy. He would kill the bastard and be done with him, for good.

****

"Halt, Gavin, halt," Mary cried. The pain seemed to go on and on without ease. Her back felt as though it might split asunder beneath the pressure of it. A burst of fluid came from between her legs, wetting her gown and running down her legs.

Gavin reined the animal to a stop and dismounted. Mary fell into his upraised arms as she slid from the horses back. With cautious haste, he eased her down on the ground.

The men behind came to a halt, their horses milling the ground around them. Collin circled, then came within a few feet of where Mary lay. "Get her back on that horse," he snarled.

The bairn is coming," Gavin snapped in return. "What would you have her do, give birth upon its back?" He cradled Mary back against him, giving her support.

The urge to push was overwhelming. Mary grimaced as she bore down hard, a cry of anguish escaping her.

"She had best be quick about it," Collin threatened.

A murmured oath came from within the ranks of men close by, drawing Collin's attention away from the two of them.

"Where is Tira? Mary needs her." Gavin snapped his voice hoarse with emotion.

Bearach rode forward. Tira slid down from behind him and limped forward. Her lip was raw and split, her face on one side swollen and blackened by a bruise. Her hair hung about her shoulders, limp and tangled. The dullness of shock had temporarily drained her features of expression. Her green eyes remained blank, as she stood over Mary, unmoving.

"Help her," Gavin thundered.

Overwhelmed by the natural urge to bring her child into the world, Mary was only vaguely aware of the woman kneeling at her braced feet. Tira folded back the skirt of Mary's gown and kirtle, baring her legs. The MacLachlan clansmen rode a short distance away and dismounted, giving her some privacy.

Mary groaned and panted as she bore down again and again. Every muscle knotted with her concentrated effort to expelling the child from her body.

"The bairn's head is showing," Tira announced finally, her speech affected by her swollen mouth.

Mary's cries of effort grew shrill with pain as the babe's head thrust from her. Tira wiped the tiny face with a fold of the kirtle. The unrelenting pressure twisted a scream of agony from Mary, as Tira worked the child's shoulders free. The tiny body slithered pink and wet into the woman's hands.

For several tense moments, the babe made no sound. Tira cleared the child's mouth with the kirtle and rubbed his back. A high, sweet cry issued forth as he breathed his first full breath. Mary's head fell back against Gavin's shoulder as the weakness of relief swamped her. With clumsy discordant movements, she dragged the tartan shawl from around her waist and offered it to Tira.

Tira worked a long thread free from the fabric and used it to tie off the umbilical cord. Gavin offered his dagger for her to cut it. The woman's face shone wet with tears as she thrust the dagger into the band at her waist and wrapped the new life within the tartan. "He is a bonny lad," she murmured as she looked down into the child's face. She rose to carry the babe to his mother's side and placed him carefully in Mary's arms.

"He has the mark of his sire upon him," Gavin said dryly. "Poor lad."

Mary's gaze took in the crop of sable red hair with a sense of surprised familiarity. To see her husband's features stamped in miniature on the tiny face, brought a smile to her lips. The babe's eyes squinted in an effort to avoid the sunlight or to focus, or both. His tiny fist waved about in the air.

Mary's gaze went to Tira's abused face. "Thank you, Tira."

The woman's tears came more quickly.

"Be done with it, and be quick," Collin ordered, disrupting the joy of the moment.

Tira rose to return to the business at hand. She pressed down hard on Mary's abdomen as she pulled to help her expel the afterbirth. It came forth with a gush.

"You can not mean for Mary to ride further, Collin," Gavin protested.

"Aye, she will or I'll kill that wee Campbell bastard she has born. Give him to me." Collin rode dangerously close.

"Nay," Mary cried in fear, her arms tightening around the infant as she twisted away from the dancing hooves. The idea, of Collin so much as touching the babe, brought with it a surge of maternal protectiveness and fear.

"Get on the horse, Mary."

Gavin swore. He eased away and bent to help her to her feet. "I will kill him should he touch you or your bairn, Sister." His blue eyes gleamed with an uncontrolled rage.

Struck by the violent trembling of reaction, Mary grew fearful of dropping the bairn. She unwound the fabric of the shawl from the child and instructed Gavin to tie it diagonally across her body over her shoulder and around her waist, creating a sling. Cradling the babe protectively within the pouch against her breast, she mounted the horse with difficulty. Blood and fluid stained the fabric of her kirtle and surcoat making the gown cling to her legs uncomfortably. She ached in every part of her body.

"Clean your hands, wench," Bearach demanded as he rode forward.

With a smile of unadulterated defiance that looked more like a grimace, Tira rubbed the slimy residue on her arms and over her gown.

"You'll soon learn your place, wench." Bearach charged at her, but she jumped aside. "'Tis not on my horse you'll be riding."

Tira laughed aloud. "You snuffling pig, I would rather walk to hell than ride with you again."

Collin motioned to one of his men and he rode forward to offer her a hand. Tira shunned him.

"Kill her," Collin ordered, then urged his horse forward.

"Take his hand, Tira," Mary pleaded.

With open reluctance, the woman complied and allowed the man to swing her up before him.

Mary wanted to weep in protest as Gavin kicked his mount forward. The jostling wracked her body with pain.

They topped the rise and below them spread the

camp of a large force of men.

"Greetings, Collin MacLachlan." John Campbell's voice carried easily across the distance. His imposing figure and red beard stood out amongst the rest of the men. "Have you mayhap become confused and journeyed in the wrong direction? 'Twould seem you have lost something along the way." He motioned to a band of men sitting on the ground close by.

Joy and relief danced in Mary's heart. "'Tis John, Alexander's father," Mary breathed to Gavin.

****

"Dear God, she's had the babe!" Alexander exclaimed in shock, his horse dancing around the puddle of blood and matter left behind in the road. His concern for Mary became a driving force wreathing within the depths of his being. His heart was filled with fresh anguish.

"She's alive, Alexander, but she will not survive for long if we do not catch them," Anne said, the agony of her own worry easily read on her face.

He kicked his horse forward without further delay. They crested a rise in the trail and just below them were the band they followed and beyond them his father's men.

"We both have something the other wants, John Campbell," Bearach shouted across the field. "You have my men, but I have your grandchild."

"And for what will you bargain with me, Bearach?" Alexander shouted from behind them, his men spreading out to surround the company of men from behind. His desperate gaze found Mary seated before Gavin on his horse. The hair about her face, dark with sweat, clung to her cheeks and brow. Deep hollows surrounded her eyes and her features were etched with pain. One tiny hand appeared from beneath the tartan she had wrapped about her and her arms shifted the weight of the child to a more secure position.

Collin dismounted and ran forward to grab her by the arm and jerk her down from the back of the horse. Mary twisted and fell onto her back, holding the bundle against her with protective determination. The babe began to squall in protest to such treatment.

Gavin jumped down from his mount, his shout of protest a snarl of rage. Collin drew his sword and posed the blade above Mary in a threatening posture, staying his son's defense of his sister. "I will have Anne and Bearach's men, and safe passage from this glen or I will kill them both," Collin's voice carried easily.

The lust to kill surged strongly through Alexander. "Bring any more harm to my wife and child, MacLachlan, and you and your men will die a thousand times this day," Alexander threatened as he drew his sword. One movement of his hand had his men doing the same. The sound of weapons being drawn on all quarters rang out clear and deadly.

"Give me Anne and the men and we will leave in peace," Collin insisted.

"Nay, you will not take Mary or Anne. Be grateful to leave with your life alone."

Bearach dismounted and strode forward as though to offer council. A movement within the ranks of MacLachlan clansmen had Alexander and his men tensing in readiness.

"'Tis Tira," Gabriel said from behind him.

A feral high-pitched growl split the air as Tira launched herself at the barrel shaped man, her arm raised. She plunged a dagger once, twice, then thrice into his back in a frenzied lust of rage. The man shook her off and staggered backward trying to ward her off with a raised arm. She slashed at him again imbedding the blade to the hilt in his chest. He jerked away, the knife protruding from him as he wove forward several feet. Like a great oak that had just received the final cutting blow, he stiffened and fell sideways. He lay on the ground motionless, his shirt blooming red with blood.

Tira turned and ran toward the Campbell forces.

As though in slow motion Alexander watched as Collin's gaze moved from the fallen man back to him. In the older man's face, Alexander read defeat, but also something else. For a moment, his sword seemed to swing away, then suddenly the MacLachlan Laird roared a war cry and raised his sword then brought it down with all his might.

Mary turned to shield the baby with her body. Alexander's shouted cry of denial was drowned by the sound of metal against metal as Gavin's blade halted the descent of his father's sword. The hiss of an arrow split the air and a look almost of relief crossed Collin's face before he crumbled to the ground, the shaft of the crossbow bolt protruding through his torso to his back.

Alexander's gaze swung to his right as Anne lowered the crossbow from her shoulder. Tears streamed unheeded down her face. "He killed my husband, I could not allow him kill my sister, too."

Alexander leaped from his mount. His heart pounding, he ran down the bank. He wove his way through the MacLachlan clansmen and horses unchallenged as they began to throw down their swords.

His steps flagged as he reached Mary's crumpled form still curled defensively on her side. "Mary." His voice sounded hoarse to his own ears as he kneeled beside her and cast his sword aside.

She turned, her features pale and etched by suffering, had never looked as beautiful to him. Alexander gathered her close, his chest and throat constricted by emotion.

"I knew you would come," Mary murmured, her voice shaky with tears.

"Always," he managed unsteadily.

A squealing high-pitched sound of protest came from the bundle between them and he drew back. Mary shifted to uncover the child, allowing him the first glimpse of his son. His hand shook as he smoothed the burnished fuzz covering the tiny round head. He could not speak for the fullness in his chest. He had come so close to losing everything dear to him. His gaze rose to her face. "'Twas Bearach who was to come to you that night. He was in the passageway outside your chamber when I secured the door. I could not allow him to take you from me."

"Shh." Mary pressed her fingers over his lips. "'Tis of no concern anymore."

"I would see my grandchild before the two of you smother him betwixt you," John demanded as he stood above them.

Mary laughed, the sound laced with uninhibited joy. She slipped the tartan shawl from over her head and arranged the child within its folds. John knelt to scoop up the bundle with expert care. A smile flashed white against the reddish bristles of his beard as he cradled his grandson.

"A shelter has been built, and water has been readied for you, Mary. I will take the babe." His tawny gaze swung to Gavin who still stood close. "Come, lad. You have waged a war with only one blow, and won. You look as though you could use a drink." He turned and walked down the hill with Gavin in tow.

Alexander frowned at his father's back not entirely pleased with being separated from his child so quickly. He turned to see Mary smiling at him. He scooped her up from the ground.

Mary sought his lips for a long sweet moment, then looked into her husband's face.

"I have found home in you, Mary," he murmured, his tawny gaze alight with love.

She looked out over the congress of Campbell clansmen, both Alexander's and his father's. Their families stood together, waiting for them below. Her heart felt free and light and so full she could not contain her joy. "We are home, Alexander. We are home." She rested her forehead against his cheek. "I love you, Alexander Campbell," she said softly.

He turned his head and his lips brushed her brow. "And I love you, *leannan.*"

A word about the author...

By day, Teresa Reasor works as an Art Teacher of six hundred and fifty elementary students, and by night as a part time college professor. But every other moment---she lives in worlds bound only by her imagination, with characters she knows as well as her own family. Now that two of her three children have left the nest, she resides in a small town in Kentucky with her husband of thirty-one years, her daughter, and a menagerie of animals.

Visit Teresa at www.teresareasor.com

Printed in the United States
125910LV00001B/11/A